ALSO BY R. J

The Face of Fear: A Powers and Johnson Novel

No Mercy

A POWERS AND JOHNSON NOVEL

No Mercy

R.J. Torbert

TWO HARBORS PRESS, MINNEAPOLIS

Two Harbors Press
322 First Avenue N, 5th floor
Minneapolis, MN 55401
612.455.2293
www.TwoHarborsPress.com

This story is a work of fiction.

ISBN: 978-1-63505-097-4
LCCN: 2016903232

Distributed by Itasca Books

Follow @RJTorbert on Twitter.

Printed in the United States of America

For Katherine

Faith is being
sure of what we hope
for and certain of what
we do not see.

—Hebrews 11:1

ACKNOWLEDGMENTS

The Author is grateful to the following for their assistance during research of this book.

Detective Kevin M. Cronin (Retired SCPD)

Dr. Dennis O'Brien, MD

Dr. Martin Dominger, DDS, MD

Dr. Jerry Kowitt, DDS

The Riverhead Correctional Facility/Correction Officer John Roche

Port Jefferson Village Free Library

SUNY Empire State College

Front/Back Cover Design: Jason Lash
Back Cover Photograph: Shannyn Torbert

The Marchese Family,
Owners,
the Henry Hallock House

Thanks for the continued Support and Inspiration

Roseann Torbert	Lorin Santospirto	Betty Thomson	Kristin Pace
Henry Coppola	George Lynagh	Sharyn Kampmeyer	Scott Tillchock
Anthony Masi	Lois Meyer	James Ward	Barbara Kantz
Bob Konoski	Katherine Healey	Joey Z	Jeffrey Lambe
Ken August	Kathy Tillchock	Jo Ann Kowitt	Andi Wolos
Barbarie Rothstein	Stanley Geller	Karen Wolf	John Valeri
Mindy Kronenberg	Allan Longobucco	Cathy Laton	Joseph Santospirto
Brittany Tillchock	Tara McDonald	Jason Lash	Kathy Daley
Maria Robison	Silvia Chilala	Dagen McDowell	Tim Wagstaff
Ricky Roth	Ki Ceniglio	Denise Vece	Doug Niedrich

To All My Good Friends in Hong Kong and China

The Entire Staff at Fun World

Alan Geller,
your creation of the mask will forever be
the ICON of Halloween.

Finally, to

WES CRAVEN.

Whose work and accomplishments continue to be an inspiration. I'm so honored to have had regular communication with Wes, over the years including during his illness. He trusted me as he described his battle and I will honor him with that discretion. He wanted to read the manuscript to this book so he could give a review and support this piece of work. This is the type of man he was. He passed away the day this book was finished in the editing process so it was not meant to be, however the friendship that he gave to me, as well as encouragement is something I will always treasure. His fans would be proud to know that during his illness and communication to me, he was very brave, and grateful for the time he was given. He was very appreciative of his life, his family, his friends and his fans. A remarkable man who honored me with his time, his words, and his friendship. You will always be the Master. May God bless you and your family. Rest in peace,

September 28

Rachelle went into the kitchen tying her hair back as her coffee maker automatically turned on. She had an hour and a half before meeting Deborah to drive out to the Riverhead Correctional Facility to see her sister Madison who had now been incarcerated for over eighteen months. The Face of Fear investigation made headlines around the world and gave notoriety to Rachelle, the police officers involved, and the Village of Port Jefferson. The young woman handled it well and could have gone on to bigger and more financially rewarding opportunities but rather chose to stay in her home at the top of Prospect Street. Rachelle also became a "local celebrity" in the town by writing more local stories about the history and local events of the village she loved, while maintaining her work with Joey Z in the restaurant. She had about four inches high worth of notes from what had happened the previous year and knew one day she would write a movie script.

She had begun taking part-time courses in creative writing at Empire State College and had decided she would take a script-writing course as well, with Professor Mindy Kronenberg at the Hauppauge location. She knew that while she wanted to stay in the village, she felt strongly about the need to grow and continue to better herself. Rachelle had even met with the mayor of Port Jefferson a few times about the possibility of writing a book based on the Dankleff murders in Belle Terre over twenty-five years ago. The novel she had started writing during the Face of Fear investigation, *Vanished: The Port Jefferson Murders*, had never progressed the way she had wanted. Although her friends encouraged her to write a novel about what had happened eighteen months prior, each time she started, she became too emotional to continue. Thus, the reason she decided to take part-time courses at Empire State College. She did manage to write *The Story of a Village Called Port Jefferson*, which sold over three thousand copies in the surrounding area of the village. Many were surprised it didn't sell more copies, with all the notoriety the village got, but with time, people forget and move on with their lives. She was now twenty-eight years of age and deeply committed to Detective Paul Powers. Their relationship became cemented with the conclusion of the famous case, and they now spent as much time as they could together based on their schedules.

This morning, their time would be limited. She visited her sister Madison twice a week at the facility and she was accompanied sometimes by Paul, and sometimes by Deborah, who had become her closest friend during the past year and a half. It was Deborah whose life was saved when Madison went on a vigilante killing spree wearing the Ghost Face mask and she, as well as her father, William Lance, the former county executive, never forgot it.

Rachelle finished her coffee and walked her two dogs, Wes and Craven, down the hill toward the apartment above the restaurant to say good morning to Paul. She used her key to open the door as the two King Charles Cavaliers ran up the stairs and jumped on the bed to awaken him, a ritual of which he and Rachelle never tired. Paul rolled over as Wes licked him until he yelled, "I surrender." He half opened his eyes as he noticed Rachelle was wearing her Ben Franklin $100 bill sweatpants. He reached out his hands to her as she jumped on the bed and immediately started kissing him first on his forehead and working her way to his lips. Paul moved his hand under her sweats within seconds as she raised her head to stare at him.

"Hmm, really? You want to do this while Wes and Craven are watching?"

"Well," Paul answered, "that does have a strange ring to it," and they both laughed. They kissed again as Rachelle moaned but got up quickly.

"I have to get back to the house, change clothes, and meet Deborah to go out to Riverhead to see Maddie."

Paul raised himself up and said, "Tell her hello for me. Give my best to Deborah as well."

"Will do," she replied. "I love you," she said as she kissed him again. "Please check on the dogs before you go to work." Paul saluted her as he walked down the stairway to accompany her.

"I'll see you later in the restaurant." Rachelle turned around and blew him a kiss as she closed the door behind her with a smile on her face.

Rachelle was a few minutes late as she drove onto Cliff Road in Belle Terre to pick up Deborah. At twenty-nine years of age, Deborah was more beautiful than ever. Her life as the kidnapped victim that started the Face of Fear investigation seemed like a lifetime ago, despite the seemingly daily reminders. One of which was visiting Madison, Rachelle's sister. Deborah believed she would not be alive today if not for the actions of Madison, or Maddie as they affectionately called her. Maddie was responsible for killing six people who were involved in her kidnapping, the murder of a police officer, and the attempted murder of Rachelle and a twelve-year-old girl during the investigation, and she was in jail for taking the law into her own hands.

The public outcry for Madison was so strong that Deborah's father, William Lance, was able to pull strings after the trial was over, keeping Madison in the Riverhead facility jail close to her sister instead of going upstate to prison. The Riverhead facility had always been a temporary home until a trial was over and an inmate was sentenced, but in this special circumstance, an exception was made. Madison was sentenced to ten years with a chance to get out in six to seven years. Her attorney, Al Simmons, prepared a brilliant case for the jury and Judge Green, against the state, and with the plea bargain and public outcry she was convicted of manslaughter in the first degree.

Deborah and Rachelle could have taken a stretch limo to the facility because of William Lance's wealth, but it wasn't Deborah's style. When she was in a limo she didn't know who her friends really were. She became close with Rachelle for the bond they would always share. As Deborah jumped in the passenger seat, she kissed Rachelle as she backed out in her 2013 silver BMW 328i that she leased.

The drive to Riverhead was approximately thirty-five minutes, which allowed plenty of time for girl talk between the two young women.

"Well, girlfriend," Deborah spoke, "it's approaching about a year and a half since you and Paul finally came to your smarts. What's the latest?"

"Well," Rachelle smiled as she turned onto Route 83 South toward the expressway. "You mean since yesterday when I spoke to you?"

Deborah laughed but tugged at Rachelle's blouse. "You haven't talked about you and Paul for a while," she said with a concerned half-grin. Rachelle looked at Deborah while they were stopped at the red light.

"I love him with all my heart," Rachelle said. She paused as Deborah waited for her to continue. "I wish sometimes he would be a little more romantic, I wish we could spend more quality time together. I mean, we spend time together, but our lives are so crazy busy I just wish we had more time to be with each other." She looked back at the traffic light before speaking again. "I hope we have a long life together, but I . . . " She stepped on the gas as the light turned green.

Deborah said, "But I what?"

Rachelle spoke again as her eyes remained on the road. "I thought I was pregnant about six months ago, and I was afraid to tell him."

"Why?" Deborah asked.

"I thought," Rachelle answered, "that he would be upset with me and I was worried it would be too much of a stress on his mind and job. He has never brought up marriage to me. I mean, I know he loves me, and don't get me wrong, the sex is beyond good," she said as she started to laugh with her friend, who was amused. "But now he is a part of me and I sometimes worry he doesn't think about me in any other way."

Deborah looked out the window, then back at her friend as she spoke.

"You need to have a talk with him. You guys have gone through so much, but now life is back to normal. His career got a boost after the Face of Fear case was over. The task force created for the cops involved is the envy of most cops everywhere."

Rachelle asked, "Do you think there is something about the reward of the task force being created because of my sister being involved that is holding Paul back from making more of a commitment?"

Deborah put her hand on Rachelle's leg as they passed Exit 68 on the expressway, and said, "No, I don't, but perhaps you need to ask him that question."

"Enough about me," Rachelle shot back. "I noticed you and Bud don't go out as much anymore."

A smile came back to Deborah's face. "Well," she said in a long breath. "He's a wonderful man, a funny man, a great cop, but it just seems like we became good friends this past year. I don't know how to explain it."

"And?" Rachelle asked.

"And what?" Deborah replied.

Rachelle began shaking her head and said, "Come on, details, details. There isn't anything wrong under the sheets, is there?"

Deborah covered her face with her hands. "Oh, I can't," she replied.

"You tell me!" Rachelle shot back. "Or I will pull over and we won't move until I know." Deborah looked down and then out the window as the Pine Barrens started to disappear as they approached their exit for the facility.

"He is the most caring and sensitive man I have ever known. There has only been one other man I have wanted to be so close to, and Bud is so sweet and tender. It's just that it seems like our relationship changed since the task force was created, and I have to say that when I started dating other men, I just began to look at Bud as my big brother. He did make me realize that I wasted too much time on Robert, and I didn't know any better having fallen for him at such a young age."

Her thoughts turned to him. Robert Simpson was her father's personal assistant and Deborah's first love from the time he was hired until it was exposed he "stepped out" on her with her then–best friend, Patty Saunders. It was during her kidnapping for ransom that her world fell apart, and was only saved with the love and support of the new people in her life: Rachelle, Madison, Detective Cronin, Paul Powers, Bud Johnson, and Sherry Walker, who resigned from the force six months ago to concentrate on starting a family. However, it was Bud who would always be special to Deborah. She looked at Rachelle and asked, "You know what I mean?"

"Yes," her friend replied as she took one hand off the wheel and touched Deborah's hand.

"What a great big brother to have. Besides," Rachelle continued, "the best thing that ever happened to you is that you, I, all of us never heard from Robert again."

The BMW pulled into the front entrance of the correctional facility and the young ladies were asked for their names, whom they were going to see, and their identification. Rachelle could see the slight change in the sheriff's facial expression when she said the name Madison Robinson. She was granted entry and parked in the visitors' parking lot, and the two began the sixty-yard walk to the visiting section of the facility. They sat in the beige bleacher-like seats with the rest of the visitors, and since they were regulars now, they did not react with surprise when the K-9 dog walked through the area to ensure no one was bringing any illegal firearms or drugs with them during their meeting with the inmates. For first-timers, the K-9 dog, the correctional officers, and the signs posted could be very intimidating. Bright red and white signs, specifically stated there would be no yelling or loud talking, children must stay seated, and there would be no noisy behavior. Lockers were also in the area so all visitors could put away all their belongings before being allowed to enter the area to visit. On the opposite side of where the inmates greeted their visitors was the attorney room, where Madison met with her attorney, Al Simmons, twice a month or more, depending on the need.

The correctional officers announced it was time for the visiting hour and reminded everyone only two visitors at a time were allowed. Rachelle and Deborah went into the room that contained a row of stools on one side of a low glass panel and stools on the other side of the panel. They sat and watched as Madison came into the area with her yellow Velcro covering on backwards. This was done to eliminate the opportunity for inmates to hide anything in their private parts of their bodies. Madison smiled as she hugged and greeted both her sister and Deborah. The low glass panels enabled them to embrace and kiss, which was allowed at the beginning of the meeting and at the end of the visit as well. As they sat down, Rachelle and Madison held hands over the top of the glass and did not let go until the hour was up. Rachelle had tears in her eyes, which had become normal and expected during her visits with Madison.

"How are they treating you?" Deborah asked her.

"They treat me fair," the inmate replied. "They don't have much choice but to treat me in a professional manner. I get extra food if I want it. They look the other way if I take a few extra minutes on a phone call. Let's put it this way, they don't treat me like I'm a murderer," she said as she looked at Rachelle. "I will do my time, and thanks to your dad, Deborah, I will be here so I can be close to Rachelle," she said as a tear came down her face. "I have church service here, Al Simmons checks to be sure I'm treated right, and Paul even checks on me. I miss having human contact, but they're afraid to have me mingle with the other inmates."

Rachelle spoke up. "It's probably safer for you, Maddie. It's been almost eighteen months already; another four years, and this will be behind us forever."

Madison looked at her older sister and asked, "Are you going to make me an aunt before I'm out?"

Rachelle smiled as she squeezed her sister's hand.

Madison began to tell Rachelle how much she loved the book she wrote about Port Jefferson. "I'm so proud of you, Rachelle; so much great history and information. They let us read, and they even sneak newspapers in to me so I know what's going on."

The hour was up so fast that no one noticed it was five minutes past the hour except the officers. They all knew who Madison Robinson was, and while they kept their personal opinions to themselves, they needed to show professionalism in the rules. A few extra minutes here and there for Madison was their way of silently letting her know they knew she wasn't a cold-blooded killer, but someone who was a masked vigilante that not only saved innocent lives, including Deborah's, but also millions of tax dollars that would have been spent in court cases. The police and correctional facility could never publicly show their support for her, but between trusted friends and co-workers they admitted they agreed with her and would express it if they had civilian clothes on instead of a uniform.

As Rachelle and Deborah left the facility, it was almost 11:30 am, and Deborah told Rachelle she was treating her to lunch at one of her father's favorite places for steak. The Rendezvous Restaurant on Main Street in Riverhead had been famous in the area for years. William Lance found the place during a stop when he was running for town supervisor and had remained a loyal customer for the past twenty years, and always enjoyed the New York sirloin marinated steak. As Rachelle drove up to the little restaurant, she noticed it looked like a little dive bar. Her feelings were validated when they walked in. A bar to the left, about eight tables to the right, and another group of tables in a lower area reminded Rachelle of little Irish bars in the city. They had a chance to speak to the servers, who had worked there for over thirty years, including Janice, who had become friendly with William Lance over the years. Rachelle admitted she was not much of a meat eater, but it was one of the most enjoyable steaks she ever had.

"The marinade is the reason," Rachelle said as she put a small bite in her mouth.

"I'll tell you a secret," Deborah replied, "but you can't tell anyone!" Rachelle crossed her heart while she chewed, as Deborah continued, "You're right, the marinade is the secret, but my dad can only come here once a month because it gives him bad gas and no one can be around him for twenty-four hours." Rachelle started choking on her food as she laughed so hard Deborah thought she would have to perform the Heimlich maneuver on her.

Madison was back in her orange outfit, walking back to her section cell when she asked Officer Bay if she could stop by the church to pray. Putting her circumstances aside, Madison was always very respectful and polite to the officers, and they treated her the same way. They had gotten to know her a bit and read her story; particularly after they were informed she would be serving her entire time in Riverhead instead of being moved upstate. Madison was in just as good of shape as when she entered the jail eighteen months prior. At twenty-seven years of age her body was slim and toned from the years of being a dance instructor, and her workouts in the prison four times a week kept her in top physical condition. Officer Bay was thirty-four, single, 6'4" and was Madison's escort on Wednesdays, Fridays, and Saturdays, as well as on alternate Sundays. He was what most young women called tall, dark, and handsome.

The commissioner of corrections who gives directives and mandatory instructions to the facilities regarding all the prisoners informed the chief that Madison Robinson would never be alone while in or out of the building. Her security and schedule were so tight that the officers didn't know they would be escorting her through the underground tunnel to the courthouse until fifteen minutes beforehand. The officers were always available due to the "lockdown" policy. Once they started their shift, they were not allowed to leave the building until it was over. The facility needed to have all officers available and ready in case of an emergency. It was rare, but no chances were taken in case an officer or another inmate was in need. Officer Bay escorted Madison to the church, where she sat down in the back row, bowed her head, and prayed. Other female and male prisoners were in the first few rows paying no attention to the most famous vigilante in the United States. A priest was standing at the front talking to a few of them while a nun was in a small corner of the room speaking to a female inmate. Maddie sat in the back as Officer Bay stood about ten feet away against the back wall.

Sergeant Donna Small, who was responsible for the section, stood next to him as they looked at Madison facing forward.

"She wasn't scheduled to be here now; just be careful," Small said.

"I know," Bay replied. "We were in the area, she asked politely, and I gave it to her." Officer Small looked at him as he stared forward. She shook her head and spoke before she walked away: "We all feel the same way, John. Just be careful."

He knew what she meant. Keep cool, keep professional,

and even though the human side of him liked her, the law could not accept she had taken matters into her own hands. Regardless, Officer John Bay was going to give her a few minutes here and there whenever he could. He politely tapped Madison on the shoulder after fifteen minutes and told her they needed to get back to her section. She got up, smiled, and began the walk to her cell with John following closely.

She turned her head to Officer Bay as they turned the corner and said,

"I don't bite."

He smiled as they approached the separate building cell for her. "Yes, I know," he replied. "This I know."

The woman inmate turned her head to look at him and said, "I guess you would know that."

The drive back to Port Jefferson was fairly quick. Rachelle called on her speakerphone to be sure Paul took the dogs out for their walk and asked him if he could set the DVR for Suze Orman's show at 7:00 pm.

"You're still into her?" Deborah asked.

A smile came over Rachelle's face as she said, "More than ever. I never miss it."

Deborah laughed as she looked at her phone and saw a text from a phone number she did not recognize: *You are still beautiful.* She began to laugh as she told Rachelle someone had just sent a love note to the wrong number.

Paul answered his cell with a "Hello Bud" and with no surprise apparent on his face started listening to his partner singing to him, but quickly interrupted him. "If you want me to help you move into your house next weekend, you better stop." That did the trick. Bud was moving to the village after thirty years of living in Miller Place. He fell in love with the Henry Hallock house at 116 South Street. He first read about the house in Rachelle's book, *The History of a Village Called Port Jefferson,* and he promptly drove to the house, convinced the owner how interested he was, and after a walk-through and inspection of the house made an offer that couldn't be refused. The Henry Hallock house, according to the Port Jefferson Historical Society, was originally owned by Captain Henry Hallock, who built seven coastal schooners between 1855 and 1878. His grandson Albert became a noted local historian in the village. The economy was still tough, but he was able to sell his home on Parkside Drive and with the profit made from the house bought this beautiful quaint little home built in 1848. The tub in the bathroom was from 1890, and although there was much work to do to fix it up, Bud loved the history of the house and without admitting it, wanted to be closer to three of his favorite people: Paul, Rachelle, and Deborah.

While Paul, Bud, Deborah, and Rachelle were already friends, the Face of Fear investigation made them a family. Once the investigation was completed and the news media found other news to exploit, the Suffolk County Police Department rewarded Detective Lieutenant Cronin and his detectives, Paul Powers and Bud Johnson, with a task force called Priority 1. The task force was directed by the chief of police as to which case would be given to them as a Priority 1. The task force consisted of Officers Lynagh, Healey, Dugan, Franks, Chapman, and a new detective, Ellyn Baker. Kevin Cronin chose his team and brought his closest allies with him from the Face of Fear investigation. This included Sherry Walker, who decided after six months on the task force that it was time to possibly teach and look forward to starting a family. Enter Ellyn Baker, 27, tall, 5'8", brunette, with blue-grey eyes that lit up rooms that already had the light on. Many throughout the precinct thought that Ellyn reminded them of the character Kate Beckett from TV's *Castle* program. The main difference was that Ellyn liked to walk around the Priority 1 area with her shoes off. At first Detective Lieutenant Cronin balked but soon gave up, as it added variety to his team of personalities.

Even Bud once asked Ellyn about the shoeless thing, and she laughed with her reply: "I think better without my shoes. Sometimes I hold off going to the bathroom for an hour because I don't want to put my shoes back on."

Bud's face had that look of puzzlement, not sure if she was just messing with him or if she was a little crazy. He even thought about asking her why she would go to the trouble of putting on her shoes to go to the ladies' room but decided against it until he knew her better.

The Priority 1 team did not rest on their success from the highly publicized case eighteen months prior. They had solved two murder cases, two cold cases, and four robbery investigations during the past year and a half. Priority 1 stood for more than just what case was most important at the time. It was looked upon as the top task force team and something to aspire to if you were a cop who wanted to further your career.

The offices for the task force were in Yaphank headquarters, which now had a new correctional facility as their neighbor. Attorney Al Simmons had already inquired as to the possibility of moving Madison to the Yaphank facility to be fifteen minutes closer to Rachelle, but so far his request had not been approved by the DA's office and the sentencing judge. The Riverhead facility was becoming overcrowded to the point that bunk beds were on the outside walls of cells and as much as two hundred inmates were already transferred to other jails at a cost of $200 per day to the taxpayers. The Priority 1 task force utilized about four thousand square feet in a separate locked area of the building.

Once Detective Lieutenant Cronin was promoted as head of Priority 1, he had provisions added that only authorized personnel could get into the area. This way there would be no "ears" and no Monday morning quarterbacks while he was working a case with his team. The only time there was outside interference was when the chief of police, the DA, and Kevin Cronin's old friend ADA

John Ashley came into the Priority 1 unit to review the current case being worked on. During the past eighteen months there were a few periods of time when there was not a Priority 1 case assigned and Cronin had no problem lending out a few of the men to help out here and there.

The relationship between Priority 1 and the media had become a strong one and something that the detective lieutenant was initially fond of. He realized, however, the need for the relationship after *LI Pulse* published his statements and interview, which escalated the solving of the famous Face of Fear case. He never forgot it and has remained available to this day when the magazine and Nada Marjanovich, the publisher and editor, requested it.

Cronin stood up and saw Powers and Johnson at their desks. He couldn't believe a year and a half had gone by since the killing spree that left Police Officer Davis dead and six more killed at the hands of Madison Robinson wearing the blood-splattered Ghost Face mask. Yet most likely she saved the lives of Deborah, Rachelle, and Officer Sherry Walker. Former FBI agent Jason "Jack" O'Connor was now serving a life sentence at Bedford Hills Prison upstate, and his cohorts had been killed during an attempt to eliminate twelve-year-old Lindsey Wilkerson. All three were shot by Detective Powers and Officers Healey and Lynagh.

The detective lieutenant believed no other squad could have saved more innocent lives than those he had on the case. Cronin was criticized by some for his manipulation of the investigation that put many people's lives in jeopardy, but those were subjective opinions. The outcome of the case ended with lives saved and the case solved.

The team, especially, Johnson and Healey, had grown close to Lindsey Wilkerson but honored the request of her parents who wanted time to pass to where it was comfortable for them to slip out of their child's life. Lindsey, then a twelve-year-old with a photographic memory, was heavily traumatized by the home invasion. Her bodyguard or "protector," as she called him, Officer Justin Healey was badly injured, and she stayed by his side at the hospital till sleep took over and her parents put their foot down by taking her home. The scene at Stony Brook Hospital looked like a war zone with Officer Dugan injured as well. Officer George Lynagh was there as well, holding a shotgun in the hallway the entire time Lindsey was at the hospital and wouldn't leave her side until they found Phil Smith dead in the storage barn on Morgan Lane the following morning. They were taking no chances on Lindsey at the hospital, but when it was over, the questions of who killed Phil Smith and how, and where the ransom money went to, were never answered.

The team missed contact with Lindsey, but they agreed that the young girl deserved a chance to be a child as she entered her teenage years. However, it was Bud that held her close in his heart. The teasing, the trivia, and Lindsey being wise beyond her years were all part of why Bud Johnson became fond of her, and showed great affection for her. During his private time he had expressed desire in his prayers that he would see Lindsey again and requested of God that he be around to see the man she eventually married. He would smile at the thought and felt that God had a sense of humor.

Four months after the case was closed, Bud received a package in the mail from Lindsey and he became teary-eyed as he pulled out a little book called *Jesus Calling* by Sara Young. Inside were devotions for every day of the year. He never started his day without reading the daily passage from that day. Lindsey had signed the first page with the inscription,

For Bud, the presence of God is always with you. When things start to overshadow your thoughts, focus on the promises of the Lord. You are always in my thoughts and prayers. Love, Lindsey.

Bud treasured the book and kept it on his desk and always took it with him when he would be out of the office for a few days. He never mentioned it, but it was something Paul noticed.

Cronin's thoughts were interrupted by Gina, his assistant, asking him to review his schedule. Gina had become so invaluable to the detective lieutenant that she not only maintained the schedules of his team, but helped him with his personal schedule as well. She was, simply put, the "director" of the Priority 1 Task Force. She knew where everyone was at all times.

Detective Powers was still at his desk reading the book aloud that Rachelle wrote. He was interested in the Henry Hallock house that Bud was moving into, and began to get lost in Rachelle's writing.

"Hey, my partner," Bud yelled, "you don't have to read aloud to me. I looked at the house because of the book."

Paul didn't even realize he was speaking but quickly started reading to himself. After a few minutes of reading he looked up at Bud and said,

"You know, I'm surprised, you of all people are moving into a house built in 1848. I bet the place is haunted. Did you ask if anybody died in the house?" Bud dropped his pen as he stared back at Paul.

"OK, OK, let's hear it; give me your best shot," he said as he leaned back on his chair.

Paul leaned forward. "No, I'm serious; someone as nervous as you buys this old rickety house with tubs from the 1800s and tires in the basement from the '50s. You don't think there are ghosts in the house?"

He had Bud's attention, who now leaned forward and asked,

"How did you know about the tires in the basement?"

Paul smiled and replied, "You took a nap last week and you were talking out loud." Paul got up to go to the men's room but made it a point to say one more thing as he walked by Bud: "Ooh, the ghosts of Port Jefferson love that house," and he raised his hands and shook them in the air.

Bud stood up and asked, "You don't really think the place is haunted do you?"

Paul acted like he didn't hear Bud as he turned the corner, but he had a big smile on his face. Bud sat at his desk as he looked at the photos he had placed there, one of his mother who had passed away and one of Lindsey with her dog, Monty, and one of Deborah. A small bowl of gummy bears in small packets was also a mainstay on his desk. He picked up the book Rachelle wrote that included the house he bought and tried to convince himself the place was not haunted. "Nah," he said to himself as he dropped the book back on Paul's desk.

Al Simmons had been waiting for Madison for about ten minutes in the attorney room when she was let in by Officer Bay.

"Thank you," she said to the officer as he closed the door to give them privacy. She gave her attorney a hug as he asked her how she was being treated. "They treat me well, as always, Al," she replied. "Thank you for coming every couple weeks, but I understand you are busy. My sentence is for the next five to six years; it won't change," she said with a forced grin on her face.

Al Simmons took her hand. "You are my client, and I will be here every couple weeks. One, to give you a chance to get out of your cell; two, I want the officers to see you are being looked after; and three, for you to know that many of us support you."

Maddie bowed her head and looked up again at her attorney. "You never told me who compensated you for all this . . . the trial, the work."

He smiled at her as he replied, "If I knew who, I don't think they would want me to tell you anyway." Al Simmons had his feelings about the matter. Someone had left $300,000 in his house to handle her case, with a note telling him to use discretion. He never spoke about it with anyone except Madison and did a nice spin job with Judge Green before the trial started. Every time he thought about his confrontation with the judge he couldn't help but laugh.

Maddie asked, "What's that grin for?"

Simmons shook his head. "Sorry I was just thinking about being called into Judge Green's office before your trial started."

"Tell me, please," Madison said as she grabbed his hand.

"Please, I need a good story."

"OK," he laughed. "Looking back, it's humorous, but at the time I was very, very concerned about you. It was six months after the Face of Fear investigation ended, and the trial was set to begin when Judge Green called in ADA Ashley and me. He sat down in his chair, let out a belch, drank some water, and said,

'What the fuck is going on here?' We both looked at him puzzled because we didn't know what he meant.

"'Gee,' Judge Green said as he tapped his temple with his forefinger. 'First you clowns get me to release Patty Saunders to bait the killers. She gets herself sliced open, and now look who is here defending her murderer, the attorney who represented Patty Saunders.'"

Judge Green's concerns were accurate. Simmons was the attorney for Patty Saunders who was responsible for the kidnapping of Deborah Lance on the Cross Island Ferry. He took her case pro bono in the hopes of building his résumé and it paid off. He earned the respect of the detectives involved in the case, including the grumpy Detective Lieutenant Cronin. They all agreed he was the best choice to represent Madison, but Judge Green was not happy he was preparing a case for someone who murdered his client.

"'Your Honor,' Ashley replied, 'Mr. Simmons had nothing to do with setting up Patty Saunders's release. It was at the request of Detective Lieutenant Cronin and the DA's office.' 'Bullshit,' Judge Green replied. 'He was sitting in my chambers with you and Cronin agreeing to let Saunders out on bail. She is killed by Madison Robinson, and here he is again. Just what in the hell are you guys up to?'

"Green looked at Ashley and said, 'So now you're defending Simmons,' and then looked back at me. He asked, 'Just who the hell is paying you for this?'

"I looked over at Ashley, then back at the Judge, and said, 'They are anonymous.'

"'Oh shit, here we go again,' Green replied. 'This is giving me gas pockets, excuse me,' he said as he got up.

"When he left the room, Ashley remarked, 'Some things never change,' and we both laughed. Judge Green was back within a few minutes and sat down.

"I had started to take a seat when the judge said, 'Please don't get comfortable. Listen you two; I won't be allowing cameras during the trial. There will not be any grandstanding in my courtroom, and if I think for one second you two are conspiring a verdict together, I will not only throw both of you in jail, I will have you disbarred. Do I make myself clear?'

"'Yes, Your Honor,' we both answered at the same time. We both stood there as Judge Green continued to stare, until finally he spoke again: 'Will you two please get the fuck out of my chambers?'"

Madison laughed as Simmons finished telling the story. The truth is Judge Green was as off-the-wall as most considered. It was a favor called in from DA Steinberg's office to have him preside over the case. He kept things moving, hid his sympathy toward the defendant, and reminded everyone of the letter of the law many times during the trial. He made himself available to the jury for their questions and scolded them when he felt interpretation of the law was misunderstood by them.

Madison's face became serious for a moment, and she asked,

"Was it difficult for you to defend someone who killed your client?"

"Yes," the attorney answered right away. "I only accepted the case because people I respected asked me to take it. I couldn't understand why detectives such as Powers, Johnson, and Cronin wanted you represented, but as time went on and I got to know you, I understood. While the law doesn't agree with you, it can't change that people care about you, Maddie."

She brushed her hair off her face and said,

"Well, Powers loves my sister, so that's part of it."

"No," Simmons answered, "Detective Johnson told me he was going to shoot you while you had the mask on. It was Powers that stopped him, and you know Johnson, he has no problem shooting people." They both laughed.

"Listen," Madison said, "tell Paul that many of the women in this facility are here because of drugs."

"So?" Simmons asked.

Madison replied quickly,

"They're getting the drugs from licensed, professional doctors."

Simmons looked confused, and Madison said, "Listen, these girls are making appointments to see their doctors and once they are alone in the little room they slip the doctor a few hundred dollars and they get their prescription for oxycodone or samples that doctors have. These girls have no chance, and the doctors are part of the problem. This is not a rehab center. They get out, and because of background checks, they get no jobs and end up back here 80 percent of the time. All that is going to happen is the jails are going to get more and more overcrowded."

Simmons tilted his head and asked, "And what do you expect Paul to do?"

Madison shook her head at the attorney. "Don't you think the doctors should be held responsible for being part of the problem?"

Al Simmons nodded and replied,

"I will speak to him."

Officer Bay opened the door to tell them their hour was up. Madison looked up at the tall guard and remarked,

"It's been an hour and ten minutes, Officer Bay, thank you."

He looked at her and Simmons and said,

"Oh, guess my watch is off."

Madison hugged Simmons good-bye, and she started to go to the changing area to put on her regular orange coveralls. As Maddie and Officer Bay walked back to her housing cell she turned and thanked the officer for being polite and courteous to her.

"It's my job, ma'am," he replied.

As they continued to walk she spoke again, asking,

"What is your first name, Officer Bay?"

"It's John, Madison."

"You have escorted me on and off for eighteen months and I never knew that," she replied.

"You never asked," the officer replied.

As he put her back in her cell, Madison replied,

"That's interesting."

"Why is that?" the officer asked.

"Oh, nothing I guess," she answered, "other than I killed a man named John." Officer Bay stopped in his tracks and looked at her as she began to laugh. "I'm sorry; I guess I have a sick sense of humor."

The officer nodded as he began to walk away, and said, "I will see you Wednesday."

Madison sat down on her bed and had a flashback about the day she killed John Winters in the abandoned building across from St. Charles Hospital. They had since torn down the building and converted it into a parking lot. It seemed like yesterday that she cut him deep for bringing misery to her sister. Unlike in movies, she wanted her victims to see her face before they died. She felt so much anger that, depending where she was, she would pull off the Ghost Face mask just to see their expressions before taking their last breath. She could still go over each killing in her head. Sometimes she couldn't believe she was the vigilante, but as her thoughts showed her taking the mask off to see their faces, reality would set in. John Winters, the leader, his brothers Kyle and Mason, as well as Wayne Starfield were responsible for Deborah's kidnapping. Her thoughts were broken by Officer Bay's replacement, Officer Gates, a pretty young female officer, petite at 5'4" and one hundred pounds, who had been a regular escorting Madison during the night shifts as well as alternate Sundays for the past three months.

"Dinnertime," Gates announced as she put the tray of turkey, mashed potatoes, corn, and bread through the opening.

"Tell me, Officer Gates," Madison asked, "why is the food so bland?"

The young officer laughed as she replied, "The cooks don't know everyone's diet restrictions and possible stomach problems. So poof, everything is cooked with nothing added."

"OK," the inmate answered. "May I ask your name? I just found out Officer Bay's name is John."

The young officer had a look of puzzlement.

"Um," she hesitated, "I'm not sure that's a good idea." As she began to walk away, she added, "I'm sorry." Madison looked at her dinner and began to pick up the turkey slices with her fingers. After a couple bites she put her hands over her face and cried. She didn't see Officer Gates looking at her.

As Simmons was driving back to Yaphank headquarters he was upset with himself that he didn't ask Madison how she knew about the drugs being handed out from doctors. He remembered Officer Bay's name badge and called the facility. Officer Bay was unavailable during the lockdown on his shift but would return the call when he left the building. Simmons made it back to Yaphank in thirty-three minutes and asked to speak to both Powers and Johnson. There was no need for a private room because everything about Priority 1 was private. While the relationship between the detectives and the attorney had gotten off to a rocky start eighteen months before, it had transformed into a mutual respect for their work and accomplishments. The attorney told them of his discussion with Madison and wasn't sure if there was anything that could be done but felt they should know. They thanked him and told him most likely it would be given to one of the other squads. Paul warned Simmons that nothing may happen, due to priorities.

"That sucks," Detective Ellyn Baker remarked. She was

doing paperwork across the aisle and couldn't help but overhear the conversation. "Doctors are giving away pills for cash and getting away with it?"

"Allegedly, yes," Simmons answered.

"Well, that bites the big one," the detective replied as she walked away in her stocking feet.

As Powers and Simmons looked at each other, Bud spoke. "Now, there's a girl after my own heart, even if she doesn't wear shoes," he said, as he smiled.

Paul waved at Bud as he spoke to Simmons: "I'll bring it up to the boss, Al, and I'll be in touch."

"Come on," Bud remarked, "I'll walk you out. I have to pick up something in the car." Detective Johnson walked out with the attorney as he received an update on how Madison was holding up. They shook hands as Bud picked up a note pad and entered the precinct just in time to see a loud confrontation between a perp and an officer.

Bud walked by and yelled,

"Shut up, shithead!" There was total silence in the room as the cops stared at Bud and the young man arrested was shocked by the detective's remark.

Bud put his fingerprint on the screen to enter into the Priority 1 area. When he got back to his desk, Lynagh, Healey, Franks, Chapman, and Dugan had just walked into Cronin's office for a briefing on the past week. He saw Cronin point his finger at him as well as Baker and Powers to come to his office. Once they were all in his office, Cronin informed them that things were pretty calm and it might be a good time to take some personal time before they were loaned out for other cases. Detective Baker spoke up and told Detective Cronin the story about Simmons and Madison at the jail.

"OK," Cronin replied. "I need to see schedules within the next forty-eight hours on vacation time." As everyone left the room,

Powers, Johnson, and Baker stayed behind to give Cronin specific info on what Simmons had told them.

As Al Simmons' iPhone started playing classical music he was pleased to find Officer John Bay returning his call. They exchanged pleasantries, and finally the attorney came to his point and asked, "John, how would Madison Robinson find out how the girls are getting drugs from doctors by slipping them a few hundred here and there?"

There was silence at the other end of the phone, and finally the correctional officer answered,

"While Madison is kept separate for her own safety, she does have access to the church, the priest, the nun, and on very special occasions, if we have enough officers outside to protect her, we let her have access to other female inmates. She's a human being and we try to give her a chance to speak to others."

"No, don't misunderstand me, Officer," Simmons replied. "I appreciate the treatment of Madison. I just wondered where she got the information."

John Bay spoke again. "Why would she care about this?"

"Well," Simmons replied, "that's Madison. She cares, sometimes too much, which is why she is there right now."

"I see," Officer Bay answered. "Anything else I can do for you?"

"No, no, thank you, Officer. Maddie is a good person in case you are wondering."

"I know," came the reply. "And off the record, she is right about the doctors; they don't care about these girls, all they care about is the cash."

Before Simmons could reply, there was an end-call sound. He wanted to call back but thought better of it. He would stop and make it a point to see Detective Cronin tomorrow morning. He knew Powers and Johnson were going to speak with him but decided he would speak directly with him as well.

September 29

The nightclub called the City was the place to be in Setauket. It was combination circular dance floor on the lower level with a balcony on the second level that would allow people to stand against the railings and look down at the gathering on the dance floor or move to semiprivate tables and booths in the thirty-five extra feet behind the railings. The decor on the walls was illuminated photos of Los Angeles, New York, Chicago, San Francisco, and New Orleans. There was even a private room for a $1,500 rental fee for the entire evening. Privacy when you wanted it, and party and dancing when you opened the door.

Kate Summers was a regular at the City. She was beautiful, brunette, twenty-five years old, and kept count of all the men she had sex with at the club in the private room. Her goal was to live life to the fullest and snag a millionaire by the time she was thirty. Her schedule tonight was a blind date set up by one of her friends in the private room. She said good-bye to her girlfriends with the hand motion of her finger going in and out of her mouth slowly. Her friends, Linda and Jackie, just shook their heads and gave her a wave. The music was so loud that patrons either used sign language, hand signals, texts from their phone, or the old-fashioned way of putting your mouth directly on the ear of those with whom you were trying to communicate.

Kate gave her name to security and checked to be sure the other name on the list for the room matched the name given to her from Linda and Jackie. The burly security guard bellowed the name Jake Wiley. With a smile to the guard and a friendly touch to his biceps, Kate started to walk to the room, but turned around and spoke to the guard again, saying, "You know, there is something very sexy about a man whose biceps are bigger than my thighs." The guard flinched for a moment and asked if she wanted to be disturbed. She quickly answered,

"Only if no one shows up, and then only by you." She winked at him as she entered the room with a grin on her face, thinking how anxious the guard would be for the next few minutes.

Inside the room, two sofas, a long black sectional, a coffee table with fruit, and a large flat-screen TV complemented the music system that included Bose speakers. Kate looked through the selections and dimmed the lights as a song from a group called Mystic Strangers started playing through the speakers. She closed her eyes as she moved her hands and body to the music. The young woman took her shoes off and unbuttoned her blouse, as the intense song was getting her aroused. She raised her hands in the air as the song lyrics said, "Never ask why, just be ready when it's time to die." With her eyes closed and a sexy grin on her face, a pillowcase came over her head as she started screaming.

The song and the pillowcase drowned out her voice as her body fell to the floor. The assailant put his hand over the pillowcase to speed up the process and finally punched the young woman in the stomach to weaken her fight. The young woman fought hard to resist but could not breathe. The assailant became more excited and aggressive as Kate raised her legs to try and fight him off, and the pain she was experiencing excited him. His hands pressed harder against the pillowcase as her hands reached for his hair. He could feel her desperation to stay alive, and it made him stronger to feel her lose life. Within a couple minutes it was over. Kate was placed on the sofa with her blouse half undone. Her body was positioned to make it look like she was sleeping. As she lay there, the killer moved in closer and kissed the dead woman's lips and then her forehead while leaving a folded piece of paper in her hand before walking away.

After the murderer opened the door with his gloves, he would look for a chance to walk away when the guard was distracted. Two minutes seemed like forever, when finally the guard's cell phone vibrated with a text. As his eyes went down to the cell, the assailant put on a baseball hat. Inside the hat was cloth that he pulled out and it came down as a black mask. It covered his head completely except for the eyes and mouth. The club was so crowded no one paid attention to him. When he got outside he moved the fabric inside the hat as he walked into the darkness of the night.

It was fifteen minutes later when the guard realized that no one had entered the room with the woman who found his biceps sexy. He walked in and smiled as he saw Kate Summers sleeping on the couch with those thin thighs. He turned the knob to lock the door, approached the couch, and noticed there was a piece of paper folded, lying in her hand. He picked it up and opened it, and it said in cut-out letters, *If I can't have you, no one will.* Bruce Roberts, a strong, muscled man, looked at Kate Summers and feared the worst. He checked her pulse, then stepped back so fast in horror that his leg hit the coffee table and he fell on top of it as it smashed to the floor with the weight of his body. He was injured with glass cuts and going into shock as he reached into his pants and pushed 9-1-1. He passed out before he could say anything, but the operator began tracking his phone. Within ten minutes there were cops and medics at the scene treating the startled guard.

Detective William O'Malley stared at Bruce Roberts as he was being treated in the room, and went up into his face. "You are in a world of shit, my friend."

"Wait," the guard said, "I didn't touch the girl."

O'Malley answered, "You are either a moron or just a bad liar." He kept his face in Bruce's face and said, "You didn't touch her, you just happen to be alone with her with the door locked." Roberts began to shake his head but was in too much pain to continue. O'Malley nodded as he told his men to get the club's films from that evening. "Get me the owner!" O'Malley yelled. "It's time to talk!" The medics took Bruce Roberts out to the ambulance with a police escort as the owner, Brian Branca, came into the room. "Mr. Branca," Detective O'Malley said as they acknowledged one another.

"Please," the owner replied, "call me BB."

O'Malley hesitated for a few seconds, trying to digest what he had just heard. "Mr. Branca," he said again, "I would like to see the films you have on that room during the evening. We know Ms. Summers entered the private room about 11:00 pm so I would like everything in the club from 10:00 pm until an hour after the 9-1-1 call."

"Of course," Branca replied. "Do you have any idea when my club will be reopened?"

His question caught Detective O'Malley by surprise, and he replied, "We will let you know."

"No," Branca replied, not liking O'Malley's tone. "You can let my attorney know. I'm not going to let you guys put me out of business because of egos. Do your job and we will cooperate, but I need my club opened." His strong remarks caught the detective by surprise again.

"Yes, BB, we will let you know." The club owner, who had had enough, replied,

"No, let my lawyer know. Second request, call me Mr. Branca." He walked out of the room.

O'Malley looked over at Detective Hansen and said,

"Let's get a background check on Mr. Branca as well."

The crime scene unit went over the room, and eventually it would come back with fingerprints of only Kate Summers, Bruce Roberts, the maid who kept the room spotless, and the bellboy who had delivered the fruits and drinks to the room. O'Malley instructed his team that the club would remain closed until the films were reviewed. No one was allowed in the private room without his authorization.

The detective was only in his car for ten minutes as he drove to Stony Brook Hospital when he received a call from Branca's attorney. "Hello, Detective O'Malley, this is Edward Larson, Mr. Branca's attorney. We will cooperate as much as we can, but we ask for cooperation in return to get the club reopened within a few days. An incident like this can destroy a business."

O'Malley's first instinct was not to care about their business but common sense prevailed within the experienced detective.

"Yes, Mr. Larson, we will do everything as quickly as we can to get your client back in business."

"Thanks very much, Detective, and please call me Edward." As he disconnected, O'Malley just shook his head as he drove into the parking lot at Stony Brook Hospital. His first thought was, *I didn't think you wanted me to call you Eddy, dickhead.*

Detectives Wyatt and Hansen stayed behind at the club until the body was removed and had the task of informing the next of kin. It was 4:00 am, and most likely the parents or relatives would be waking up in the next couple hours. "What a waste," Hansen spoke.

Wyatt just shook his head as he replied,

"More dreams that will never come true."

SEPTEMBER 30

Simmons walked into headquarters in Yaphank, presented his ID, and requested time with Detective Cronin. The desk receptionist was surprised when she was informed to give him a four-number code for guests to enter the Priority 1 area; normally someone would come to guests and escort them in. Simmons came in with a pleasant greeting to everyone before Cronin waved him into his office.

There was much more respect between the attorney and the Priority 1 Task Force. This was particularly true when it came to Detective Bud Johnson. He didn't like or trust the attorney and continued to push his buttons until he realized that he was actually a good hardworking man who genuinely cared about his clients. While they were not friends, there was a mutual understanding for each other. Bud particularly gave his respect and support to the attorney after witnessing how diligent he was before, during, and after the trial of Rachelle's sister, Madison. Bud was thirty-one years of age and he was about twenty pounds lighter with the encouragement of Paul, Rachelle, and Deborah. He dated Deborah for a few months after the Face of Fear investigation, but it was difficult to keep momentum with the cases that followed. They were close, but the relationship became platonic. He never understood why it did, because his heart would stop whenever he saw her. Emotionally, he loved Deborah and the bond they had. He questioned himself if he was "in love" with her and felt it played games in his head.

Al Simmons stretched out his hand to Kevin Cronin as he sat down in the chair in front of the detective. "I would like to speak to you about Madison Robinson in the facility in Riverhead," he said.

Cronin stopped scribbling on his desk and replied, "Oh, why do I not want to hear this? What did she do now, start beating up the guards?"

"No, no," Simmons replied, laughing. "I told Detective Powers and Johnson yesterday that many women in the jail, not a few, but many, are getting themselves in trouble because of our wonderful doctors in Suffolk County. I guess the insurance companies aren't paying enough so they are taking cash from these women behind closed doors and in return they are giving them samples of Vicodin and oxycodone. The more brazen licensed professionals are actually writing prescriptions for them."

"Yes," Cronin replied, "they spoke to me briefly about this yesterday." Cronin put his hand to his head, rubbing the side as he spoke. "So you think we should do something because you believe Madison that this is really going on. We can't forget she killed six people, Al."

"Yes," the attorney replied. "I figure she saved the taxpayers about $4 to $6 million in court costs while saving lives at the same time." Cronin acknowledged the attorney's comments with the nod of his head and pushed the button at this desk.

"Gina, please have ADA Ashley stop by my office before the end of the day."

"Thanks, Al," Cronin said as he got up. "No promises."

The attorney shook his head and stopped at the door before exiting. He said,

"I've been visiting Madison every couple weeks for almost a year and a half. These prisoners, they do their time, they get out, and with the technology for background checks, are stopped from getting any kind of job. They have nowhere to go but break the law again to survive. If they get caught, they are back in prison until they do their time again and they are back out on the streets again.

Once you are in prison, you are done."

Cronin started to speak but was interrupted by the attorney. "I'm not talking about the pharmacy killer and rapists, etc. I'm talking about women who made bad choices about themselves with drugs and were enabled by dishonest doctors. It will be a vicious circle for them with the beginning and the end at the jail. In fact, 80 percent of these prisoners will be back in the prison. Hell, one of the guards told Madison he has seen teenagers turn into old ladies during his thirty-five years as a correctional officer. Kevin, did you know the facility is so overcrowded they are getting variances approved to have sixteen-year-old girls in the same cell block as adult women?"

Cronin stood up as he dropped his pen and replied,

"I hear you, Al. Let me see if there is anything we should be looking at." Simmons just stood there as the detective lieutenant raised his hands and continued, "I will see what I can do, but I don't think the DA or the chief would assign it to the Priority 1 team."

Simmons tapped the door frame as he spoke again. "Rachelle is a writer, she can ask for a tour of the facility for a story she's working on."

"No," the detective answered. "No way, I'm not getting the sister involved in this, but I do have an idea. Let me speak to the DA's office." The attorney smiled as he waved good-bye.

He walked over to the desks of Powers and Johnson, and exchanged glances at Lynagh, Healey, and Detective Baker.

"How are things?" he said. Bud looked up and started singing lyrics from "You Can Call Me Al." Simmons laughed as he grabbed a packet of gummy bears from his desk before he left.

Paul Powers leaned forward and spoke. "You are losing your edge, my friend; you used to annoy him, now he laughs when you sing to him."

"Yes," Bud answered, "he knows that I like him, my partner, and that makes all the difference. Shit, I've got to figure out another way to get under his skin."

Paul nodded as Officer Lynagh walked by and said, "Maybe he just figures he should laugh or you might shoot him in the balls or the ass," then continued walking toward the men's room. Paul had a smile on his face as Bud was taken by surprise.

"Ha, ha, everyone is the comedian now. That's my job," Bud said as Lynagh raised his arm up to acknowledge he heard him before pushing the men's room door open. Bud was shaking his head thinking about Lynagh's remark. It was during the chase of Kyle Winters who had just assassinated a police officer in the attempt on Rachelle's life. He caught up with the cop killer on Daniels Deck at the Red Onion Café and shot him in the groin when he didn't follow directions during the arrest. Bud smiled to himself as his thoughts turned to shooting former FBI agent Jason "Jack" O'Connor in the ass at the climax of the investigation. He never told anyone he actually aimed for his leg. Who wanted to hear more jokes that he wasn't the greatest shot? The capture of the man who was known as the Voice by his associates resulted in three life sentences with no chance for parole. Bud thought about paying him a visit a few times but decided it wasn't worth the gas money in this poor economy.

Cronin's phone rang and it was ADA Ashley, who said he couldn't make it till 5:00 pm and offered to meet him at Cavanaugh's for a drink and a bite to eat. With Cronin's family visiting relatives in California, the date was set. Paul, on the other hand, had plans to see Rachelle and his father for dinner and touched Bud's shoulder as he left, saying,

"I love you, man. See you tomorrow."

Bud looked over as Paul was walking away and said,

"Don't forget next Saturday, Henry Hallock house."

"Yeah, yeah," Paul yelled back. "I'm sure the ghost will be there."

Bud yelled, "Not funny, not funny," as Paul disappeared

from sight. It was fifteen minutes later when Lynagh and Healey left the building. Detective Ellyn Baker came over to Bud's desk and offered to help with the move the following week. He thanked her, and she replied,

"Can you tell me about the person I replaced, Sherry Walker, sometime?"

He seemed surprised by the question but replied that he would be happy to tell her. He said,

"She was a good cop who was part of Rachelle Robinson's protective detail during the Face of Fear investigation. She saved Rachelle's life and was an integral part of the investigation from her hospital bed until it was completed. She was promoted to Priority 1 Task Force when she was healthy enough to come back to work. A knife through the abdomen will put you out of commission for a while. She was here for about six months but decided her heart was no longer in it. We speak about once a month still, but she needed to move on. You tend to look at life different when you have faced death."

Ellyn seemed totally engrossed in what Bud was saying and said, "That's deep, about facing death. Are you and Deborah Lance an item?"

The detective leaned back on the back two legs of the chair and replied, "We are close friends."

"Oh," she replied.

"Why?" he asked back.

"Just wondering," she replied. "I see the way she looks at you when she is around and I see the way you are when you answer a call or text from her. I'm a cop, but more important, I'm a woman."

"Well," Bud answered, "maybe we should change the subject." Ellyn Baker smiled as she went back to her desk. Bud thought to himself how attractive she looked without shoes on. He shook his head to clear his focus.

"Good night!" Detective Cronin bellowed as he left the Priority 1 section. He went out to the parking lot to meet ADA Ashley for dinner and found a folded piece of paper on his windshield. He opened it to read in cut-out letters.

An express assurance
on which expectation
is to be based.

He folded the paper and went to the ground to search for any possible bomb under his car. He opened his car door carefully as he searched for wires. He went back underneath the car again and found nothing. He turned the ignition on with his eyes closed. Nothing. He drove to Cavanaugh's in the town of Blue Point not knowing if he should be angry or happy he didn't blow up in a million pieces. He couldn't get to the restaurant/bar fast enough to meet with the ADA.

Bruce Roberts was getting ready to be released from the hospital when Detective O'Malley came into his room and said, "OK, tell me the whole story again."

As Roberts explained to him what happened, O'Malley took notes and waited until he finished before asking, "Why were you injured on top of a smashed glass coffee table? You keep leaving that part out."

Roberts shook his head, hesitated, and spoke. "It's not good for my reputation, but I was slightly frightened when I realized Kate was dead. I panicked."

O'Malley replied,

"You use her first name?"

The muscleman quickly answered, "Her name was on the list with Jake Wiley."

O'Malley tried to call his detectives, but his BlackBerry would not work in the hospital. He had tried the iPhone but returned to his BlackBerry within a few months. He was just more comfortable using the keys instead of the screen for emails.

O'Malley left the hospital telling Roberts not to leave town for a while. The detective felt Roberts was not responsible, especially for the fact that he called 9-1-1 while in the club. O'Malley called Detective Bob Wyatt and told him to take Hansen and bring Jake Wiley to the Fourth Precinct.

O'Malley got into his car and started driving back to the squad room. There would not be much sleep tonight. William O'Malley, a thirty-year veteran at the age of fifty-six, was considering retiring soon to become a teacher. The political red tape with the new administration was becoming unbearable to him and he was getting concerned he would lose his patience, especially with the new round of detectives who wanted to be the next rising star. Six feet tall and once very slim, he had put about twenty-five extra pounds on his frame and looked older than his age. He arrived at the precinct and decided to take a nap before his detectives brought in Jake Wiley.

ADA John Ashley was already sitting at a corner table in the back of Cavanaugh's when Detective Lieutenant Cronin walked in. He knew the detective had arrived by all the patrons yelling,

"Hey Kevin!" "Hey, Detective!" Cronin's booming voice could be heard replying,

"Hi, guys! Nice to see you!"

He was always well-known in the communities of Blue Point, Bayport, and Sayville, but ever since the Face of Fear case his face had become well-known throughout Long Island. In fact, it was just another reason to put him in charge of the Priority 1 Task Force. The chief of police felt it would have much more impact with someone with a track record who could easily demand respect. Kevin was within two weeks of turning fifty, but his emotional outlook on life and desire to be a great cop kept him performing at the level of the younger cops.

He shook hands with ADA Ashley as he sat down and ordered a Bud Light. The history of these two men went back almost ten years. Detective Lieutenant Cronin proved he was the master of solving puzzles and games during the kidnapping of Deborah Lance and the Ghost Face vigilante killings. Ashley had always regarded Kevin as a top detective, but he gained a new respect for him by the time the case was finished. There was only one question in his mind, and he had not raised it for the past six months. Tonight he would have his opportunity.

Detective Cronin ordered the prime rib special while Ashley ordered the smothered burger and Fries. After the menu was given back to the server, Kevin said, "I was originally going to speak to you about one specific thing, but after what happened in the parking lot at headquarters there will be two things to talk about." Ashley took a sip of his beer as the detective began to tell him about the visit from Al Simmons in regards to the correctional facility and the drugs being received by what he called "dirty doctors." He explained to the ADA the information was given to Simmons from Madison. Ashley stopped eating after the word *Madison* was mentioned.

"Oh, shit," the ADA said. "Oh, shit. I'm getting a bad case of indigestion. I'm not ready for this. You say 'Madison Robinson' and it brings back a shitload of crap I don't want to think about."

"John," the detective said, "that was over eighteen months ago and it was a crime spree. This is a chance to put away licensed professionals who are not ethical and a big part of the oxycodone and Vicodin problem. I want to send Bud in there on a private tour with a writer from the *LI Pulse* as a writing team doing a story. If he thinks it is safe enough I want to put Detective Baker undercover for about a week to ten days and see what she comes up with." Ashley dropped his silverware as he put his napkin to his mouth.

"Kevin, what if something happens to Baker or one of the prisoners? And besides, Bud will have the prisoners either dancing to Lady Gaga or shots will be fired."

"Look," Cronin answered, "this is small potatoes compared

to what we have asked your office for help on in the past."

Ashley nodded and replied,

"Why? Why is this so important?"

Cronin leaned back on his chair as he spoke. "Tell me why it's not important; give me ten days."

Ashley asked the server for coffee as he told the detective he would get back to him after he spoke with DA Steinberg. Then he asked,

"Now, what's the second thing you wanted to talk about?"

The detective took out the folded piece of paper and handed it to the ADA, who opened it and read silently to himself the note left on Cronin's car.

"Would you happen to know who would give me a note like that?" The detective asked.

Ashley dropped the note, saying, "Now what the hell is that supposed to mean?"

Cronin's frown on his face became more pronounced. "Well, let me ask this, do you have an idea what it means?"

The ADA looked around the restaurant like he was in disbelief over the questions.

"Again," he said a little louder, "what the hell are you getting at?"

Cronin looked at the ADA and said, "This has nothing to do with our conversation in the parking lot in the village after the Face of Fear investigation?"

"Ah," Ashley replied, "now I know where this is going. I ask you to keep your word on finding out what really happened to Phil Smith and the money and here it is a year and a half later and you're being asked to cash the check, and you're wondering if I have anything to do with it."

Cronin shook his head and said, "Getting a note with one of the definitions of the word *promise* will do that to you." It was during the Face of Fear investigation that Phil Smith was eliminated by someone after the attempt on Lindsey Wilkerson's life.

"Kevin," the ADA spoke up, "I spoke to you directly about what happened to that asshole on the final night of the case. I asked you because I was worried that you felt you needed to end it no matter what had to be done!" There was silence at the table, and Ashley spoke again. "Was I right?" Again there was silence. It was becoming awkward at the table when the ADA said, "Besides you are forgetting my interview with the *New York Times* a week after the case closed." He had pressure from the FBI to the attorney general's office. Everything was accounted for in the entire case except the timing of Phil Smith's death by a bullet hole to the throat. There was silence at the table again until the ADA changed the subject. "I will get back to you on sending Baker in undercover. We would have to let the chief of the facility know. We just can't risk it without anyone knowing. Things are getting a bit busy, wait, sorry, I know how much you hate using that word busy."

"Yes" Cronin replied "when people use that word, it makes me feel they are overwhelmed and not in charge of their time."

Rachelle and Paul were holding hands over the table when his father came in to greet them at Twilight Café, a small, little '50s-themed café inside Harbor Square Mall in the village. Rachelle tried to keep away from Z Pita Restaurant when the meetings were personal. She felt as part owner and hostess that it was best to have some separation when she could. She liked the café because it had a piano in the corner and it was nice when a patron would sit and play and sometimes even sing. They were sitting by the pinball machine sharing a large James Dean salad when Paul excused himself to use the men's room.

"So," Anthony Powers said as he took Rachelle's hand, "how's it going!"

"It's great," she answered as her eyes moved away.

"Is it?" he asked.

"I guess," she replied. "I have my job at Z Pita, I write, I'm fulfilled. I love and adore your son, yet sometimes I worry about where we are going. I want and need him, and I get scared sometimes there is nothing more. I need him to express more to me, do more than what Paul would normally do to show me how he feels about me."

Anthony Powers squeezed her hand and said,

"Rachelle, give him time. He loves you more than life itself."

Paul walked back to the table and asked,

"Am I interrupting something?"

"No, no," his father answered. "Rachelle just asked me to tell her something she didn't know about your father, so here it is." He pulled out his wallet and opened up a piece of paper that had a pencil rubbing of the name Ronald L. Bond. Rachelle looked at the paper and asked him why.

"Well, my dear," Anthony Powers replied, "back in the early '70s they sold POW/MIA bracelets, which I wore for Ronald Bond until it fell apart. It didn't feel right to me, so I carried his name with me until I got to the Vietnam Memorial in DC and I made a rubbing of his name. I even communicated with his father until he passed away a few years ago. I still have the card his father, Errol Bond, wrote to me before he died. He never gave up that his son might be alive as a prisoner in Southeast Asia. So for his father and for his son, I keep his name in my wallet."

Rachelle looked at Paul and grabbed his father's hand, saying,

"That is so sweet. I would love to know more about him. Maybe I will look him up on the Internet."

"Yes," the elder Powers said, "it's all just a small part of keeping his memory alive." Rachelle mouthed the words 'Thank you' to him for keeping their conversation private as she leaned over and kissed the side of Paul's cheek.

She looked down at her watch as she said,

"I told Joey Z that I would close the restaurant tonight and be there by eight."

Paul stood up as he said, "Well then, we should go," with a grin. They stopped at Rachelle's favorite store in Harbor Square called Sea Creations. She loved all the trinkets in the store but the one thing she bought the most were the signs of the towns in Long Island with the longitude and latitude coordinates. It was always a hit when it was given as a gift. They walked Paul's father over to Danford's Hotel on Broadway and then walked back up Main Street so Rachelle could close up.

Paul pulled Rachelle to his body as he spoke. "After you close up come on upstairs. Spend the night with me."

She put her finger on his mouth and said,

"Only if you walk Wes and Craven tonight and let them stay in the apartment," and kissed him before walking in the back door of Z Pita.

The detective smiled as he walked through Trader's Cove parking lot up to Prospect Street to Rachelle's and Madison's home to walk the dogs. Paul grew to love the King Charles Cavalier dogs. They were originally given to him and Bud from Lindsey Wilkerson, the young girl who was the center of the Face of Fear investigation with Deborah and Rachelle. Both Bud and Paul thought Rachelle should have the dogs for company and some security while Madison was in jail. Paul smiled as he thought about the day Rachelle surprised him by naming the dogs Wes and Craven. She knew how much he admired the director, and he thought it was how she was expressing that she wanted to start a life with him. Whenever locals asked their names, it always brought a smile to their faces when he told them. Wes was the happy-go-lucky dog who would lick a burglar to death, and Craven would bark at anyone who got too close to Rachelle unless he knew them. Rachelle spoiled them by allowing them to sleep in her bed, which made it a problem when intimacy was desired between her and Paul.

Paul finished walking them and brought them back to his apartment, saying, "Mommy will be back soon." When he reached the top of the stairs to his apartment above Z Pita he sent Rachelle a text that he had walked the dogs and asking her to please stay for the night with the dogs. He turned on the TV and saw his favorite; Monica Crowley was substituting for Sean Hannity tonight. "Let them have it," Paul said to the conservative warrior princess.

The Pajama Club in Huntington had been busy since they opened it the previous year. What made this club different was that the doors opened at 10:00 pm and once you were in, there was no leaving until 8:00 am. You were not allowed to come in with regular street clothes, only loungewear and pajamas with an overnight bag. A $100 cover charge to get in, plus the cost of drinks, and you got the overnight party of your life for Thursdays, Fridays, and Saturdays. A private room and shower were yours for an additional $500. The club was closed Sundays once the Saturday overnight party was over at 8:00 am and did not open again until Tuesday for the regular music scene from 8:00 pm to 4:00 am. On Tuesday and Wednesday nights the club was known as Decades. A decade of music was selected and the clientele would get in free if they dressed appropriately. Last Tuesday was the '70s decade, which continues to be the most popular among the crowd during the week.

The twenty-five-thousand-square-foot club was once a movie theater, and the investors had done a magnificent job with total reconstruction of the inside. The music tonight was current, for it was Friday night. There always seemed to be many more young women on the dance floor than men. While many women danced with the opposite sex, there were even more women dancing with other young ladies. The music never stopped as the DJ was masterful in syncing up one song after another while talking and rapping to the crowd.

A figure standing up against the railing had his eye on a

young woman by the name of Michelle Cartwright, who was moving her slim body on the dance floor. The way she shook and touched her body and hair while moving her legs was giving him great pleasure. As the song "A New Life" by Mystic Strangers came on, his heart pounded with excitement as he watched her slim body move as if she had no bones. Her eyes closed yet her body language was that she wanted to do this with her clothes off. The man moved closer, as he couldn't take his eyes off her. He could feel his heart beat through his chest as the words "You cannot hide from me, you will see. I can give you a new life," were sung. Just twenty feet from her, he moved and bobbed his head so he didn't lose sight of her as the other dancers were getting in his way.

The lyrics to the song were a turn-on to Michelle. He could sense it. The darkness of the music to the haunting lyrics was making his heart pound. He couldn't take his eyes off her as she touched her body during the song. He didn't move until it was over, and as if he was no longer hypnotized he moved back over to the side and would not take his eyes off the beautiful young woman. Her long, flowing brunette hair almost made him approach her too soon. It was another twenty minutes before Michelle had enough of dancing and decided to go to the ladies' room. The man in the shadows of the crowded room watched her go into the ladies' room and planned how he would pretend to go through the wrong door if he was caught by others coming out.

He was lucky. He stepped in and caught Michelle stepping into the middle stall as he walked in behind her and covered her mouth with only a second-long scream coming out of her mouth. She was not strong enough to handle him as he snapped her neck and sat her down on the toilet seat. He kissed her lips, the side of her face, and forehead before leaving a note in her hand. He took out his baseball hat with the fabric that came down to hide his face from the back of his pants, put it on, and walked out of the ladies' room just as a group of women came in. Their smiles were wiped off their faces as he rushed out, and they looked inside to be sure nothing happened. They heard a trembling sound coming from one of the stalls as they tried to open the door, but it was locked.

"Are you OK in there?" one of them spoke. The trembling and crying continued as the leader of the group tried to convince whoever was in the stall to open the door. Suddenly one of the other girls let out a scream as she pushed the other stall door to find Michelle Cartwright lying against the wall on the toilet seat with her eyes open with the stare of death. As the other girls ran out of the ladies' room Wanda, another patron of the club, convinced whoever was in the next stall to unlock the door. As she pushed it open, she saw it was twenty-four-year-old Taylor Black, who had her legs on top of the toilet seat with her arms wrapped around them. Tears ran down her face as she shook uncontrollably. Wanda continued to hold her tight for comfort when management came into the bathroom and called the police.

As Rachelle locked up Z Pita, she went up the back stairs and climbed into bed with Paul. He was half asleep, but she loved the challenge of getting him awake and aroused. Without saying a word to each other they kissed and touched each other's bodies until only the sounds of their moans could be heard during their lovemaking. Paul enjoyed late-night sessions with Rachelle because it seemed he lasted longer to give Rachelle more pleasure when he was a little tired. They started laughing when they brought up the subject of the dogs, because it seemed like Wes liked to watch them while Craven didn't care and slept. The difference in their personalities was quite fascinating to them.

Detective O'Malley was still up looking at the film of the City nightclub and finally spotted the man coming out of the private room. He was wearing a baseball hat with the fabric hanging down, so he knew there was a camera in the general area inside the club. O'Malley moved the film faster to see Bruce Roberts also go into the room about fifteen minutes later, according to the timer. He looked at his watch and knew Detectives Wyatt and Hansen had probably informed the parents of Kate Summers of her murder. They also spoke to Jake Wiley, who was supposed to meet Kate in the private room set up by her girlfriends, but he was forty-five minutes late due to traffic and parking. By the time he got to the club there was such a commotion, he had sent Kate a text to meet some other time.

O'Malley wrote a text to Wyatt and Hansen to bring Kate Summers's girlfriends in for questioning. He told them to also bring Detective Caulfield along. He was getting ready to go home when his cell phone rang. It was Detective Wyatt, who was awakened from bed to get to the Pajama Club. The only thing O'Malley had eaten all evening was his pumpkin seeds. He became addicted to them ten years earlier and could now eliminate the seed shell, eat the seed inside, and spit out the outer white shell without the use of his hands if he wanted to. O'Malley told him he would be there in twenty-five minutes and told him to bring Hansen and Caulfield with him.

As Detective O'Malley entered the stall to look at the beautiful young woman, he picked up the paper on her lifeless body. It had the same message that was on Kate Summers: *If I can't have you, no one will.* He could tell by the condition of her dress that it was strictly a killing and not something sexual. The crime unit had already taken photos and sealed off the bathroom to check for prints of any kind. Detective Wyatt brought O'Malley to a separate room to speak to Taylor Black who was in the next stall when the murder took place. She was still accompanied by Wanda, who stayed at the request of the young woman.

"Hello, Ms. Black," O'Malley said. "I'm sorry for what has happened here, but you need to tell me the unfolding of events here while it's still fresh in your mind."

Taylor Black hesitated for a moment then told the detective she was in the stall when she heard Michelle open the door and a man startle her by coming up behind her. She tried to scream but

NO MERCY | 49

he muffled her voice and then there was silence. She explained to him she was so scared she raised her feet and put her hands over her face as she heard the man position the body.

"How do you know it was a man," he asked her.

"His legs and shoes," Taylor replied.

Wanda interrupted her. "Oh, it was a man all right. I saw him leave the bathroom with the strange-looking hat with a mask on his face. It was a man all right."

"OK," the detective said, "anything else you think might interest me or you think was odd?"

Wanda spoke up again, saying,

"I think killing someone in a bathroom stall is odd, don't you think?" O'Malley frowned at Wanda as he turned his head back to Taylor.

"Well," she said, "after he killed her, it sounded like he was kissing her."

O'Malley moved in closer to Taylor.

"Keep going."

The young woman looked at Wanda then back at the detective. "The sounds of kissing are unmistakable. It was more than once. Very creepy."

The detective kneeled down to be at the same level as Taylor before speaking again. "Have you ever seen the woman in the club before?"

Taylor looked at Wanda, then back at the detective, saying, "I don't know. I haven't seen her yet."

O'Malley knew what he had to ask, but he was afraid of the answer. "Are you up to taking a look at her now?"

Taylor started crying before she spoke. "I've never seen a dead person before other than at a wake."

"OK," O'Malley answered. He looked at Wanda. "Are you up to taking a look?"

Without hesitation Wanda got up and spoke. "Honey, if it

will help catch that motherfucker, absolutely."

"I'm not surprised," O'Malley said in a low voice as he escorted Wanda to the Women's room. On his way out of the room he said, "Thank you, Taylor. I'm going to have one of the officers take you home. Go and get some rest."

"I have a car," the young woman answered.

"Fine," O'Malley spoke again. "One of the officers will follow you home."

He looked at Wanda, smiled, and said, "Let's go to the restroom."

He asked her, "If I showed you a video picture would you be able to tell me if it matched what you saw coming out of the bathroom?"

"Honey," Wanda replied, "I won't forget what he was wearing on his head. Good thing he didn't try and kiss me. I'd break his motherfucking penis in half." O'Malley shook his head as he had Wyatt and Hansen get the tapes of the club, while Caulfield was questioning other patrons. Too bad, he thought, that no filming was allowed in the bathrooms. O'Malley went home at 2:30 am with such a stress headache that he slept in the guest bedroom so he wouldn't wake his wife. He had told Wyatt and Hansen there would be no day off tomorrow.

OCTOBER 4

"**G**ood morning, my partner!" Bud said as he ran up the stairs to greet Paul, only to find Rachelle hiding her naked body under the covers up to her head.

"Oops," the detective said. "Ah, is Paul hiding somewhere?" A big smile came on his face.

Rachelle just giggled. "Bud, you are too funny. He's in the bathroom getting ready to go to work with you!"

"Well," the detective answered, "at least he wasn't so preoccupied that he forgot about me."

Rachelle replied, "I'm just glad you didn't come up those stairs ten minutes ago."

The detective nodded, "I'm sure Paul is also. OK, tell him I'll be in the car waiting for him." As Bud shut the door downstairs, Paul opened the door to the bathroom as he approached Rachelle still with the covers up to her head. As he looked at her she found she was still amazed by his good shape.

"Are you being shy all of a sudden, missy? I've seen your body a few times."

"No," Rachelle replied, "but Bud hasn't seen my body, and I would like to keep it that way." She explained to him that Bud ran up the stairs while he was in the bathroom. He laughed as she said, "Can you imagine if he came up a few minutes earlier?"

"You mean," Paul said, "like right now," as he gazed into her eyes and started to move the covers from her.

"Oh God," she said as she put her arms around him. "He can wait another ten minutes." It was twenty minutes before Paul came out to meet Bud to go to the precinct. As he got in the car Bud started singing, "You were always on my mind."

Paul looked at his partner. "Yes, my friend, life is good!" Paul wanted to bring Deborah up, but he felt if it wasn't his place since life had taken them in different directions. Still, he wished for his friend and his partner to be happy. As they drove to Yaphank headquarters Bud was explaining how excited he was about moving to the Henry Hallock house in a few days.

"Yes," Paul said, "the haunted house. We will be there to help you."

Upstairs in the apartment Rachelle was still in bed and called Deborah.

"Hey you, if you haven't had breakfast, meet me at the Coffee House." Deborah was happy to make plans with Rachelle for more girl talk. "Give me an hour," Rachelle said, "I have to take care of the dogs and have to work in the restaurant until 5:00 pm today, so let's eat before my shift. OK?"

"See you in an hour," Deborah replied as she hung up. She was amused, as she thought Bud would be jealous if he knew she would be having breakfast where his favorite server worked. He had become so fond of Brittany at the Coffee House that the only times he had breakfast there were the days she was there. He even met her boyfriend at the bar Country Corner where he worked in Setauket, because he wanted to be sure he was OK for her. That was Bud, always concerned and looking out for others. Deborah shook her head to try to stop thinking about Bud, but all she could do was smile.

As the ride continued to headquarters, Paul opened the paper to read about the City nightclub murder. He could not focus clearly because he had a tendency to get headaches while the car was in motion.

"What a shame," he said. "A beautiful young girl's life snuffed away, so many animals in today's world." His Samsung Galaxy smartphone buzzed as he finished his sentence. "It's Cronin," he said as he picked up the call.

"When are you guys getting here? Let's go!"

"On the way, Boss, give us ten minutes."

When they walked into the precinct and into the Priority 1 area, Detectives Cronin and Baker, as well as Officers Lynagh, Healey, Chapman, Franks, and Dugan were waiting for them in the conference room.

"Have a seat," Cronin said to them. They took a seat and remained silent, as they were surprised to see Police Chief Bob Jameson sitting next to Cronin looking over paperwork for a few minutes until Detectives O'Malley, Wyatt, Hansen, and Caulfield walked in and took a seat. Police Chief Jameson stood up and began to speak.

"Good morning, gentlemen. I asked all of you here because in the last week there have been three murders. Two on Long Island and one in Manhattan, that seem to have a connection. Three girls between the ages of twenty-three and twenty-eight, all brunettes, all same body type, all killed in nightclubs. All with a note on them in cut-out letters that read, *If I can't have you, no one will.*"

He motioned for his tech man to show images of the three girls on the screen. "Now," the chief continued, "to the dismay of Detective O'Malley, I'm assigning this case to Priority 1. It's one thing to have a homicide, but now it appears we have a man wearing a baseball hat connected to a mask on a rampage. We have video of him coming out of the private room at the City nightclub and the bathroom of the Pajama Club."

"Sir," Paul spoke up, "the third girl. Where was she killed?"

The chief answered, "Outside of a place called Skyline. He broke her neck, laid her outside of the club, and placed the note that he left with all three victims: *If I can't have you, no one will.*"

"Chief," Cronin spoke up, "can we have a closer image of the girls?"

The chief nodded to his tech man, and the three girls' faces were enlarged on the screen. Bud looked at the screen, at each of the girls; he studied them as his face dropped and his heart started pounding. He stood up as he continued to look at the images.

"Bud," Paul said, "what is it?"

Detective Bud Johnson started walking to the screen as Cronin stood up and also asked, "Bud, what is it?" Bud touched the screen as he turned and looked at everyone in the room.

"Bud!" Paul yelled.

"Chief," Bud said, "what were the height and weight of all the girls?"

The chief scrolled down his paper and said,

"All between 5'5" to 5'7" and 110 to 120 pounds."

Bud took out his wallet, pulled out a photo, and held it up for all to see.

"Tell me that Deborah Lance doesn't resemble these girls." He put the photo back in his wallet as Paul stood up and looked at Cronin.

Bud spoke up, "We have to put protection on her until this is resolved."

"Wait, just wait," Detective Wyatt spoke up. "Are we going to put protection on any pretty brunette that is 5'5" to 5'7" and between 110 to 120 pounds?"

"Not every one, but this one we are," Bud said as he started to walk out the door.

"You're not going anywhere," Cronin remarked. "Sit down!"

Paul walked over to Bud and gently led him back to a seat next to him. "Bud, calm down, we are here to help if there is anything to this."

Detective O'Malley stood up and spoke. "Chief, I would like a temporary assignment over to Priority 1 until this case is resolved."

"Listen up," the chief spoke up as he motioned for O'Malley to sit down. He looked at Detective Lieutenant Cronin, who stood up and spoke.

"We can only have a certain amount of people assigned to this case. There are ten people in this room, not counting you, of course," he said, pointing at the tech person. "Paul, you will have the lead on this case. Take four people with you plus Detective O'Malley, while Officers Healey and Lynagh, for now, will be with Deborah Lance until we get a handle on this case. Baker, you and Chapman are assigned to the correctional facility case, which I will discuss with you separately. The rest of you will be at your normal stations and responsibilities. Paul, see me in my office with your team in fifteen minutes."

Paul had wanted Lynagh and Healey as part of the four for his team, but he also knew they were the best to keep Deborah safe just in case. He had his doubts, but he wanted to be sure like Bud. Paul looked over at his partner and asked, "Are you going to keep calm?"

"You need me!" Bud said. "Why even ask that?"

"OK," Paul answered. "Bud, Dugan, Franks, Wyatt, and of course you, Detective O'Malley."

Detective Hansen spoke up.

"Everyone has a job except for me, I guess."

"Not true," Detective Powers said. "I will speak to Cronin to have you on the team as well." He looked at Caulfield and said, "Sorry, we need someone to keep the paperwork moving at your precinct."

"No problem," Caulfield answered. "I enjoy dinners at home."

Paul went to his desk to sort things out before bringing in the team to Cronin. O'Malley wasn't happy that he was no longer the lead on the case, but Paul Powers's reputation as an interrogator as well as a detective was difficult to top. The national media coverage of the Face of Fear investigation and the outcome of it was clearly an overmatch for O'Malley to fight. He did, however, walk into Cronin's office while Chief Jameson was still there. As he started to speak Cronin noticed Lynagh and Healey walking by and, ignoring O'Malley for the moment, threw a ball of paper against the glass and waved for them to come into the office.

As they entered the office, Lynagh spoke. "Boss?"

"Listen up," the detective lieutenant said. "For now, keep your distance. There's no need to have Ms. Lance get shaken up right now. This may be nothing other than they look like her. I will call the father and speak to him."

O'Malley spoke up. "The girl is in her late twenties; why speak to the father?"

This time Cronin didn't ignore him. "She went through a life-changing event about a year and a half ago, plus she lives in the father's mansion. He should know. If this turns out to be something that involves her safety, we will speak to her." He looked back at Lynagh and Healey and said, "Let's give this a week, watch her 8:00 in the morning until she's home at night. If she goes to a dance club, give me a call, and we will send in some backup." He stood up as he spoke again. "For now report directly to me. We want to be absolutely sure there is a connection between her and the murders before you report to Detective Powers as the head on this case." The officers nodded and left the office on their new assignment.

O'Malley started to speak again as he looked at the chief. "Sir, I've been a lead detective for over twenty years, and now I'm in a support role. While I respect Detective Powers's and Johnson's record, I would like a little support here to work in the direction we need to go."

The chief frowned and answered,

"Sorry, Detective, you are a good cop, but you haven't seen the shit that went on here eighteen months ago and don't know the half of it. The people on this task force need your support. This is now a Priority 1 Task Force case. The decisions will be made by Cronin and his lead detective, Paul Powers. Get right with that."

He turned to Kevin Cronin and reached out his hand to

shake his, saying, "Good luck, Detective."

Chief Jameson then walked out the door.

As Paul was walking toward Cronin's office, he tapped Bud on the shoulder. "Just keep your cool on this."

Bud snapped back, "You mean like when Rachelle's life was at risk?"

"Whoa," Paul fired back, "that's not fair. There have been no attempts on Deborah; her life has been quiet since Face of Fear was over. Let's not jump the gun yet. If there is something here, I will be the first one by your side." He hesitated for a second as he saw Bud weakening. "Just like the last time," Paul finished.

Bud nodded and said, "OK, my partner, OK." Paul was referring to the many times they have counted on each other, especially when their lives were in jeopardy, but it was the Face of Fear investigation that forever bonded them. Bud had become suspicious of Paul as the evidence accumulated during the case, and even handcuffed him to his own bed. The detective escaped with the help of Joey Z from downstairs in the restaurant and ended up saving Bud and Officer Dugan's lives as well as others in the Wilkerson house. Bud played it over and over in his mind so many times and never forgave himself for having doubts about him.

The case went down in history as the most famous on Long Island, and it was Cronin, Powers, Johnson, Lynagh, Rachelle, Madison, Deborah, Healey, and Lindsey that received so much publicity there was worry their lives would never be the same again. Lindsey's parents respectfully asked the media to let a twelve-year-old girl have her privacy and grow up. Rachelle gained the most notoriety from her writings and tweets and promised she would one day write a book about it all. Madison was known worldwide as the vigilante Ghost Face killer, which helped the county break the rules and keep her in the Riverhead facility even after her trial. It had never been done before, but the exception was made with the political pressure and public sympathy to keep her on

Long Island close to her only family, Rachelle. The former Suffolk County executive William Lance, a powerful businessman with extraordinary wealth—and also the father of Deborah Lance—pulled all the strings to keep Madison in a jail, not a prison.

Bud fell for Deborah during the case, but his insecurities kept them from progressing. Her wealth and status was his problem, not hers. She never changed toward him, but behind the jokes and the humor there was some truth. Now, as her name was being mentioned in this case, he wondered why his confidence with her left him. Still, everyone in the room, including the one closest to him, Paul, noticed he carried a photo of her in his wallet and had one of her on his desk as well.

Powers and Johnson walked into Cronin's office and Paul convinced the detective lieutenant he needed Hansen as well on his team for the case. Cronin asked Powers what he was assigning the team to do. Paul started to give instructions, and it was always Bud's favorite part to watch how he continued to be smooth no matter what was happening.

Detective Powers looked at O'Malley and said,

"Detective, I'd like to see your reports on the case to date. Then you and Wyatt go to the City and speak to the club's owner and employees at Skyline. Make sure you speak to them before you speak to the lead detectives about their thoughts and notes on the case. Also, you have video of the masked man coming out of the rooms at both the City and Pajama Club. What about the video of them going in the rooms? Check it out."

He looked at Cronin and continued, "Boss, please call the City and let them know our men will be speaking to the appropriate people at the club, then ask them for notes that may help us with the murders here. We need to find out if there is a connection not only to each other but to pretty brunettes, or if there is a link to Deborah or something else."

He looked at Franks and Dugan and said, "Talk to the

relatives, friends, and parents of the two Long Island victims. Did they know each other? Are there six degrees of separation somewhere? Find out."

He looked at Hansen and instructed, "Speak to anyone who dated or was a boyfriend of the two girls. You will have to coordinate with Franks and Dugan, most likely."

He turned around to Bud and said, "You are with me, but first look at all the tapes in the club from the night of the murder. If there is a link, then it's on those tapes. Maybe you will save O'Malley time by finding the men who walked in, not just walked out. Get all phone records and have the techs check their computers. Get close-ups and printouts of the hat with the mask that was worn in both murders, and let's see if it was in the Manhattan murder."

O'Malley stood up and asked Paul, "And you, what are you going to do?"

"Well," Paul said, "I'm going to read your reports when I get them, and once you leave the office I'm going to request to the boss here"—he pointed to Cronin—"that nothing about our investigation of this case gets out to the papers. What I do after that will be my decision and my choice as I supervise the investigation, especially when it comes to following up with my detectives." He looked at O'Malley with a blank stare and asked, "Any other questions?" O'Malley just walked out of the office without saying a word.

Paul looked back at Cronin as the detective lieutenant said,

"Paul, let's get this done quickly. If by some chance there is a link with Deborah Lance, it will be all over the national media again and we don't want that, right?"

"Yes," Paul answered. He looked around and saw everyone except O'Malley was still there. "Let's get started, guys." As they all started moving out through the door, he looked back at Cronin and said, "See ya."

As he approached the door he heard the detective lieutenant

say, "Paul, keep close to Bud on this one. He looked out for you a couple years ago when Rachelle was in trouble."

"Don't worry," Paul replied and then added, "You took over the lead on that case. What about this time?"

Kevin Cronin stood up and said,

"I had to; all of you were too close and emotionally involved to think straight. You have the lead unless I don't believe you can handle it. You have proven yourself over the last two years, but I want to know what's going on."

Paul nodded and said, "You're right. I'll be in touch." As Paul left, Gina walked in with Cronin's mail and told him ADA Ashley was on his way in.

"Damn," Cronin said, "I never have any peace anymore."

"Also," Gina spoke again, "Brian Branca's attorney is on the line."

"Who the hell is Brian Branca?" he replied.

Gina said with a smile, "The owner of the City nightclub. He wants the club to reopen."

"Pass the call," Cronin replied as she left. He thumbed through his mail and found an envelope with no return address but with cut-out, typed letters with his name on it. He opened the letter carefully and opened the paper up and read:

A declaration that
something will or will not
be done.

He folded up the paper as ADA Ashley came in. Ashley said, "Kevin, we got the approval for your undercover detective at Riverhead. We are going to have to speak to Chief Samuels at the facility, but it looks good."

"Thanks," Cronin replied. Ashley could see his head was somewhere else. Cronin figured he would get the OK, which is why he had already assigned Detectives Baker and Chapman to the case. In fact Ellyn Baker was already on the phone with Al Simmons,

Madison's attorney, to tell him the news.

"What's going on?" Ashley asked.

Cronin looked up at the ADA and said, "Close the door." A look of concern came over John Ashley's face as he shut the door.

Officer George Lynagh and Officer Justin Healey were no strangers when it came to protective detail. They got in the squad car and started driving toward the Village of Port Jefferson. They already knew that Deborah Lance was at the Coffee House in Port Jefferson Station having breakfast with Rachelle. Paul had sent Rachelle a text and discreetly found out she was with Deborah. Both Lynagh and Healey had never spent much time together until they were handpicked by Detective Lieutenant Cronin to be on the Priority 1 Task Force.

Justin Healey was thirty-three years of age, 6'2", and as disciplined and hard-nosed as they come. His jet-black hair and chiseled features made him look like a model when he had civilian clothes on. He was also the bodyguard of Lindsey Wilkerson before and during the bloodbath of the attempt on her life a year and a half earlier. He too missed her, but respected the parents' wishes to keep her life away from what was extremely traumatic for her. Many times his thoughts would be of her, and he never forgot how she wouldn't leave his side when he suffered severe wounds from a shotgun blast. He was smiling thinking about her, and it wasn't noticed by his partner, George Lynagh, because his thoughts were on the current case. At 5'10" Lynagh was built more like a tank with husky shoulders and short, cropped blond hair. At thirty-four years of age he looked more like a marine than a cop who had been in numerous situations that could have resulted in serious injury or death, but he had never even had a scratch. Sometimes he wondered if and when his luck would run out. Though Lynagh was a family man with two kids, while Healey was single, both of them were married to the job. They were loyal to Cronin as well as Powers and Johnson, and sometimes bending the rules was a necessity to keep people alive.

"Gina," Cronin said as he pushed the intercom button. "please get William Lance on the phone, and after I speak with him please get Nada from *LI Pulse* on the line." It was only a few minutes before the call came in from William Lance. The detective didn't mention that ADA Ashley was still in his office during the call. "Hello, William," the detective spoke. They had been on a first-name basis for over a year now.

"Hi, Kevin," Lance spoke. "It's been a while."

"Yes," Cronin replied, "it sure has. Listen, we don't think it's anything to be concerned about at this point in time, but I wanted you to know that we put a protective detail on Deborah for a few days. We have a case that has a slight chance of a connection, and Bud doesn't want to take any chances."

"Well," William replied, "thanks for telling me, but are you going to tell her?"

"No," the detective replied, "not unless we know there is a connection for sure. I don't want to unnecessarily alarm her."

"OK," Lance answered.

Detective Cronin spoke again. "One more thing. Does Deborah go to dance clubs?"

"Yes, on occasion," the father answered. "I don't follow her every move at twenty-nine years old, but I know she will go with a group of friends on occasion."

"OK," Cronin replied, "give me a call the next time she goes."

"I will," Lance replied, "but she doesn't always let me know her business." They hung up, and within two minutes it was Nada from the *LI Pulse*. Cronin explained to her that he would like one of her reporters to go on a private tour of the Riverhead facility with one of his officers to do a reconnaissance mission for him. There could be an exclusive story for the magazine in it for them. The magazine had always done fairly well, but it was the case of

Deborah's kidnapping and the vigilante killings that brought the magazine to an even higher level of prominence. Nada, Bud, and Cronin had been in touch with each other on a biweekly basis since the Face of Fear case ended. Yet as fate would have it, Bud and Nada had never met in person.

Lynagh and Healey were parked outside the Coffee Shop when they saw Detective Bud Johnson drive up, park his car, and walk into the restaurant.

"What the fuck is he doing?" Lynagh said as he looked at Bud through binoculars. Deborah and Rachelle had finished their breakfast and just had coffee mugs in front of them when Bud walked to the back booth and greeted Rachelle with a kiss and hugged Deborah, who was surprised but happy to see him.

"Hi," Deborah said with excitement. "It's been a while. How have you been?"

Rachelle was caught off guard by the "been a while" comment.

"Yes," Bud answered. The truth was that during the past six months they had gone out together only a couple times. "I know, too long. If you're not busy next Saturday, you can help me move into the Henry Hallock house on South Street with Paul, Rachelle, Lynagh, and Healey. It will be fun, plus I will take you to dinner any day of the week that is convenient for you before the move-in. Any place you want to go."

"Hmm," Deborah answered with a giggle. "Are you trying to bribe me?"

"No," Bud answered nervously, "but I would like to spend more time with you if it's OK."

Deborah smiled and replied, "Maybe we should talk. Is everything OK?"

"It is fine," Bud answered. "I would just like to see you more if you are up to it."

The young woman replied, "That's very sweet. Maybe we

can get together Friday, and yes I will be happy to help Saturday."

"Great," Bud replied as he hugged Brittany. "How are you, sunshine?" he asked his favorite server, who just patted him on the shoulder as she hustled back to her tables.

"Well," Rachelle said, as she thought the exchange she witnessed was awkward. "I have to get to work. I will call you later, Deborah." She got up and kissed both of them good-bye.

As Deborah and Bud walked out of the Coffee House, Lynagh said again,

"What the fuck?" He called Cronin's office, and the detective lieutenant promptly called Detective Powers to his office. He said, "I told you we were keeping the Music Club Murders separate from the detail of Deborah Lance for now." Already the case had its file name.

"Yes," Powers replied.

Cronin started yelling, "Don't 'yes' me! Then what the hell is Bud doing with the Lance girl right now!"

"He cares for her, Boss, he's worried, and I'll talk to him."

Cronin stood up and started for the door. "Paul, this is your case. Let's not let this get out of hand." With that he walked out of his own office, went out to the parking lot, and jumped in the car with ADA John Ashley behind the wheel, and they drove off.

Cronin looked at Ashley as he exited the parking lot and said, "I assume your office is going to get the paperwork ready for Detective Baker to be thrown in jail."

"Working on it now," the ADA replied. "Chief Samuels of the facility will be notified by DA Steinberg himself tomorrow."

Bud kissed Deborah good-bye, and within fifteen minutes of leaving her, he sent her a text: *Please keep in touch XXX.*

She replied, *It goes both ways, Detective Johnson.* She added a yellow smile to the text. As Deborah drove up to Belle Terre, the exclusive village above the Village of Port Jefferson, her phone buzzed again with another text: *I meant it when I said you were still beautiful.* She smiled, but because she was driving she didn't notice it came from a different number. Just like the first time she had received the message. She also didn't notice Lynagh and Healey were sixty yards behind her as she drove into the gates to the famous Pink Mansion on Cliff Road.

Jason "Jack" O'Connor was playing solitaire in his cell when the correctional officer came to the door and unlocked it. "You have visitors, let's go." The former FBI agent who was sentenced to life in prison with no chance of parole rarely had visitors, especially unannounced visitors. He was led to a small room with a one-way mirror. He couldn't wait to see who was there to see him. He was in the chair for only five minutes when ADA Ashley and Detective Lieutenant Cronin walked in and sat across from him.

"Hmm," he said as he smiled, "you must need me for something, to drive all this way. I'm sure it's not because you missed me."

"No," Cronin replied, "but Bud Johnson said to send you his regards and to tell you he misses your ass." The smirk disappeared from O'Connor's face. He didn't appreciate the remark made by Cronin. ADA Ashley did think it was funny.

O'Connor spoke firmly.

"What do you want?" It was a metamorphism of his attitude. One comment that got the best of him and he had a hard time dealing with it. The comment by Cronin was in reference to Detective Bud Johnson shooting O'Connor in the ass the night of his capture. It was Cronin who figured out the investigative puzzle, and it was Johnson who made him pay by shooting him in the backside. Both Cronin and Ashley were there to find out if O'Connor had anything to do with the notes to the man who put him behind bars, and that man was now sitting across the desk from him. Ashley looked at Cronin, then back at O'Connor.

"Enjoying the food? You put on some weight since you've been here," the ADA said.

O'Connor nodded as he said, "So you've become a comedian since the last time I saw you."

Ashley didn't miss a beat, saying, "Many true things are said in jest."

Cronin threw the notes on the table for O'Connor. He picked them up and read them. As he finished the second one he couldn't help but bring back the smirk on his face. Ashley watched him carefully as he read the notes. It was true that the former FBI agent known as the Voice had put on weight, but he had also aged ten years in the last two. The lines in his forehead were more prevalent, and even though he was forty, the grey was just starting to show on his sideburns. He puckered his lips, as he continued to glance at the poems once he had laid them on the table.

"Interesting," he said, "two definitions of the word *promise*. Very nice."

Detective Cronin reached for the papers and asked, "Why is that?"

O'Connor leaned in toward the detective and said, "Anybody that can put stress on your life is a friend of mine."

"*In* your life," Ashley said, "you mean *in* your life."

"Oh," O'Connor answered, "now you're an English teacher."

Cronin put the three images of the girls who were killed on the table and asked,

"Do they remind you of anyone?"

"Hmm," O'Connor said in a voice carefully disguised as sarcastic. "Gee, let me think, gosh, ahh, no, I can't think of anyone."

Ashley spoke up. "Do you know anything about these girls?"

The prisoner laughed and said, "Gentlemen, I'm in prison. How in the world would I know anything about this?" He spoke with such a superior, sarcastic tone in his voice that Detective Lieutenant Cronin asked Ashley to leave the room. The ADA complied but reminded Cronin he would be in the next room watching.

Cronin and O'Connor were sitting in silence staring at each other by the time Ashley reached the next room to view from behind the one-way mirror. He put his hands up to his chin as his thoughts ran wild as the two continued to stare at each other. Finally, Cronin moved his hands as O'Connor jumped from nervousness but tried to cover himself. Cronin stood up and walked over to the other side of the table. ADA Ashley was sweating bullets, hoping he would not have to run into the room.

He whispered to himself, "It's on tape, Kevin."

Cronin bent down to O'Connor's ear and spoke in a tone that was a little bit louder than a whisper.

"You don't want me to find out that you're involved in all this, and I will tell you why. I'm smarter than you for one, and two, I have many people I know who are prisoners here that don't like inmates that beat up the elderly. You see, if you beat the elderly, then you wouldn't think twice about beating up their own mothers. Do you understand me?"

O'Connor looked up at the detective and replied, "I didn't beat up the elderly."

As Cronin walked around to his side of the table again, he replied, "They will believe me over you, and besides, even a twelve-year-old girl got the best of you." He was referring to Lindsey Wilkerson's photographic memory. O'Connor stood up angrily as Ashley opened the door to the room again.

"OK, I think playtime is over."

"Listen, O'Connor, if you have anything to say, now is the time," Cronin prodded.

"Go to hell," the inmate replied.

"No," Ashley replied as he pushed Cronin toward the door, "you ruined your life as well as others'."

As the officer escorted Cronin and Ashley toward the front, Ashley requested the list of all the visitors that had signed in during the eighteen months O'Connor had been at Bedford Hills Men's

Prison. The facility was only three years old and only a mile away from the famous Bedford Hills Women's Prison.

"Sir," the officer answered, "Detective Lieutenant Cronin asked for this yesterday, and it was faxed to him." Ashley looked over at him as he walked out the front door. They had much to talk about on the drive back to Long Island.

Only ninety minutes had passed when the guard came back to O'Connor's prison cell to tell him the police were back. They led O'Connor back to the interrogation room and he sat alone looking around the room.

Finally he spoke to the mirror facing him. "I told you guys that I don't know anything." His voice got louder. "Screw you! I'm not going to talk anymore!" The figure behind the mirror moved toward the door and walked into the room and sat down across from the startled former agent. It was Bud Johnson.

"Hello dickhead, or maybe I should say *asshole*." Another reference to O'Connor being shot in the ass continued to be humorous to the detective.

"What do you want?" O'Connor yelled.

"Shut up!" Bud answered. "I drove two and a half hours just to see you today, just to say some words to your face, so listen up." Bud turned around at the mirror, which was a sign to the officer to turn off the video as a favor. "I don't know if you have anything to do with the Music Club Murders or not, but I will tell you . . . look at me!" he yelled as O'Connor moved his eyes.

Bud stood up and got in O'Connor's face as the officer behind the mirror grew nervous. Bud forced O'Connor to look directly at him. "If I find out you have anything to do with this or if Deborah Lance is harmed in any way, I will hurt you bad," he said as he moved his lips toward the prisoner's ears. "And then you will suffer. Death would be painless, so I will make sure you suffer. Do you understand me?" There was silence from O'Connor as the detective looked for acknowledgement on the prisoner's face.

"Speak up," Bud said. "I want you to tell me you understand me."

The man once feared as the Voice simply said, "Yes, I understand."

"OK," Bud said. "I have to go catch more bad guys, so you have a great day, and maybe I can come back and visit you again and maybe even sing a song for you, but if I do come back it will be very important for you that Deborah Lance is alive and healthy." The detective walked out of the room as O'Connor just sat there not believing what had just happened. Bud collected his belongings, including his firearm, from the locker and signed out on the log sheet to make the two-and-a-half-hour drive back to Long Island.

During his ride back, he confirmed the videos from the three clubs on the night of the murders were waiting for him at the precinct. Confirmation was also given that phone records from all three girls were also waiting for him. He pulled over after about an hour and did something he hadn't done for over eight months. He sent Deborah a text message with a trivia question: *What is the most successful sequel franchise in history?* He was still sitting in his car when she answered, *You are silly, but it's James Bond.* He laughed out loud, as he knew many people thought the James Bond franchise was the most successful due to the longevity, but by box-office standards he knew it was the Harry Potter movies that had the most success.

He pulled back onto the road as he started speaking aloud, and looked up at the sky. "It's me again. I have kept my word about keeping the lines of communication open. I have done my best, and now there is still work to do on my language. You must admit it's been better. Life is full of challenges, with both good times and bad, and I'm asking for you again to give me the strength. Dear Lord, protect Deborah. I don't know if this is about her, but my gut tells me it might be. My heart wants me to be sure. I've kept my promise to you. Please help me again. Your presence gives me peace, and I am thankful for you. Strengthen me according to your word." It was one of his favorite psalms, Psalm 119:28, that Lindsey brought to his life.

His concentration broke as his phone rang. It was Paul, who demanded,

"Just where in the hell are you?"

Bud replied, "I will be in the office in one hour, Paul."

Paul fired back, "Where have you been?"

"Visiting some fat ass," Bud said as he hung up.

Paul just stared into the phone as he shook his head and continued to read O'Malley's reports on the case, to which Paul assigned the name the Music Club Murders.

Deborah Lance was upstairs going over grading papers for her class when her father walked in to give her a hug. "Everything OK, sweetheart?"

Deborah gave her father a kiss and answered,

"Gee, all of a sudden I'm starting to get all this attention from some of my favorite men."

"Who else?" her father asked.

"Well, Bud, as you know. We have become more about being friends this past year, but he actually asked me out to dinner tomorrow night. He wants me, with his other friends, to help him move in and has been sending me texts like he used to when we were a couple."

"Well," her dad replied, "maybe he has missed you, love."

"Maybe," she replied.

As her father walked out of her office, he knew why Bud was in contact with her. He was happy about it, but he worried about his daughter's emotions about Bud.

Deborah continued to grade her students' papers with written notes. She found out early in her career that her students responded better when they received more than just a grade. She dropped her pen and started thinking about what had happened today with Bud. He always made her laugh, which is what she had always liked best about him. She picked up her phone and sent him a text: *I heard the Henry Hallock house may be haunted.* She laughed out loud when she heard back from him, thanking her and Paul for all the wonderful information they had given him.

As Bud pulled up to headquarters he was remembering what attracted him to her in the first place.

Cronin and Ashley had been back for over an hour when Detective Bud Johnson was called into Cronin's office. As he stepped in, both Ashley and Cronin stopped their discussion and looked at him. Bud's head was moving sideways as he was alternating looking at them when the boss spoke up, asking, "Anything you would like to tell us, Detective?"

Bud had a look of puzzlement on his face, but before he could speak the ADA spoke.

"Do you think it was a good idea to visit O'Connor and let it slip that you would 'make him suffer' if something happened to the Lance girl?"

Bud raised his hands up as he replied, "Who said that?"

Ashley answered quickly, "O'Connor."

"There you go," Bud replied. "I visited him to see if he was aware of anything, but he's a killer who's angry I shot him in the ass. It does not surprise me he said I spoke those words to him."

Ashley just nodded as he looked at Cronin. "I've got work to do on the other side of the building, Kevin. I will call you later."

"OK," Cronin replied. "Shut the door on your way out."

As the door shut the detective lieutenant spoke to Bud. "Stay away from O'Connor, Detective, no good can come from it for you." Bud just stood and wanted to ask how he knew so fast but decided against it.

"Yes sir," he said as he opened the door and walked out. He walked into the tech room and asked them to prepare the videos from the club. He knew it was going to be a long night. He was in the room for fifteen minutes when a bag of popcorn tapped him on the shoulder. It was Paul.

"I know how much you like your popcorn while watching movies, partner."

Bud smiled as he took the bag and said, "Let's get together in the morning."

Paul spoke again. "We can discuss the tapes and the reports I read today."

Bud answered, "Thanks for the popcorn."

The films started, but Detective Johnson's mind was elsewhere as he sent Lynagh a text about where they were. He got an answer that they were outside the gate at the mansion and it was apparent Deborah was in for the evening. He sent a text back to them to let him know if she left the house before they left the detail for the evening.

Paul was exhausted by the time he left headquarters for the evening. He drove to Rachelle's house to check on the dogs before visiting her while hosting at Z Pita. He would get into trouble if he verbally said "Rachelle's house" in front of her, because there was sensitivity about it actually being Rachelle's and Madison's house. He didn't want to deal with that, so he tried to remain disciplined on the ownership of the house.

As usual, as he entered the house Wes was the first to greet him, and Craven took his time to say hello with the attitude of "What took you so long?" He checked their water dishes and found a note left for him that said, *I love you*. He picked up a pen and wrote, *Me too, XOXO*. He decided to take the dogs down Prospect Street to Main Street so they could see Rachelle, whom he called "Mama" to the dogs.

"Let's go see Mama, boys." When he reached the back of the restaurant, Joey Z was in the back trying to help a regular find a parking spot. It was early October, but traffic still created a parking issue in the small village. In fact it was becoming a heated subject at times. Many customers had stopped coming to certain restaurants due to the lack of parking. During the summer the village had decided to repave a section of one of the parking lots, which created even less space. Yet the constables were driving around looking for tickets to write. It was making many proprietors in the village upset over losing customers over the issue.

"Joey Z, when you go in, ask Rachelle to come out back for a minute. Don't tell her the dogs are here," Paul asked.

Joey Z went inside, giving Paul the thumbs-up, and it was only three or four minutes before Rachelle came out to greet her family.

"Ahh," she said, "all the boys in my life," and she hugged Paul. Even Craven was excited to see her as the dogs jumped in her arms as she went down on her knees.

Officer Justin Healey sent Detective Cronin a text that they were leaving the Lance mansion for the evening. They waited for ten minutes before Healey said, "Should we leave or wait for Cronin to confirm?"

Lynagh answered quickly,

"We wait for his blessing."

It was four minutes later when they got a reply from Cronin: *Enjoy the evening.*

OCTOBER 2

Paul requested to have a meeting Sunday at headquarters to review the case and check on the status of everyone's progress. He had a bulletin board of the three young women who were killed and a blackboard to make notes as each detective reported to him. Detective O'Malley was first. He reported the young woman killed in Manhattan, Alicia Hudson—5'5", long hair, brunette, aged twenty-five—was a grad student at New York University. A regular at Skyline every Saturday. She had a boyfriend, Arthur Winston, twenty-four, also a student at New York University. Alicia had no record and was an excellent student throughout her life. O'Malley went on to explain that unlike the other two women, she was outside the club when she was killed. He continued to speak as Paul made notes on the blackboard. Alicia was from Stony Brook, Long Island.

"Excuse me for a second, Detective," Paul interrupted. "Where are the other two victims from?"

Officer Franks and Dugan flipped the pages of their notes, and Franks said, "Kate Summers was from Setauket and Michelle Cartwright was from Huntington Station." Paul stared at the photos, turning his head at an angle as he focused on them.

Detective Lieutenant Cronin stood in the room and remained silent as Detective Powers took command of this case. He asked O'Malley more questions about the detectives on the case in New York City. He asked about the background of the boyfriends of the girls to Franks and Dugan. They looked over at Detective Hansen, who found no connection between the boyfriends and nothing unusual about their backgrounds.

Paul looked at Dugan and Franks again and said, "Jobs, what did the girls do?"

"We know Michelle Cartwright was a New York Film Academy student, who worked at Hour Glass restaurant in Hell's Kitchen, dormed at the school but was from Huntington Station. Kate Summers was a teacher in St. James, and Alicia Hudson lived in Smithtown and worked at Luso's restaurant near her apartment as a hostess. One of the common threads was they all were from Suffolk County, Long Island."

"OK, guys, listen up. There are other common denominators here. They all had notes left with them, they were all pretty brunettes, they were all in dance clubs the night they were murdered—except Alicia, who had just left the club. They were all between the ages of twenty-three and twenty-eight."

Hansen spoke up. "They all lived on the North Shore and commuted west to work or school."

Paul turned around to Bud and asked,

"Anything on the tapes?"

"We have a masked man with a baseball cap coming out of the room at the City club and the women's room at the Pajama Club. There was nothing like that at Skyline. I will be reviewing the tapes all day today without interruption. There has to be more. One thing is for sure: it's the same guy. The two videos with the mask are clearly the same guy."

"What about . . ." Paul started to speak then hesitated. "What about their vehicles?"

Hansen spoke up. "Only Kate Summers had a vehicle, and even then she got a ride to the club from her friends. They all commuted to work or school on the Long Island Rail Road."

Paul nodded and said, "There has to be another common denominator. OK, listen up. Bud, look at these tapes really closely; there has to be something we are missing. Did they give you all the tapes? Detective O'Malley, check if the railroad has any video.

Pick up Arthur Winston and the other boyfriends for questioning, find out any connection between them. Question the friends who brought each of the girls to the clubs. Report anything back if you have concerns. I have sent the images of these victims to all the music and dance clubs on Long Island. They were asked to report if there is a hit on a young woman filling the description. In the meantime Detective Lieutenant Cronin, sir, I would like to get Detective Baker made up and dressed up in the style of the victims and see if anything starts to happen. We will find out if the clubs are cooperative in reporting her to us, and we will see if this is just random killing of brunettes. I know she is scheduled to go to the correctional facility, but until then I think we can use her."

Cronin hesitated before he spoke. "Go ahead and get her ready."

Paul smiled and extended courtesy to the boss, asking, "Any comments or suggestions?"

Cronin moved away from the wall toward the table of police officers and detectives as he said, "Be careful. What bothers me the most about this case is the notes he is leaving with the bodies. *If I can't have you, no one will.* He is directing anger toward one individual, yet killing women that look alike. My opinion is this is about one person angry at someone and they won't stop until the real person is out of the way. Also, don't inform the clubs you're sending someone in undercover. You don't want them to be or act any differently than they would normally."

"Boss," Bud asked, "why go through all this trouble with the other girls?"

"Because," Cronin replied, "it's about hurting others he feels hatred toward. That's where we come in. We have ourselves another puzzle, gentlemen." He looked at Paul and asked, "What are you doing today?"

The detective answered, "Hansen and I are going to each of the victim's homes and apartments to take a look around. Then we are going to visit the clubs when they reopen Tuesday. I would also like to pull Lynagh and Healey off the Lance detail tomorrow and put Hansen and Wyatt on it." Bud looked up with interest, but Paul put out his hand for Bud to please stay quiet. "No offense to anyone, but I would prefer they were used in the clubs for the next few nights as we check into them further, especially with Baker being there."

"Granted," Cronin said as he left the room.

The detective lieutenant went to his desk and enjoyed the slow pace of phone calls, emails, and people interruption that went along with normal hours of the week. His thoughts were broken up by a phone call from the sergeant at the front of the headquarters building. "Sir, there is mail addressed to you marked personal that's been here since yesterday." Cronin stood up and left the Priority 1 area and took the five-minute walk to the front. He would normally have Gina get it, but he felt like taking a walk. As soon as he arrived the envelope was handed to him and he opened it up. He unfolded the paper and read:

Promises, Promises,

Always Keep

Your Promise

He folded up the paper and walked back to his office and called John Ashley. Instead of saying hello the ADA answered with,

"It's Sunday for shit's sake."

Cronin answered him, "The conversation I had with you in my office behind closed doors. Well, we have to get ready." The phone clicked without Ashley saying anything.

Bud went back to the video room and had the tech man who wasn't happy he was called in on a Sunday put the three club videos side by side on the large wall as he sat down with a pad and paper and watched intently. He was getting bored after about an hour when he noticed on one of the videos a man with long hair handing a piece of paper to the DJ. The man playing the music nodded his head as the man walked away. Bud scanned the crowd to see if he could find Kate Summers. He saw her dancing on the screen when he yelled up to Bob the technician and asked if the video played the music. Bob turned it on and it was a song Bud had never heard before. He scanned the crowd on the video to see who was dancing and to find the man who requested the song.

He started yelling up to Bob to close in on some of the patrons when his eye caught a man with long hair handing a piece of paper on the other video. "Stop!" he yelled. "Just play the other two." He watched intently as the DJ started playing a song. Bud moved up to the screen to watch Alicia Hudson at Skyline dance to a song that sounded like the same group as the Summers video but with different lyrics. Bud was feeling anxious as he watched the man eyeing Alicia dancing to the song.

"Who the hell are you?" Bud spoke aloud as he tried to get a good glimpse of his face. The man had so much hair that it was difficult. He fit the body type of the man who walked out of the private room with the hat and mask on. Whomever he was, he was aware of how to avoid facial recognition from video cameras.

Bud called Paul with his findings. "I think you should get a hold of the DJs, get them in here tomorrow, and show them the video of the man requesting the songs. Also, the City club, go to the private room and check the playlist in the room of the songs played. It may be a long shot, but there may be a connection."

As Bud was talking to Paul, he had Bob rewind the tape to one hour before Kate Summers entered the room. "Well," he said to Paul, "I'm feeling better that there is most likely no connection to Deborah. I just will have to make sure she doesn't go to any club until this damn thing is over."

"Good job, partner," Paul replied. "Take the rest of the day off." Paul couldn't help but laugh when he said it. There was always something funny about telling someone who came to work on a Sunday to take the rest of the day off.

"Gee," Bud replied, "thanks."

He sent Deborah a text: *Hello, Deborah, this is your detective just saying hello.* As he prepared to leave, his eye caught the bouncer, Bruce Roberts, being handed a bill discreetly on the tape. "Roll it back ten seconds Bob." The video ran again. "Stop!" It was a $100 bill being slipped into his hand. Bud called Paul back and told him he needed to bring in Bruce Roberts as well on Monday.

The detective asked Bob to play it again after his call to Paul ended. He moved in closer to the screen as he spoke to it, saying, "What the fish is going on?" Bud had been working hard on the use of his language since Lindsey's influence on him and the *Jesus Calling* book. He began to substitute the word *fish* whenever he really wanted to say the other four-letter word. He would slip at times, but he was aware and tried hard. He stayed for another ten minutes looking at the films again and asked Bob to have them aligned up from all three clubs running based on the same time from 8:00 pm on for Monday. He was hoping to see one common denominator of all three clubs.

As he walked through the Priority 1 area to collect some things from his desk, he sent Deborah another text asking if he could see her in an hour. As always she answered him within a minute; she could punch the keys as fast as he read. *See you in an hour,* she wrote back. *It will be nice to see you outside of work again.* Bud smiled, but he was glad Deborah wasn't there to see the confused look on his face as he struggled to convince himself whether it was pleasure or work. He smiled again when he decided it was a combination of both. He left the building in a good mood, feeling confident this was about a serial killer and not about Deborah.

Paul didn't want to wait until Monday to find out why Bruce Roberts was slipped a $100 bill. He knew Bud was meeting Deborah in an hour, so he called Lynagh and Healey to question him first. He looked at Hansen and told him to go home for the evening but to take Wyatt and pick up the DJs from the clubs

Monday morning and bring them down to headquarters. Paul would normally send a text to O'Malley, but the senior detective was not the greatest at utilizing BlackBerries and iPhones. When O'Malley picked up Detective Powers's call, he was told to get with the city detectives to coordinate bringing the DJ who worked the Skyline to headquarters. O'Malley was already won over by Paul Powers's ability to run an investigation and had resigned himself to being an integral part of a Priority 1 investigation now known by the name Paul assigned to it, the Music Club Murders. He made his calls to set up the pickup for the next day. He had already decided to bring in both the DJ and his setup man who was responsible for the equipment and insuring all the electronics ran smoothly in case there was a need.

Lynagh and Healey were parked on Cliff Road by the dead-end circle three-quarters of the way around facing south so they could see anyone driving toward the house and have the harbor in back of them.

The time spent waiting for Bud to pick up Deborah was not even noticed as George Lynagh said, "Do you miss the girl?"

Justin Healey looked over at his partner and immediately knew who he meant.

"Yes," he said, "I do miss her. I wanted to see her grow up; I wanted her to tell us all the things that she has remembered forever. I wanted to see her and Bud go at it with each other while not having to worry about her life at the same time, but most of all I would have liked to be a part of her life. I became very fond of her." He hesitated for a moment as he looked around searching for words. "Here we are less than a half mile from her house, and both Bud and I haven't seen her in well over a year. I understand the parents' wishes, I do. She doesn't need to be reminded of what happened as a twelve-year-old."

His voice cracked a bit, which surprised Lynagh, and then he continued to speak. "She is becoming a beautiful young lady, and I know she is driving all the boys and teachers crazy by now." Healey forced a nervous laugh. Lynagh smiled as he saw the pride in Healey's face as he continued to talk about Lindsey Wilkerson. She had been twelve years old at the time of the Face of Fear investigation. It was her photographic memory and high IQ that was the downfall of the Voice, former FBI Agent Jason "Jack" O'Connor, and put him away for life behind bars. It was Officer Lynagh and Paul Powers who were downstairs in the house while Officer Healey was in the upstairs bathroom with Lindsey and her parents, who were hunkered down in the hot tub when the attackers came. Healey, suffering from serious wounds from shotgun blasts, sat against the wall with his shotgun ready to protect the family. This was only minutes after Healey saved the girl's life by shooting one of O'Connor's cronies through the head after climbing through her bedroom window.

Lynagh continued to let Healey express himself even though this was the longest answer to a question he had ever asked, but it was OK. He saw a side to Healey he had not seen before. It was an emotional side that indicated genuine feelings about the girl who would always consider him her protector. Lynagh looked out the window as he saw Bud drive up to the gate, punch in numbers, and go in, but he let Healey continue to speak anyway.

"I hope one day when she's old enough to make her own decisions that she would want to come by and say hello, that's all. She was great at the trial, wasn't she?" Healey looked at Lynagh for validation. His partner nodded as he watched Healey keep going. "The faces of the attorneys, Judge Green, the jury as Lindsey recounted the dates in chronological order. I thought the defense was going to pee their pants," he said as he started laughing. "She held up, she wouldn't let anyone get one up on her. She wouldn't break. Shit, she had O'Connor's attorney nervous. Their only chance was intimidating her with fear by hurting her or her parents or her dog. I was so proud of her. It's amazing to me how respectful the media was to her. They can be wild animals on stories, but they kept her name out of the papers. I suppose it's another reason her parents didn't want her to keep in touch with us. I understand."

Healey giggled like Lynagh had never heard him before and added, "Besides, I don't think the world is ready for Lindsey Wilkerson just yet, but look out, America, when she is ready." He put his head down in the car as he took a long breath. Then silence. Lynagh put his hand on his shoulder as Justin Healey looked at him.

"Listen up," Lynagh said. "The best thing about a girl with a photographic memory is it's a certainty she won't forget you, but something tells me she wouldn't anyway. I have a feeling you haven't seen the last of her." Healey nodded as he saw Bud's car pull out of the front path of the house.

"Shit, Bud's been here."

Lynagh laughed and said, "Yes, you were going on so much about Lindsey I didn't want to stop you. Let's go check on this asshole Roberts." They drove down Cliff Road toward the entrance of Belle Terre, and other than a glance from Justin Healey, nothing was said when they drove by the house of Lindsey Wilkerson.

It was a twenty-minute drive to Bruce Roberts's house in Lake Grove, and the officers were surprised he wasn't home on a Sunday evening with the club closed. They looked through the windows and even considered checking the door.

"Maybe we should hear a noise inside and have probable cause," Healey said as he put his hand on the knob of the door.

Lynagh laughed. "Nah, let's give him ten minutes and come back tomorrow." They sat in the car, and within five minutes Bruce Roberts got out of his car and started walking toward his front door.

"Christ," Healey said. "Look at the size of this guy. Reminds me of Schwarzenegger from Commando."

"Excuse me, sir," Lynagh said as they got out of the car. "Suffolk County Police."

"Yea, I got that," Roberts said. "You have nice uniforms."

"Well," Healey replied, "sometimes we forget we are wearing them."

"What's up?" Roberts replied.

"At the City club, the night of Kate Summers's murder, you were slipped a $100 bill an hour before she got there. Could you tell us why, please?"

"You know," Roberts answered, "you guys are so polite, it really makes it difficult not to answer your questions."

"Then please do so, sir," Healey interjected.

"No," Roberts answered. "I'd rather just say no, thank you sirs." He smiled and started to walk away.

Healey looked at Lynagh and said, "You know, this is the part where Bud would say, 'No, shithead or dickhead or shit for brains or just shoot him in the ass and get things done, but no, we are given a hard time for being polite."

Lynagh just raised his hand to Healey while looking at Roberts, who by now had turned around and was just squinting, trying to comprehend what was going on.

"Sir," Lynagh replied, "you can either answer the question, or we will take you to the precinct and ask questions all night."

Roberts took out his phone and called the owner of the City club.

"Mr. Branca," Roberts said, "I have two police officers who want to take me to the precinct to ask me questions about the night of the murder."

Lynagh and Healey could not hear what the owner was saying to him, but they could tell that Bruce Roberts was a puppet on a string.

Roberts said, "Yes sir." As he hung up he looked at the officers and told them he would be down at the precinct the next morning sometime with an attorney.

He turned around and started heading for his door when Lynagh said,

"You left out the part of kissing his ass when you spoke to your boss."

Roberts turned around and stared at the officer, who didn't flinch a muscle while Roberts, who was twice his size, continued to stare at him with ice in his eyes.

"You are a very small man, Officer." Lynagh inched closer as Healey moved his hand closer to his weapon.

"Go ahead," Lynagh spoke, "give me a reason to prove size really doesn't matter."

Roberts was surprised by the statement and decided to turn back around and head for the door. He stopped and turned around again, looking at Lynagh with a puzzled look on his face. He said,

"It's easy to be brave when you have a 9mm Glock strapped to your waist."

Lynagh moved a few steps closer as Healey kept his hand on the top of his gun. Lynagh stopped with both his arms straight down away from his firearm. He said,

"I don't need a gun with you. Being smart wins every time over being big."

The tension became so thick that Healey moved up and gently put his hand on the back of his partner's shoulder. Bruce Roberts was now angry over the officer's comments, but he was under strict orders from Branca not to get physical.

Lynagh and Healey stood their ground as Roberts reached for his keys, looked back at them, smiled, and opened the door. Suddenly, a fireball explosion lit up the night as both officers went to the ground and crawled back to the car to avoid debris landing everywhere.

After thirty seconds that seemed like five minutes, Healey spoke. "I think we have probable cause now."

Lynagh picked up the radio to report as he said, "No shit."

Paul had just arrived at Rachelle's house for dinner and was playing with Wes when the call came in about the explosion.

Lynagh reported Roberts was blown to bits before the question was asked.

"OK," Paul said, "let the crime unit do their thing. I'll send Chapman and Franks to relieve you in an hour. Meet me in the morning to review everything." He hung up as Rachelle moved in for a hug.

"What's wrong?" she asked.

Paul shook his head. "We got a real mystery on our hands, love."

"Well," she said, "let me help relieve a little stress." And she kissed him.

Bud was just finishing up his whole-wheat rigatoni at the Pie in the Village when the call came in about the explosion.

He shook his head as Deborah grabbed his hand, saying,

"No work tonight, please." She always made him smile.

"No work," he replied, "just an update." She was a good influence on him and had encouraged Bud to eat healthier and lose some weight over the past eighteen months. The Pie restaurant on Main Street had become another of Bud's favorites when it came to his food. They had the best margherita pizza, the salads were really good, and he loved the tortellini soup with spinach.

As usual, he also got attached to the servers. He always had trivia for them, and sometimes they would have one for him. Bud would also tease the staff on occasion, especially over the beer selection the restaurant had. Here they were in the middle of the village and not only did they not carry the local Port Jefferson beer from the brewery down the street, but also the Long Island beer Blue Point, which Bud loved. He got over the disappointment with the service, the food, and the beer on draft they did carry, Brooklyn Lager. Yet every time Bud went into the restaurant, he would ask for the local Port Jefferson just to be funny.

The owner, Kristen Pace, would also come over and speak to Bud on occasion. A beautiful blond woman whom he would tell

Paul belonged on Fox News with all the other female anchors. His partner would just shake his head and smile at Bud, and say, "You are a funny guy, Bud Johnson." He thought to himself, *Justin Healey would have a crush on Kristin Pace if he met her.*

Yet it was true. The woman whose family also owned the famous Pace's Steak House was an attractive woman who raised a family and spent many hours making the Pie one of Long Island's best restaurants for pizza. Since its opening in 2003 its growth from just serving pizza, calzones, and meatball heroes to when Kristin took over as sole owner in 2008 was limited. She expanded the menu in 2009 to a full menu, and now you couldn't get in the place without a wait after 6:30 pm.

The 3,500-square-foot restaurant had become a favorite of Bud's, which meant Deborah, Rachelle, and Paul would also patronize the eatery. Rachelle, who had become a critic of local restaurants in her articles, wrote about how good the food was for alternatives such as the grilled vegetable salad, the caramelized pear salad, and the gorgonzola salad. It was Bud's love for the classic margherita pizza that kept him coming back. There was no one like Bud when it came to his food, even with losing almost twenty pounds. It continued to be a challenge for him.

"Come on," he said to Deborah, "I want to show you the house you are going to help me move into next Saturday." Bud would not allow Deborah to share the bill.

"No," he said, "I asked you out, this is my treat." Bud was always refreshing to her. He was the only man she ever met that didn't treat her like she was worth over $20 million. They drove to 116 South Street and he pointed it out to her.

"Wow," she laughed, "you will enjoy this old house. I hope the ghosts don't mind sharing with you."

He touched her shoulder and said, "Oh, don't start this again, you and Paul," as they both laughed.

"You know what I like best about this house?" Deborah said.

"Tell me," Bud replied.

"That you will only be about five minutes from me." Bud was very touched by the remark and hugged her with his hand touching the back of her head.

"That's so nice," he said as he kissed her cheek. She noticed he didn't kiss her anywhere else. They got out of the car and walked around the house that looked small from the front.

Madison lay in her cell making noises as Officer Gates moved to her space to make sure she was OK. She had been working the overnight shift for six months and had witnessed Madison having nightmares before during her stay at the facility, but this seemed unusual. The young woman moved her leg as her thoughts played on her mind as she slept: No windows, just rooms connected that seemed endless. Somehow she was touched on the leg and she would run to the next room, then was touched on the back of the neck. She would run to the next room, which was in total darkness. Being blinded from the dark would frighten her even more. She began to run again until she ran into the blood-splattered Ghost Face mask. She couldn't move forward because of the figure in front of her, she couldn't move backward because there was a knife in her stomach. The figure took off the mask, and it was her own face looking at her. "You did this to yourself, Madison." The knife was pushed deeper as Madison started screaming.

Officer Gates opened her cell door and put her hand on Madison as the young woman put her head in her chest.

"It's OK," Gates said, "it was a nightmare. It's OK." She sat with Madison for thirty-five minutes until she was calm and went back to her station. Madison had told her what her nightmare was about, and Officer Gates was conflicted over what to do.

OCTOBER 3

The following morning John Bay came in as a substitute for Officer Cane to be Madison's escort. He walked up to the cell as Gates was serving Madison a tray of food for breakfast. Officer Gates motioned to John Bay to hold his thoughts until she was finished and as the two of them walked away from Madison's cell, the inmate spoke,

"Officer Gates, thank you for last night."

The correctional officer turned to her as Officer Bay watched the exchange and said, "You're welcome, Madison."

As Madison turned her head toward the tray of food she heard the officer speak again, saying,

"Janet."

Madison looked up at her. "Excuse me?"

The guard spoke again. "My name is Janet; when we are alone please call me Janet."

Madison grinned. "Nice to meet you, Janet."

The officer walked back to her desk as John Bay said,

"I hope you are going to tell me what this is about."

Janet Gates looked up at the tall guard. "She had a nightmare last night that she was murdered by herself disguised in the bloody Ghost Face mask. I stayed with her until she was OK, but I think she should talk to a doctor."

"Janet," the male officer said, "try to keep it professional. I know it's difficult." She looked at John Bay with an appreciative smile as she spoke.

"Keeping things professional doesn't change our thoughts, John. Thanks for the advice. I won't disrespect the facility or my job, but I am human. We all know the real story here. I will see you tomorrow."

John Bay understood the conflict of being a person, but they were trained that once the uniform was on all inmates had to be treated the same. *Easier said than done,* he thought.

Paul woke up and turned over to see Rachelle was already out of bed. She had mastered the art of his weakness, which was intimacy with her. They now spent 50 percent of the nights together, and Rachelle often wondered when and where the next step would be. Paul put on his boxer shorts and walked out to the kitchen, where Rachelle was making breakfast. All she had on was his shirt, and it was such a turn-on for him. There were times he couldn't take his eyes off her when she had nothing on but his Yankees jersey. He thought it was even sexier than when she had nothing on at all. He poured himself a cup of coffee while Wes moved in for a petting. He looked over at Craven, who barely left Rachelle's side. It never ceased to amaze him, the difference in their personalities. He took a sip of his coffee and asked Rachelle what her plans were for the day.

"Well, my love, I will be at the restaurant from nine to four in the afternoon today and Joey Z will work the night shift, and then I will be here writing for a bit. I'm going to visit Madison tomorrow if you would like to come with me."

She looked at him half expecting him to say no because of work, but he said yes. She kissed him on the lips and said, "Great, I have to shower and get to the restaurant."

Paul finished his breakfast, walked the dogs, and stopped by his apartment above Z Pita to shower and get to the office. *It is going to be a very long day,* he thought.

Cronin was at his desk when ADA Ashley walked in and gave him information on all forty-two visitors Jason O'Connor had had in the last eighteen months. The detective looked over the names—ex-wife, daughter, son, lawyers. He scanned the names and chose twelve names to have photos of them sent to him. Ashley made the call to the prison and had them email photos of the twelve men. One of the best things the prison had ever done was to take photos of all the visitors that came to visit as a permanent record.

Gina came in to Cronin's office to bring him some papers, and the detective asked her to bring the photos in once she printed them out. Ashley and Cronin were only discussing the explosion the night before for five minutes when Gina brought the photos in. They looked at them, and still nothing stood out. Cronin then asked Gina to send the photos via email to everyone working the case to see if anyone looked familiar.

Ashley started speaking. "Are you sure you want to go ahead with this?"

"Yes," Cronin said, "I believe it's the best way."

"Well," the ADA said, "the only reason why I'm agreeing to this, as well as the DA, is because you were right during the Face of Fear case."

"If," Cronin replied, "anything happens to me, you will have to get with Paul. He's a good man and a leader as you can see."

"Maybe, but he's not as full of surprises as you are," Ashley said. Cronin laughed as Officer Chapman came into his office to tell him the DJs and his set up man or as some called equipment manager, as well as the club cleaner were in separate rooms.

"The club cleaner?" Cronin replied.

"Yes, sir," Chapman answered. "Detective Johnson requested the pickup after reviewing the video feed from the clubs."

They both stood up as Ashley said, "Well this should be fun."

Paul Powers met with Cronin and Ashley in the main interrogation room. It was state-of-the art. In the eighteen months between them, there was no comparison between the interrogation rooms for the Priority 1 Task Force and the Face of Fear case. The monitoring room was a square with four one-way mirrors on each side and speakers to control each room. This could be viewed from the window or from a video feed. You could walk to each window and see what was going on within seconds. Each interrogation room had its own separate entrance from a back hallway. The three DJs and the tech person were in four rooms, while the City club's private room cleaner was in the conference room with Officer Dugan as an escort.

"OK," Cronin said to Paul. "Good luck, but bring these photos of people with you to show them."

"What for?" Paul asked, looking confused. Cronin had not mentioned the notes he was receiving and did not want to distract from the case, especially if there was no connection.

"Just a safeguard," the detective lieutenant replied. "These people have visited O'Connor upstate."

"Fine," Paul answered, still looking a little confused. Bud entered the room as Paul looked at him.

"Ready, Bud?"

"Always, my partner," Bud answered.

As they entered the room, Ashley looked at Cronin and asked,

"Bud doesn't have his gun with him right?"

He expected Cronin to laugh and say, no but instead he answered,

"I hope not."

The references to Bud Johnson's shooting of Kyle Winters in the groin and O'Connor in the ass during the prior famous investigation would forever create conversation and inside jokes the rest of his career. The two detectives sat down in front of the DJ from Skyline. Paul took the lead during the interrogation, which was the norm.

Ron Royal, better known as the Master, was a twenty-eight-year-old club mixer and seemed only able to talk about music. He didn't seem to know about anything outside of his ten-by-twenty-foot area where his equipment and tapes were. He was a genius when it came to his playlist, video screens, and speakers.

Paul showed Ron the video of the man who had made a request on paper to him.

"Yes," he said, "he requested 'Kiss of Death' by Mystic Strangers."

Bud perked up.

"How do you remember that?"

The Master replied, "I got many requests, and if there is one thing that I remember in my life, it's my music, but this was different. The request came with a $100 bill in it. I'm sure about the song he requested."

Paul asked him if he still had the bill on him, and the Master laughed, saying it filled up his tank on his van the next day.

Paul brought out the photos from the jail and asked him if anyone looked familiar. The DJ shook his head, telling the detectives he had never seen them. Bud asked him if he had seen or knew Alicia Hudson, and again his answer was no. They thanked him and asked him to stay for a while during the interviews. Ron Royal looked at his watch and promptly said, "The Master will wait for a bit, however, time is money, my friends."

Bud, never at a loss for words, replied,

"Well, then it's good the club is closed on Monday nights."

The two detectives then went into the second room, where Ken Anker from the Pajama Club was ready for them.

"Please," he said, "feel free to call me Sir Entertainment."

Paul smiled and replied, "Ken, we have some questions for you. Thank you for coming down."

"OK," the DJ replied with a big smile on his face, "call me Sir for short." He held his hands raised up in the air.

Bud promptly replied, "How 'bout I call you Dick, short for Dick Head?"

Paul hit his partner on his shoulder to get down to business.

Paul knew Bud's reply stemmed from his annoyance at the request from the DJ to be called Sir.

Cronin, in the monitoring room, was shaking his head watching the exchange, while Ashley noticed in Room 3 the DJ from the City club now had an attorney in the room with him. He motioned for Cronin to take a quick look and his only reply was,

"Interesting."

They both went back to Room 2 and turned up the volume to listen in. The questions were the same for Ken Anker as they had been for Ron Royal. The answers were the same too, including the $100 bill for a request to play a song. Yet they were surprised it was a different song title. This one called "The Thrill" by the same group, Mystic Strangers.

Paul asked the DJ if the song was an unusual request and the DJ responded,

"Yes, I had never heard it before."

"If," Bud asked, "it was so unusual, why did you have the song available?"

The DJ was surprised the question was asked, but he answered,

"Man, in today's technology you can download anything quickly and play it. No big deal."

Paul brought out the photos given to him by Detective Cronin, and again there was no recognition of who they were.

Paul and Bud excused themselves and went into Room 3 with Lawrence Stone and attorney Michael Corbin. ADA Ashley walked into the room to lend some support to the detectives, with the lawyer in the room.

"Gentlemen," Attorney Corbin stated, "why is there a need for an ADA to be in the room during a simple questioning?"

Ashley replied, "I was thinking the same thing about your client", Cronin smiled behind the mirror as he watched.

Ashley looked over at Mr. Stone and asked, "Mr. DJ, may I

call you Lawrence?"

The man promptly replied,

"My show name is Ace of Clubs. Get it?" He laughed and said, "Ace of Clubs, it's a double meaning."

Bud quickly spoke up. "Pretty bold for a guy with his fly open." The DJ looked down at his fly.

The attorney yelled back,

"That's uncalled for, Detective!"

Paul whispered in Bud's ear while Ashley touched Bud's arm to calm him down as the ADA spoke.

"Mr. Ace," as he looked at the DJ, "have you ever seen this man before in your life? Yes or no?"

Attorney Corbin stood up. "Don't answer that! What is this? This is not a trial. We are leaving this instant unless you are charging my client."

Ashley stood up to be on Corbin's level. "How do I know you are really his attorney and not someone trying to keep him quiet, take him out of here, then kidnap him, and kill him to keep him from talking?"

Cronin was laughing loudly behind the mirror, enjoying the show. Lawrence Stone looked up at Ashley as he caught Bud nodding yes in agreement to what the ADA was saying and then blew into his finger like it was a smoking gun.

The DJ yelled "Wait!" as he looked up at the attorney. "Really, who are you?" The attorney just shook his head like he couldn't believe his client could be so dumb.

Ashley looked at Michael Corbin and said,

"Let's just all put our egos aside, sit down, and work this out. Ace here is not going anywhere without answering a few questions, or he will be charged as an accomplice."

Corbin and Ashley both sat down as Paul continued to look at the DJ's reaction. The ice was broken as Bud spoke up that he was hungry and they needed to finish up. They all looked at Bud before starting up the questioning.

Paul spoke first. "Mr. Corbin, who is paying you?"

The attorney replied,

"I am on retainer for the City club."

"So," Ashley said, "the owner, Brian Branca, is your client?"

"Yes," the attorney answered, "but Mr. Stone here is an employee of Mr. Branca, therefore I am here to protect his interests and those of the club."

"My friend," Ashley replied, "we were told Edward Larson was Brian Branca's attorney."

Corbin replied, "We are both on retainer."

Ashley was quick to respond, "We have been in this room for over thirty minutes and have established nothing because of all this spin. Now, let's just ask a few questions and everyone can be on their way."

As it turned out, Stone knew nothing. Not even a request was given to him. No money was exchanged, and there was no recognition of any of the photos. Attorney Corbin smiled at the three gentlemen across the table as if to say sorry but that he really didn't care. Ashley got up without even saying good-bye to his counterpart and opened the door to the back hallway to join Detective Cronin in the viewing room.

"Kevin," he said, "I think it's OK to let the three DJs leave for now. Besides, we can bring the cleaner from the club in here, and who knows, with any luck Corbin doesn't even know we brought the young man in."

Cronin agreed and called Gina to have Chapman escort the three DJs out one at a time. He didn't want them talking to each other. As Chapman was escorting the first DJ out, Cronin got a call from Gina that she had an urgent call from Hansen. She put the call through as Hansen began to speak.

"Sir, the twelve photographs you sent to us through email, do you have them in front of you?"

"Yes," Cronin replied. "Let me put you on speakerphone so the ADA can hear you. OK, go ahead."

Hansen began to speak again. "The Jerry Wakefern photo. You had me look for the boyfriends of the victims, including the man Jake Wiley, who never showed up for his blind date with Kate Summers. Well sir, the photo of Jerry Wakefern is the man I interviewed as Jake Wiley."

Cronin slammed his fist on the table and exclaimed,

"I knew it! O'Connor is mixed up in all this! Good job, Detective!"

ADA Ashley yelled into the speaker, "Pick him up!"

"Yes sir," Hansen replied.

"Wait," Cronin replied. "Hold on. You are at the Lance mansion right now, correct?"

"No," Hansen replied, "Ms. Lance is at the school right now, so I am in the parking lot."

"Hold on, Detective," Cronin said as he pushed the *mute* button. "John, if O'Connor is involved, why? His only beef over the last two years was the money, Deborah Lance, Bud, myself, and the young girl. He's already in jail for life, so Lindsey Wilkerson doesn't mean anything to him. Revenge against Bud and me means something to him, and if money could be the pot of gold for his accomplices, then Deborah could possibly be a target."

Ashley shook his head and said, "Pretty thin, but maybe?" He made the statement in the form of a question.

"Listen," Cronin said, "he's killing brunettes that look like Deborah to have a reason for killing the target all along. He kills her, he gets revenge on Bud. He kills me, he has revenge on Bud. He kills us all, he gets what he wants with nothing to lose, and how could we prove it with him in jail?"

Ashley held up the photo of Jake Wakefern and said, "We start with him."

The detective pushed the *mute* button again while Hansen waited.

"Detective," Cronin said, "take a walk into the school and tell the principal it's nothing serious but as a precautionary measure you are to remain in the building until school is out. Don't say anything about Deborah at this time. When she drives home, identify yourself and ask her to come to the precinct in the morning before school. Stay with her until Franks relieves you in about four hours."

Cronin then pushed the intercom button and said, "Gina, have Chapman pick up Jerry Wakefern. Have him take Officer Dugan with him."

Detective Hansen got out of his car and walked into the entrance of the school. He was met by a woman behind a glass partition who requested identification. The schools on Long Island were no different than the rest of the schools across the nation. Shootings across the nation of children in schools had everyone taking precautions. When Hansen flashed his badge, the woman behind the glass paged security, who happened to be an off-duty police officer. Hansen gave the officer general details as a courtesy but told him he would remain in the building as a precautionary measure.

Paul and Bud moved to another room where the tech man—or music engineer, as he liked to be called—was. Bill Tillman went through the same list of questions as the others. He was of no help to them, and they released him within twenty minutes.

By this time Gina had escorted the young man that worked in the City club as the service man, maid, or house engineer. Paul told Bud to take the lead on questioning him since he was brought in at Bud's and O'Malley's request. He asked the same questions they discussed with the others, and as they expected there was no information the young man named Rodrigo Hernandez could offer. Then Bud showed the video showing Rodrigo coming in and out of the private room, including the video of Bruce Roberts getting a $100 slipped to him.

Bud continued, "The video shows Roberts going into the room while you were still in the room cleaning before the girl got there. Tell us what was said."

The young man shrugged his shoulders and said,

"Nothing, he just gave me twenty dollars to make sure a certain song would play while the client's date was in the room with him."

Paul looked anxious. "What song?"

Rodrigo answered, "'Alone in Darkness' by Mystic Strangers."

Cronin called Gina on the intercom and said, "Make a note to get the lyrics from all three songs and give a copy to myself, Paul, and Bud, please. Also, get Wyatt, who is parked a block away from the Wilkerson house, to be relieved by Franks and O'Malley. No need to notify or bother the family at this point."

Ashley looked over at the detective and asked, "Are you taking over the lead in this case?"

Cronin looked up at him and replied,

"You know that will be impossible."

Ashley shook his head as Cronin pushed the intercom button again and said,

"Gina, all these instructions I'm giving to you, make notes and give them to Detective Powers so he is aware of everything, please."

Chapman and Dugan reached the home of Jake Wiley aka Jerry Wakefern in Centereach to bring him down to the station, and as they expected, he wasn't there. They walked around the building to peek through different rooms in the back of the house and saw nothing out of the ordinary. Officer Chapman noticed the old furniture in the house and the wallpaper looked like it was from the '70s. Even the carpet on the floor was shag.

"This guy lives in a time machine," Chapman said.

In a split second time stopped. A figure wearing the baseball hat with the mask draped down stepped out and fired his shotgun, hitting Dugan in the face, instantly killing him, and shooting Chapman before he even got his hand on his gun. The man wearing the mask calmly walked around the building and drove off in the squad car, only to park it in a nearby 7-11 parking lot. No one paid attention to whoever got out of the squad car.

Chapman was lying on the ground shaking, trying to reach his radio. He was bleeding, but he had his bulletproof vest on. Still he was going into shock. Officer Dugan didn't have a chance. There was no vest for the face.

Bud looked at Rodrigo across the table. "Any other contact with anyone else the night of the murder?"

"Only," Rodrigo said, "the man in the bathroom in the private room."

The detectives looked at each other as Bud said, "Rodrigo, help us out here. Why didn't you tell us about the man in the bathroom?"

The young man looked at Bud and replied,

"You didn't ask me, but he said he was waiting for his blind date."

Paul spoke up. "Did you get a look at him?"

"Yes," the young man answered. "He had long hair, slim, 6'1", maybe 6'2", about thirty-seven or thirty-eight years of age."

Bud played back the video showing the man leaving the private room with the mask on. "Look at his body, his hair, his height. Is this the man you saw in the room?" he asked.

"Yes," Rodrigo answered, "but he didn't have a mask on." Bud nodded as he looked over at Paul.

Detective Hansen walked over to the classroom where Deborah was teaching and looked in discreetly as he saw the young woman talking to her fifth-grade class. He stayed around the area until he knew her workday would be ending and even checked with the administrative office which vehicle was hers so he could park accordingly. He was getting bored after an hour of this and decided to get back to the car and get closer to her vehicle. He couldn't believe that a woman who had a father worth over $20 million would want to spend her time teaching. He thought to himself, *That's why you have to be dedicated to be a teacher.*

He smiled as he got in his squad car and turned the ignition, and in an instant he was gone. The explosion was so loud that some of the windows shattered in the classrooms, scaring the kids. Calls came into 9-1-1, and they were soon transferred into Cronin when Gina found out it was at the school. Cronin hung up the phone and told Gina to get Lynagh and Healey to the school immediately to pick up Deborah. She was not to leave alone.

Justin Healey and George Lynagh raced through the streets with the lights and siren blasting to get to the school. Gina called the principal's office to be sure no one left until the officers were there. When they got to the school there were two ambulances and three squad cars of officers from nearby precincts. Healey drove up over the curb and parked near the front entrance of the school. They walked in calmly, found out where Deborah Lance was, and asked for an administrative person to replace Ms. Lance, for she would be coming with them. As soon as they got to the classroom, Deborah knew something was very wrong when she saw it was Officers Healey and Lynagh.

"Is my father all right?" she asked.

"Your father is fine, Ms. Lance, but you will have to come with us to the precinct," Lynagh explained.

"What's wrong?" she asked nervously.

"All will be explained at the precinct," Lynagh said as he grabbed her arm.

"Detective Cronin, Powers, and Johnson are waiting," Healey added.

Deborah told her class good-bye and left them with the administrative assistant. The officers politely put her in the car as she started to send Bud text messages. She called her father, who was in Manhattan and said he would be leaving to join her but wouldn't get there for a couple hours. Deborah called Rachelle at Z Pita and began to get choked up as she spoke.

"Rachelle, they are bringing me down to the precinct. I'm scared, please come, my father can't make it for a couple hours."

"I'm leaving now," Rachelle answered.

William Lance called Kevin Cronin. Rachelle called Paul and Bud, who were trying to get answers from the boss as to why Deborah was picked up at the school and being brought down.

"Listen up, everyone!" Cronin yelled, but before he could begin, an emergency call was transferred to him. It was Stony Brook University Hospital.

"Detective, this is Eddie Sharp, the hospital administrator. I'm sorry to tell you that we have two of your officers here. One is dead; the other is in serious condition with a shotgun blast that the vest only partially caught. Alive is Officer Chapman, but I regret to tell you Officer Dugan was dead before he hit the ground."

Cronin sat down as Powers, Johnson, Ashley, and now O'Malley, who had just arrived, were listening. Detective Lieutenant Cronin hung up the phone and looked at everyone as Gina stepped in.

"Dugan was killed at the Wakefern house, Chapman is in serious condition, and now," he looked at O'Malley, "Hansen was killed in an explosion at the school. His car was . . ."

He was interrupted by O'Malley, who snapped,

"Goddamn it! He was with me for ten years, never a problem like this!" He sat down with his hands covering his face.

There was silence in the room except for Gina's soft cry. She had grown fond of Walter Dugan over the past five years, and although she had only met Detective Hansen the week before, he was a fellow officer.

"Boss," Bud said softly and respectfully, "what does this have to do with Deborah? I'm not sure about the connection. At first maybe, but now I'm not sure."

"Bud," Paul said, as he looked at Detective Cronin for his blessing to speak up,

"Wakefern has visited O'Connor four times in the last six months. Three women have been killed that look like Deborah, to give the impression of a serial killer. Dugan is killed at Wakefern's house, and now Hansen is killed while he was checking in on Deborah. Do we really think this is a coincidence? Bud, if O'Connor wanted to get back at the three of us, he would come after us and the people we love." As he heard himself speak, his heart started beating faster about Rachelle.

"Listen," he spoke again, "we need to talk to her. She may know something that she doesn't think is important to this case."

Bud stood there and looked around at everyone and sat down. He looked up again and said,

"What about the girl, Lindsey?"

Cronin spoke up. "Wyatt is at the house right now, but we are going to have to borrow two squad cars to relieve him. He is shaken up over losing Hansen." Detective Baker came into the room to tell Cronin that Rachelle Robinson was in front and wanted to get into the Priority 1 area to see Paul.

"Shit," Paul said, "what is she doing here? Let her come to my desk. I will be out in a second." As they were finishing up, Lynagh and Healey brought Deborah into the room and would stay with her until Powers and Johnson were ready.

"Wait, guys," Paul said. "Let me see what's going on with Rachelle. Bud, go talk to Deborah and reassure her we are not sure just yet but we are concerned. Don't ask questions until I'm back."

He left the central monitoring area and met with Rachelle at his desk. He greeted her with a hug and a squeeze of her hand as she asked, "Why has Deborah been brought here?"

"Rachelle," Paul said, as his disapproval showed.

She interrupted him,

"Why, Paul? Tell me. I'm not leaving."

The detective took her hand again and said,

"We think she may be in danger and need to be certain."

Rachelle started moving toward the interrogation room. She knew where it was due to her many visits to the new precinct over the past year.

"Where are you going?" Paul asked.

Rachelle turned around and said,

"I don't want her to be alone; I want to be there with her."

Paul reached for Rachelle as she stopped and looked at him. "I will not abandon her when she needs support. Take me to her, Paul, please."

"Rachelle," Paul spoke, "if there is a connection, I would worry about you being with her until this is resolved."

Rachelle moved his hand from her arm and said, "I am not leaving her."

Paul looked at her for a few seconds and relented.

"Come with me," he said. He opened the door to the room where Lynagh and Healey were with Deborah. Rachelle smiled as she hugged her friend, and Deborah would not let go of her.

Rachelle spoke. "It's going to be all right, and I am here with you. Come on, let's sit down."

Cronin, Ashley, Bud, and Paul watched as Rachelle held Deborah's hand tight on the table.

Detective Cronin looked at both Detectives Powers and Johnson and asked,

"Are you two going to be able to be objective?"

Paul started walking toward the door and said, "Don't insult me."

"Answer the question!" Cronin yelled.

"Yes," Bud answered. Cronin looked over at Paul, who started to nod a weak yes.

"John," Cronin said to Ashley, "I suggest you go in there on behalf of Deborah. She's not a suspect, but you need to be sure nothing is violated. She is a friend, and I think it is the wise thing to do."

Paul and Bud came in and sat across from Deborah and Rachelle as John Ashley walked into the room and took a chair and sat on Deborah and Rachelle's side of the table. Paul immediately knew the reason. ADA Ashley told Lynagh and Healey to see Cronin in the monitoring room. Ashley began to explain to Deborah why he was there and noticed how Rachelle continued to hold her hand. When Lynagh and Healey reached Cronin, they were instructed to get to the hospital with the other officers to show support and respect for the families of the fallen officers.

Paul looked at Rachelle, and then turned his attention to Deborah.

"Deborah, we need to talk about a few things. We don't know or understand everything that's going on, but we need to be sure there is no connection to you."

Deborah started to speak, but Ashley asked her to be quiet for now.

"Deborah," Bud said, "we have a problem."

Ashley interrupted, "Guys, is there a question anywhere?"

Cronin behind the mirror started talking out loud to himself. "Jesus Christ," he said, as he shook his head.

"Deborah," Paul asked, "in the last week has anything unusual happened?"

"Well, other than Bud starting to text and call me again, no," she said with a smile. Paul looked at Bud as he spoke again.

"Deborah, nothing else besides Bud?"

She shook her head and said, "No, seriously, other than that. Missing me, I'm still beautiful, no nothing else."

Bud frowned as he said,

"Deborah I never sent you any texts like those. May I see your phone?"

The young woman reached for her smartphone and pulled up the text messages to show Paul and Bud. Bud turned the phone back to Deborah to show her it wasn't from his number.

"I guess," she replied, "I assumed it was from you because it was around the same time you started communicating with me on a regular basis."

Paul spoke up. "We knew there was a slight possibility there could be a problem, so I'm sure that's why Bud was keeping an eye on you." Deborah looked over at Bud as Rachelle gave Paul a look of disappointment at what he said.

"Of course," Paul said to try and save the situation, "out of concern for you."

"Listen," Bud said, "anything else other than these texts? We are going to check the number, but I'm sure they are disposable phone numbers. What about at work? Anything out of the ordinary happening at work besides what happened today?"

"No," Deborah answered, "nothing."

Paul spoke up again. "What about your dad? Anything unusual going on with him?"

"No," she replied.

"What about the men you have dated?" Paul continued. The young woman was silent. "Deborah, please," Paul asked again.

Deborah Lance finally spoke, saying,

"I can't talk to you about that in front of Bud."

Bud looked at Deborah and wanted to speak, but his thoughts were interrupted by Ashley, who said, "Bud, please leave the room."

The detective was starting to speak again when the PA was used. Detective Cronin's voice said,

"Detective Johnson, I need to see you, please."

Bud got up slowly, and as he reached the door he heard Deborah's voice say,

"Bud, is that why I started to hear from you again, because of this?"

The detective put his hand on the doorknob and replied, "I was worried about you, Deborah."

She shook her head and said,

"OK, I guess I just thought you wanted to be with me, that maybe you missed me."

Bud started to speak again when the PA was used again, but this time Cronin used a much firmer voice: "Detective, now!"

Bud went into the monitoring room and stood by Detective Cronin without saying a word.

Rachelle continued to hold Deborah's hand as Paul said again, "Deborah, talk to us about the men you have dated over the past six months."

Bud stood behind the mirror as the young woman he cared about explained in detail the three different men she had dated over the previous six months. There was nothing out of the ordinary.

Paul pushed a little harder. "None of them ever became aggressive with you?"

"No," she answered. "Only," then she hesitated, "well, one of them sexually, but I stopped it before it got out of hand." Bud moved closer to the mirror.

Paul patiently asked for his name. Deborah looked at Rachelle as she answered,

"His name was Sean Martin; he is from East Hampton."

Cronin pushed buttons on the PA and said, "Gina, have Officers Lynagh and Healey pick up Sean Martin from East Hampton first thing tomorrow morning."

"Yes, sir," she replied, and Cronin's attention went back to the interview.

Paul asked, "Deborah, did he ever ask you to do anything that made you uncomfortable?"

Ashley spoke up. "Don't answer that, Deborah. Next question, please."

Paul continued, "Why did you break up?"

The young woman hesitated and then answered, "I just didn't feel it could go any further. I've never been one to waste time. Besides, sex isn't the most comfortable experience since the kidnapping."

The kidnapping Deborah was referring to was her own eighteen months prior. She was beaten and almost raped and killed until Madison barged in with the Ghost Face mask on and killed Wayne Starfield, who was holding her hostage under the orders of John Winters and Jason "Jack" O'Connor.

"OK, Deborah," Paul said, as he caught Rachelle giving him the eye to be careful about what else he asked her.

Paul continued, "This is going to be a really crazy question, but I need to ask it. Does the group Mystic Strangers mean anything to you?" Deborah's eyes widened as she looked over at John Ashley. Paul was surprised by her reaction, especially to a question he almost didn't ask.

Ashley got out of his seat and went to the other side of Deborah. She whispered in his ear as Paul turned around to face Cronin and Bud with a questioning look on his face.

Cronin looked at Bud and said, "I guess Paul hit on something here."

Ashley looked up and spoke to Cronin through the mirror. "Please have Bud leave the monitoring room."

Bud raised his hands. "Oh, come on!" he yelled.

"Bud," Cronin said, "there's something here that she doesn't want to say in front of you. You have a personal relationship with her. Go ahead and leave the room for now."

He rubbed the side of his head as Bud spoke again, saying,

"I'm scared that she's in trouble again, and I need to be there for her."

Cronin pushed the PA to the interview room and said, "Hold up, John, we are having an issue here."

Detective Cronin walked over to Bud and put his hand on his shoulder. "I have a feeling, Bud, that you will be there for her at the right time."

As Paul, Deborah, Ashley, and Rachelle sat in the room waiting, Paul tried to break the ice by saying to Rachelle,

"What time is Suze Orman on tonight?"

Rachelle just gave him an angry look. Paul knew things would be tense with her for bringing Deborah in, so he felt he needed to speak up again and be clear about why she was brought in.

"Deborah, you do realize you were brought here as a precaution in case there is a threat to you, right? We are only here to see if there is any connection to your safety and the case we are working on."

Deborah nodded as the voice of Kevin Cronin came over the PA, saying,

"We are ready to continue."

Ashley went back to his chair as Rachelle gave Paul another stern look. Still she was holding Deborah's hand.

"Deborah," Detective Powers said, "please tell us why the group Mystic Strangers means something to you."

Deborah looked at Paul and answered, "It was Robert's favorite group."

Cronin hit the wall with his fist and said,

"Damn it!"

Robert Simpson was Deborah's former boyfriend and worked as her father's personal assistant from the time she was thirteen years old. He became her lover when she was eighteen and their relationship continued until the Face of Fear investigation and Bud came into her life.

Paul continued, "Have you heard from him at all since he left eighteen months ago?"

"Never," she answered.

"Deborah, other than liking the group, and this is real important, is there any meaning to any of these songs?"

"Yes," she answered. She took a long breath and spoke. "He

loved to have sex while the music was playing. It turned him on."

Behind the glass Cronin caught himself talking out loud. "Holy mother of hell."

Deborah continued, "He wasn't rough with me, but we were intimate at least three times a month with certain songs playing. He liked the dark, Gothic sounds, especially when there was no light."

Cronin began talking to himself again. "Where have you been, Robert Simpson?"

Paul shook his head and could understand why Deborah had wanted Bud out of the room. "Deborah, do you think Robert Simpson is capable of killing women who look like you?" he asked.

She shook her head and said, "Not the Robert I knew, but I don't know him anymore."

Paul continued, "Do you think he would hurt you physically in any way?"

Deborah teared up as Rachelle put her arm around her friend, and answered, "I'm not sure of anything anymore. Do you think women are being killed because of me?"

"OK," Ashley said, "this interview is over. Detective Powers, please give us a minute."

Paul got up and touched Deborah on her shoulder before he walked out of the interview room.

"Excuse me, John," Cronin's voice came over the PA. "Deborah, this is Detective Cronin. I'm sorry to have to ask you this, but does the phrase 'If I can't have you, no one will' mean anything?"

The young woman looked up to the mirror.

"No, Detective. Robert was upset about not being a part of our lives anymore, but he did not specifically use those words."

Cronin spoke again. "What about the words 'You are still beautiful'? Does that sound like something Robert would say?"

Through her tears, Deborah replied, "He always said I was beautiful, since I was thirteen years old."

"OK," Detective Cronin answered, "thank you."

Cronin released the PA button as he spoke to himself again: "Sick motherfucker." He looked over at Paul and said, "Have one of the uniforms take her to her car at the school. We should get to the hospital; fill in Bud on the details on the way. I'll see you later; I'm on my way there now." Paul nodded as Cronin left.

Paul met with Rachelle, Deborah, and Ashley in the hallway.

"Come on, Deb," Paul said, "someone will take you to your car."

Rachelle spoke up. "I will take her."

"No," Paul sighed as he spoke again, "not without an escort." Bud walked up to Deborah and took her hand as she acknowledged him. ADA Ashley asked for Detective Cronin, and Paul told him he was on his way to the hospital. The ADA acknowledged that they should also make an appearance, which included him as well.

As they left the Priority 1 area, an officer came running around the corner shouting, "There's been an explosion outside!"

As Paul, Bud, and Ashley reached the parking lot and raced to the explosion, they soon realized it was Detective Kevin Cronin's car.

"No!" Paul yelled. Bud fell to his knees, as he could not believe what he saw.

"No!" Paul kept saying. ADA Ashley stood there in silence as he tried to pull Bud up, who was crying. The sirens could already be heard from the fire trucks as Ashley escorted Bud back to the building, where he sat in the nearest chair as Deborah came over to him, held him, and began crying with him. Paul stood up against the wall in the precinct and starting banging the wall with his fists as Rachelle reached for his arm.

"Stop, please stop," she said, as tears came down her face. He looked at her and then put his head to rest against the wall.

Rachelle put her arms around his waist and could hear Paul struggling to hold his tears back as he said, "His family is in

California."

Rachelle continued to hold him as Ashley said, "I will take care of it."

Just then Gina ran out to the front area as the ADA caught her and held on to her while she cried uncontrollably. John Ashley walked Gina back to her office and stayed with her until an officer could drive her home.

He pushed the buttons on his smartphone when he was alone. He waited till the call was picked up. He said

"Let the games begin," then disconnected the phone call.

The ADA shook his head and waited for the news to break on television. It took only fifteen minutes for the *Long Island News 12* anchor, Mary McKenzie, to break into regular programming to announce the killing of Officer Dugan, Detective Hansen, and now Detective Lieutenant Cronin. Ashley sat there as he waited for Commissioner McGuire, Chief Jameson, and DA Steinberg to get to what had been Kevin Cronin's office only forty minutes earlier. It was another ten minutes before the DA and the chief came into the office as Ashley quickly shut the door.

The chief looked at the ADA and said,

"I gave this case to Priority 1 to solve it, not get everyone killed, for Christ's sake!"

"Chief," Ashley said, "there will be no more killing. Now it's time to solve the case."

The chief looked at DA Steinberg for support and asked,

"What do you think of this?"

"I say," the DA answered, "based on their track record, let them have some time with this."

The chief looked back at ADA Ashley and asked, "Can Detectives Powers and Johnson handle this?"

"Sir," the ADA said, "there is no one else I would dare have handle this."

"Listen," the chief replied, "we can't have any more bodies, especially our own." He looked back at DA Steinberg and continued,

"I'm getting too old for this shit. Let's call Detective Powers in."

Ashley went to Paul's desk, and Rachelle was still with him.

"Paul, the chief and DA need to see you," He said. Bud didn't care that he wasn't asked to enter the office.

Powers walked into the office to dead silence and stood there waiting for someone to speak to him.

Finally the chief said, "Son, are you and Johnson up to closing these cases? We have two dead girls on Long Island, one in Manhattan, and three dead cops."

Paul answered quickly. "Why plural, Chief? They are not two separate cases, it's one case. It's all connected to Deborah Lance. They look alike to give it a serial murder feel. When they finally got to Deborah Lance, she would just be one of the girls. This is Robert Simpson getting payback to the girl who dumped him, the cops trying to protect her, and Cronin, who he believes destroyed his life. We find Simpson, we find out who else is involved and why."

The chief looked at the DA, then back at Detective Powers. He said,

"You've got five days to get this thing closed. I don't want to put any more pressure on you than you already have, but this is what happens when we have more bodies in a few days than in the past two years. Barry, please come with me." And with that he was out the door with the DA.

Paul opened the door and yelled for Bud to come in. Detective Johnson left Deborah and walked into the office as Ashley shut the door behind him.

"Bud, we have to pull ourselves together and get working," Paul said.

Bud was clearly annoyed, and replied, "What the fuck are you talking about? We just lost three cops today, including Kevin Cronin just an hour ago. What the are you preaching to me about!"

"Hey!" Paul yelled back. Both Rachelle and Deborah heard the yelling and looked in the office as Bud rushed for Paul. Ashley moved in between them and struggled to pull them apart.

"Stop this shit! You guys get your act together right now, or do I call and have you removed! Christ! You guys haven't been alone for ten minutes with Cronin gone, and you're already at each other's throats. I have no problem pushing for O'Malley to handle this!" He held up his phone as if to make a call.

Bud walked away from Paul toward the wall. He stood silently staring at a blank wall until he said, "Paul, we have lost good cops. I'm human, Paul, and so are you. We have work to do, but our lives are changed forever. We won't solve this without each other, but don't tell me we have to get our act together. Damn it, let's just solve this."

Paul put his hand on Bud's shoulder and said,

"Let's get to the hospital. Get a uniform to keep Deborah company."

They left the office and said good-bye to Rachelle and Deborah. Paul hugged his lover as she looked at him with worry. Bud's good-bye was a little more awkward, but as they approached the front door he said,

"Deborah, it's true I started to keep contact because I was worried about you, but isn't that enough for now? I had forgotten how special and fun you are. So just know how much you mean to me, OK?" Deborah nodded as she put her hand on his face.

As she walked down the stairs, her father, William Lance, pulled up and greeted his daughter. Officer O'Brien was assigned to Deborah until further notice. Paul and Bud said good-bye to Ashley, who told them to keep in touch. They drove to Stony Brook Hospital to meet the families and other officers who had gathered there.

They even requested to see the body of Kevin Cronin. Doctor Thompson told them it would be impossible.

"First of all," he said, "the body was badly burned, and I think it's inappropriate until his family returns from California."

After an hour of paying respect to the families of the fallen officers, both Powers and Johnson pulled Officers Justin Healey and George Lynagh aside. Paul spoke just above a whisper to them as Bud looked around to make sure there was no one being nosy.

"We need to find Robert Simpson, and we need to find him fast. Am I making myself clear?" Paul said. Both officers acknowledged and left the hospital.

Powers and Johnson went to visit Officer Chapman, who was in serious condition.

The news came over Monday night at the Bedford Hills Prison in Upstate New York regarding the deaths of Officer Dugan, Detective Hansen, and Kevin Cronin, the detective lieutenant who had put Jason "Jack" O'Connor away for life. O'Connor sat in his cell on his bed with his eyes closed, meditating on the news of the death of his nemeses. He sat there breathing slowly, with a grin coming over his face; the expression on his face was one of reaching an orgasm. He was in a state of euphoria over the deaths. Finally, a huge grin climaxed minutes of arousal. He would sleep well tonight.

Paul called Detective Baker to cancel her plans to be a decoy at the music clubs. Instead he instructed her to relieve O'Brien in four hours at the Lance mansion. His phone rang as soon as he hung up from Baker. It was Franks telling him that it appeared Rachelle Robinson would be staying with Deborah Lance.

"Why do you think that?" Paul said.

"Well," O'Brien replied, "she brought her dogs over to the house, so I assume she's going to stay over."

"Damn it," Paul replied. "Thanks, Officer, you will be relieved in four hours by Detective Baker. Listen, there is a squad car parked near the Wilkerson house, correct?"

"Yes sir," O'Brien replied. "Officers Blake and Santiago are there."

"Good," Paul replied, "I'll be in touch."

It was safe to assume Lindsey Wilkerson was not in any

danger. Nothing unusual had happened to her over the last week and there had been no incidents involving the house. Paul got himself to a private room at the hospital and finally broke down and cried. He knew Officer Dugan well, and although he did not know Hansen well, he was working with them. But it was the sudden loss of Detective Lieutenant Cronin that deeply affected him. Bud had been looking for Paul at the hospital and saw him through the skinny clear glass on the door crying. He decided to give him a few more minutes before walking into the room.

Madison was trembling in her sleep as her nightmares were getting worse. She was driving along a road when she came across a hitchhiker. The only problem was he was wearing a Ghost Face mask. She stepped on the gas, and the faster she went, the more hitchhikers would appear on the side of the road. Finally one of them was standing in the middle of the road and she decided she would not stop. As the car came upon the hitchhiker in the middle of the road, he pulled off his mask and it was herself again. The car hit Madison as she sat up screaming. Janet Gates came running over as Madison was in a deep sweat and shaking again. She was torn over what was happening, but she couldn't ignore it. She opened the door and sat and held Madison again. She knew her job would be in jeopardy, but she couldn't stop herself from trying to calm Madison down and help her.

Their relationship changed at this moment, for they sat and talked for over two and a half hours. Madison spoke to Gates and told her the story that made national news. Janet listened with very few interruptions. She thought if Madison got it all out of her system, then maybe, just maybe, the nightmares would end. The correctional officer knew that her sister Rachelle would be visiting her tomorrow and she would make sure to talk to her. Janet held on to Madison as she spoke about the vigilante justice she took against the men who threatened her sister. Janet broke protocol again by telling Madison that others in the facility empathized with her but would never openly admit it.

"I guess," Janet said, "I will be the one who will lose her job," and she let out a little nervous laugh.

"No," Madison replied, "no one needs to know you have shown compassion to me. Thank you."

Bud made it home and there were boxes all over his house, for it was only five days until he was supposed to move into the Henry Hallock house in the village. It didn't really seem to matter anymore.

He lay on his bed for a few minutes, then sat up and walked outside and began to talk: "Well, Lord, it's me again. I spoke to you only a couple days ago, but I need to chat. You have been such an influence on my life in so many ways, and yes I know I'm not perfect, which is why I need you to guide me again. You have brought Deborah into my life, and I let things slide because of my job. I want her . . . no, I need her to survive this. Her life is more important than mine. Let it not be her. As you sacrificed for us, I am willing to do the same. So I guess that means I would rather you take me." He smiled and looked down for a second before looking up again and continuing, "If that isn't love, I don't know what is. Besides, if anyone knows anything about sacrifice, it's you, Lord. You have encouraged me not to be discouraged by the difficulty by helping me keep my focus on you. I am aware of your presence. Thank you, Lord, and good night."

Paul sent Rachelle a text when he got back to his apartment above Z Pita: *Please be careful, Rachelle. I love you.* Rachelle was already sound asleep and wouldn't see the text until the morning. Paul took a shower and then played his messages. One from his father, who told him if he didn't hear from him by Tuesday morning he would be flying back up to New York from Florida. The news had reached Florida in regards to the three cops, including Cronin and the seriously injured Chapman still holding on.

The second message was from Rachelle: "Hi Paul, it's

Rachelle. I'm staying with Deborah, and I don't want to leave her. I know you're worried, but our lives were bonded together a couple of years ago. I love you, Paul, and I'm very worried about you as well. I'm so sorry about Kevin Cronin. I'm so sorry for the others as well. Call me tomorrow." The sound of a kiss came over the message before the sound of a *click*. He sat down on the bed and played her message again just to hear her voice. He missed her already.

OCTOBER 7

It was now 11:00 on Tuesday morning, and Rachelle got ready for her morning visit to Madison at the jail. Deborah told her she would also be going. Detective Baker had been relieved at 2:00 in the morning, and she was back at 11:00 for another shift to keep an eye on Deborah Lance. Baker found it ironic that she would be at the facility as an escort instead of an inmate. It was only a couple weeks earlier that Cronin was ready to assign her at the facility as undercover. They did not know that Al Simmons, Madison's attorney, would also be there at the request of Janet Gates. She had contacted him with the number given to her by John Bay. Attorney Simmons assured Officer Gates that no one would ever find out she called him.

Paul had already been in the office for a few hours and caught himself looking through the photos that were on Cronin's desk. He was now in charge of the case, and the fact that he was getting text messages from Ashley proved it. Autopsy results would take a few more days due to requests, and Ashley had already informed Paul that Cronin had told him if anything happened to him, he did not want a burial until the case was closed. Paul thought that even in death Cronin knew how to keep the pressure on. Detective Bud Johnson was at the hospital with Officer Chapman, who had awakened from surgery.

The gang hanging out at Jerry's Deli in Port Jefferson Station was the same old group of guys there every day. They were there every day but usually up to no good by night. Singing, laughing, and high-fiving, they were legends in their own minds yet very dangerous when their turf was disrespected. Their banter suddenly came to a screeching halt when they saw Lynagh and Healey get out of the police cruiser. They all knew who the two of them were. If you did not, they would check your pulse to see if you were alive. The news media and the papers had made the two of them almost as famous as Powers and Johnson.

As the two officers approached the gang, Lynagh received a text from Powers to get to Rodrigo Hernandez and show him the photo of Simpson to verify if he was the man Rodrigo saw in the bathroom of the private room at the City nightclub.

"Hello, boys," Lynagh greeted them. "We need your help."

The leader of the pack spoke up. "And why should we help you, mother . . . " He caught himself before finishing his sentence.

"Oh," Lynagh replied, "I thought this was going to be a friendly conversation, but I will tell you why. Because we have a cop killer on the loose and we are going to turn every building upside down, every gang member, meeting place, home, and their families inside out till we find who is responsible. Now are we going to get some help or do we start right here?"

One of the other members of the gang took off his sunglasses as he spoke to Lynagh.

"Does your partner here speak, or is he just a silent sidekick?" he asked as he and his friends all laughed. Healey put out his hand to shake the young man's hand but instead knocked his glasses to the sidewalk. He bent down to pick them up but instead stepped on them, breaking them into hundreds of pieces.

The gang member looked at Healey with fire in his eyes as he said,

"You must be fucking crazy, man. You know what it means to make me lose face in front of everyone."

Healey picked up the pieces he could and gave them to the gang member, saying, "I'm sorry."

Lynagh looked back at the leader and asked, "Does anyone else have anything to say about my partner, or can we continue?"

There was silence. "OK, good," he spoke again. He passed around photos of Rodrigo Hernandez, Jerry Wakefern aka Jake Wiley, and the video still of the man wearing the baseball hat with the mask and Robert Simpson. "Take a good look, my friends," he said, as the photos were passed around.

The leader in the dark purple bandana spoke up.

"We are not your friends, Mr. Cop."

Lynagh put his arm on Emanuel, better known as the Man, and told him he needed to speak with him privately. They walked over to the side of the building, leaving Healey with six others.

The young man who no longer had sunglasses spoke again to Officer Healey.

"There are now six against one; you must not feel safe."

"Yes I do," Healey responded. "I've killed people with this gun I'm wearing." The small grin disappeared from the gang member's face.

On the side of the building Lynagh spoke as firmly and politely as he could.

"You see, Emanuel, I don't want you to lose face in front of your friends here like your asshole buddy over there, but we will not stop until we shake down everything. Now I want to know where I can find these people, and if you don't know, I want you and your crew out there to help find out."

Emanuel looked at the officer and asked, "And if I don't?"

Lynagh moved closer to him. "Listen, there's a reason you and I are on the side of the building. We are out of earshot of everyone else, and there's no one filming us. You agree to help us now, or I swear you won't be the leader of this group when they see the condition you are in when you leave the side of this building."

The gang leader looked at the sky, then back at Lynagh. "Let me look at the photos again." He stared at Rodrigo Hernandez and knew he worked at the City club.

"He lives in Selden, over on Perry Street."

Lynagh took the photo back and asked,

"Why would you know that?"

Emanuel paused then answered, "I know him from the club; someone I know got him the job there. He lives with a cousin, which is why you didn't have the address."

Lynagh showed him Jerry Wakefern aka Jake Wiley. Emanuel answered, "He is the boyfriend of Linda Tangretti, who goes to the club often."

Lynagh showed him the photos of Robert Simpson and the figure with the long hair wearing the baseball hat with the mask.

"Never seen them before," Emanuel answered.

Lynagh took the photos back and said, "This is what I want you to do. The club reopens Wednesday night. I want you there working the club, and I want you to be in touch with me if you think there is anything we need to see."

Emanuel shook his head and said, "You are one crazy motherfucker getting me involved in this."

Lynagh went up to his ear and whispered, "You have no idea."

The officer then approached Healey and said,

"Let's go."

One of the members said, "OK, silent man, time to go." Healey moved toward the car and stepped hard on the man's foot and dug in.

"I'm sorry," Healey said as he moved to the car.

As Lynagh pulled away they could hear the young man yelling that his foot was broken. It took the two officers twelve minutes to drive to Selden. Perry Street had twelve houses on both sides as the officers began asking questions of the neighbors as to the house Rodrigo Hernandez lived in. They were directed to the grey-and-green house at the end of the block, and as they approached the door, Lynagh remembered the explosion that had just happened at Bruce Roberts's house.

He looked at Healey and said, "Remember, door explosions and people running out of front doors with shotguns."

Lynagh and Healey each took a window and peeked in. Lynagh saw nothing, but Healey spotted a body on the floor in one of the rooms. They wanted to go in, but the explosion at Bruce Roberts's house and Cronin's car prevented them from entering. They called for backup and walked around to the back of the house and smashed one of the windows to get inside the house. Lynagh kept moving his nightstick around the rim of the window opening to ensure they would not get nicked by a piece of glass.

Once inside the house with their guns drawn, they could hear both Detectives O'Malley and Wyatt outside. Healey touched his radio to tell them they were inside of the house and for them not to use the front door and only to come in the house through the open window if shots were heard. Normally the ranks of O'Malley and Wyatt would not take directives from officers in uniform, but there was a different acceptance level from those on the Priority 1 Task Force. Lynagh pointed for Healey to check the body while he stood guard with his weapon pointed at whoever may be in the house.

"He's gone," Healey said. "It's Rodrigo."

Lynagh looked over and said, "Time for whomever to keep cleaning house. Where was he shot?"

"Dead center chest," Healey replied.

"Well," Lynagh said, "we know it wasn't Bud that shot him." It was inside jokes like this that kept them from losing their sanity.

Lynagh checked the front door and found no explosives, so he opened it for Wyatt and O'Malley to come in. "We are going upstairs," Lynagh said. "If you guys keep an eye downstairs, it would be a help."

As they prepared to go upstairs, Healey sent Powers a text about Rodrigo. The two officers went from room to room and found nothing. They came downstairs and asked the two detectives to stay with the body while they went back to headquarters to meet with Powers and Johnson.

Once they arrived at Priority 1, the four of them went into the conference room to review the entire case. The three girls' photos were still up on the wall. Rodrigo's photo and Bruce Roberts's photo were placed with them. On the other side of the wall, Powers put photos of Robert Simpson and Jerry Wakefern up.

"There has to be more," Bud said. "We need to know who this guy is," he said, as he posted the photo of the long-haired man with the masked baseball hat. "Chapman told me at the hospital it was this asshole that blew away Dugan. He kills three girls, cops, and we think Simpson is involved because of the notes and the music he liked to have sex with Deborah to."

"Are you OK?" Paul asked, looking at his partner.

"Yeah, I'm fine, thanks," Bud replied. "This is not making sense." Bud added, "The young girl in the bathroom stall, Taylor, she said she heard the man kissing the girl after he killed her. Yet the man that was in the private room at the City club also had the hat and long hair. The only connection to Simpson is the music and the possibility of the notes."

Paul spoke up. "Wait a minute," he said as he approached all the photos. "Wait a damn minute." He looked at Lynagh and asked, "Do we have Simpson's body stats? Look at this closely." He pointed at the video still. "Is it possible? Put twenty pounds on Simpson, give him long hair, could it be?"

"Paul," Bud spoke up, "if you are right, then Simpson has suddenly reappeared as a killer and puts Deborah in more danger than we originally thought."

"Unless," Lynagh said, "he could never kill her, just those that look like her."

"But why?" Paul said. "There's more to this than Simpson. He's not smart enough to do this on his own." He thought to himself it was times like these that he missed Detective Lieutenant Cronin.

"It's him," Bud replied as the officers and detectives looked at him. He spoke again, looking down at his notes. "Only Simpson would say, 'If I can't have you, no one will.' He's going to attempt to kill Deborah as he works himself into a frenzy. If he takes a few of us out along the way, then so be it."

Rachelle and Deborah's visit lasted an hour with Madison, and they decided to wait around until after Madison's meeting with Al Simmons so they could talk to him. As the young women waited for him, Officer Janet Gates came out into the waiting room to meet with Rachelle and Deborah and introduced herself.

"Listen," Janet said, "this is highly irregular, but I wanted to let you know you need to speak with Madison's attorney and your sister." Rachelle's face became very intense as Officer Gates continued, "Madison is having nightmares, bad nightmares. Instead of her killing the bad guys and executing vigilante justice, in her dreams the one behind the mask doing harm to her is herself."

Deborah spoke up. "She told you all this?"

"Yes," Gates answered, "but I've been there with her on and off for the past three months. They are getting worse. The other night I held on to her for a couple of hours. It is really against protocol here, but I could not help myself. I just want to be sure she gets the help she needs."

Rachelle grabbed her hand and thanked Officer Gates for the information and help as they waited for Al Simmons to exit from the attorney-client room. Rachelle handed him a note as soon as he met her, and she asked him to read the note and go back to Madison in the room. Now he understood why Janet Gates requested he pay Madison a visit.

Al Simmons sat with his forefinger on his left temple as he began to change the subject, as he folded up the note from Rachelle. Madison had been talking about the treatment she had been receiving at the facility. It helped that she was not treated like a serial killer. Both Officers Bay and Gates could not have been better under the circumstances.

"Maddie," Simmons said, "I need to speak to you about a few things." The serious look on his face and the fact that he did not respond to what she was saying worried her. As she started to speak, the attorney raised his hand for her to hold up till he spoke. "First," he said, "Officer Gates has informed me that you are having nightmares about what happened a year and a half ago. If this is true and it's getting worse, I want to have a doctor treat you."

Madison sat there silently as her attorney continued, "There is something else going on that you should know, but if you can't keep yourself calm I will limit the information access to you. If you are having nightmares, we certainly don't need more stress on you while being locked up here."

Madison sat up straight as she prepared herself for the next bit of information from Simmons. "It seems that there may be a threat to Deborah Lance as a repercussion of the Face of Fear case. The Priority 1 squad is convinced Robert Simpson has revenge on his mind and may have collaborated with former Agent O'Connor to kill women that resemble Deborah, as well as Officer Walter Dugan and Detective Cronin and a detective you don't know named Hansen. If all of this is true, then you need to know that Rachelle is involved, because she rarely leaves Deborah's side."

The attorney sat silently as he looked at Madison's face with a blank expression. Her eyes moved about the room as tears rolled down her face. Simmons pulled out a couple tissues he had in his suit pocket as he waited for her to speak. Finally, after about another thirty seconds, she spoke. "I just saw them before you. Why didn't they tell me?" she asked as she put the tissue to her eyes.

"Maybe," he replied, "for the same reason you didn't tell them about your nightmares." The attorney leaned forward to comfort her as he spoke again. "Maddie, we are going to get you help."

"I don't care about me," she replied. "Just make sure my sister and Deborah are OK. She doesn't have me now, and Rachelle needs her, and needs Paul. Don't let anything happen to them." Even now, all she cared about was Rachelle and Deborah.

"OK," Simmons answered, "I will be in touch about a doctor to speak with you."

Janet Gates opened the door and saw the red surrounding Madison's eyes and asked if everything was all right.

"Yes, Officer Gates," Madison replied as she hugged her attorney good-bye. Simmons walked out of the attorney-client room and headed for the lockers to pick up his personal belongings when he saw Rachelle and Deborah waiting for him. He started walking toward them as he thought to himself, *This just keeps getting better all the time.*

As Officers Lynagh and Healey got out of the squad car at Sean Martin's house, they waited out of courtesy for the local East Hampton Police to question him. When Officers Blair and Lawrence pulled up, they were asked to back them up in the rear. Another unmarked vehicle pulled up to the cars, stopping Lynagh and Healey. Jumping out of the car was Detective Ellyn Baker.

"What's going on?" Lynagh asked.

"Powers," Baker answered. "He asked me to back you up." Lynagh and Healey looked at each other before answering her.

"OK," Officer Lynagh replied. "Come in behind us, but give us ten seconds." The East Hampton local authorities went behind the house as Healey stepped to the side of the door and knocked on the door. There was no answer.

"The car is in the driveway," Baker whispered. Healey banged louder on the door but still got no answer.

"Shh," Lynagh said, "do you hear that?"

Healey shook his head as he replied,

"No, let's not pull that shit here."

Lynagh spoke again quickly.

"I'm serious, listen. Put your head to the house and be quiet."

The officer did just that and heard moans coming from inside the house. He nodded *yes* to Lynagh as the senior Officer said,

"We are going in."

He turned the doorknob, and it was that easy. The door was unlocked. With guns drawn Healey and Lynagh walked in as Baker stayed by the door. Toward the back of the house the moans were getting louder as both officers moved toward the back bedroom. There, on the bed was a young woman on top of Sean Martin as he lay underneath her with his eyes closed. Lynagh and Healey walked inside the room, put their guns in their holsters, and stood there with their hands on their hips. Healey, with a stone face, eyed the room while Lynagh, with his sunglasses on, was contemplating how to break up the fun.

Finally, he just spoke. "We are sorry for the interruption, folks, but we have a test of the emergency broadcast system."

The young woman on top started screaming as she got up and ran to the bathroom and shut the door. Sean Martin tried to get up to cover himself, but Lynagh wouldn't have any of it. The officer said, "Stay where you are with your gun out for a moment; we have some questions for you."

Healey was amused by Lynagh's reference to Sean Martin's penis as his gun. He introduced himself and Healey, as Martin was clearly agitated that his sexual adventure had been prevented from having a climatic ending.

Lynagh spoke again as Healey started to walk around the room. "Have you been sending Deborah Lance text messages lately?"

"What?" Martin answered. "I wouldn't give that stuck-up bitch the effort!" Lynagh moved closer to him as he lay naked in the bed and now seemed to enjoy the attention.

"When is the last time you communicated with her?" Lynagh said in a louder voice.

Martin shook his head as he answered, "That little bitch only liked sex one way. She was a bore in bed. You heard of a whore in bed, well she was a bore in bed."

Lynagh moved closer as he spoke quietly to Martin.

"If I were you, I'd be careful."

The officer started to walk away from the bed as the bathroom door opened, with the young woman still naked but this time with a gun in her hand. She fired and hit Healey. As Lynagh turned toward her, more shots rang out. Ellyn Baker had been standing by the door and fired two shots into Holly Moore's chest and then turned and fired two more shots at Sean Martin before Lynagh had a chance to react. He turned and saw a gun near his hand and looked at Baker, still pointing the gun as the backup from the rear came rushing into the house.

"Justin!" Lynagh yelled as he rushed to Healey on the floor. "Damn it!" Lynagh yelled as he opened Healey's shirt and saw he wore his vest. It had caught the small-caliber .22. He stared at Healey. "Justin, you're OK, your vest caught it." He looked up at Baker, now leaning against the doorframe still holding her gun by her leg.

"I only have one question," Healey said from the floor, holding his chest.

"What's that, buddy?" Lynagh asked.

Healey spoke as he looked at Lynagh's eyes.

"Why am I the one who is always getting shot? It's always me, never you."

Lynagh smiled as he replied, "Lynagh luck, I guess." He looked up at the East Hampton authorities looking at two dead, naked bodies. "Guys, help my partner to the car, please, we've got to call this in."

Lynagh walked over to Ellyn Baker, who was still staring into space holding her gun, and put his hand gently on her firearm and slowly took it away from her. "Talk to me," he said.

She turned her head to look at him.

"I never killed anyone before. I read about it. I've seen it in movies, TV, and newspapers. I thought I would be OK when the day came, if it ever came, and what happens? Two at the same time with no clothes on."

Lynagh put his arm around her.

"You saved our lives today, Ellyn. We got sloppy and Powers sent you in as a backup. We are alive right now because you are one hell of a shot. Come on. We've got to call this in, and I'm going to hold your piece for now."

Lynagh called Powers to inform him of what happened and the detective sergeant told him to have Baker take Healey to get checked out medically. "You stay at the scene with the other officer's till the crime lab is finished and photos taken at the scene." Power's hesitated and spoke again. "George, before you leave there, we need to know why two naked people pulled guns on you today to kill. Then you get Baker back here. Internal affairs will want to talk to her, and they will most likely require her to speak to a professional about what went down."

"Yes sir," Lynagh said as he approached the room again.

He put his phone back in his pocket as he looked at Detective Baker sitting on the chair on the front porch. He walked up to her and spoke in her ear: "I know this is tough, but you have to be strong here for the next couple hours. It is important we find out why these two were willing to kill cops while they had no clothes on. You go in there and act like you just saved two cops' lives and don't take any shit from anyone. I will back you up. Keep in mind one thing. We are not leaving till we find out what they didn't want us to see or have."

Baker bit her lip as she continued to stare at empty space in front of her.

Suddenly she turned to Lynagh and said, "Let's go." When they entered the room, the dead woman was covered with a blanket courtesy of Officer Blair. Lynagh picked up the blanket to take a look, and two bullet holes were dead center in her chest. He dropped the blanket and looked over at the body of Sean Martin. Officer Blair covered only his private part, but the two bullet holes in the center of his chest made him look over at Baker as she went through jewelry boxes and drawers in the room.

Lynagh thought about Rodrigo Hernandez being shot dead center in the chest. He sent a text to Powers to compare ballistics from Rodrigo's body to the bodies in East Hampton. He didn't like where this was going, but he wanted to be sure that Baker wasn't taking matters into her own hands. *Then again*, he thought, *we are alive right now at this moment because of her*. The officer continued to look at Sean Martin and thought about how close his life was to ending today. It gave him a sense of mortality he had not felt for a while. Thinking too hard about whether or not this is your last day on earth is not productive for a police officer, but this time Lynagh and Healey let their guard down and they almost paid for it with their lives.

The crime unit from Riverhead arrived and everything was overturned and taken, including the computers. Lynagh and Baker stayed for another two hours and the only thing they found out was that the woman Detective Baker killed was Holly Moore. According to her license, she was twenty-five years of age, was from Center Moriches, and was employed at, of all places, the City nightclub in Setauket. She had a pay stub in her clothing from the club that one of the East Hampton officers found. As Powers sat in his new office space, the phone rang and as he thought about being in Cronin's former office he picked up the call on the second ring. ADA Ashley walked in and shut the door behind him as Powers listened to Lynagh telling him what they found and that they had a set of photos of the crime scene.

"OK," Powers replied, "get in here and hold on to Baker's gun till you get here. We may send Baker to the club tonight as a decoy." When he disconnected he looked up at Ashley.

The ADA spoke. "We need to talk."

Officer Lynagh looked at Baker and told her she may have an assignment that night at the club. Blair and Lawrence just stared at each other, not sure what to make of what was going on.

Ashley looked at Powers before saying, "Baker can't go to the club. She just fired her weapon, killing two people."

Powers ignored the comment as they both stared at each other.

It was 11:00 at night when Madison got up and called to Officer Janet Gates. The correctional officer walked over to her cell as Madison spoke.

"Janet, I will understand if you can't do this, but if you could make a phone call it would mean a lot to me. I need your help."

Janet started looking the other way with her thoughts, knowing she would be overstepping her bounds of professionalism again, with no going back, if she made a call.

She looked back at Madison and said,

"Madison, you can make a call, you know that."

Madison spoke quickly.

"Janet, my calls are monitored. Please, I need your help. I'm sorry to put you in this position, but I need this, please."

The correctional officer started to walk away as she said,

"Madison, I can't."

There was silence for fifteen minutes, then she walked back to Madison's cell and said, "Tell me what you need, no promises."

The night shift at the jail was rather quiet as Janet Gates checked on Madison every fifteen to twenty minutes with a walk-by. The hour of 8:00 in the morning came fast, especially with all the things inside the correctional officer's head. She served breakfast to the most famous inmate on the East Coast and said good-bye to Madison. The young woman behind bars did not mention the conversation between them.

Janet Gates picked up all her personal belongings, signed out, walked to her car, and hesitated as her hand touched the cold silver from sitting there overnight. She looked back at the facility as if she could see Madison. The officer was clearly struggling with her emotions. Finally, she opened the door, turned the ignition, and drove out of the facility parking lot. When she reached the traffic circle on Route 24 she kept going in a semicircle and headed up toward Main Street in Riverhead. When she passed the Chase Bank she slammed her hand on the steering wheel and turned left into the parking lot away from view. Janet Gates stared into space outside her windshield for about five minutes, then picked up her phone and pushed the buttons. It rang three times and then the call was picked up.

She said, "Hello, you don't know me, but I was asked to give you this call from Madison Robinson."

The call lasted for about three minutes before it was disconnected. Janet Gates turned her vehicle around and turned left, heading east toward Flanders. On the receiving end of the call, the figure walked into the bathroom. The drawer was opened as the hand reached in for paintbrushes. Inside the bottom drawer was red paint. To the right in the bottom drawer the figure reached in and pulled out a Ghost Face mask. Delicately and patiently, little by little, specks of red were painted on the mask to give the appearance of blood splatter. The hand holding the paintbrush was slow, as the artist was meticulous in giving the blood splatter effect. After forty-five minutes, the mask was moved to the basement to dry.

Janet pulled over again on Route 24 and made a second call and spoke when the voice came on. "Listen, I know you won't get this till after work, but you need to call this number I am going to give you. Please, I know we shouldn't, but please call and hear them out. The decision is yours. Please help her." She pushed the *end* button, dropped the phone on the front seat, and began to breathe heavily as she said, "God, please help me." Within minutes she was calm and got back onto Route 24 and let out a forced smile as she passed the landmark Giant Duck on the side of the road.

Paul shook his head and started yelling at ADA Ashley, which got the attention of only Gina. With everyone out of the office, it was an opportunity for Detective Powers to let loose on everything that had happened to the Priority 1 team and the Music Club Murders investigation.

Ashley would not back down. "You don't have to agree with it, but get right with it. You need to let your team know as soon as possible." With that, the ADA left what once was Cronin's office.

Paul called Bud and had Gina call everyone else to get to Priority 1 as soon as possible. He also called Detective Caulfield to tell him he would be assigned to Priority 1 until the case was finished. His first assignment was to get to Stony Brook Hospital and watch the room of Officer Robert Chapman.

Bud Johnson, George Lynagh, and Ellyn Baker were in the precinct within forty minutes, while Franks, O'Malley, and Wyatt needed an hour to get replacements for the security detail on Deborah Lance and the Wilkerson house. Paul explained Caulfield was with Chapman at the hospital. There was no need to shut the office door because no one else other than the Priority 1 squad or the DA, ADA, commissioner, or precinct commander could walk by and hear what Paul had to say. He sat back in his chair, tapped the desk with his pen, and looked at his squad. All were sitting down with the extra chairs Gina brought in except for Bud, who was moving his feet from left to right with his arms crossed over in front of his chest.

Paul suddenly stood up and spoke.

"I've been advised that what is happening with the Music Club Murders is unfortunately connected to . . ." He hesitated for a moment as Bud became alert. Paul looked over at his partner and finished, "the Face of Fear investigation."

Bud's face became flush as Lynagh stood up. Paul raised his hand to stop them from talking and continued speaking. "Deborah Lance, Rachelle Robinson, and Lindsey Wilkerson are fine, but we will have them watched just in case. This is not about them. This is about the Priority 1 squad. We solved the case; we killed O'Connor's team and put his sorry ass away in a cell filled with photos of lives he destroyed. Somehow, from his jail cell, he managed to reach Simpson, who apparently claims Cronin ruined his life by allegedly forcing him to be a part of a plan to bring the Face of Fear investigation to an end."

Bud looked over at Lynagh as Paul continued to speak, saying, "Simpson is out for revenge on the rest of the Priority 1 squad for allegedly threatening him to go away with additional threats to stay away from Bud and Lynagh. Keep in mind this is a killer's allegations that with O'Connor and some kind of connection with the music clubs have purposely killed innocent young women to set up the case that would be assigned to Priority 1."

Bud unfolded his arms as he spoke. "Three girls lost their lives just so the case would be assigned to us, to make it easier to eliminate us?"

Paul nodded in agreement as he replied,

"That's not all. There is a $100,000 bounty on all Priority 1 cops, which is why Dugan and Hansen were eliminated, why Chapman is in the hospital with Caulfield at his door, and why the attempt on Lynagh and Healey was made before Detective Baker here saved their lives. Holly Moore worked at the City nightclub, and it has been confirmed that Sean Martin worked part-time as a bouncer there, which is where he met Deborah Lance. This whole thing has been a setup, to get us both emotionally and professionally."

Detective Baker stood up to speak to Powers. "Sir, how do you know all this?"

Paul nodded as he replied,

"ADA Ashley informed me a few hours ago. The DA has a very reliable source from Bedford Hills Prison, where O'Connor is being held. It appears that his lips have gotten a little loose since he was successful at eliminating Cronin. The bounty on Detective Cronin was $200,000. We are all at $100,000 with the exception of you Bud." He looked at his partner and then left the area behind his desk and walked up to him. "It seems you are the grand prize of $250,000. Now why would he put such a high bounty on you?" he said with a slight sarcastic tone.

Bud gave a slight nod and moved his lips a little, then smiled as he said,

"Maybe he doesn't like my singing."

Paul walked back to his desk as he replied, "Always the funny one."

Bud just stood silently as Paul called in Gina. There was silence in the room to the point of being uncomfortable when the woman who had worked for Detective Cronin for years walked in. "Gina," Paul said, "I want you to get Officer Shepard from the Sixth Precinct to stay with ADA Ashley. Get Officer Whitson from the Sixth as well on attorney Al Simmons. They will have twelve-hour shifts with Officer Leonard replacing Shepard and Buckley replacing Whitson. Franks, you stay at the Lance mansion. I know Rachelle Robinson is staying with Deborah Lance."

He turned his attention to Lynagh and said, "Pick up Healey, make sure he's up to it, and have him fifty yards from the Wilkerson house. No contact until I approve, or there is an emergency. Got It?" Lynagh nodded.

"Once he is set there, get back here for further instructions," Paul continued.

He pushed the intercom for Gina and asked her to call ADA Ashley's office to get O'Connor at Bedford Hills completely shut off from the rest of the prison population. No news, no newspapers, no one. He took his finger off the intercom as he looked at O'Malley and Wyatt. "You guys are part of this case, and being assigned to Priority 1 is hazardous to your health right now. Do you want out?"

Wyatt looked over at O'Malley and said,

"I've been with Detective O'Malley for five years. I'm in if he's in. I won't leave him now."

O'Malley stood up, put a pumpkin seed in his mouth, smiled at Wyatt, and looked over to Paul.

"Well, I've been thinking about retiring, so why not go out with a bang. Besides, it's the least I can do for Hansen. We will see this through. It started as our case, and we will be a part of it until the end of it."

Paul nodded as he replied, "Nice to have you on board. O'Malley, you will be in charge of Wyatt and Caulfield, but you will report to me. Let Caulfield stay with Chapman and have him relieved through Gina's office in six hours. No one is to get to Chapman's room except for the doctors, nurses, the ADA, or members of Priority 1. You schedule the shift through Gina here on in. Also, we are missing something with Kate Summers's murder. She was there with friends and set up to meet Wiley on a blind date. Yet he never showed up. Your reports show you spoke to her girlfriends who were with her at the club. Speak to them again. How long did they know each other, and more important, did the girls she was with have a connection to anyone from the club? If so, it can give us a trail. Also, we never saw video of who walked into the rooms, only who walked out. Find out why." O'Malley nodded and looked at Wyatt to get up and follow him.

Paul looked at Ellyn Baker, who was sitting down again. "How are you feeling?" he asked.

She looked directly at Paul when she answered,

"Like I killed two people."

"OK," Paul answered, "maybe you should feel like you saved two cops' lives. I have your gun. Keep your backup for now, but I want you to see Dr. Watts for a session."

Baker nodded her head and said, "Whew, Dr. Watts, now there is an idea. What kind of name is that for a psychiatrist?"

Bud smiled, appreciating her sense of humor. He couldn't help but notice her shoes were already off.

"Very funny," Paul said. "I get it, the name Watts and the word idea, ha ha. Now get yourself checked out. You know I will be speaking with you tomorrow before you get your piece back. Regardless, we will have to get a replacement for you tonight, we can't let you work till the doctor OKs it."

Baker started to protest, but Powers interrupted her.

"You're on desk duty till further notice. Go home, relax, and see the doctor."

Baker got up to leave and started getting near the exit when Bud yelled,

"You forgot your shoes!"

The detective turned around, picked up the pair, and walked out with her shoes in her hand. Bud just shook his head with a smile as he thought, *I could never get away with not wearing shoes.*

As Baker got close to the exit, Powers yelled, "Don't forget to give your schedule to Gina. She needs to know where everyone is."

"Yes, Boss," Baker answered as she opened the door to the main part of the building. It was now just Powers and Johnson left in the office.

Paul shook his head and looked up at Bud as he said, "Just you and me now. We got a lot of work to do."

Bud started singing,

"You and me against the world."

Paul just stared at his partner.

"You have a bounty of $250,000 on your head, and you're singing a song by Helen Reddy?"

Bud's face turned serious. "I don't care about me. I do care about what could happen to people I care about. Let them come looking for me, but they hurt Deborah, Rachelle, Lindsey, or you, and I'll give them a war they won't believe." He walked out of the office and went to his desk.

Ashley hung up the phone, looked at DA Steinberg, and told him what Gina said. Detective Powers's request was on Jason "Jack" O'Connor's line of communication being 100 percent completely shut off until further notice.

Steinberg leaned back in his chair and stared at the ceiling as he said,

"Maybe Cronin was right. Powers can handle a case like this." He moved his eyes to the ADA and said, "Be careful, John, you were as big a part of the Face of Fear investigation as the squad from Priority 1."

The ADA nodded. "I trust these guys, Barry. They know what they're doing, and with me keeping the legal guidelines in perspective, this will be resolved once and for all."

The DA stood up. "It better be. This whole thing with undercover at the Riverhead jail, I assume this is on hold, or is *Long Island Pulse* willing to put another writer undercover without a cop in there?"

The ADA replied, "Let me have Bud ask Nada how they feel about it. He and Cronin have had the relationship with her."

Steinberg sat down again as he replied, "What about the female cop who put bullet holes dead center in the chests of naked people?"

"Yes," Ashley replied. "You left out the part that they had guns. One running out of the bathroom, the other had a gun under the pillow, and reached for it when she came out shooting."

The DA continued to be inquisitive. "Where did Baker come from?"

John Ashley was prepared for this. "Cronin selected her from the Third Precinct when he saw her scores on shooting. He interviewed her and requested the transfer after Sherry Walker left the task force."

The DA nodded. "That was probably the smartest thing she ever did." He looked out the window as he spoke again, saying, "Get Powers ready and prepared in the case. Both of you have to give a press conference. Place a call to East Hampton and make sure the incident that happened is not released to the media until further notice. Once this gets out, there will be a panic if the public finds out this is related to the Face of Fear investigation. Madison Robinson may be behind bars, but if by some chance Robert Simpson is telling the truth, he was forced into all of this and it gets out, Priority 1 will be in danger of being dissolved."

Ashley looked at the DA and replied, "Enough said," as he left his office.

It was two hours later when Lynagh called Powers to tell him Healey was home resting and that Gina had assigned another officer to the Wilkerson house until that night, when Healey would return. "Also," he said, "Emanuel called me to tell me he heard through the grapevine that people we may be interested in will be at the Pajama Club, which operates as Decades on Wednesday nights."

"OK," Paul said. "Bud and I will be there tonight, but I would like you and Officer Carol Wright at the City club in Huntington. Go in separately. They will make you as a cop, but not Carol. She will need to go in as someone who just wants to have a good time."

Lynagh replied, "Where did we get Officer Wright from?"

"She's from the Third, twenty-five, pretty, brunette, and ready to be undercover. Keep an eye on her."

Bud was at his desk exchanging texts with Deborah when Paul walked over to him and told him they were going to the Decades club aka the Pajama Club.

"Bud," Paul said, "we've got to try to keep our distance from the girls until this bounty thing is resolved. We don't want them around us while this is going on." Bud agreed and said he looked forward to checking the place out. He looked at his phone and sent Deborah a text.

Rachelle curled up on the couch as Deborah brought in the popcorn as they prepared to watch a few episodes of *Pawn Stars* on On Demand. Both Deborah and Rachelle loved the show and enjoyed all the historical information they learned from it. Priority 1 had asked Deborah to take a few days off from school, and Rachelle was staying with her. Rachelle took some popcorn as she told Deborah she had an hour before she had to get ready to be at work for the evening.

"Joey Z is leaving at 7:00 pm tonight. I'm closing, so I can't be late," Rachelle said. There was no reply from Deborah as Rachelle looked at her. "He cares for you, Deb. You need to give him time if you feel the same way."

Deborah looked down at her iPhone and saw the message from Bud. She smiled as she read it to Rachelle. It said, *You will always be a part of me no matter what the ending shall bring.* She put her phone down as Rachelle continued to look at her.

Deborah cleared her throat before she said, "He is the only man I've ever met that made me feel like he didn't care about who I was or where I come from. He has never asked me for anything other than to spend time with me and create memories. All he cares about is me, nothing else."

She started laughing as she continued. Even Wes, who was at Rachelle's feet while Craven laid by the front door, raised his head to look at Deborah as she continued, "He is the funniest, most romantic man. One minute he is so ridiculous and silly and I don't know what to expect, whether it's finding a pair of his socks in my pocketbook just to tease me or sending me a trivia question."

There was about thirty seconds of silence as Rachelle petted Wes, waiting for her friend to continue. Finally Deborah said, "And yet there are times I feel like no one can protect me like he can. I just feel so safe when I'm with him. My dad has always been there for me, but you know what I mean?" She looked at Rachelle, who by now was nodding her head with squinted eyes.

"Oh God," Rachelle said, as she put her hand on Deborah's arm. "You are so in love with him." Deborah tried to resist as Rachelle squeezed her arm more. "Oh no, don't you try to avoid this. You are crazy in love with him!" Deborah turned her head away from Rachelle.

"No, no, no," Rachelle pressed as she put her hand out to her friend's head to sway it back to her.

"Look at me, Deborah Lance; you look at me."

As she finally got Deborah to look at her, she noticed her eyes were filled with water.

Rachelle held on to Deborah as her friend sobbed into her chest.

"It's OK, honey," Rachelle said as she stroked her hair. "It's OK, I'm here for you. Until you speak with them, some men need a little more than a clue to pursue things."

Deborah looked up at her friend and used profanity for the first time. Rachelle had never heard her use it.

"He's a fucking detective. He needs more than a clue?" It was so comical the way she said it that they both began laughing hysterically. Even Wes got up and started barking.

Rachelle said, "Listen, I've got to get ready to go to the restaurant. Why don't you come with me? You can sit in the back and go upstairs to Paul's apartment for a few hours, relax, and I will feel better that you are close by, and the dogs will have company."

After a couple minutes of persuasion Deborah agreed, and within thirty minutes they were out the door. As they turned right on East Broadway in Rachelle's BMW, Officer Franks followed them from fifty yards behind. Once Rachelle parked, she brought the dogs upstairs and gave the key to Deborah so she could come and go between the apartment and the restaurant as she pleased.

As Rachelle ran down the stairs she yelled back,

"Don't forget to come down later; it will be good for you to get something to eat" Deborah sat down on the bed as Craven settled in at the top of the stairway and Wes jumped on the bed to lie down next to her.

"You are such a mush," she said as she kissed the King Charles Cavalier. The dog began to lick her face to express mutual affection as she giggled and turned on the TV. Within minutes she fell asleep from all the stress of the past few days. Rachelle spotted Joey Z in his normal routine of walking from side to side for the dinner crowd, but as soon as he spotted Rachelle he greeted her with a hug and was gone within minutes. He always left with a comment that made Rachelle laugh. This time it was, "Tonight I have a mini vacation. I will be by myself." Rachelle just shook her head with a smile.

It was 8:30 pm, and Powers and Johnson parked about a block away and walked inside the nightclub operating as Decades for the evening. It was '70s night, and Bud apologized to Paul that it wasn't '80s night. They were stopped in the front by the tall bouncers as both detectives flipped open their badges. They were completely out of place, as most of the patrons were in '70s apparel, mostly reflecting the disco era: silk printed shirts for the men and dresses in either black or white for the women. The club had two levels with the top level serving as an overhang of the bottom level. You could dance, sit, drink, or just stand against the railing looking down on the main dance floor when you were on top. Paul pulled out photos from the videos from the night of the murder from all three clubs and started scanning the crowd.

The music was so loud he pulled Bud's ear to his mouth and said,

"Let's check out the bathroom where the murder took place."

They were directed to a long and narrow hallway away

from the dance and bar area and found the men's room, which had the international symbol for men's room but right above it had a sign that said, *Elton John*. Both detectives didn't get it until they got to the women's bathroom with a sign that read, *Olivia Newton-John*.

Bud shook his head and said,

"Oh no, not this shit; you have to be kidding me," as he looked at Paul, who had a big smile on his face. Paul's affection for Olivia Newton-John had now become an inside joke and Paul loved getting under Bud's skin.

A young woman came out of the bathroom, and as Bud showed her his badge, he said, "I have a question, ma'am. What's the story with the bathrooms being called Elton John and Olivia Newton-John?"

The young woman was caught off guard but answered,

"When the clubs have '70s and '80s nights the bathrooms are always designated that way."

"Thank you, ma'am."

Paul interjected as he looked at Bud, "I like this place already."

The doctor told Ellyn Baker to stay home for a few days. So, since she was now on her own time, she decided to go dancing at the club as an off-duty cop.

As Carol Walker was getting ready to enter the club, Lynagh spotted Ellyn Baker going in. Lynagh yelled into Wright's earpiece, "Hold up! Don't go in until advised. Confirm copy!"

"Copy that," Wright answered.

"Shit!" Lynagh said aloud. He called Powers to inform him of Baker entering the club.

"Damn!" Powers answered. "Send Wright in to the bar to keep an eye open, give her ten minutes, once you go in even in civilian clothes you will be recognized as a cop. Let's play this out now that Baker decided to spend her off time there. Damn!" he said again before pushing the *end* button.

Baker's silk, sequined dress outlined her almost perfect body, enhancing her breasts and waist. The back was so low-cut that Detective Lynagh wondered if you could see the top of her ass if you were close up. He found himself talking to himself as he watched her go into the club. "Good thing she doesn't have a gun," he said. "There would be no place to put it."

Ellyn Baker cleaned up nice, he thought. In civilian clothes and makeup she was in the same class as the young women who were killed. Lynagh wasn't sure if he could wait ten minutes as he instructed Officer Wright to go in and stay at the bar.

Ellyn Baker made heads turn. She moved to the music and enjoyed the atmosphere of the club, which included beautiful people watching both men and women. She ordered herself an iced tea as she walked her way through the round tables of people to get a glimpse of the area where the private rooms were. She did not notice the bartender telling one of the bouncers that he just had an attractive sexy customer who ordered a drink with no alcohol.

As the detective walked by the private rooms she heard a voice behind her say,

"May I help you, Miss?" She would not have heard it, but the DJ was making an announcement and no music was playing.

Ellyn turned around to face an obese man who must have weighed over four hundred pounds, with long, black, greasy hair. As he walked toward her she couldn't help but notice that he kept pulling up his pants. The bouncer noticed the look on her face as he stepped in front of her.

"What's a beautiful young woman like you doing here all by yourself, walking around the club with an iced tea in her hand?"

"Listen," Ellyn said, "I was looking around the club. I've never been here before, so I would appreciate it if you and your fake Izod shirt would leave me alone." Ellyn walked around the bouncer, which seemed like forever, but once her back was to him he grabbed the back of her hair and pulled her inside the closest private room.

Within seconds Lynagh walked in the front door and the bouncers in front notified the owner, Brian Branca, they had a visitor. Lynagh spotted Carol Wright at the bar sipping a drink.

Inside the private room the large man wouldn't let go of Baker's hair as she reached to open her pocketbook. The bouncer swatted it away as the contents of it slid across the floor, including her backup piece, which was a 32 caliber semiautomatic pistol.

"What are you doing here, bitch?" Baker tried to get out from under his hold as she struck his stomach with her knee. He promptly hit her harder in the stomach and she went down to the floor. Baker could not catch her breath even as he grabbed her hair again.

"What are you looking for here?" he asked as he spotted the pistol on the floor.

Baker caught her breath and said,

"If I was looking for you, it would not be so difficult."

The obese bouncer hit her hard again in the stomach as she was gasping for her breath. Lynagh couldn't find Ellyn anywhere and went inside the women's bathroom as some women screamed as he called out her name. There was no reply, and he realized there could be a very serious problem. He called Powers, who said he was on the way with Bud, but it would take twenty minutes to get to Setauket.

"Get the owner immediately," he told Lynagh, who was in civilian clothes tonight. "If she's in trouble, he most likely can get it stopped."

As they disconnected, Lynagh went up to one of the bouncers, flashed his badge, and said,

"Bring me to the owner now, or I will start shooting bullets in the ceiling, causing a mass panic." The bouncer looked at him in disbelief until Lynagh yelled "Right now!" as he pulled out his weapon.

The bartender moved his head away from Officer Wright and started to send a text when the young officer took ahold of his ear until his head hit the bar. "No texting on the job, handsome. Stay here with me or I'll be insulted and may shoot you." He looked at her with his head sideways on the bar and couldn't believe such a young, petite women was pinning him down on his bar.

The young bouncer put up his hands and replied, "OK, OK, calm down. I will bring you to his office now." Lynagh put his gun back in its holster under his jacket as he was led into a hallway with a hidden door that looked like part of the wall if you did not know it was a door. He looked back at Wright, and she nodded to him.

Ellyn tried again to get out of the grasp of the oversized man, but he would not let go of her hair. She twisted her body and maneuvered her legs to where she was able to kick his face so hard with the heel of her shoe that it knocked out his front teeth. He was enraged as he let go of her and she got up to run for the door, but he was able to grab her again, and this time he hit her hard in the face as she went down to the floor and didn't move. The man got up breathing hard for he had hit her so hard he lost his balance and almost fell on her, which would have most likely killed her. He went to the bathroom inside the private room to wash up as he tried to contact the boss, Brian Branca, who had his hands full with Lynagh. The officer pulled out his weapon again and held it down on his pant leg as he spoke to Branca and his cronies.

"We have a friend here who disappeared. I want her found now before I start doing things you may regret."

"Tell me about your friend," Branca said. "Is she a cop with a gun on my premises?"

"Stop stalling!" Lynagh yelled as he raised his gun. "I've already had two of your employees try to kill me today. I'm insulted because I'm only worth $100,000. I guess if I shoot you I'll be worth more."

"You are threatening me, Officer?" Branca yelled back. "In

front of my attorney?"

Edward Larson put out his hand and said, "Nice to see you again, Officer."

Lynagh ignored him as he pointed his weapon at Branca and said,

"Where is she?"

Branca looked at one of his employees and said,

"Open up the videos." A button was pushed as twenty-four monitors opened up, sharing all parts of the club.

Lynagh still had his gun on Branca as he spoke again. "Find the brunette in the black glitter dress, and make it fast." Two employees looked but were not getting anywhere.

Lynagh was persistent. "Find her in the next sixty seconds or start emptying out this club."

Branca's attorney began to speak. "Officer, you shut this club with no proof that your coworker friend is here against her will, and we will sue you and the police department for damages. The club just reopened; it will destroy our business."

Ten minutes had already gone by, and Lynagh did not know how much longer he had left if Ellyn was in trouble.

He spoke again. "Where are the videos for the private rooms upstairs?"

Branca quickly answered,

"We can't use them while they are occupied. Four of the seven rooms have clients in them."

Lynagh spoke louder. "Put them on the screen now!"

Branca looked at his attorney, who said,

"Show him, Brian. We will use it in the damages case, and the clients in the rooms will have a case as well."

The first video was opened and it was a woman performing oral sex on a man.

"Oh great!" Branca yelled.

The officer wasn't deterred and said,

"Keep going."

The second video showed the room empty. "Move it!" Lynagh yelled. The third video showed a group of people making out and singing karaoke. The next room video opened up and showed Ellyn Baker on the floor motionless as Lynagh called an ambulance and yelled at Branca, "Bring me to this room now!"

Larson, now nervous, said,

"Officer, we can't go out there with a gun in sight; it will cause panic in the club."

Lynagh raised his gun and replied,

"Do you think I give a shit right now?"

There were six men in the room, all ready to make a move as Branca continued to sit looking for guidance from his attorney. Lynagh called Powers back requesting backup at the club and informing him of what was on the video. The two detectives were minutes away as Bud called for more backup while Paul kept Lynagh on the line. The detective sergeant told his officer he didn't want him moving from the room while he was the only cop in the club. It was another three minutes when George Lynagh spoke again as he looked at the video.

"She's not moving." He looked back at Branca, still sitting, and said, "For your sake you better hope she is taking a nap."

Brian Branca began to speak but his attorney put his arm on him to remain silent. Larson looked back at the officer and said, "Mr. Branca had no knowledge of this unfortunate situation, and we are very concerned for your friend. If this is the result of one of our employees, they will be fired immediately and we will also press charges. We are very sorry for what has happened."

As he finished his sentence one of the other employees moved his leg from getting stiff and Lynagh pulled out his backup gun and now had two guns extended in two different directions.

"All of you move over here to your dipshit boss. I'm very angry right now. Quick, move!" he said as he waved his gun. The rest of Branca's entourage walked over to Branca and Larson.

The bartender begged Wright to let go of his ear, for he had drinks to serve. The place was so busy that only a few patrons who were close by noticed what was going on.

Wright let go of his ear as she said, "Serve your drinks, but if I see you go for anything other than a glass or bottle, I will shoot you. I am a police officer and I have partners here in the club. They better come out of here tonight breathing." It was eerie to the bartender how she continued to talk so tough with such a disingenuous smile on her face.

Powers and Johnson pulled up to the front of the club at the same time as four squad cars did, as well as O'Malley and Wyatt. Paul stood at the door and started giving orders for officers to guard all the exits and to inspect everyone leaving the premises. He ordered O'Malley to supervise the outside perimeter and the officers while he went inside with Bud and Wyatt. O'Malley started selecting officers for specific locations at the back and second levels. Before going into the building as he looked at his watch, Paul turned around and looked at the elder detective. "William, if you don't hear from me within ten minutes, come in after us with everyone."

O'Malley nodded as Paul asked, "In your long career have you ever shot anyone?"

"No," O'Malley answered. "I never had to, but I would not hesitate if things had to change." Paul turned around to head into the building as the ambulance pulled up. O'Malley met with the medics and sent them into the building. Powers called Lynagh to get directions to where he was. It was not easy because the club was full and the noise was getting louder. Bud went up to the DJ, flashed his badge, and told him to take a break from the music. There were so many people in the club drinking and talking that the only change was people leaving the dance area.

They reached Lynagh within three minutes and Paul started yelling to Branca,

"Where is Baker? Bring us now!"

He told Wyatt to stay in the room with the entourage as Branca got up and brought Paul, Lynagh, Bud, and the medics to the room where Baker was still lying on the floor. Bud went over to her with the medics and determined she was still alive. Bud put his hand on her head as he looked at the black eye that was forming on her face.

The senior medic who was examining her spoke. "Someone beat the shit out of her. From the way she is breathing she probably has broken ribs as well."

As Bud gently took his hands off her face he thought about Deborah. It seemed like only yesterday he first met her after being held in the house, but this was a physical beating. Bud was getting emotional as Ellyn opened her eyes and tried to talk to Bud. The senior medic motioned for his crew to put her carefully on a stretcher as Ellyn tried to speak to Bud again.

"Hold on," Bud said as he put his ear to her mouth. Paul kept looking around the room for any clues about what may have happened, but he could see from Ellyn's throat she was speaking in Bud's ear. Bud moved his mouth over to Ellyn's ear as he whispered to her then touched her forehead with a gentle rub. He got up as the medics put the young detective on a stretcher as Paul ordered Lynagh to escort the medics and Baker to the ambulance.

"If anyone gets in your way, shoot them."

Branca started yelling, "You can't shoot in here. You'll ruin my club!"

"Your club?" Bud answered. "You have bigger problems, my friend, right now. And speaking of bigger, who is the large four-hundred-pound man that looks like a slob that you have working here?"

Branca hesitated as Bud spoke again. "I'm not going to ask you again, because I think you are resisting arrest."

Branca replied, "I had nothing to do with this!"

Bud got in his face as he yelled back,

"This is your club! I want a name right now!"

Paul started to leave the room, and suddenly Branca realized he would be alone in the room with Bud.

"His name," the club owner replied, "is Kevin Sysco. I will get him."

"No," Bud said, "no you won't. I have a better idea. Set it up with your tech man to get me on the PA system from here."

Branca shook his head and said, "I want my attorney here. What the fuck do you guys think you are doing?"

Paul called O'Malley outside to get Lynagh back to the owner's room after the ambulance left and to bring Edward Larson back to the private room.

After disconnecting, he handed his phone to Branca and said,

"Get your man from the control room to let the PA system come through here now." Branca took the phone and called Steve Lewis, who was near the DJ waiting for the authorization for the music to start again.

"Never mind that, make arrangements to allow a PA system to be controlled out of Private Room 4. Now!" Branca said as he disconnected.

Within five minutes Lewis was up in the room with a cord and a microphone, and in minutes they had a PA system hooked up to the stereo system. It was ready. As Bud took the microphone, Lynagh brought Larson to the room.

Bud tapped the microphone as Branca asked,

"What are you doing?"

Paul looked over at Larson. "Are you going to advise your client to be quiet, Mr. Attorney?"

"Yes," Larson replied.

Bud had a puzzled look on his face as he looked at Paul and said, "I have a question. Should he be advising Bullshit Branca here if the attorney is also a suspect?"

Paul took a deep breath and shook his head. "I really don't know. I think we should check with the ADA on that one," he said, looking back at Larson. "But I don't want to take any chances, so let's leave him here for the moment."

Then he called Wyatt into the control room and said, "We are sending down Steve Lewis. He is going to turn on the master control and then he is going to make a copy of the video from the cameras here."

As Lewis started to leave the room, Bud called to him, "Excuse me, if the video accidently gets deleted, I just want to let you know I will find a way to tie you into the murders of Detective Cronin, Hansen, and Officer Walter Dugan. So be careful."

Steve Lewis stared back at Bud as he looked at Brian Branca and left the room. It was another five minutes when Wyatt notified Powers that the PA was on. Paul looked over at Bud and nodded. Bud tapped the microphone a few times, which caused most of the people to look up at the ceiling with a puzzled look as if they were not sure what to look for. Bud began to speak as Branca looked at his attorney for help, but Larson just shook his head in silence.

Bud put on his radio voice and said, "Good evening, boys and girls, ladies and gentlemen, drug users, parole violators, prostitutes, pimps, underage drinkers, and all-around shitheads. This is Detective Bud Johnson of the Priority 1 Task Force in Suffolk County. I'm sorry for the interruption tonight, but I did want to bring to your attention that in addition to a murder that happened here a couple days ago, we also had a lovely young lady beaten up tonight who just happens to also be a detective with Suffolk County."

The club was dead silent as everyone was listening. Officer Wright continued to sit at the bar as she looked around for suspicious behavior from anyone.

Bud continued, "Now, this woman was physically beaten by one of the employees here, who by the way has been fired but is most likely still here in the club at this moment."

The women in the club were now setting down their drinks as the detective continued, "The coward who beat our detective up . . . well, you can't miss him. He happens to be a big, fat man who smells bad and looks like a complete slob. This is important, because it will make it harder for him to hide due to his girth. Oh, by the way, his name is Kevin Sysco. It is spelled S-Y-S-C-O, which is funny because it's the same name of a company that sells food, but in this case he eats it."

He continued as people in the club started walking toward the door to leave and gather their belongings. O'Malley and his officers were ready to inspect everyone coming out. Bud looked at Branca, who edged over to the couch to sit down.

Some patrons were enjoying the speech and were giggling as Bud continued, "So we ask for you cooperation. If you know where this man is, please let one of our fine officers know as you leave the building, or better yet, Mr. Kevin Sysco, you can get your big, fat, ugly ass up here to Room 4 and save us all a lot of time and effort. Again, everyone, I'm sorry for your evening being cut short, so to make up for it I would like to sing for all of you."

Paul started shaking his head as Bud started singing a popular, classic song by War, "The Cisco Kid."

After Bud sang the entire first verse, he made up his own lyrics for the second verse but was still in tune to the music of the song: "Sysco kid is not a friend of mine. Your ass is so big you won't be hard to find."

Even the guys in the master control room had puzzled looks on their faces as Wyatt said to himself, "One crazy motherfucking cop."

Officer Wright tucked her lips in to hide her amusement at Bud Johnson's PA speech.

Bud spoke again into the PA after he finished his singing.

"Thank you, ladies and gentlemen and the rest of you

degenerates. I hope you all have a wonderful evening and also hope never to see you in this club again. It is a bad element here, and I and the other fine officers of the Suffolk County Police Department will be keeping an eye on this place for quite some time. Good night, good luck, and good riddance. PS, all of your handbags will be inspected on the way out, so if you have anything you shouldn't have, please leave it in the club."

Everyone thought Bud was finished, but he went back on the PA, this time in an airport voice: "Mr. Sysco, paging Mr. Kevin Sysco, please come to Private Room 4. You are wanted in Private Room 4. Mr. Kevin Sysco, please get your huge bodily self up to this room in the next thirty seconds or we will tear this club down with every officer we have. Thank you."

Bud shut the PA off as he asked for alone time with Branca. Paul started to object, but Bud reassured him, "Paul, I'm fine, really. I just want to talk to him for a moment."

"I object!" Larson yelled.

"Come with me," Paul said as he and Lynagh went to the master control room. It was apparent that Bud's PA speech had the entire club emptying out.

Bud approached Brian Branca, who spoke as the detective approached him. "You crazy fucking cop, you just destroyed my business!"

Bud moved in closer as he replied, "I guess my bounty just went up."

Branca was silent as Bud looked at him. The club owner's eyes spoke a thousand words as the detective spoke again. "I want to know where the fat man is. I want to know where Robert Simpson is, and I want you to call off all the bounties on my fellow cops. Put it all on me and raise mine to a million, I don't care, but if another cop is killed in or out of prison, I assure you my mission will be to be a part of your life until there is no life."

Branca looked down as he said, "Sysco lives on Grant

Avenue; Simpson, I don't know where he is. I had nothing to do with what Sysco did tonight. Why would I bring attention to my club like this?"

The detective spoke again. "Where is all the bounty money coming from?" Branca shook his head in the motion that he could not speak. Bud picked up his phone and called Lynagh in the control room. "Did you see the video of Baker and Sysco?" he asked.

Lynagh replied, "Bud, it's ugly. He beat the shit out of her, but she caught him with her high heel right in the mouth before he laid her out. From his reaction she might have knocked his front teeth out."

Bud replied, "Can you turn off the video camera for this room?"

Branca raised his head in concern when he heard the question. Lynagh informed Paul of Bud's request. The detective sergeant grabbed the phone and said,

"No, Bud. I'm not shutting the camera off. For your own good, no," and he disconnected the phone.

Bud disconnected the phone, realizing that Branca did not know his request was turned down. He said, "The camera is off. Tell me where the money is coming from or you won't be leaving this room in one piece."

Branca spoke. "Simpson, he skimmed, a little at a time while he worked for William Lance. Over the course of fifteen years it was over $4 million, and Lance never noticed it."

Bud stood up and grabbed Branca's arm, and they went back to the control room. Paul had just gotten off the phone with ADA Ashley and requested an alert for all dentists and oral surgeons to be notified within a twenty-five-mile radius with a description of Kevin Sysco. Bud informed Paul about the information from Branca as Lynagh and Wyatt controlled the rest of the entourage in the room. After their conversation they were all informed that they were being placed under arrest.

Officer Justin Healey, was back on duty after being cleared and was sipping on his coffee. He noticed the light flickering in Lindsey Wilkerson's bedroom. He was getting a little nervous as his concern heightened. He studied the lights and realized it was Morse code. It was a message coming from Lindsey's front bedroom. He turned on the car and drove to get a closer look at it. The message said, "Hello, Officer Healey. Thank you and God bless you."

He sat in his squad car and looked at the message flickering in the night a few more times. Healey was overcome with emotion that Lindsey would repeat the message as many times as she did to ensure that he saw it. His thoughts took him back to the night eighteen months prior when he was her constant bodyguard, or as Lindsey called him, her protector. It was the night in the house when O'Connor's men made a bold move to eliminate her in her own home. It wasn't just at the house that night. He stayed with her during the day in school and during the night, 24-7. He was within twenty feet of her at all times. He laughed to himself as he recalled her banter with Bud. It seemed she was the only one who could get the best of him in conversation and trivia. Healey's thoughts had taken him so far away from the present that the knock on the glass window startled him. It was his replacement for the evening. As he drove away, he flashed his headlights to say good night to Lindsey. For a fleeting moment he wondered how she knew he had knowledge of Morse code. He smiled as he thought he probably told her on June 22, 2012, at 8:00 at night, during a conversation. He shook his head as he continued to think about the little girl with the eidetic memory.

The drive back to Paul's apartment above Z Pita had the detectives exchanging theories as Lynagh, Wyatt, Caulfield, and O'Malley brought Branca, Larson, and four of their entourage from the control room to the precinct for booking.

Paul looked over at his partner and said, "You know they're going to get out on bail quickly. All they're going to say is that Sysco acted on his own and he is fired."

Bud nodded and said,

"Yeah, we'll see. We need to find the fat man, Wiley, and Simpson quickly, before the hit list gets more check marks next to their names."

Paul turned right on Arden Place, then right again into Trader Cove behind the restaurant and parked his car.

"Listen," Bud said, "mind if I borrow your bathroom before I go?"

Paul nodded and replied,

"Go on up. I want to check in on Rachelle. It's close to time to shut down the restaurant."

Bud had a key of his own and headed up the stairs as Paul walked into the backdoor of Z Pita and greeted Joey Z, who had returned, and also hugged Rachelle. Her face glowed when she saw him, and the three of them sat down to have a conversation.

When Bud reached the top of the stairs, Wes was at the top moving around in a circle, expressing his excitement to see Bud. Craven was curled up on the bed with not a care in the world. Bud loved the dogs, which had been given to him and Paul after the incident at Lindsey Wilkerson's house in Belle Terre. Paul and Bud were so worried about Rachelle being alone after the arrest of her sister Madison that they gave her the dogs to raise. Yet the presence of Lindsey remained, and part of it was these two beautiful dogs given to them by the young girl.

What puzzled Bud was why the dogs were so calm when it was apparent someone was in Paul's bathroom. He could hear the movement of water faucets being turned on and off and towels being taking off the door, as well as a toilet seat cover being dropped. Bud took his 9mm Glock out and stood by the door waiting for someone to come out. He took his phone out and quickly texted Paul a note asking him if Rachelle was downstairs with him at Z Pita. Paul quickly answered him that he was sitting across from Joey Z and

Rachelle. The detective wanted to text him back that someone was in his bathroom, but there was no time. The door opened and Bud grabbed the woman wrapped in a towel and threw her across the room onto the bed. Deborah was screaming so loud that Paul, Joey Z, and Rachelle could hear her through the ceiling due to the quiet of the late night in the restaurant.

Paul jumped up, yelling "Stay here!" to Rachelle and Joey Z, but like many times lately Rachelle did not listen.

Rachelle could hear Joey Z in the background as she went out the back, saying,

"I'll stay here. Too much excitement for me."

Paul ran up the stairs, gun drawn, as the dogs were barking, and he heard the sound of crying. He stopped at the top to keep himself covered in case he had to fire his weapon and saw Deborah Lance lying on his bed with a single towel barely covering her while Bud was trying to comfort her.

"Jesus Christ!" Paul yelled. "What the hell is going on?" Rachelle ran right by him as she went to Deborah.

Bud shook his head and said to Paul,

"I heard a noise in your bathroom. You sent me a text back that Rachelle was sitting across from you downstairs when I asked you. It did not cross my mind that Deborah would be in your bathroom taking a shower at 11:30 at night."

Paul looked over at Rachelle with an expression on his face that said Bud should be forgiven.

As Rachelle held Deborah, she spoke to Bud.

"May I ask why you came up here when Paul was downstairs?"

Bud answered quickly. "Two reasons: to give you and Paul some private time and, second, to use the bathroom."

Rachelle brushed her hair back as she replied,

"There is a bathroom in the restaurant, Bud." He looked over at Paul as his partner smiled and Rachelle noticed.

"What?" she asked.

Suddenly Deborah spoke. "Bud has a phobia about using public bathrooms." With that Deborah Lance started giggling as Rachelle looked at Bud, sheepishly grinning, and Paul's smile.

She looked back at Bud as she spoke again.

"Seriously? Super cop, crazy cop, hero cop has a problem with public toilets?"

Bud sat down on the bed next to Deborah as he replied,

"I don't expect to see this in one of your articles. It's a private thing." They all started laughing.

The gathering was interrupted by Joey Z from downstairs: "Is everything OK up there?"

Paul yelled back, "It's all good, Joey, just a misunderstanding."

The owner of Z Pita replied, "OK, I'm closing up everything and moving forward with my boring life. Good night." They all laughed again as Paul's ringtone started playing "Let's Talk About Tomorrow" by Olivia Newton-John.

Bud got up as he heard it and said, "Oh fish, I swear he put that ringtone on just to antagonize me."

The smile from Paul's face disappeared as he said, "Pick up Linda Tangretti and have her down at the precinct for the morning, and make sure Gina keeps an eye on the alert bulletin for all the dentists and oral surgeons in the radius to notify us if they get Sysco in their chair."

He disconnected as he looked at Bud and said, "It was O'Malley. He did some checking after he spoke with Linda Tangretti, who set up Kate Summers's blind date with Jake Wiley aka Jerry Wakefern. She herself has a relationship with him. O'Malley and Wyatt noticed pictures of them on their visit to her house before tonight's show that you put on at the club. She came to Long Island last year from Connecticut. She is the second cousin of Patty Saunders. If we dig deep enough, she is most likely involved with the calls that were being received from Connecticut during the Face of Fear investigation."

Bud shook his head and said, "And the hits just keep on coming."

Paul continued to speak, ignoring his comment as Deborah and Rachelle were on the bed sitting quietly. "We have Branca, Larson, and his four cronies locked up for at least twenty-four hours. Tomorrow we find Wakefern, Simpson, and Sysco or we could lose more cops with the bounties. It's not safe to have the girls with us."

Rachelle stood up and said, "What's going on Paul?"

The detective started to answer her but was interrupted by a text from Lynagh, who had gone to the hospital. He read it out loud to Bud: "Ellyn has a fractured cheek, concussion, three fractured ribs, and a broken arm. I have assigned two officers from the precinct to stand guard at her room. Advise if you disagree."

Paul scratched his head as Bud only said,

"Damn."

Rachelle spoke louder this time. "Paul, what is going on?" Paul looked at Rachelle and couldn't believe how beautiful she was even in a state like this. "Paul!" she yelled again.

He hesitated as he looked at Bud, then spoke. "We believe there is an aftermath of questions unresolved from the Face of Fear case that has created repercussions that we have to handle. We are on what we call the Music Club Murders that has a link to Face of Fear. One of the links is bounties on the cops from Priority 1, especially those connected with the case."

He looked at Deborah as her face became more concerned. And he continued, "We believe Robert Simpson has become involved with O'Connor and a few others, and his contacts murdered three innocent young women to draw out the Priority 1 Task Force. Simpson was tipping DJs to play certain songs, getting turned on thinking about you, Deborah, and killing them. With this case becoming a Priority 1 assignment, we became targets that resulted in the deaths of Hansen, Dugan, and Cronin, while Baker and Chapman have been severely injured."

There was silence in the apartment until Deborah said, "I would like to speak to Bud alone if I could." She said it in such a soft tone that it surprised Rachelle.

Bud put his hand on her shoulder, almost forgetting she had been wrapped in a towel the whole time. He said, "Deborah, now is not really a good time."

She looked at him without hesitation. "Excuse me? I have always been available for you. I answer your texts. I never said no to you when you've wanted to see me. Talk to me now, Bud, or you will never see me again."

Bud was startled by the determination in her voice, and it became awkward for Rachelle and Paul. Finally Rachelle got up and asked Paul to walk the dogs with her for a few minutes, which he quickly obliged just to get out of his own apartment. The door shut downstairs as Deborah tightened the towel around her body. Bud looked at her, waiting for her to speak, and it became uncomfortable until finally she sat down on the bed and said, "Were you ever going to tell me that it's apparent I may be the inspiration of three girls getting killed or there was a bounty on you?"

Bud tried to speak, but the young woman interrupted him. "Bud, I need to know what you think about when you think about me. I don't know what I mean to you. Are we friends? You are the kindest man I have ever met, but I don't want to be hurt anymore. It hurts me to be around you because of the way I feel about you. I don't know the real reasons you are with me sometimes, whether it's to protect me or that you really care about me. We were so close, and now I have to drag things out of you. Tell me once and for all how you feel about me." The timing couldn't have been more perfect. It was midnight, but William Lance sent his daughter a text that he had not heard from her and wanted a reply or phone call to be sure she was OK.

Deborah started answering her father verbally in a trembling voice. "I'm OK, Dad. I'm just standing naked in Paul's apartment asking Bud to love me. Gee, I wonder how well that would go over with dear old Dad."

Bud stood silently as Deborah actually typed in, *I'm OK, Dad*, and *I'm with Rachelle, Bud, and Paul. Love you.* He returned a smiley face within thirty seconds as Deborah looked at Bud and adjusted her towel again.

"Deborah," Bud said, "the truth is I rarely stop thinking about you. My feelings for you scare me for so many reasons. If anything were to happen to you as a consequence of who I am, what I do, I could never forgive myself. It's true our relationship cooled as we settled into our careers, but it doesn't change my feelings, especially when I see you like this," he said with a smile.

His attempt to make light of the situation did not work with Deborah this time.

"It's not funny, Bud," the young woman answered. "I want to know what you want from this relationship. I tried to move on, and yet here we are again. Do you want to be with me? Do you even think about the times we were intimate? You mean the world to me, Bud. I am literally undressing my love for you, but I need to be happy."

Bud put his hand on her cheek and said, "I'm afraid of being close to you because of who I am. This job and what has happened and what is happening now. I would sacrifice myself for you. That's how much you mean to me, but I worry what if I'm not there. At the very least we need distance until this case is finished. I can't let people get to me through you, but don't ever think I don't love you."

Deborah raised her hand to take his hand that was on her cheek as she replied, "You're worth the risk to me. I will create distance, but when this is over I need you to come to me. We will move forward together, or release me. I don't want to have the ache anymore." For the first time in eight months Bud kissed her on the lips and held her tightly as they heard Paul, Rachelle, and the dogs running up the stairs.

By the look on Rachelle's face, she was nervous to ask Deborah but did anyway, "Are we good?"

Her friend smiled and said, "Yes, I should probably get dressed now."

Rachelle turned to Paul and said,

"I'm going to stay with Deborah for a few days till this thing blows over." She then turned to Bud and reminded him they would be there Saturday to help with his move into the Henry Hallock house on South Street.

"Thanks, Rachelle," he answered.

Everyone was out of Paul's apartment within fifteen minutes. Paul sent Rachelle a text as they walked into the Lances' Pink Mansion: *I miss you already*. She held the phone to her chest as if to say, "I love you without saying the words."

As Deborah laid down on her bed for the night in her room, her phone vibrated, and when she looked at Bud's name on the screen she pushed the *connect* button.

"Can't sleep?" she asked.

"No," he said. "I would like to tell you more of what's going on, Deborah, so you understand this case. If it's too late I will call you tomorrow."

"No, no," she answered, "please tell me."

For the next hour the detective told her everything about the case. The people involved, including the names, and his feelings about who was to blame and why it was happening. He needed her to know everything and why, especially that it involved Robert Simpson, the first love of her life. He even told her how he himself threatened Simpson to stay away from her after the case was over. Regardless of Bud's threats or Cronin's pressure to have Simpson draw out O'Connor in the face of fear investigation against his will.

Deborah reassured Bud that she understood why.

"Rachelle told me about Cronin asking her to meet with Simpson at the Red Onion Café to cause confusion to O'Connor. Bud, Robert brought all this on himself. If he is killing innocent people, then he will suffer the consequences—if not in this world then in the next world when his soul leaves his body." Bud felt better after they spoke and said he would be in touch.

"Be careful, Bud," Deborah said as they hung up.

Bud walked outside on the back deck of his house in Miller Place for what would be the last time before he moved to the village in a few days, and prayed. He picked up the book Lindsey had given him called *Jesus Calling* and read the passage for October 5 since it was past midnight. A calmness set over Bud as he got to the last sentence of the devotional passage: *If you make problem-solving secondary to the goal of living close to me, you can find joy even in your most difficult days.*

OCTOBER 5

D r. Martin Dominger had been an oral surgeon for fifteen years and had been located in Port Jefferson Station in Davis Park for ten years. He was a well-educated man who graduated from Columbia Dental School and had four years of dental training, from 1988-1992, two years of medical school from 1995-1996 and completed 4 years of residency in 2000. At 5'11" he looked almost like a midget compared to the size of Kevin Sysco, who had come in as an emergency. He had never seen a man the size of Kevin Sysco who could still walk around normally. In fact, the Surgeon was worried about his chair being damaged by the big man sitting in it too long.

He cleaned Kevin's teeth and proceeded to take X-rays of his mouth to verify the extent of the damage. When the results came back, Dr. Dominger knew the roots had to be taken out and he would have to tell the big man that implants would be necessary. As he had Kevin open his mouth for further damage confirmation, all of a sudden, the big man in the chair made a loud noise as he felt something hard in his groin. As Dr. Martin Dominger stood up from the sudden jerk of Kevin Sysco, he saw Bud Johnson holding his 9mm Glock in the big man's groin.

"What the hell?" he said as he was tapped on the shoulder from behind. It was Paul Powers showing his badge as he ordered the doctor to move away from the patient. Doctor Dominger's mouth was opened with shock at what he was witnessing.

"Dr. Dominger," Powers said, "your services are no longer needed. Please leave us alone and shut the door." The surprised oral surgeon walked to his receptionist, who promptly showed him the police bulletin and had called the police number shown. Martin Dominger nodded as he asked for the schedule of patients for the remainder of the day.

Bud kept his gun on Sysco's groin area as Paul said he was going to get a cup of coffee. When he reached the door he turned around and said, "Now there is an ass you couldn't miss, Bud."

His partner looked up at him and said, "Everyone is a comedian these days. Keep trying to take the title away from me."

Paul shook his head. "That would be impossible. I will be back in five minutes, got it?" As he stared at Bud, his eyes widened a bit. The door shut as Bud kept his gun pressed hard into Sysco's groin. He straightened his arm out so he could reach Kevin Sysco's face.

"Listen to me very carefully and don't move or I will blow off most likely the only small thing on this body of yours. Do you know who I am?" The big man nodded his head yes and Bud continued, "Then you know I will blow your worthless dick off if I say I will, correct?" Sysco nodded again. "OK, good," Bud answered. "I'm going to ask you some questions, and if I don't think your answer is sincere and honest, then you will become dickless. Understood?" Sysco nodded again. "OK," Bud said, "let's get started. And be careful, I am not patient. First, are you proud of yourself for beating up a young woman?" Kevin shook his head no. "Tell me why you did it," Bud replied.

Sysco began to talk. "She made fun of my clothes."

"Not good enough," Bud answered, as he pulled back the chamber pin.

Sysco jerked again in the chair and started begging in an almost comical manner, "Wait, wait! Don't shoot my dick off! Please! OK, I'll tell you everything!"

Bud released the chamber back to its original position as he instructed Sysco he was running out of time. "Why did you beat the shit out of our female detective?" He pushed the gun harder into the groin area.

"I was ordered to from Jerry Wakefern. He got information and an image that she would be in the club last night."

Bud slapped the side of Sysco's face with his free hand. "Where did he get the information from?"

The big man answered right away. "We paid for the information from an officer on the East Hampton Force who was at the house when Baker shot and killed two of our employees. Plus, I was told I would have gotten a $25,000 bonus on her bounty if I was able to hide the body till the following morning. I didn't count on the other officer making it into the control room and the cop knocking my front teeth out."

Bud nodded as he asked, "Where are you getting information from? O'Connor to Branca to Wiley?"

"No," Sysco said. "O'Connor to Wiley to Simpson to Branca."

Bud knew his five-minute time limit from Paul was getting tight and asked, "Is it Simpson who killed the girls in the clubs?"

"Yes," Sysco answered.

Bud shook his head. "Where can we find Simpson and Wiley?"

Sysco answered, "I don't know, really, but it's someone other than O'Connor making the decisions. O'Connor devised the plan for payback, but there is another involved that is communicating with Branca through his attorney." Bud heard Paul yell on the other side of the door that there was one minute left.

Bud turned his attention back to Sysco. "You know, I should shoot you just for the way you smell. What the fish kind of cologne are you wearing?"

"No!" Sysco answered, confused over the fish comment. "Please, I told you everything you asked!"

Bud took the gun off his groin and spoke.

"We are going to take you down to the precinct and talk about the bounty list or the hit list. Before we get there and things become official, I want you to know I have my own list. I call it the shit list. You, my friend, are on my shit list. That means it is in your best interest to cooperate. If you think you can get up, now is the time to get up out of the chair."

As Sysco stood up Bud punched him hard in the stomach as Sysco bent over to catch his breath. The detective kneeled over to be next to Kevin Sysco's face and said, "You know what that was for, right? Tell me or I'll do it again."

Sysco could barely talk, but he said, "Baker."

Bud nodded as he hit Sysco hard again. "I don't like people that beat up on girls, especially when they're a quarter of your size. Understood?" Sysco nodded as Bud put his knee in his groin as Sysco went to the floor.

The detective bent down and asked again,

"Do you know what that was for?"

"For you," Sysco answered.

Bud shook his head and said, "Wrong, that was for Baker's broken ribs. This is for me," and he kneed him in the groin. Paul opened the door as Bud walked out and motioned for Lynagh and Healey to take him in.

"Wait!" Dr. Dominger interrupted the arrest. "You can't just take him out. His mouth is too damaged."

Powers and Johnson brought the surgeon to another room as Lynagh and Healey stood guard over Sysco.

"What's up, Doc?" Johnson asked. Powers looked over at Johnson and gave him a half smile for the Bugs Bunny reference.

The doctor didn't notice and responded seriously, "I can't let you take him out of here until I at least take his roots out. His nerves are still alive, and if they get infected there could be some real problems. This procedure needs to be done."

Paul looked at Bud then turned his head back to the doctor. "How long, Doctor?"

"It's at least another hour, but if he has eaten or drank in the past six hours, I have to wait before I begin."

"Damn," Bud replied. "Look at him, Doc, he probably doesn't go twenty minutes without a drink or food of some kind."

Bud's eyes suddenly widened, and he said, "Wait. You would have to use that medication on him. What do they call it? The stuff that they claimed killed Michael Jackson."

"You are thinking of propofol," Dominger replied.

"Yes," Bud answered. "I heard it works like a truth serum?"

Dominger answered, "It helps with putting patients to sleep. I think you may be thinking of Versed. Patients are more likely to speak."

"OK," Paul interjected. "If it's safe to use Versed on him, use that instead. We have some questions."

The doctor shook his head as he responded, "Listen, this is a serious procedure. I will administer the Versed and take care of his roots, but I can't have you guys talking to him while I am working."

"He's a dangerous man, Doctor," Bud answered. "You do your job while Officer Lynagh and Healey are in the room. Just make sure we have time to question him."

They all went into the room, which was now crowded with six people. The doctor explained to Sysco what was going to be performed on him. Bud made sure Sysco understood that only the roots would be extracted and new teeth or implants would have to wait until he was a prisoner.

Powers and Johnson left the room while Healey and Lynagh stayed, Lynagh with his shotgun he had taken out of the back of his vehicle.

"Good old Lynagh," Bud said as they walked back to reception. "Him and that shotgun."

Paul smiled as he remarked, "Cronin told me once he picked up that habit from his father, George Lynagh Sr. He was a cop for over thirty years, and it seemed that the atmosphere always got a little quiet once they heard him clank the chamber to his shotgun. They called him Duke."

Bud nodded as he said, "Never met him, but I like him already."

Dominger came out and told the two detectives they would have to wait at least another hour before they could start. Powers and Johnson picked up a couple magazines and sat down while they waited.

Once the oral surgeon started working on Sysco, it was another thirty minutes until he came out and told them the medication had not worn off.

Bud jumped up and went to Sysco in the chair and started asking questions as Paul and the doctor entered the room.

"What's your name?" Bud asked.

The big man half smiled and said, "Kevin Michael Sysco."

"Did your mom have a nickname for you?"

"Bud," Paul said, "stay on track."

He held up his hand to Paul to motion he wanted to see how the medication worked.

"She called me Sweetness," the big man answered.

Bud shook his head and replied, "She must have known what your weakness would be. Listen up, Sweetness, who informed the club about Ellyn Baker coming there?"

"Officers Blair and Lawrence from East Hampton. They were paid for the info."

"Where is Robert Simpson, Sweetness?" the detective asked.

"He moves around, but he stays in touch with O'Connor through Jerry Wakefern."

"Who is the man in charge, Sweetness?"

Sysco smiled as he spoke. "Everything goes through Branca, Linda, and O'Connor. We don't know."

"Who killed Kevin Cronin?" Bud asked.

"The tech man at the club. I don't know his name."

Bud was getting agitated as he said, "Repeat after me: 'I am a big fat son of a bitch.'"

A chuckle came to his face as Sysco repeated the sentence.

Bud continued as Lynagh and Healey tried to keep from chuckling. Even Paul was smiling.

Bud continued, "What is your favorite food?"

"Lamb," Sysco answered.

"I bet," Bud answered.

Dominger was now shaking his head. "You are a bit stressed yourself, Detective. Another ten minutes and you can have him all to yourself." He walked out of the room. Paul left the room as he heard Bud having Sysco sing "Mary Had a Little Lamb."

Dominger looked at Paul in the hallway as he held up his hand.

"It's best you don't ask," Paul said.

It was time to meet with Ashley and interrogate the men arrested from the club the previous night. On the way back, Powers sent O'Malley a text to get priors on all the men ready, including Sysco's. O'Malley responded it would be taken care of and reminded Paul that Linda Tangretti was also in custody. He also sent a full report of who was with Chapman, Baker, the Lance girl, and Rachelle, who was now opening up at the restaurant.

When Powers and Johnson arrived at Priority 1, John Ashley was waiting for them in Cronin's former office. He had been informed from Gina they were on their way back with Kevin Sysco. Both detectives walked in with a greeting as Powers waved a hand to Lynagh and Healey to place Sysco in one of the interrogation rooms. Bud added his two cents by telling Lynagh to put him in the largest room. Bud could tell by Ashley's face that there was another issue to be dealt with. Ashley took Cronin's old chair, which was a sign the DA's office was losing confidence in how the case was being handled. Paul and Bud took the seats in front of the desk as ADA John Ashley spoke.

"We have been informed from Brian Branca's attorney that you, Bud, put on such a show last night that the entire club emptied out, and based on your singing performance and announcement it is fair to say that his business is destroyed."

Just as he finished his sentence, Edward Larson knocked on the door and motioned for ADA Ashley to come to the door. He whispered in his ear so Powers and Johnson would not hear. Ashley looked at Bud as Larson continued to whisper in his ear. When Larson left, Ashley took his seat back at Kevin Cronin's former desk.

Ashley stared at both of them for a few seconds before adding,

"Is there anything I need to know? Gentlemen?"

Bud leaned back and said, "First things first. How is Officer Chapman doing? How is Officer Baker doing? I won't ask about Detectives Cronin, Hansen, and Officer Dugan because we know they are dead. We have a situation here that if we don't get this case under control fast there will be more killings! So what were you saying? Oh yes, the nightclub. Look at our record, Mr. ADA. I think we know what we are doing." Powers put his hand on his partner's knee as Bud looked away.

Ashley leaned forward while looking at Bud and said, "Anything you want to tell me about Sysco? His attorney claims you put a gun on his dick and threatened to blow it off."

He looked at Paul to comment, which he did. "I wasn't there, so I don't know, but I will tell you he sang like a bird. We got a lot of information."

Ashley interrupted him, "So you just happen not to be in the same room with your partner, who it could be argued that we need a linguistic anthropologist to understand his comments and behavior. How convenient is that?" His inflection in his voice indicated the level of sarcasm as he looked at Bud. The room was silent when Gina walked in to tell the three men everyone was set up in the interrogation rooms.

As ADA Ashley stood up, he spoke again. "Is there anything

I need to know before we sit across from them with their attorneys?"

Bud raised his hand and said, "Sysco, we should bring in a couple of pizzas to his room. It might help us in the questioning."

Paul shook his head as Ashley said, "Ha ha, very funny, Detective. I'll see you guys in Room 1, and let's work our way down." He was out of the office before Powers and Johnson even got out of their chairs.

Bud looked over at Paul with a puzzled look on his face and said,

"Linguistic anthropologist?"

Paul got up to leave as he replied, "Yeah, well, you have to admit we all wonder at times what culture you came from."

Bud just shook his head as he said, "Linguistic anthropologist? Where is Lindsey when you need her?"

The mention of the young girl they all shared a bond with put a smile on Paul's face as they walked into Interrogation Room 1, where Brian Branca and Edward Larson were sitting. Detective Powers sat down next to ADA Ashley. Bud decided to stand in the corner so he could get a better view of everyone's responses to the conversation. As usual during interrogations, Paul was accepted as taking the lead during the questioning. He looked down at his notes and started speaking while keeping his eyes on his paper.

"Mr. Brian Branca, we have the murders of Kate Summers, Detective Hansen, Detective Cronin, Officer Dugan that all seem to be connected to your club. I'm sorry I forgot to mention the murders of Alicia Hudson and Michelle Cartwright in Skyline and the Pajama Club and, oh yes, your employee Bruce Roberts being blown to bits as well as Rodrigo Hernandez being killed."

Edward Larson spoke up. "Is this a news update, or is there a question coming soon?"

Powers answered quickly, "Yes, are you sure, Mr. Larson, that you don't want an attorney for yourself since you are a person of interest as well?"

The attorney shook his head and said, "No. I will be representing both Mr. Branca and myself."

"OK," Paul replied as he began his line of questioning. Detective O'Malley walked into the control room, pumpkin seeds in hand, at the request of Paul to witness and suggest anything. Detective Powers remembered it was O'Malley that had first contact at the club with Brian Branca the night of the murder.

"Mr. Branca," Paul spoke. "Take a look at the video."

Edward Larson spoke. "Again, is there a question anywhere?"

John Ashley felt it was time to speak. "Mr. Larson, one of our detectives was badly beaten at your client's club. Or should I say your boss's club? Be patient with the question part of this interview, or we can end this and hold both of you for twenty-four hours as possible suspects." He looked at Paul to continue as O'Malley popped pumpkin seeds in his mouth on the other side of the glass. Normally, he would eat the seed without the seed shell, but at this moment he was not concerned about the extra sodium content.

"Mr. Branca, take a look at this man coming out of Private Room 4 with the baseball hat and mask. Do you recognize this man?"

Branca answered, "No." The questions continued with videos of Kate Summers going into the private room after talking to Bruce Roberts. A video was played showing someone paying the DJ to play a specific song. Still Brian Branca had nothing to add as he looked at his attorney before every "yes," "no," or "I don't know" answer. Paul asked over thirty questions, and not one answer was helpful.

The detective looked over at his papers and said,

"Mr. Branca, you are free to go for now, and take your cronies with you, except we are holding Kevin Sysco for attempted murder of a police officer. He has implicated your involvement so I look forward to seeing you and your attorney again. Oh, one more question. Since Kevin Sysco beat the shit out of one of our fellow cops and Sean Martin and Holly Moore attempted to kill Officers Lynagh and Healey, is this just a strange coincidence that they both worked at your club, or you just simply don't want to acknowledge the bounties?"

"No," Branca answered.

Powers came back strong. "No what? No you don't want to acknowledge the bounties or no you don't think it's a coincidence."

Larson tried to interrupt, "Don't answer!"

Branca fought to answer anyway, saying, "He's confusing me!"

Paul slammed his hand on the table. "Tell me why!" he pushed harder. "What is going on in your club?" O'Malley was now enjoying this as he leaned against the glass to get a close look.

Branca leaned forward as Larson pushed him back. "No! No I don't know why!"

Paul got in his face. "You don't know why what!"

Larson stood up and said, "Don't answer that!" He looked over at Ashley and added, "Charge us with something now or we are leaving."

Ashley replied, "You can leave, but don't go anywhere. We know your client and you are up to no good. Once we can prove it, you will see us again."

As they approached the door Larson turned around and said, "By the way, we will be suing your department for Detective Nut Ball over there destroying our business. We will have to close for a month and reopen under another name just to get going." Bud stayed in the corner and started singing "Don't Worry, Be Happy." Larson rolled his eyes as O'Malley used the PA to speak to the room.

"ADA Ashley, I need to see you in the control room, please, with Detective Powers." Paul looked at Bud and asked him to sit in Sysco's room with Lynagh in the room till he got there. When

Powers and ADA Ashley walked into the control room, O'Malley spoke. "As you know, we have videos of Sysco and Baker and we have the video in the room with Bud and the fat man as well. What we didn't know was that there was a separate hidden camera that our tech man found in Branca's office that shows the private room from another angle." O'Malley started playing the video from the back wall camera, showing Bud talking to Branca. The camera showed Bud clearly.

"Do we know what he is saying?" Ashley asked.

O'Malley turned around and looked at them with an unhappy expression. "I took the liberty of calling in Jackie Smith, a lip reader we have used on a regular basis. Bud is telling Branca to take the bounties off everyone in the task force and to put the whole amount on him."

Paul shook his head. "What? No! Why? What is he doing?"

Ashley looked over at Paul. "I think we need to keep this to ourselves right now. Bud is trying to draw fire away from the rest of us, but I'm not sure if it means anything to these guys. The answer is to find Simpson and Wiley, and then we will get to the one pushing all the buttons." Ashley walked over to the door and added, "Let's keep this to the three of us for now. We need to get to Sysco before Bud gets himself in trouble in the room."

They walked in and saw Bud singing to Kevin Sysco, with the big man begging him to stop. Paul motioned for Lynagh to leave and asked him to join O'Malley in the control room to watch the interrogation.

Paul sat down and started talking right away. "Well, well, well, you're looking at ten to fifteen years for your display of affection toward Detective Baker. However, it will most likely be life for the murders of Kate Summers and three other police officers. So if you do not cooperate right now, we are going to walk out of here, put you in a jail cell, and throw away the key. You will have bread and water for the next thirty to forty years."

Bud sat up as he said, "Think of all the weight you will lose."

Ashley and Powers ignored Bud's comment as the ADA spoke up. "Start talking and we will only pursue the attack of Detective Baker, but only if you were not involved in the murders."

Sysco was not as dumb as he looked as he stared at Powers and ADA Ashley.

"Put it in writing and I'll talk with an attorney here."

Ashley replied, "We have a deal, but only if you had no involvement in the murders and the attorney you use is not employed by Brian Branca."

Sysco looked up at Bud as he spoke again. "And protective custody from my friends at the club and this sick cop," he said, as he pointed to Bud. Powers looked at the ADA and their eyes were in agreement.

Bud spoke again. "Would you like a side rack of lamb with that written agreement?"

Sysco replied, "This is what I mean. Keep him away from me and I'll talk." Bud walked out of the room singing "The Cisco Kid." O'Malley and Lynagh smiled from the control room, for it appeared that Bud accomplished what he wanted to do, which was get a reaction from Sysco.

Bud walked into the control room and greeted them and the tech man, Bill. He went toward the PA button and said,

"Watch the fat man's face very carefully." He pushed the button and in his best radio voice said, "Hello, gentlemen, I hope you are having a nice day. I would just like to remind you that in Interrogation Room 2 Miss Linda Tangretti is waiting for you to tell her side of the story. Thank you for your attention."

The PA button was released as Sysco's face became flushed and he said,

"You made a deal with me. I want to talk. I will speak now if you give me your word. This is on video, right? I'll talk now!"

Bud nodded in the control room. "That's right; don't pee

your pants just yet." Lynagh and O'Malley were trying to hold back their giggles. Ashley looked down at his notes on Sysco's priors that O'Malley had gathered. It showed that he assaulted his mother five years prior.

"You're a regular woman beater aren't you?" Ashley asked.

"No," Sysco answered, "she pissed me off, made a comment I didn't like."

Bud pushed the PA button again and said,

"True, she must have told you to stay off the couch."

Sysco ignored Bud's comment and said, "Do we have a deal or not?"

Ashley spoke. "We have a deal. If we find out you were involved in these murders, it's off the table."

Paul started his questioning. "Who killed the three girls, and why?"

Sysco answered without hesitation. "Robert Simpson killed them in coordination with Jason O'Connor to get the Priority 1 Task Force assigned to the case. They knew if they killed girls that resembled Debbie Lance that another connection would be made."

Paul continued, "The other connection being?"

"Bud Johnson," Sysco answered. "Simpson said he was forced by Detective Cronin to get involved in the vigilante killings to draw out O'Connor and his gang. According to him, Johnson humiliated him by the way he spoke to him and treated him."

Bud stared through the window as O'Malley chewed on pumpkin seeds with an occasional glance at Bud as the interrogation continued.

Paul scratched his head for a moment and looked at Ashley, then moved a piece of paper and a pen in front of the large man and said, "Write down the names and amount of each person that has a bounty on them."

Sysco took the pen and said,

"As of now or including everyone?" Sysco explained, "The

initial bounties once the task force was involved were for Deborah Lance, Rachelle Robinson, and Lindsey Wilkerson. O'Connor called off the bounties once Cronin was gone. He only had a reward on their heads to punish Cronin for the way he handled the case. He figured with him out of the way there was no need to waste the bounty money on them." Paul nodded as he told Sysco to start writing.

While the big man was putting pen to paper, Ashley and Paul exchanged a few whispers. In the control room O'Malley called Wyatt to verify that Deborah Lance, Rachelle Robinson, Lindsey Wilkerson, Baker, and Chapman all had someone in the vicinity of them. As he was speaking on the phone he saw Powers wave him into the interrogation room.

When he got to the door, Paul got up and met him there and said, "Get Lynagh, Healey, and yourself home for some rest for a few hours. We are going to be busy late tonight. Make sure Healey is replaced at the Wilkerson house. Also don't mention this to Bud; just tell him I asked you to go speak to Linda Tangretti in the next room for a few minutes before we get to her."

O'Malley nodded and wasn't sure what Paul was up to, but he had learned and accepted fast that things were done a little differently at Priority 1.

Sure enough when O'Malley got back to the control room Bud asked what was going on, and O'Malley handled it well.

He waved at Bud and said, "Your boss wants us to sit with Linda Tangretti for a bit and extended courtesy to me since I was the first one to speak to her." Bud nodded and accepted the explanation.

Lynagh was asked to stay in the control room and witness the interrogations with the suspects. When they entered Interrogation Room 2, O'Malley mentioned he forgot his notepad and went back to the control room. Once he arrived he told Lynagh to pull Franks into the control room, replace Healey at the Wilkerson house with

Officer O'Brien, and to get home for some rest. He explained to Lynagh, Powers wanted discretion with Bud about that night and that's all he knew. Lynagh pushed the intercom button for Gina to find Franks as O'Malley went back into Interrogation Room 2.

Kevin Sysco pushed the paper over to Ashley and Powers and they looked at the names on the list.

Rachelle Robinson	$150,000 bounty
Deborah Lance	$150,000 bounty
Only with Robert Simpson present	
Lindsey Wilkerson	$150,000 bounty
All canceled upon death of Detective Lieutenant Kevin Cronin	
Detective Paul Powers	$100,000
ADA John Ashley	$100,000
Officer George Lynagh	$100,000
Officer Justin Healey	$100,000
Officer Dugan	$75,000 (killed)
Officer Chapman	$75,000
Officer Franks	$75,000
Detective Kevin Cronin	$200,000 (killed)
Detective Bud Johnson	$250,000
Sherry Walker	$75,000
Canceled after her retirement from the force.	
All other Priority 1 assigned officers:	
Detective O'Malley	$ 50,000
Detective Hansen	$ 50,000 (killed)
Detective Wyatt	$ 50,000
Detective Baker	$ 50,000

Powers and Ashley looked at the list, and then Paul turned to Sysco and said, "There is over $1.3 million here in bounties. Where is all this money coming from?"

Sysco looked around the room to collect his thoughts before answering,

"Simpson took money over the years from William Lance, a few thousand here and a few thousand there. It added up. He had a good gig. He figured whatever he could sneak away while he was banging his daughter. When he married her it would be the pot of gold at the end of the rainbow. All that changed when you guys brought him into the limelight of a case he had nothing to do with."

Paul replied, "So he doesn't take responsibility for screwing the girl who kidnapped Deborah Lance in the first place. Anyway it really doesn't matter, he is a killer now."

The detective's comment was in reference to Patty Saunders, with whom Simpson had an affair during his relationship with Deborah Lance. It was Saunders who initiated the kidnapping of her and set off the most famous case in Long Island history. Paul continued to look at the list. "So it was no fun for O'Connor to kill the girls once Cronin was out of the way."

Sysco nodded.

Paul continued, "What about Sherry Walker. Why the bounty to begin with?"

Sysco tried to move forward but forgot his huge belly prevented him. "She saved Rachelle Robinson's life in the village and the boss man was pissed beyond belief. When all of this was planned and she left your task force, he figured she wasn't worth the bounty money as well."

Ashley interjected, "For someone who wasn't involved in the murders, you sure know a lot."

Sysco answered quickly,

"I work for Branca. I never killed these people. I will admit I was angry and upset with that chick—what's her name, Baker? Well, I smelled the $50,000 with the $25,000 bonus, plus she fought back and I couldn't stop myself. Look what she did to my mouth." He showed his teeth. "She knocked my fucking front teeth out with one of her heels."

Powers was very soft and quiet when he replied,

"Don't call her a chick again or I will have the video turned off. You don't want that. Who ordered the bounties? Branca?"

Sysco shook his head and hesitated. "Simpson, O'Connor, and Wiley, but I think there is someone else involved that we don't see. I mean Brian Branca acts like the boss, but I think he is getting his information and directions from someone else."

Ashley spoke again. "How is Simpson getting money back? Does he plan to just spend the bounty, and that's it."

Sysco explained that Simpson had stolen over $4 million from Lance over the fifteen years he worked for him and it was worth it to him to spend the million. He said, "In return Branca would give him interest in the club, which of course your crazy detective destroyed on the PA."

Paul spoke quickly. "He didn't destroy it. You guys did." Paul looked down at the list again and stared back at the big man, asking, "If you were not involved in the killings, how do you know so much?"

Sysco laughed. "Because I'm a trusted employee. Hey, do you guys serve dinner?"

Paul ignored his question. "How did Holly Moore and Sean Martin fit into all of this?"

Sysco tapped his fingers on the table for about twenty seconds before answering, "They worked there part-time, and when the original bounties were given, he found a way to get close to Deborah Lance. He was going to kill her but he said he wanted more opportunities with her in the sack. Plus there was no killing her without giving Simpson a chance to speak with her. When she wouldn't get freaky with him and broke it off, he was moving in for the kill, but it seemed like Detective Johnson was close by, or her father, whenever there was an opportunity. He figured it was a matter of time, but then of course the bounties were eliminated and he concentrated on others. I'm sure when he saw those two cops in East Hampton, he thought of the $200,000 bounty, but the chick

. . . er, I mean pretty detective . . . shot them both, which is another reason I felt compelled to teach her a lesson."

Just as he spoke those words Paul's cell buzzed with a text from Caulfield at the hospital that Baker had taken a turn for the worse and she was having trouble breathing. The doctors were thinking it was a tear or puncture in her lung but that would be confirmed later. Paul showed the text to Ashley and noticed it had also been sent as an email with ccs to O'Malley and Bud.

He looked back at Kevin Sysco and said,

"You better hope Detective Baker doesn't lose her life, fat man. It would be difficult not to let go of the leash on Bud Johnson. You don't want that."

Paul pressed on as he tapped the table that separated them.

"How did you know that Detective Baker was going to be at the club?"

Sysco shrugged his shoulders. "Branca told me."

Paul tapped harder on the paper as he asked Sysco who told Branca the detective was going to be there.

Sysco smiled and said, "I already told you; it was Blair and Lawrence."

Paul looked over at Ashley as the ADA said, "Yes, you did."

Lynagh moved closer to the one-way mirror as he told the tech man, Bill Tillman, to move in closer on Sysco's face with the video as he spoke.

"Officer Blair called Branca to tell him about Martin and Holly being killed and that the woman detective called Baker would be in the club. They overheard you guys in East Hampton after your detective shot Holly and Sean."

Powers sent Bud a text that there may possibly be a leak in the squad and that they couldn't assume it was only Blair and Lawrence. Bud didn't mention anything to O'Malley during the interrogation of Linda Tangretti. For all he knew the leak could be from him or one of his men. He thought to himself, *There is no way the leak came from one of the cops permanently assigned to Priority 1 Task Force.*

Paul continued his questioning as Sysco repeatedly asked for something to eat. Lynagh, who was told to go home for some rest, would not leave even when Officer Franks came into the control room.

Detective Powers asked Kevin Sysco who the explosives expert was, and the big man replied that it was Joseph Brenner, one of Branca's entourage at the club. When asked directly if Joseph Brenner wired Kevin Cronin and Detective Hansen's cars, he answered yes, but wasn't positive about Cronin's vehicle.

Ashley quickly spoke. "Why was Bruce Roberts killed off?"

Sysco replied that Roberts was not the target, that they assumed Lynagh and Healey would bend the rules and try to get in the house, thus more bounties would be collected. He explained that Roberts was collateral damage and a risk the boss took. "The boss wins either way."

Paul replied, "Get bounty on the two cops or get rid of a liability in Roberts."

The interview continued as Paul asked how Linda Tangretti fit into all this.

Sysco continued to show his knowledge of all that had happened. "Linda lived in Connecticut and was a cousin of Patty Saunders." Paul clenched his fist as the big man continued to talk. "Linda helped Patty when Deborah Lance was first kidnapped on the ferry by placing calls from Connecticut and being an alibi if she needed it. When the case was over and Patty was killed by Madison wearing that fucking mask, she was devastated. Detective Johnson told Robert Simpson to leave Long Island and never come back unless Deborah Lance asked him to. He added a slap to his face when he threatened to sue the department and have Cronin's job for all he put him through. He waited for almost eighteen months. All that time he was planning to come back into her life, but he wanted people to pay. He wanted her to feel guilty, as well as Johnson. Anger set in and he decided she would have to die if he couldn't have her."

Ashley replied, "Then why was the bounty taken off of her?"

Sysco shrugged and said,

"He was told to leave her alone after Cronin evaporated."

Paul interjected, "Is that supposed to be funny?"

Sysco replied, "Sorry, I meant to say after he was killed."

Paul looked over at Ashley then back at Sysco. "Well, Sysco Kid, that's it for tonight. We are going to hold you here for a while until we get you in front of a judge."

Paul motioned for Franks to send in an officer to take Sysco back to lockup. Officer Lynagh shook his head as he walked out of the control room and precinct to get some rest to meet up with everyone later that night.

As Sysco got up to leave, Paul spoke again. "One more thing. If the club is closed, then what would Branca, his attorney, and his entourage of stooges need to be at the club for?"

"Easy," Sysco answered, "it's used as an office and central point for everything they do. They are there till almost midnight every night, which is why they don't come in till 1:00 or 2:00 in the afternoon." Paul nodded as the officer took him away.

The detective looked at Ashley and said,

"I will be in Room 2 in a minute. I need to make a call. Do me a favor and send O'Malley in here, please. I will review the tape of their questioning Tangretti later." Ashley nodded as he left the room.

Paul pushed the buttons on his cell and waited for the third ring and smiled when he heard Rachelle's voice say, "Hello Detective Powers." He realized how much he missed her and her voice the second he heard it.

Paul was thinking so long that Rachelle spoke again. "Paul, is everything OK?"

The detective was able to get his thoughts back when he told her how much he missed her. He couldn't see the smile on her face, but he knew it by the little change in the inflection in her voice when she was smiling from ear to ear. It had been a while since they were able to speak on the phone at great length, and now wasn't the time either. There were times when Paul wished his life wasn't so complicated. He wanted to stop what he was doing and not have a schedule and just go and do whatever he wanted to do. He thought about how Deborah Lance had the money and the opportunity to be like that, yet here she was, on Long Island teaching fifth-graders when she could be under the sun in Hawaii.

Finally, he heard Rachelle trying to get his attention: "Paul? Paul? Is everything OK?"

"Yes," he answered. "I just wanted to tell you I love you and miss you."

"Well," she answered, "maybe I will come over and wake you up tomorrow morning before we go to work if you would like."

The detective hesitated, then said,

"I wish you would, Rachelle. I have to go. Say hello to Deborah for me." The phone disconnected before Rachelle could say good-bye. She stared at her iPhone in surprise.

He disconnected so fast that she then sent him a text: *I love you too.*

It was only seconds later when she got the reply from him: *I have always loved you.* Tears filled Rachelle's eyes as Deborah came over to her to be sure she was OK. Rachelle showed her the text as Deborah smiled and hugged her. It was difficult for Paul to fight his emotions, which had become conflicted. He knew he should keep his distance from Rachelle to protect her, yet he felt she was most protected when he was with her. He shook his head with his thoughts as he tried to understand what he should do when it came to Rachelle.

OCTOBER 6
12:01 AM

I t was after midnight when Brian Branca, Edward Larson, Joseph Talison, one of the bouncers from the club, Joseph Brenner, and Michael Corbin walked into the parking garage in Setauket after a long night in the empty club. The entourage that worked for Branca got into the backseat as Branca got in behind the wheel with Larson in the shotgun seat.

They were laughing when suddenly the back window of the car was smashed by the butt of Officer Lynagh's shotgun, which he turned around quickly to point at the three startled men in the back of the car. The front passenger door opened as O'Malley grabbed the already frightened Edward Larson by his collar and pulled him out of the car and onto the pavement about ten feet away from the vehicle. As Larson tried to get up, the elder detective put his foot on the attorney's throat and put just enough pressure that the air passage was threatened. Keeping his foot on Larson's throat, O'Malley looked over at the vehicle and took out a bag of pumpkin seeds and started eating them, letting the seed shells fall on Larson. At the same time O'Malley pulled Larson out of the car, Justin Healey jumped on the hood of the dark grey Mercedes and in a kneeling position with a stretched-out leg held his 9mm Glock on Branca through the front windshield. With Lynagh pointing a twelve-gauge shotgun at the three men in the back, Healey on top of the hood, and O'Malley eating pumpkin seeds over Larson, Paul Powers got in the passenger seat next to Branca.

"Well, well, well," he said, "what have we here?"

Branca started to speak. "What the fuck are . . . "

He couldn't finish his sentence because Detective Powers

put his hand on Branca's chin and squeezed so hard the club owner's lips looked like a fish. Powers pressed harder as he spoke. "Listen very carefully. Take the bounties off, and I might let you live. Get with whoever it is that is telling you what to do, and lives will be saved, including these morons in the back."

The men in the backseat were keeping their eyes on Lynagh pointing the shotgun at them at close range and could not even be concerned about what Powers was saying. Paul shook Branca's head and held on to his face as he continued to speak. "I saw the video of Bud speaking to you in the private room. I know he told you to take the bounty off all of us and to put all of it on him. I'm telling you right now if anything happens to Detective Johnson, and I mean anything, I will hunt you down. I will find you."

He squeezed his face harder as he continued to speak. "Bud Johnson talks tough, but he has a heart, he prays for guidance on how to deal with people like you." Paul moved closer to Branca's face as his voice got stronger. "As for me, I will show you no mercy. I will make you suffer, and you will have a slow death. Do you understand me?"

Branca's eyes moved to the corner and looked at Healey pointing his Glock at him through the windshield, then moved back to Powers as he tried to say yes through his fish lips as he nodded at the same time.

The detective would still not let go of his face as he spoke again, saying, "Make no mistake, Brian Branca, I will find you." Paul Powers continued to hold Branca as he stared into his eyes and he let the club owner look into his eyes. "Now I have one question for you, and I want a straight answer or I won't let go." Paul spoke to Branca's ear and loosened his hold on his chin so the club owner could answer him. Suddenly Paul let go of his chin, which had imprints of Powers's fingers left in his face.

The detective got out of the car, leaving Lynagh and Healey, and for a moment the men in the car thought they were all going to be executed when Lynagh started backing off. After a few seconds, he nodded for Healey to back off as he jumped down from the hood of the car. By this time O'Malley had eaten about twenty pumpkin seeds and the white seed shells were spread over Larson's body.

O'Malley spoke when he saw Powers, Lynagh, and Healey leave the vehicle. "You know, Ed Larson," he said as he snapped another pumpkin seed into his mouth, "I'm really getting too old for this shit, but I'll give you a piece of advice. I would do whatever Detective Powers suggested to your partner over there, because I have to tell ya, they look really pissed off; you know what I'm saying? Now I'm going to take my foot off your throat and you are going to get up, get in the car, and this here incident never took place. Understand?"

Larson nodded his head the best way he could. O'Malley walked away and met up with the other three cops as they drove away. Larson held his throat with his hands, trying to force more air into his lungs. Branca had his head on the steering wheel, trying to pull himself together. His three friends were restless in the back and Joseph Brenner even got out of the car to stretch his legs and bend over to think about what had just happened. It was another few minutes till Branca finally pulled his head from the steering wheel and yelled for Larson to get back in the car and spoke,

"What did he say?" Branca said as he looked in the back seat at Talison and Michael Corbin. "He threatened my life. Did you hear him?"

Talison replied, "You're kidding, right? We had a double-barrel shotgun pointed at us from one foot away by a cop who looked like he wanted to blow our heads off. We weren't concerned about what he was saying to you."

Larson shook his head as he spoke. "Clever, very clever. Powers sat next to you," he said as he pointed at Branca. "One cop stood with his gun pointed at the back, the other on the hood in front of the windshield and the other grabs me, the attorney, outside the car. No one, including the other cops, can verify what he said to you. His word against yours."

Branca suddenly changed his facial expression and said,

"Except," he hesitated then and his cocky smile returned, "except for the digital camera from the monitor station." He looked at Brenner, who was still walking outside the car, and said, "Joseph, get to the central office downstairs and have the guard play back the tape. We'll be right down to pick you up."

Brenner took the stairs to the lower level. Brian Branca took out his cell phone and punched in the numbers. He wasn't surprised the call went to voice mail, since it was now after midnight. "We have a problem; we were ambushed by the cops. I thought they were going to kill us. We need to talk, call me as soon as you can."

He disconnected and started shaking his head as he looked at Larson and said, "What do you think?" The attorney looked at the spot where O'Malley dropped pumpkin seed shells on him and analyzed all the little white specks on the concrete before answering Branca.

"Screw Wiley, screw Simpson, screw O'Connor. It's time we speak face-to-face with the boss. Somehow we have to get rid of Sysco. He's talking too much. We have an in with the cops, let's get with the boss and do nothing until we meet with him."

Joseph Brenner made it to the monitor station only to find no one there. He walked around the equipment until he found what he was looking for. He pushed the eject button only to find there was no disk or chip recording the events in the parking garage. He slammed the chair against the monitor as he yelled, "Son of a bitch!"

Behind him a voice startled him, saying,

"Wrong."

Brenner turned around to see a figure dressed in black slacks and a tight black top wearing the mask with blood splatter on it.

"Did you enjoy blowing up Cronin?" the masked figure asked.

Brenner replied as he pulled out his weapon, "I've had enough of this shit tonight." But it was too late. The figure wearing the mask pulled out a gun and fired three shots. The first in the left leg, the second in the other leg, and then the shooter pulled off the mask as Brenner looked at his killer. The gun fired and hit him squarely in the heart. As the assailant put the mask back on, Branca drove up to pick up Brenner. The occupants in the car started screaming when they saw the Ghost Face figure running toward the car. They were like babies crying for candy as they screamed for Branca to drive faster in the garage. The steering wheel was so erratic at the hands of Branca that he knocked off the side-view mirrors on two cars as he drove. From the rear seat Talison looked at the masked figure running toward the car and suddenly stopping and firing toward the car.

"Christ!" he yelled. "Get us out of here!" Branca tried to turn the corner in the garage but he was going too fast and hit the side wall and had to stop to reposition the car. It was enough time for the masked figure to jump on the trunk of the car as the men screamed louder. Talison pulled himself together and pulled out his gun and started firing at the back, but the Ghost Face attacker was too fast as he rolled off the back of the car onto the concrete. Talison continued to fire as the masked attacker took cover between the cars.

Larson kept yelling at Branca,

"Keep going! Go! Go! Go!" As the grey Mercedes reached the lower level of the garage Branca did not want to wait to insert a ticket and pay with his credit card. Instead he circled around and started circling to go up in the garage.

Talison was still sideways on the backseat when he yelled, "What the fuck are you doing?"

Branca sped up as he replied, "No time to stop. If I went through without paying, my tires would have been destroyed."

The Mercedes kept going up as Larson dialed 9-1-1. He said,

"We are in the parking garage in Setauket located next to the City music club. We have been attacked and fired at by a masked man. We are circling the exit and entrance ramps to avoid being killed."

The operator informed Larson that the police were on the way.

Larson shouted back,

"It is the fucking police that are trying to kill us!"

The operator answered back, "Sir, you said it was a masked man."

Larson bellowed back as the car reached the top of the garage, "It has to be a cop!" Talison looked through the back window, which was now shattered, and spoke. "The stance he took before firing at us. It had to be a cop." The Mercedes with dents, scratches, and bullet holes in it moved slowly at the top of the garage.

Corbin moved his head from left to right as he moved forward and back at the same time. He said,

"Just stay here till the cops get here; fuck this."

Larson looked over at Branca. "No, just keep moving. Whoever is behind this won't keep up with us if you keep moving the car."

Branca moved the car slowly toward the down ramp when the masked figure jumped in front of the car and fired twice into the windshield and struck Larson in the head with the second bullet. Branca stepped on the gas to run him down, but again it was too late.

Talison yelled, "Keep going! Just go!" With Larson slumped over and leaning toward the driver, Michael Corbin grabbed the fatally injured attorney to keep him off the driver as the car swirled to get down to the lower level. The sounds of rubber squealing were so loud it would be hard to believe it was only one car making the noise. Talison had his gun out and was turning left to right, back to front, so much he could feel his neck aching with pain. The now-damaged Mercedes made it to the lower level within sixty seconds, and this time when they got to the exit Branca stopped as Talison looked out, gun drawn, as the credit card was inserted and the paid receipt was issued. The car made it fifteen feet past the exit gate when three squad cars pulled up and blocked its path.

Rachelle and Deborah were at the Pink Mansion sitting at the kitchen table with William Lance discussing plans for the upcoming Halloween season, which was only three weeks away. Both Deborah and Rachelle had become afraid of this time of the year due to the events that had taken place in their lives. They had been staying together since the day Hansen's car was blown up a few days earlier. While it was clear that Rachelle was the stronger of the two emotionally, she too was worried and fearful about the case Paul and Bud were working on. They were very open and honest with Deborah's father. He was a good listener and he even held his daughter's hand as she spoke about her feelings for Bud.

She told him, "I guess you never really know what someone means to you unless there is a chance it will never be the same again."

Her father got up to go to bed as he kissed her forehead and said,

"Dating is a very powerful and emotional force in life, my love. Be patient."

Rachelle looked at Deborah and grabbed her hand and continued where her father left off, saying, "It's not clear exactly what is going on. Sometimes I think Paul tries to protect me from what's going on. I know he is upset about Cronin and Hansen and that Robert is on the loose, but Deborah, I'm here with you and you know Bud won't let anything happen to you."

Deborah smiled at her remarks and seemed satisfied, when Rachelle spoke again. "OK, time to walk the dogs before going to bed." Deborah picked up her phone and sent Bud a text. *It's late,*

Bud, but I wanted to let you know that I was thinking of you.

She looked at Rachelle, smiled, and said,

"Sorry, I couldn't help myself."

As they got up from the table her iPhone buzzed. It was Bud answering already. *I miss you. Do you want to see me?*

She answered quickly, *It's almost 2:00 am, but I would love to see you.*

Rachelle and Deborah collected the dogs and went to the front door, opened it, and saw a figure standing there. They both screamed as Bud stepped through the door. The girls moved back as they held their chests while Wes went on two paws to greet him. Rachelle sat down in the foyer chair with Craven trying to comfort her. Deborah, still trying to collect herself, placed herself on the first couple steps leading up to the bedrooms.

Bud walked over to Deborah to greet her and said,

"I'm sorry, Deborah. I was on the grounds talking to the officer on Cliff Road when you sent me the text and asked me over. I knew I could get to your door in less than a minute. I thought you would find it funny."

He began to speak again, but Deborah jumped in his arms and put her arms around his neck with her head against his chest. The detective put his hand on the back of her hair and massaged it while he spoke. "It's OK, Deborah; everything is going to be fine."

The young woman held on tight while Rachelle said,

"Bud, what are you doing here at 2:00 in the morning?"

He stopped massaging Deborah's hair as he turned around to look at Rachelle and said, "I can't get ahold of Paul. I've been trying since 11:00 pm. I thought he may have been with you, but your phone is off." Rachelle had a puzzled look on her face as she grabbed her phone. The battery was dead.

Bud continued to speak. "I called Lynagh, Healey, O'Malley, and no one is answering their phone."

Rachelle's facial expression changed as she asked Bud to go

with her to the apartment above the restaurant to check on him. Bud turned to Deborah, who was disappointed he was leaving so soon, but he reached out his hand for her to come with them and she took it. They put the dogs in the lit front area so they could take care of business till they got back. Bud waved to the officer outside the gate and stopped for a second to wave at the officer parked thirty yards away from the Wilkerson house. They turned right on East Broadway down to Main Street in front of the ferry, turned left on Main Street, then another left on Arden Place, before making a quick right into Trader's Cove parking lot behind Z Pita. Bud saw Paul's car in his spot when he stopped the car behind the apartment door at the back of the restaurant.

Rachelle jumped out and headed for the door with keys in her hand when Bud yelled,

"Wait! You're not going in there just yet." He got out of the car and told Rachelle to wait until he took a look. He motioned to her to stay put as he started walking to the door, and he pulled out his gun.

Rachelle started walking again toward Bud when he gave her the *stop* sign and said,

"Wait, Rachelle. Wait till I let you know it's safe."

She looked back at Deborah still sitting in the car. "Now I'm getting scared."

Deborah got out of the car to be with her. They both watched while Bud opened the door with his key, his gun drawn as he went up the stairs. Rachelle saw a light go on upstairs and started moving closer toward the backdoor when Bud waved them to come up from the window. Rachelle raced up the stairs, for all she could think about was Paul. There was no one there. Bud looked around to be sure there wasn't anything that looked out of the ordinary, when he heard the answering machine go on.

Rachelle had pushed the button to listen, and they heard Paul's father: "Son, give me a call. I need to speak to you."

The next voice was Bud's: "Hey, my partner, been trying to reach you. Give me a call back or I'll start singing to you in this thing."

The answering machine clicked again and it was Rachelle: "Hi, it's me. I just wanted to let you know I will be working the early shift at Z Pita in the morning. Please stop down. I would love to see you."

The next message that came on was from ADA Ashley and was in total contrast to Rachelle's voice and tone: "Paul Powers! I've been trying to reach you and Johnson!" Bud looked at the phone with a puzzled look as the message continued. "Where the hell are you? Ed Larson and Joseph Brenner from the City club are dead. You were there a few minutes earlier. They're talking about a masked killer. Shit, Paul, I know you were upset about Bud telling Branca to move the bounty all to him, but don't do anything dumb. We have a case to solve. Give me a call right away. I can't get ahold of O'Malley either." The call disconnected as Bud moved to the stairway.

Rachelle grabbed him and asked,

"What's going on, Bud? Where is Paul? He's not responsible for these people getting killed, is he?"

Deborah stood there looking at Bud and he noticed it as he answered Rachelle.

"I'm not sure, Rachelle."

He regretted he said it the way he did. Rachelle's face became flush with worry as she reached out to Bud and said,

"Please, please find him."

The detective looked at Deborah when she asked,

"What are they talking about, Bud?"

He shook his head. "I don't know, but I'm going to find out what's going on. I'm going to take the two of you back to Deborah's. Get some sleep, and when you wake up this will be over." His thoughts added the words *I hope*. He took the girls back to the mansion in Belle Terre, got in his car, and called ADA Ashley.

As soon as John Ashley picked up the call, he was yelling. "Where the hell are you guys!"

Bud replied, "John, I've been here. I've been trying to contact Paul as well."

The ADA calmed down but still spoke in a hurried voice. "Bud, listen carefully. Ed Larson was shot and killed in the garage next to the club. Joseph Brenner was killed in the control room of the parking garage. Branca claims it was a masked killer and it was a cop. Talison, one of his cronies, said it was a police stance when he fired and that Powers and his team threatened him."

Bud replied, "What was the build of the killer? What mask was he wearing? What does the video show?"

The ADA answered quickly, "The digital feed was destroyed, and for the build, they claim they were too scared and too worried about saving their lives to notice, and as for the mask, well . . ." There was dead silence on the phone for a few seconds.

Finally Bud said, "Hello?"

He finally heard the words he was afraid to hear: "The Ghost Face mask."

Bud let out a heavy breath before saying, "Shit."

Ashley continued, "And Bud, it had the red blood splatter on the face."

Bud's heart started beating faster as he spoke. "And why do we think Paul is connected to this, other than we can't find him for now? For all we know they could have been injured, kidnapped, or killed."

Ashley replied, "Bud, listen to me. We saw the video where you told Branca to take the bounty off of everyone and put it on you. Paul was upset; he paid Branca and his boys a visit five to ten minutes before they all started getting shot at."

Bud started driving faster and said, "John, I need to wake fat-ass Sysco up and we need to speak to Linda Tangretti now."

"Bud," Ashley answered, "it's after 2:00 in the morning. These prisoners have privileges and rights."

Bud answered quickly, "John, I don't give a rat's ass about their rights at this moment. I need to talk to them now. If Paul, Lynagh, Healey, and O'Malley are hunting down Simpson and Wiley and whoever is involved in this, we are going to have more bodies on our hands. I don't give a flying fish right now about Sysco; he is probably snoring up a storm, keeping everyone else awake."

Ashley told Bud he would make phone calls to get Tangretti and Sysco available in the rooms. He also told him he would call Wyatt and Caulfield to meet him at the precinct. They disconnected and Bud tried calling Paul. It went straight to his voice mail.

Bud spoke into the phone when he heard the sound to leave a recording: "Paul, this is Bud. Don't do anything crazy. Don't throw your career away. Rachelle is sick with worry. She was in your apartment and played the messages, including one from Ashley about Larson and one of the other assholes being killed. I'm worried, Paul. You call me. I want to hear from you. We have always been partners. Call me. I'm on my way to the precinct to talk to Sysco and Tangretti. Call Rachelle. Don't do this to her. Don't do this to me."

He pushed the *disconnect* button and then he called the dispatch room at the precinct. He took a chance and asked the technician if one of the vehicles assigned to O'Malley, Lynagh, or Healey were in use. The answer came back yes on O'Malley's vehicle. Bud asked for the GPS location of the car. The answer came back the vehicle was on the Long Island Expressway, exit 64 heading east.

Bud started yelling,

"Have Caulfield and Wyatt go to the precinct and have them put Sysco on speaker to me. Call ADA Ashley now. I need a police helicopter ready for me in fifteen minutes."

"Sir?" the dispatcher replied.

"Just do it!" Bud yelled.

The message was relayed to Ashley, who immediately made a phone call to clear it through channels for the chopper. Caulfield and Wyatt arrived half asleep at the precinct and brought Sysco in.

"Christ!" Wyatt said. "You smell terrible. Take a shower twice a day instead of once, will ya?" Sysco ignored the comment as they made the call to Bud Johnson.

Wyatt spoke first. "Bud, this is Wyatt. We have your man here. Go ahead." Caulfield looked into the monitor room and gave a signal to the tech man to accidently have trouble starting the recording.

Bud's voice was heard on the speaker: "Kevin Sysco, Sweetness, listen to me very, very carefully. If you are not straight with me, I will have the two detectives there with you let you go and I will get the word out you were let go because of your total support in this case. You will live in fear the rest of your sorry life. Do you understand me?"

Sysco looked at the two detectives, then at the camera in the room. He noticed there was no red light flashing, so he replied that he did understand. Bud got out of the car to walk to the chopper, which was still getting prepared for the flight.

"Why would Detective Powers be heading out east after 2:00 in the morning with three fellow officers?" Wyatt and Caulfield looked at each other with surprised looks on their faces but moved their attention back to Sysco, waiting for the answer. Sysco hesitated as Wyatt put his hand on Sysco's large shoulder.

Finally, the big man answered.

"My guess is they are going after the two guys who were with Sean Martin. They wanted in on the bounties on you guys and informed the club your pretty little detective was on the way to the club that night."

Bud asked, "Who did they tell?" He couldn't wait any

longer for an answer and started yelling, "Who?" Sysco was getting more pressure on his shoulder from Wyatt.

"I told your friends earlier; they told Branca and the boss."

Jackson in the tech room had beads of sweat coming down his face as he tried to look frustrated getting the linguistics of the taping to work.

"They told Branca, and he told me."

"The two East Hampton officers?" Bud yelled.

Sysco leaned back on the chair and spoke in a surrendered tone. "Yes, the two officers who were with Lynagh and Healey when they killed Martin and the girl. They got paid $50,000 for each in cash for the info."

"That's a lot of cash for information like that," Bud replied.

Sysco answered quickly, "East Hampton officers are well paid. That's what it took to make them talk."

Bud jumped in the copter by this time, and it was so loud he could not hear. He yelled for them to be dispatched to the radio in the chopper as it took off. It was another five minutes before Tillman connected the call back in the room. He asked Sysco how Tangretti was connected to all this, and the big man told him she was the cousin of Patty Saunders who was killed by Madison Robinson. It was her with Simpson and O'Connor and the boss man who put up the bounties on the Priority 1 Task Force.

"So," Bud said, "three innocent girls and two cops were killed to get revenge. Who is the boss? Branca?" Sysco shook his head even though Bud couldn't see him from the copter.

"No, only O'Connor, Branca, and now Simpson know who he is."

Bud asked Wyatt to take him off speaker and pick up the phone. The detective picked up the phone and listened to Bud's voice: "Call O'Malley and see if he picks up the phone. If he does, tell him to have Powers call me. Go back to Branca and his men and bring them all back in. Their attorney is dead, and Sysco just implicated Branca with the two officers that were with Lynagh, Healey, and Baker."

Wyatt replied,

"What about Tangretti? She is sitting in the next room."

Bud replied,

"Put her in a holding cell. It's more important to pick up the boys from Setauket. Call Ashley to get a warrant for their arrest."

Caulfield could tell by listening in on the conversation what was going on, so he said,

"It's almost 3:00 in the morning; we are not getting a judge up at this time."

Bud heard him in the background and yelled, "Wake up Judge Green and have Ashley tell him it's connected to the Face of Fear case!" Wyatt acknowledged Bud and disconnected. He looked at Sysco and Bud kept shaking his head as the helicopter traveled through the air. His thoughts went to Linda Tangretti; this missing link from Face of Fear caused all this. Anyone could have guessed Simpson would have lost it, but no one thought Linda Tangretti was capable of being connected to this kind of revenge. Bud's thoughts consumed him as the helicopter flew to East Hampton.

"Let's go," Caulfield said as he brought the big man back to the jail across from the precinct.

Wyatt called Ashley, who was still awake sitting in his kitchen. Ashley listened as Wyatt spoke for a few minutes and told the detective to pick up the men as Bud instructed, but to wait to hear from him on the warrants. John Ashley got up and walked over to his counter. He turned on his coffee machine, figuring he would be up from here on in. He placed his hands on the cool marble of his counter and shook his head with his thoughts at what was happening. He heard the click of a gun behind him and figured he had nothing to lose at this point if he spoke.

"It won't bother you to shoot a man in the back?" he asked.

The voice behind him replied, "Not really, but if you would

like to turn around it is OK with me. You're a dead man anyway."

Ashley turned around slowly, wondering who he would see, and at the same time upset his mortality had caught up with him before the age of forty. He turned around, and there was Jake Wiley aka Jerry Wakefern.

Ashley spoke. "Before you shoot me, I have some questions."

Wiley, with a puzzled look on his face, started waving his gun around but was curious. "You think this is some kind of negotiation? You are worth $100,000, and I plan to collect."

Ashley replied, "Why am I so high on the list?"

Wiley laughed as he said, "It is obvious, isn't it? You treaded lightly on the Madison Robinson case, yet you came out like a bulldog against O'Connor and put him away for life. You have two questions left."

"Why kill three innocent girls? Why not just come after us?"

Wiley answered, "The boss man wanted the publicity to hurt you guys and take care of the physical part later. The best way to find you was to have the case assigned to Priority 1. The girls were collateral damage."

Ashley replied, "So Simpson was embezzling money all this time, and he wanted payback to Cronin for ruining his life."

Wiley nodded his head. "He had a good thing going. He was banging the boss's daughter plus her girlfriend for a while. He was getting extra cash from the hidden safe that he had the combination to, and all of a sudden the girl gets herself kidnapped and Cronin forces him to get involved to bring the players out, and what happens to Simpson? He loses the girl, the home, his job, all because some cop—what's his name, Johnson—falls for her and threatens him to leave town as well. How long did you think he could stay away?"

Ashley leaned up against the counter a little more as he spoke again. "What is in this for you?"

"I got the $200,000 for Cronin, and you will be another

$100,000. Once I get the $250,000 for Detective Johnson, I really don't give a shit about the rest of all this or anyone else. I will be gone. You are out of questions."

Ashley said, "Just one more."

Wiley raised his arm and said, "Sorry, no more."

The shot rang out as Wiley looked at Ashley, who didn't move at all. Wiley looked down at his stomach and saw the blood pouring out. He put his hands on it to see if the blood was real. It was. He turned his head and kept saying,

"No, no, no, you're a ghost."

Detective Kevin Cronin moved closer to Wiley as he said,

"No, you will be the ghost in about thirty seconds."

Wiley dropped to his knees as he looked at Cronin again, and all he could say was "No" before he fell face-first to the floor.

John Ashley bent over as if he was going to faint. He said,

"Christ! What the hell were you waiting for? For him to shoot my head off?"

Cronin looked up at Ashley while he was confirming there was no pulse coming from Wiley.

"I wanted to be sure he wanted to shoot you and not report to you."

Ashley slammed his coffee mug down on the counter so hard it broke into pieces and said, "What the fuck is that supposed to mean? Why would I agree to have you here?"

Cronin walked over to his friend for the past ten years.

"You know why, John. When things like this happen I don't trust anyone. Besides, if I had serious doubts about you, I would have let him shoot you before taking him out."

Cronin started walking toward the door when Ashley spoke again. "Not true, Kevin."

The detective lieutenant stopped to wait and let the ADA continue with his head tilted to the side to hear him better. Ashley said,

"If I were dead, Kevin, it would be hard to explain my disappearance to the DA, the chief, and the judge. You know that. Even our guy Tillman, who set your car off with the fucking laser beam, would be suspicious of you." Ashley pushed off the counter as his voice became stronger. "You, the master of manipulation and games, even you know that killing me would put a halt to this plan."

Cronin stayed where he was and replied, "You agreed; I had to die in their eyes to get the bounties off the Lance girl, Rachelle Robinson, and Lindsey. You all agreed. What the fuck is the problem here!"

Ashley looked down at Wiley's body on the floor as he spoke again.

"It comes back to haunt a man, Kevin, when he doesn't keep his promise."

The detective turned around to look at John Ashley as he was now confronting him over the promise he made to him eighteen months earlier in the Trader's Cove parking lot in the village. Ashley took another step closer to the detective.

"Yes, you solved the case, you figured it out, but you took risks with people's lives to bring closure to a case, and now look where we are. We are crossing the line with procedural protocol, and I'm concerned that even when this is over, our badges, my license, will be taken away."

Cronin hesitated and spoke softly. "The Priority 1 Task Force was created to give us some leeway on protocol. Your office agreed to the section being locked off with no cameras other than in the interrogation rooms. If our hands are tied, a case like this would never be resolved. You know it and I know that Priority 1 operates on the grey lines when it comes to procedural protocol."

There was no reply from Ashley as Cronin spoke again in a firmer voice. "It was the only way to save the lives that we did and find out who we could trust during the Face of Fear investigation."

Ashley interrupted him, "That's the point, Kevin, it didn't stop. Look where we are now. Simpson wants revenge, O'Connor wants revenge."

Cronin moved closer to the ADA and said, "My ways may not be the traditional approach that you or the DA expects, and you may think there was another way to have handled the Face of Fear investigation, but there is one more thing that you seem to forget so I will remind you once again. You and the DA knew of my plan. No more lives were lost and some were saved. You may not like my methods, but I have never gone outside of the law."

Ashley folded his arms across his body as he replied,

"Kevin, who killed Phil Smith in the barn the night of the Wilkerson raid in Belle Terre, and where did the money go?"

Cronin walked directly up to Ashley's face as he answered, "John, I always keep my word. That's all you need to know for now."

John Ashley was referring to the night Phil Smith disappeared from sight when O'Connor was arrested, while three members of his entourage were killed during a gun battle at the Wilkerson house.

The detective lieutenant tried to walk away again as the ADA pressed,

"Kevin, if you or Paul or someone else shot Smith, we can push for a self-defense argument. You're a good cop, Kevin; we would not have known what was going to happen with the bounties if you didn't convince us and Nada at *Long Island Pulse* to put an undercover reporter in the prison for the past year to befriend O'Connor. While I worry about the grey line you follow, lives have been saved again. The problem is, this time there can't be any carryover. This has to be cleaned up. Powers at this moment is hunting down the men responsible for your death, the three girls, Dugan and Hansen."

Cronin raised his hands and said, "Isn't that what he is supposed to do?"

Ashley picked up the pieces of the mug that shattered.

"No, I'm not talking about investigating. He took Healey, Lynagh, and O'Malley with him. Even Bud is scared shitless what Paul will do. Five minutes after they left Branca and his crew, a figure with a bloody Ghost Face mask doesn't stab them. He shoots Brenner, then Larson while chasing down the car. None of this is recorded because the digital recorder is shut off and destroyed."

Cronin moved his hand closer to his gun as he asked, "And you know all of this how?"

Ashley replied, "Because I haven't had any sleep, that's why. The cops on the scene called Priority 1 dispatch and I couldn't get ahold of anyone except for Franks, who gave me the report over the phone. Chapman and Baker are hospitalized and everyone else is on the hunt."

The detective slowly moved his hand away from his holster as he spoke.

"Where's Johnson?"

Ashley forced a laugh. "He's on a helicopter heading out to the Hamptons to prevent Powers from doing something crazy. Now doesn't that sound funny? Bud is trying to save someone else from being crazy."

Cronin walked over to look down at Wiley and kneeled down to shut his eyes. "Powers had nothing to do with putting a mask on and shooting someone. I trained him. I know it's not him."

Ashley replied, "Corbin and Talison swear it had to be a cop under the mask. The way the gun was handled, the stance, the confidence. The energy felt was that he was a cop." He looked at Cronin directly in the eyes as he continued, "Sounds like someone I know."

Cronin ignored the remark as he spoke. "I'm sure ballistics will help with the signature of the gun used. In the meantime you have to get this cleaned up." He pointed to Wiley. "You are going to have to take credit for the shooting for now. If they find out I'm alive, the bounties on the girls will be back on."

Ashley took a long breath before answering, "I'll take care of it."

Cronin approached the door, put his hand on the knob, and hesitated. "One more question before I leave, John." The ADA just stood there without a word, waiting for the detective to ask his question. Cronin opened the door and spoke as he was walking out. "Where were you when Phil Smith was shot?" The door shut behind him as John Ashley felt his heart pounding and had to sit down.

"You are a motherfucker, Kevin Cronin," he said to the door that Detective Lieutenant Cronin just walked through.

The ADA picked up his iPhone and looked at the body of Jake Wiley until his call was answered. "Wiley's dead, I will need to get the body out of here quietly." The voice on the other end was DA Steinberg. Ashley gave the DA details as to what happened, including Cronin saving his life. "He was right again. He knew someone would make the attempt on me, and he was correct the bounties would be canceled on the girls, which is why I have to take the credit for killing Wiley for now."

"No," the DA answered. "We will clean it up, but no one takes credit. Let him disappear and create mystery of his whereabouts with his associates."

DA Steinberg continued to speak. "If this gets out you will need an escort, John, and whoever is the leader of the group will raise your bounty. We need to keep it out of the news."

Ashley replied, "I have to go with Cronin and Powers on this one. Simpson is not smart enough to do all this on his own. As for an escort, Cronin is staying here in the guest room, so I think it's best everyone thinks he is still dead for now."

"What about the parking garage?" Steinberg asked. "We don't think Cronin is playing vigilante, shooting suspects, do we?" There was silence on Ashley's end as Steinberg spoke again. "Your silence is not helping my thoughts."

"I'm thinking," Ashley replied.

Steinberg spoke again. "If there is one thing I learned over the years, it is that volumes are spoken when nothing is being said."

Ashley hesitated a few more seconds before speaking. "Cronin is always on the edge of the law. I don't agree with his methods, but he does get results and saves lives. We have to give him the benefit of the doubt. Besides, I don't think he would resort to wearing a mask and chasing down cars."

"OK," Steinberg said. "Keep in touch and try and stay alive, will you, please? That's an order."

"Right, boss, good night." The ADA pushed the *end* button.

It was now 2:45 am, and Powers, Lynagh, Healey, and O'Malley pulled up to the house on Winston Street in East Hampton. Paul looked at his phone and saw eight or nine texts from Rachelle and Bud to call them, and put the phone back in his pocket. They were at the home of Officer Blair.

Powers looked at O'Malley and asked,

"What info did you get?"

O'Malley pulled out his notebook. "Married, with a five-year-old girl."

"OK," Powers answered. "Justin, you make sure the girl is OK in the room and sound asleep." It was rare for Healey to be called by his first name, and he noticed it. Paul looked at Officer Lynagh and said, "You and I will pull him out of the bedroom. Let's try not to wake the wife, and if we do, we explain it's an emergency for the investigation of the Music Club Murders and the bounties." His eyes moved to O'Malley as he said, "Keep an eye out front and let us know if any problems arise."

They got out of the car and started walking toward the house when Lynagh suddenly had a flashback.

"Wait!" He said, "Check the door first." Healey examined the door, top and bottom, while O'Malley looked in the window and saw a male figure lying on the floor. He pulled out his weapon as the others followed suit. He waved Powers to the window, and there was Officer Blair sprawled on the floor. Powers looked up toward the stairway and saw a woman's head between the railings half nude and not moving. He looked over at Lynagh to blast the door open with his shotgun. He fired two blasts as the door blew off its hinges as the four of them stormed into the house, guns drawn.

Powers yelled to Healey, "Check on the daughter!"

Justin Healey ran up the stairs as he heard the cops downstairs yelling "Clear!" He stopped at the door and spoke to himself before walking in. "Dear God, please not the five-year-old." He moved in slowly and saw the little figure in the bed. His body began to ache as he feared the worst. He touched the bed, and then moved his hand over to the girl's face. It was warm and she was breathing. The officer breathed a sigh of relief as he went out to the hallway.

"They didn't touch the girl," He reported. O'Malley had already called an ambulance and the East Hampton Police. Blair was shot but alive, and his wife had a slight pulse but was in a bad way.

Powers looked at O'Malley and said, "I'm going to Lawrence's home. You are in charge here. Wait for everyone here."

O'Malley shook his head and spoke in a firm tone instead of being concerned he was speaking to a superior officer. "You're not going alone."

Powers shook his head and looked at O'Malley, who was holding firm on his remark. "I won't be, Lynagh is coming with me. Keep Healey here for the girl. Tell them to rush them out of here and to get next of kin here ASAP so the girl is not alone when she finds out about her parents. Bud sent me texts. He's in the Hamptons waiting for me. He took a chopper out here." O'Malley nodded as Powers and Lynagh left the house.

It was another two minutes when he realized they no longer

had a vehicle. The police were there within minutes, as well as the ambulance, which awakened the little girl. She was startled to see Officer Healey, but he had no choice. He wanted to keep her from seeing her parents being carried out of the house. He had tears in his eyes as the little girl cried for her mommy and he held her. It was thirty-five minutes before her aunt, the sister of her mom, was at the house to comfort her niece. Healey walked downstairs and put his hands over his face as O'Malley left the house to give his fellow officer some private time. He took out a bag of pumpkin seeds and absorbed the salt from the white seed shells as he wondered what the hell kind of case he had gotten involved in before his retirement. His thoughts were of mixed emotions as he looked back at Justin Healey shaken up over what had just occurred.

Rachelle sat with her legs up to her chest, rocking back and forth as she looked at Deborah sleeping on the sofa. She tried to stay up with Rachelle because she knew she was worried about Paul. The young woman's eyes looked at Craven sleeping next to Deborah while Wes was awake and clearly knew that Rachelle was upset. She picked up her phone, punched in numbers, then canceled the call and put the phone down. She rocked a little bit more then picked up the phone again. The call went straight to voice mail. When the sound to leave a message came on, Rachelle spoke. "I need your help. It's time you take care of Paul, because I'm not sure if I can. Please call me."

It was almost 3:15 am when Powers and Lynagh got to Officer Lawrence's apartment building in East Hampton. They waited five minutes for Bud, who threatened to sing to Paul every day for the rest of his life if he didn't wait for him. Bud showed up in a police car driven by an East Hampton officer from the helipad. In a loud whisper Bud spoke as he greeted Powers and Lynagh, "You fuckers! Lord forgive me. What the hell are you doing?"

Paul looked at his partner.

"No more. We are going in."

Bud grabbed his partner and said,

"Look at me, Paul. You have a life with Rachelle. Don't blow it. Let's do this the right way."

Paul looked over at the officer who drove Bud to the house. He looked at the name badge, which read *Blanchard*.

"Officer Blanchard, please go to the door of your fellow officer and ask him to come out peacefully."

Bud added, "Tell him we have a warrant for his arrest." He looked at Paul with a smile and said, "I got Ashley to wake up that old fish Judge Green and grant the warrant."

Paul shook his head as the four of them approached the door. Officer Blanchard knocked on the door as Lawrence came to the door and said,

"It's almost 3:30 in the morning."

Blanchard spoke. "We have a warrant for your arrest; please come out peacefully." There was silence.

Blanchard smiled and looked at Powers. "Well, I guess he's all yours." Powers looked at Lynagh to knock the door down as Bud grabbed the officer aside. A half second later a shotgun blast went through the door that would have taken Blanchard's face off.

"You saved my life!" Blanchard said to Bud as another shotgun blast came through the door, this time taking out the rest of the door. Paul motioned for Lynagh to go outside. Paul started yelling into the apartment.

"Why, asshole? Why shoot one of your own? Did you try to kill your partner Blair as well?"

Lawrence spoke. "I'm a dead man anyway. I have nothing to lose except my life. My life was nothing, The money I was making just wasn't enough for the East End of Long Island. I couldn't change my quality of life until I was offered the money for information. I didn't know how crazy these people were till it was too late."

Powers looked over at Bud before turning his head back

to the now-open doorway and saying, "Why shoot your partner? Why the wife? She's barely alive. Did you rape her too?" As he spoke, Lynagh positioned himself near the apartment window on the second floor and sent Paul a text he was in position. Paul gave Bud his phone and told him to wait until there was gunfire.

Lawrence replied, "I could never kill my partner. It was that crazy fuck Simpson. He shot my partner, and the wife was begging for her daughter's life when he started to rip her clothes off. She fought him and he claimed he couldn't get excited without the music. So he bashed her head against the railing a few times and was going for the girl upstairs when I stopped him."

Paul replied, "So why try to kill an innocent officer?"

Lawrence hesitated.

"I guess greed. I know who you guys are. If there are two or three of you out there, we are talking almost a half million for the bounties."

Paul answered, "Stephen Lawrence, there are ten of us out here. You lose. Come out now, and we'll take you in alive."

Lawrence was quick to respond, "It's too late. I've killed an officer, I took money for information on cops, and I was there when Blair and his wife were killed and beaten. I won't be subjected to prison."

"Stephen," Powers said, "Blair and his wife are alive."

"You're just saying that!" Lawrence yelled.

Lynagh had opened the window just enough, but Lawrence heard the creaking. He turned around and fired as Lynagh moved out of the way of the window in time.

Bud rushed into the apartment and tackled him before he could turn around and fire again.

"Bud," Paul yelled, "what are you doing?"

Bud just looked up at his partner from the floor as Blanchard began to put the handcuffs on Lawrence.

"Enough lives have been lost, my partner."

Powers put out his hand as Bud grabbed it to stand up. They hugged for a second as if to thank each other.

When they were back in the hallway, apartment doors began to open from the noise. Paul just stood there as Bud started waving his badge for people to get back in their apartments. One man couldn't seem to resist, and Bud had to get a little stronger with him: "Hey! I said get your fat ass back inside!" He flashed his badge again.

Lynagh called 9-1-1 and identified himself for an ambulance and police to arrive at the scene.

Paul looked around the apartment and kept shaking his head. He said,

"Money, money, money; money is the root of all evil."

Bud walked up to his side. "No, my friend, it's the love of money that is the true root of all evil. 1 Timothy 6:10"

Paul looked at his partner, not surprised he had quoted the bible. "Let's get some rest." Bud nodded as they answered questions and signed some papers for the local authorities. They took the vehicle back to the home of Officer Blair and picked up O'Malley and Healey before heading back to the precinct.

It was 8:00 am when Deborah woke up to the sounds of the dogs crying to go outside. She looked and saw Rachelle was in a deep sleep in her Benjamin Franklin lounge pants. She smiled every time she saw her in those pants and often wondered who Rachelle loved more, Paul or Franklin. She laughed a little loudly but caught herself so she wouldn't wake her up. There was a note on the front door from her father that said, *Deborah, going to the city for the day. Call if you need me. I love you. Dad.* Deborah loved the way her Dad would actually write the words *I love you* instead of *Love you.* He never took shortcuts with anything, and she loved that about him. Although she was twenty-eight years of age, she looked forward to the once or twice a week talks they had.

She opened the door and let the dogs out. The grounds were

completely gated, so there was no worry about them taking off. As she watched Wes and Craven enjoy their freedom outside, her phone buzzed with a text from Bud. *How are you doing? I found Paul last night. It was a tough night, but we are OK. We are trying to stay away from you and Rachelle until the bounties on us are taken off. This should be over by move-in day, but I'm not sure I'm up to it.* He ran out of room and continued to send another text: *Deborah, I want you to know you are the sweetest woman I have ever met and I'm thankful you care about me. Even when we are not together I think of you when something good happens to me. It proves to me how important you are.*

Deborah smiled with emotion and needed to clear her throat. Her thoughts wondered how he really felt about her when the phone buzzed again. It was Bud again. The text read, *In case you are wondering, you mean the world to me, which is why I'm moving to South Street . . . to be closer to you.* Deborah smiled and kissed the phone, then chased after the dogs for some playtime.

It was close to 9:00 in the morning when Rachelle woke up and looked at the beautiful grandfather clock in the foyer of the mansion. *Oh my God,* she thought. Deborah had just entered the house with the dogs when she jumped up to look for her phone to see if Paul was OK. There was a text from him: *All OK. I love you.*

She looked at Deborah and said, "I have to get to Joey's. I promised him I would take the 10:00 am to 4:00 pm shift. Can you keep the dogs here while I work?"

Deborah gave Wes a kiss and told Rachelle, "No problem. They won't let me teach in the school until the case is over anyway."

Rachelle hugged her with a big thank-you and said, "I'll see you later. Come down to the restaurant at 5:00. Let's have dinner together. If you're not busy tomorrow I'm going to see Madison. Please come with me if you can."

Deborah nodded and said, "See you later. By the way, are you going to shower before going to work?"

Rachelle gave her the evil eye as she walked out the door,

saying, "Why, my dear, I'm going to shower at Paul's. It's so convenient." And with those words she blew kisses to the dogs.

Deborah shook her head as she spoke out loud to herself. "Ah yes, sex, what a wonderful thing. At least I think so. It has been so long I can't remember much." Rachelle drove out the gate as Officer Carson sent a text to Powers asking whether he should stay with Rachelle or stay at the house where Deborah was. He didn't receive an answer back and the officer made the decision to stay outside the Lance mansion.

Rachelle ran up the stairs and jumped on the bed where Paul was in a deep sleep after three and a half hours of sleep. The young woman kissed him all over and even tried to arouse him, but he was totally out of it. She gave up and finally went into the bathroom to take a shower. The cool water felt good on her body as she let it soak through her hair, down to her face and down to her legs. Rachelle felt like there were times she had the weight of the world on her shoulders. Writing for the local paper, the notoriety from the first case, the restaurant responsibilities, and trying to hold on to her relationship with Paul. All these thoughts filling her head as the water sprayed over her face. Her eyes closed, yet her thoughts kept circling over and over in her head. Thoughts turned to Madison sitting in jail having nightmares. Rachelle's thoughts were going from one subject to the next thinking about how nice it would be to have a normal life, a quiet life. One where no one was being shot at, kidnapped, or stabbed. The young woman covered her face with her hands to try and wipe all the thoughts away. She put her head down to let the water spray on the back of her head as she looked at the base of the tub, watching the water hit the base in all directions from her head and body.

She turned the water off, reached for a towel, dried herself off, and went to Paul's bed. She began to kiss him all over his face until he opened his eyes and stared at her. She put her hand on the side of his face and began stroking it with the movement of her fingers. He loved waking up to her beautiful eyes staring at him after he slept. She smiled and said the words that everyone wants to hear. Those words that have been repeated over and over millions of times, yet there is only one way that we long to hear them. Rachelle was just as much a reader as a writer. One of the books that made an impression on her was *Written on the Body* by Jeanette Winterson. It was this book that expressed the clichés of love, and Rachelle agreed with the author that those words—I love you—were the most unoriginal thing one can say to another, yet they are the words we want to hear from the ones we care about the most. There is something about those specific words that give us security and makes our heart smile. This moment right now with Paul was no different. She didn't care how he said it, how fast or slow, she needed to hear those unoriginal words.

"I love you." Paul kissed Rachelle and said it in a way that made it special. It was romantic and it was good enough for her. He touched her and said, "I've always loved you." Rachelle moved over on top of him and they made love in a way they had not for some time. There had been sex, but the act of making love had diminished in their lives. The problem was that dreaded four-letter word: *busy*. Their lives had taken a course where they had been caught up in a busy world. This morning, the priority was different. The detective knew he had to be careful when Rachelle was with him, but it was times like this when he couldn't resist her. Paul hated the Face of Fear investigation, but he believed it brought him closer to Rachelle. Now, he was scared the Music Club Murders and the consequences from Face of Fear were now threatening to tear them apart. The case was violent, and while not as complicated, the fallout would be much steeper if it was not resolved. It was another forty minutes before Rachelle got out of bed and put on clothes that she kept in Paul's apartment.

The detective sat up in bed as Rachelle brushed her hair and said,

"Are you going to ask me about last night?"

Rachelle stopped brushing for a couple seconds, then started moving the brush again before saying,

"I figured you would tell me if there was something I needed to know or if you wanted me to know. I get scared, Paul. Not for me anymore, but I worry about you. I worry about your life. I worry about our future. Tell me, do you think about our future? I know what your job is, I know what the world is about today, but there are things I think about. Such as us, and having children, and I know I don't want to bring them up in a world wondering if their daddy is going to come home tonight. I'm not scared about me, Paul. I'm scared for us."

She kissed him on the lips, and as she got up and walked to the top of the stairway, she turned around and looked at her lover, who still had his back against the bedpost. The beautiful woman smiled and spoke again. "I believe in you, Paul. I always have." She blew him a kiss as she ran down the stairs and entered Z Pita through the back entrance.

Joey Z was sitting at the back table looking over papers as he asked Rachelle if everything was all right. It was his way of letting her know she was twenty minutes late. Rachelle walked over to him and kissed him on top of his head. "Everything is fine, Joey Z."

The majority owner looked at Rachelle as she walked toward the front of the restaurant and spoke to himself.

"Women, can't live with them, can't live without them."

One of Joey Z's regulars witnessed the kiss Rachelle had given to him and the owner just shook his head and raised his hands, saying, "Hey, if only I was born rich instead of handsome." The customer laughed because it was a typical Joey Z comment.

Joey Z looked at his watch as he spoke again. "Speaking of which, Mom and Dad should be coming in any minute. This will be a fun day." Joey Z's parents came into the restaurant every third day and sat at the table in the back while they read various newspapers, still going strong well into their eighties and while working part-time with their dollhouse business in Smithtown. They had become part of the extended family, and Paul would even get her a Mother's Day card to leave for her when she would come to the restaurant every year.

Upstairs, the back of Paul's head was becoming damp again. He had just told Bud to stay away from Deborah to keep them safe, and yet he couldn't turn Rachelle away when she came to see him this morning. The conflict of his convictions was making him feel guilty. He was getting depressed and was having doubts about whether he could solve the case. Doubts would set in, and he could feel himself getting emotional from being overwhelmed. He needed to get in the shower quick and clear his mind.

Deborah was playing with the dogs when her phone played the song "Always on My Mind." She laughed every time Bud sang it to Paul, so she thought it was a perfect song to let her know Bud was calling. She picked up the call. "Hello, Detective Johnson, may I help you?"

He had a smile just hearing her voice.

"What are you doing?"

"Playing with the dogs."

"I'm jealous," he answered.

"Well, you should be, because I have been rolling on the floor with them."

The detective laughed as he spoke again. "I just wanted to let you know I was thinking about you. When this is over I would really like to have a chance to speak with you at great length."

"I have always been here for you, Bud. Always. Whenever you need me. I am here for you."

"You are an amazing woman, Deborah."

"Only when I'm with you, Bud."

"Don't forget. Move-in day was changed. One week later. I want this over before moving in."

"I remember, silly."

"OK, stay put. Officer Franks will be at the gate today."

"I'm here, but don't forget I'm visiting Madison tomorrow with Rachelle and then to the mall for some shopping."

"OK, we will have a couple of officers watching just to be sure."

"You can watch me," she answered with a giggle.

"Too dangerous. I'm worth too much to the bounty hunters. I'm not sure if I'm worth $250,000 or $1 million at this point," he said with a nervous laugh.

There was silence for a few seconds when Deborah answered, "You're priceless, Bud."

The detective was not used to such kind words. He took out the photo he kept of Deborah in his wallet and looked at it while he spoke again. "I better go, but I think we should have lunch at the Pie soon. You got me hooked on their grilled vegetable salad."

"OK, Bud," she replied, "be careful."

She heard the click, but within seconds she received a text from him. *You mean the world to me, don't ever think anything else.*

Stony Brook University Medical Center is the largest academic medical center on Long Island. It is located on Nichols Road in Stony Brook, Long Island. The University associated with it is well respected with over twenty-four thousand students. On the grounds is a facility for veterans that allows about 350 honorably discharged veterans to have a roof over their heads.

Once he arrived, Detective Sergeant Paul Powers nodded at Officer Sinclair at the entrance and walked into room 218 on the eighteenth floor of the hospital, and looked at the swollen black-and-blue face of Detective Ellyn Baker. Her eyes were closed for about three minutes before she opened them to see Paul Powers standing over her with a concerned smile on his face. She was reminded just how handsome he was, and she thought it was ironic the moment she appreciated his looks, her own face looked like someone had rubbed charcoal all over it.

"Hey," Powers said.

Baker closed her eyes again, but this time she had a smile on her face when she spoke. "I'm not ready to come back to work."

Paul laughed. "I love a woman with a sense of humor."

"Well," she answered, "I'm just sorry you're seeing me before I get my facial."

The detective laughed again before saying, "Ellyn, we got the fat man, and he gave everyone up. There is not much of a mystery here except where Simpson is and if there is someone calling the shots. They have put bounty money on us, and because you are part of us, you are worth $50,000 to them. This is why fat ass, excuse me, the fat man, Sysco, wanted to take you out."

Ellyn Baker lay silently as her thoughts raced in her head. "I guess this type of thing is normal for Priority 1."

"No, no it's not," Paul answered. "This is related to a case we had about a year and a half ago. We thought it was over, but we were mistaken. This time it will be finished, once and for all. You have my number, and there will be an officer at the door. Do you have any questions or anything you need to tell me?"

Baker moved a bit in her bed to get comfortable and spoke. "How did they know who I was at the club?"

"The cops in East Hampton. They got to them with payouts. They informed Branca, Wiley, and Simpson."

Baker moved her head toward the window as she replied, "If that is true, then how do we know if they haven't gotten to any of our team?"

Powers's face lost all expression as he absorbed Ellyn Baker's words. "Ellyn, just get well; we will take it from here. I'm going down the hall to see Chapman, and will stop back to say good-bye."

As he started to walk away, the detective grabbed his hand and said, "Be careful, Detective."

Paul smiled and squeezed her hand. "You're a good cop, Ellyn, and one hell of a kicker. For someone who doesn't like to wear shoes, you sure know how to use them."

"Well," she answered, "what I need right now is someone from Mary Kay."

"You know," Paul replied, "we will have to figure out a way to resolve you being at the club after a shooting but we have time to address it."

He kissed her hand and walked down the hall to visit Officer Chapman. As he walked toward the room he called O'Malley, who answered on the second ring. Detective Sergeant Powers told him to get with Sysco again and to double-check the bounty list with the payout schedule. "I want to be sure there is no one left off the list that should be on it. Also, sit him down and see if he has been holding anything back on where Branca and his crew could be. Now that they have been implicated, they won't return to the club or their homes. Somebody is putting them up." After that he directed O'Malley to meet him at the hospital with the list.

"Paul," O'Malley interrupted the detective, "Linda Tangretti had to be released. We didn't charge her with anything yet. The fat man's confession is not enough to hold her."

"Shit!" Paul yelled as he hung up.

He called Gina to find out where Lynagh, Healey, Franks, Johnson, Wyatt, and Caulfield were at that very moment. He asked her to give him an answer within ten minutes. *Good ole Gina,* he thought, *she always stays on top of where everyone is.*

When he hung up with Gina he sent ADA Ashley a text: *When is Cronin's family coming in from California? Also let's get O'Connor out a little at a time. Maybe he will be ready to vent to our undercover reporter.* He put his phone in his jacket as he walked in to pay his respects to Officer Robert Chapman.

Gary Reynolds was a part-time reporter for Nada at *Long Island Pulse* for five years while he took mass communications at

Five Towns College in Dix Hills. It seemed the stars were aligned when he graduated, and the chance to work full-time was available. The only catch was that it would be as a prison inmate at Bedford Hills prison, undercover. Detective Lieutenant Cronin had set it up with Nada and got the approval of the DA's office that it would be for twenty-four months. Cronin did not want to take any chances with O'Connor and knew the only way to keep an eye on him was to convince him Reynolds was also a cold-blooded killer. They set up his fake name as Reynolds and even went to the trouble of creating his history in case O'Connor had his visitors check him out.

After six months of seeing Reynolds in the same circle at the prison he was able to befriend the former FBI Agent. Reynolds was being paid by the taxpayers while being on Nada's payroll for benefits. When he eventually left the prison, his story would be exclusive to *LI Pulse* and he would receive a bonus. At twenty-three years of age, he was dealing with the guards and the protocols of prison as well as the lousy food for the experience of a lifetime. Ashley had his doubts when Cronin initially wanted the setup at the prison, but once again it appeared it was the right call. It was now ADA Ashley who was communicating with Nada since the world still thought Cronin was dead.

Today was the first time since the initial order that the guards let O'Connor out of his cell. Outside there were only two others playing basketball, and Reynolds was sitting on a bench watching them.

O'Connor sat down with Reynolds, who promptly spoke.

"Hello there, stranger. You must really be a bad boy to keep you in a cell so long. You must have a lousy lawyer."

"They are pissed off that their precious Detective Lieutenant Cronin blew up in a million pieces. They have no proof, of course, that I'm involved, but they want to punish me anyway. Which makes me confused and suspicious of why I'm allowed to speak to you."

"No problem, man," Reynolds shot back. "You sat down with me," and he got up to leave.

"No, no wait," O'Connor answered. "I guess I am getting a little paranoid. You have time?"

Reynolds was a pro. "I've got another twenty years, man. What's up?"

"Fucking Robert Simpson. Our plan was to destroy the lives of the people who got me here. Then he enters the picture and convinces us to have bounties put on their heads. We have no choice because he has the money, but he can't let go of the girl. He really lost it. He starts killing young women to get Cronin's task force involved to make it easier to eliminate them."

"Why are you telling me all this?" Reynolds asked.

"Because," O'Connor replied, "I will bring you in on this by getting messages to certain people through your visitors. I'm no longer allowed to have visitors, so I'm cut off."

Gary Reynolds thought of every possible scenario to avoid suspicion. Even though he had now been in prison for fourteen months and had O'Connor's confidence, he did not want to blow it now. He asked, "If the people who visited you start visiting me, wouldn't that raise a red flag to everyone? Also, how could you get word out for them to see me with you being watched so close?"

O'Connor was impressed with the young man. "I have a guard who is a friend. He will take care of it for me."

Reynolds breathed a sigh of relief at this moment that Cronin insisted no one at the prison knew of Reynolds being undercover. He simply did not trust anyone, and he was proven right again. Now his only worry was which guard. If the wrong guard was listening in to his conversation with his visitors, his cover would be blown and his life threatened. He decided to go for it.

"I'll do it, but I need to know which guard is involved. I need to know who has my back and who I can talk to. Also, our conversations are recorded. How to plan this?"

"My friend," O'Connor replied, "will make sure the conversation is not recorded. He will be in touch with you."

Just as he finished speaking, correctional officer Gene Blakely yelled at Reynolds to get up and head back to the building. All of a sudden Gary Reynolds felt very alone. He was given pause to say anything to anyone, not knowing which of the guards was a partner with the sicko he had befriended. He returned to his cell with almost a feeling of desperation. He did not want to bring attention to himself, but he was upset by the news about the demise of Detective Cronin. He also did not want to speak to his contacts through the DA's office until he knew which guard was on Simpson's payroll. He wasn't in his cell for ten minutes when correctional officer Tom Jenkins came to his cell to tell him his attorney was waiting for him in the attorney-client room. The officer led the young man to the room and greeted Al Simmons for the first time in his life. Tom Jenkins stood by the door as Gary Reynolds sat across the table from the attorney.

"You can leave us," Simmons said to the correctional officer.

"Sorry, sir," Jenkins replied, "I can't leave you alone with him unless his hands are in cuffs to the table." Simmons looked at Reynolds, who nodded it was OK. "Go ahead then, Officer, I need to speak to my client in private."

Jenkins came over and cuffed Gary Reynolds and left the room while standing outside the door with a window so he could keep an eye on things. The undercover prisoner stared at the attorney, not sure of what to think or say.

Finally, Al Simmons spoke.

"Things are reaching a boiling point, or should I say a climax."

Reynolds just sat there in silence with his hands in cuffs, waiting for Simmons to speak again. Things started to get awkward, so the attorney spoke again.

"I was sent here by Detective Cronin to work with you."

"Why now are you in the picture?" Reynolds asked. "I've been here for fourteen months, and the only contact I have had has been with ADA Ashley and Cronin. You say Cronin sent you, yet I've been told he was blown to pieces."

Simmons reached over the table and whispered into Reynolds ear, "He's alive. I have been sent here by ADA Ashley to let you know."

Reynolds inhaled a long breath and exhaled as Simmons sat down in his chair to speak again.

"He is dead in our eyes to keep the bounties off of the women. Thanks to your information. This is why I'm here. You are now my client, and all information will be passed through our conversations."

As Simmons continued to speak, Reynolds interrupted him.

"O'Connor has a guard here on his payroll. I need to be careful. The only thing in my favor is that I've been here for fourteen months living the way the rest of the prisoners have."

Simmons was quiet as he gathered his thoughts on the new information. Reynolds continued to inform him that O'Connor would have visitors see him to communicate back to him during the brief times they were together. They spoke for another fifteen minutes before Simmons got up and knocked on the door for Officer Jenkins to unlock Reynolds and take him away. When Al Simmons got to his car he called ADA Ashley to give him the news. When they hung up the assistant district attorney ordered a background review of all the guards in O'Connor's and Reynolds's section at the prison.

While Powers was at the hospital, he sent a text to Caulfield to pick up Tangretti again. He no longer cared about her being released earlier. He wasn't finished with her.

Detective O'Malley was at the hospital within the hour and paid his respects to both Detective Baker and Officer Chapman before meeting with Powers. Gina had also sent the locations of his team to the detective. Franks was parked down the block from Deborah's house, Lynagh was at his desk looking over photographs and video, Bud was having lunch, Wyatt was down the block from the Wilkerson house, and Detective Caulfield was on his way to pick up Linda Tangretti again. Powers responded to Gina, thanking her. He sent Bud a text to meet him later at Spy Coast for dinner and drinks and turned his attention to O'Malley. He looked at the list carefully. He looked at each name and the amount of bounty assigned.

"What are you thinking," O'Malley asked as he ate his pumpkin seeds.

"I'm thinking we better find Branca, Simpson, and his men pretty fast."

"Where do you think he is hiding out?" O'Malley asked.

"Somewhere that is secure to him. He won't stop until he kills Bud at this point. I don't think he has it in him to kill Deborah Lance, but at this point I'm not sure."

O'Malley nodded as he spoke again. "The FBI is pushing hard to get involved with this case since police officers were killed. We can't hold them off much longer."

Paul looked at O'Malley, and it was like a lightbulb went off in his head.

He started writing in his notepad and O'Malley waited to ask but decided to leave it alone.

He walked away from O'Malley for some privacy and called Gina.

He told her to pick up every CD from the group Mystic Strangers and to give it to Bud to bring it to him tonight. They were going to listen to some songs tonight.

He continued, "Gina, that folder I'm working on, pull it out and listen carefully." O'Malley could see that Paul was giving a specific set of instructions for her.

Detective Caulfield was waiting for Linda Tangretti for over an hour when she entered the apartment given to her for use by Robert Simpson. As she entered the living room he grabbed the back of her hair, asking her where the hell she had been.

"It's not easy when you are wanted by the law."

"That's for sure," Caulfield answered. "You are definitely wanted by the law." With that they kissed as he started to unbutton her blouse while falling onto the sofa. The detective became impatient and ripped her blouse as he grabbed the button on her slacks. He kissed her neck as she moved her hand to the top button of his slacks. Linda tried to speak, but the detective moved his mouth to her lips as his hunger to have her prevented her from saying anything. He was so impatient to have her that they fell to the floor as he attempted to remove her slacks. It was the first time the two of them were intimate in over two weeks. They were careful as the setup began to draw out Priority 1 Task Force on the Music Club Murders Case, and they were careful to not let the chemistry they had for each other distract from the goal of eliminating the members for bounties set up by Simpson.

Linda Tangretti, the cousin of Patty Saunders, wanted revenge since Patty was stabbed and killed by Madison wearing the Ghost Face mask. Her body fell into the water next to Danfords's dock, and it was almost ten minutes before they got her out of the water. She laid low for six months until she hired an investigator to find Robert Simpson, who had moved to Marco Island, Florida, in hopes of accidently on purpose bumping into Deborah Lance at their vacation home. He had been threatened by Detective Cronin to involve himself in a murder investigation that he had nothing to do with by being a patsy. Then he was threatened by Bud Johnson to stay away from Deborah Lance. His life was in tatters and he felt he had nothing to lose by getting his revenge; in fact, he was determined he was going to get it. He knew Linda from his affair with Patty, and while he resisted at first in killing young women at the clubs, it was like a switch was turned on the moment he heard the music that turned him on. Linda knew of his desire for sex during music from her cousin. Deborah had confided to Patty and she too used it to her advantage in convincing Robert Simpson this was the best way for justice for Patty and the loss of Simpson's livelihood and relationship with Deborah Lance. Linda couldn't help herself, just like her cousin Patty. She had to find out what all the fuss was about between the sheets. She set him up one night with the right music and realized it was his equipment below the waist that made him a true "rock star" in the lovemaking department. When Robert Simpson decided to use the money he embezzled from William Lance during his employment years for the bounties, Linda wanted a share. Enter Detective Caulfield, who was easier than Linda thought to get on board. During two months of dating and overnight stays she slowly manipulated him to be a part of bringing down the Priority 1 Task Force. Her goal was to get justice for her cousin, but more important, to collect as much of the bounty as possible. Now that she had Caulfield where she wanted, she would dispose of him when he was no longer needed. She was disappointed that he didn't know everything that was going on, but O'Malley did keep him informed. After all, working with him for five years brought trust to their relationship. Linda was satisfied after being with Peter Caulfield for twenty-five minutes of rough intimacy. She was on her back as she turned her head to look at the detective.

She smiled as she spoke.

"What's next, sexy?"

"We lost the $200,000 for killing Cronin to Wiley; Simpson saved $75,000 by killing Dugan himself. Chapman is still in the hospital as well as Baker. We need to kill the rest if we want to be comfortable. As long as they don't find out about me and you, my job is safe."

"That's nice," Linda answered. "But you told me I'm

implicated from Sysco, so what happens to me?"

"You will have to disappear, Linda," he answered. "You get your cut and disappear. If things go right, I will be able to be a cop and keep the benefits."

Linda turned over on her side to look at Peter Caulfield. "I will need a lot more than half of whatever we get from eliminating these cops to disappear. I still think we should go after the girls."

"Listen," Caulfield answered. "There is no money on their heads. Leave it alone. Between Lynagh, Healey, Franks, Powers, and Johnson there is over a half million to be collected. If we get Ashley and my dear boss O'Malley, it's another $150,000. Be patient." He turned over on his side to look at Linda and asked, "Have you heard from Simpson or Wiley?"

"No," she answered.

He fell back on his side as he spoke again. "Get word to them that we want $100,000 if I get rid of that fat fuck Sysco."

"OK," she answered as she started kissing his chest. They had started to caress each other again when Linda's iPhone buzzed with a text. *Get over here now.* "It's Branca, I've got to go. He's been a bear since he's been on the run. Sysco has been a singing bird during all this."

"Like I said," Caulfield answered, "$100,000 and he's gone also."

"I will ask," Linda replied. It took the two of them ten minutes to get their clothes on and go their separate ways.

As Detective Peter Caulfield left the apartment he called Detective O'Malley to inform him he was still checking on possible leads as to the location of Linda Tangretti and Jake Wiley.

"Wiley's dead," O'Malley said. "He tried to take out Ashley and I guess the ADA can handle a gun. However, keep it quiet for now."

Caulfield was silent in his shock but managed to express a sigh of relief that the ADA was OK. "Thank goodness he is OK," he replied.

O'Malley then directed Caulfield to question Kevin Sysco and try and find out more information about where Branca, Corbin, and Talison might be. Wiley's house was now under surveillance under his alias as Jerry Wakefern, and it was apparent no one was at the club. They hung up the phone and Caulfield started dialing numbers to give the news of Jake Wiley's death.

Bud Johnson met with his attorney and the bank for his closing on the house that he would be moving into the following Saturday. He could not wait to finally be a resident of the village of Port Jefferson. He had already hired a painting service to start fixing up the outside of The Henry Hallock house as soon as he moved into the South Street community. When he left his attorney's office he called Paul to tell him the news.

"Well, partner, looks like I will be less than five minutes away from you."

Paul laughed. "Yeah, you and the ghosts; just don't bring them to my place."

"Come on," Bud replied, "no ghost jokes." Paul laughed as he pushed the *end* button.

To be safe Bud dialed Deborah's number and found her getting ready to visit Madison at the jail with Rachelle, then they had plans to go shopping at the Suffolk County Shopping Mall.

"OK," he said. "Have fun, be careful."

She laughed as she ended the call. Bud drove up to Belle Terre and to Cliff Street, where Officer Franks was at the front gate in his vehicle. "Listen," he said, "Deborah will be leaving, but I would like you to keep an eye on things here. I will get someone else to follow the girls."

"No problem," Franks replied. "Just get me some relief. I'm bored as hell after hours here today." Bud called Gina at the precinct to have Lynagh and Healey follow the girls to Riverhead and to the mall and to get another officer at the gate of the Lance mansion. Gina punched in Carol Wright's name to be that officer.

They were all impressed with the young officer the night at the club, and she was still on loan. Bud left Franks with a few trivia questions to think about and drove back to the precinct to have another talk with Kevin Sysco.

Once he had Sysco in the interview room, Detective Caulfield walked in to tell Bud that O'Malley had instructed him to question him as well.

"Go ahead," Bud replied, as he got up to find Gina. Once he did, he asked her to verify if O'Malley instructed Caulfield to question Sysco under orders from Powers. She replied that it was and it satisfied Bud that it was Paul running the investigation and not O'Malley. He liked the older detective, but he did not like the energy coming from Peter Caulfield. He decided to go to the monitoring room and watch the questioning before going in himself. He acknowledged the tech man as he sat down to watch and listen.

Bill Tillman turned on the video as Caulfield tapped his fingers on the table for a few seconds then began to speak. "If Branca and his men are not in the club or their homes, where would they be?"

Sysco smiled and farted. The room was stifling within seconds.

"Is that supposed to be funny?" Caulfield asked. Sysco farted again. Bud couldn't stop laughing in the monitoring room. There was something about passing gas that always made him laugh. Even the word *fart* would make him lose it. Though he didn't like Sysco the prisoner, watching this unfold and seeing Caulfield's expression was priceless. He was holding his stomach when Sysco farted a third time and Caulfield had to leave the room to escape the smell. He walked into the monitoring room to find Bud and Tillman laughing so hard they had tears in their eyes.

"I hope you guys are enjoying yourselves," Caulfield remarked. Bud didn't reply because he was still laughing. All

Caulfield could think about at this moment was that Bud Johnson, who was worth $250,000, was three feet away from him laughing like a hyena. Caulfield pushed the intercom asking the desk to bring air freshener to the interrogation room. Within a couple minutes the room was sprayed and Caulfield started to leave the monitoring room.

Suddenly Bud stopped laughing and said,

"Your piece."

Caulfield looked back. "Excuse me."

"Leave your gun here. You had it in with you when talking to fart man."

The detective pulled out his Glock and his backup piece and left it with Bud. Detective Bud Johnson watched the interview between them as he took notes before entering the room.

Lynagh and Healey were about fifty yards away when Deborah and Rachelle visited Madison at the facility. While they were in speaking with Madison, the detectives spoke to the correctional officers and even had an opportunity to speak with John Bay, who was assigned to Madison at the jail, as well as Officer Gates. They were pleased with their conversation with Bay and could tell he had a genuine affection for Madison, while not admitting it. He told them Janet Gates would be relieving him that night and spent most nights with her, which is how she noticed the nightmares.

Madison hugged Rachelle over the glass and held on to one of her hands as she touched Deborah to say hello.

"How are you doing, baby sister?" Rachelle asked, trying to keep her emotions from being noticed in her voice.

"I'm OK, Rachelle," Madison answered. "I'm seeing a therapist about my nightmares. They are treating me as well as they possibly can." She looked over at Deborah and asked, "And you? How are you holding up?"

Deborah smiled as she said, "Other than life getting more

complicated, I guess I'm doing fine. I guess until this is finally over my life won't be my own."

"I have a feeling," Madison responded, "that it will be over sooner than you think." Deborah wondered how Madison got her information, but she learned not to pursue it. The less she knew about how Madison kept up, the better it was.

Bud and Caulfield had spent an hour talking to Sysco when Bud got a call from Paul. He got up from the table, leaving Caulfield in the room alone with him.

"Nothing more to say?" the detective asked.

Sysco smiled and farted.

"You fat fuck," Caulfield yelled as he got up to leave the stench in the room. He could not hear Tillman in the monitoring room laughing.

Paul was dropped off at his apartment in the back of Z Pita, by O'Malley, and couldn't help himself. He pulled out the list again and kept staring at the names and the total bounty of each. He pushed his *message* button on his phone as he undressed to shower. The usual people were on it. First it was his father: "Hello, Son, I haven't heard from you. Give me a call." Rachelle's voice was next, which always made him smile when he heard her speak: "Hi, Paul, it's me, just calling to say I love you and if you get a chance please walk the dogs if you are close by during the day. Oh yeah, and hurry up, get your clothes back on." She ended the call with a laugh. He shook his head as he grabbed a towel, amazed at how well she knew him.

The messages continued as Bud's voice came on: "Hey, my partner, let's get together for dinner. Time for us to have a private chat. There is something about Caulfield that is not sitting right with me. Later." Paul heard the click. He went to the machine and replayed the message again as he took out the bounty list. It wasn't about who was on the list. It was about who wasn't on the list. Paul decided to skip the shower and put his clothes back on as the next message came on. It was Rachelle's voice again: "It's time you take care of Paul, because I'm not sure if I can. Please call me." It was a recording of the call Rachelle made from Deborah's foyer. Paul stopped in his tracks and replayed the message three times. He didn't know what to think, and for the first time in quite a long time he didn't know what to do. He was so distracted he went straight to the precinct without stopping to walk the dogs. On his arrival he asked for an update for the location of everyone. Gina started to give him the information but he interrupted her, asking her to put it on paper for him. The list was in his hands within ten minutes.

Detective Wyatt was a block away from the Wilkerson house, and while there were no bounties on Lindsey Wilkerson, Rachelle, and Deborah, Paul wasn't taking any chances. Detective Caulfield was at his desk after interviewing Kevin Sysco. Detective Bud Johnson just left the building after the Sysco interview. Officer Franks had left his shift at the Lances' Pink Mansion to go home. Officer Wright was now at the house. Detective Baker and Officer Chapman were still in the hospital. Detective O'Malley was on his way to the precinct. Officers Lynagh and Healey were in Riverhead near Rachelle Robinson and Deborah Lance. *Gina,* Paul typed in on the office email, *please send Detective Caulfield to my office.* While Cronin would bellow orders to Gina and others on the intercom, Paul liked less talking and using the email format. Detective Caulfield was in his office within five minutes.

"How's it going?" Paul asked.

"If you mean the search for Tangretti, Simpson, and the other cronies, nothing yet."

"What about the questioning of Sysco?" Paul replied.

"Well," Caulfield answered as he sat down, "we spoke to him for over an hour and he claims he told us everything he knows."

"Maybe he has," Paul answered. He placed the bounty list on his desk in front of him. "See anyone on the list that you know?"

Caulfield picked up the list and put it back down. "I know

everyone on the list except Sherry Walker."

Powers pushed the list closer to him. "What about a name you know that's not on the list." Caulfield looked at it again then recognized what Detective Powers was getting at.

"My name is not on the list."

"Why would that be?" Paul replied.

Caulfield shook his head and told Powers that he wasn't assigned to the task force unit until after the case had started. It was either that or he was just plain lucky. Powers accepted his explanation for now, and Caulfield was dismissed. As the detective walked out to go home, Gina informed Paul ADA Ashley was on his way to his office.

"Just great," Paul answered. He sent a text to Bud that he could not see him at Spy Coast at 6:00 pm to talk. He needed to speak to Rachelle about something. Bud answered back: *They are going to the mall later. You can speak to her then, and you and I can speak and get something to eat later.* Paul answered back, *Agreed. Let me know when they are there.*

Bud sent Lynagh a text to let him know when the girls were ten minutes away from the mall. Bud then sent Gina an email to get a detective to check on Linda Tangretti's actual home in Connecticut. He remembered she had a place from the Face of Fear investigation and he could not understand how all of them could manage to stay out of sight. He followed up his text to inform Gina to notify the Connecticut State Police and to take an officer with him. Run it by Powers to approve and get back to me with his approval or disapproval. It was less than ten minutes when Wyatt sent him a text that Powers had approved O'Brien and himself to check out Tangretti's home in Milford, Connecticut.

It was a long day for Officer Franks. He was exhausted and couldn't wait to take a long nap. He got out of his car, pushed the code to his apartment door, walked into the elevator, and as the doors began to shut the man who wore the baseball hat with the mask jumped in and stabbed Franks in the neck. He barely had a chance to reach for his gun. The killer was so quick he held up the doors with his left arm while he stabbed with his right. He didn't want to take a chance of Franks wearing a vest, so he went straight for the throat. Officer Wilson Franks fell to the floor trying to keep the blood from pouring out, but it was no use. He died in the elevator only to be found by a young teenage boy who yelled down the hall to his mom that there was a dead police officer in the elevator. The woman scolded her son for such a distasteful joke, but when she found the floor of the elevator filled with blood and the body of Franks, she fainted to the floor, which prompted her son to call 9-1-1. As soon as officers arrived and saw it was Franks, they called Priority 1. Gina came into Paul's office without knocking, and he could see by her face something was terribly wrong.

"It's Franks," she said. "He's been killed in the elevator at his complex."

Paul got up and told Gina to have Bud and O'Malley at the complex right away. Bud had just walked in, so Paul grabbed him to drive to Franks's complex in Smithtown. O'Malley arrived first and looked at the pool of blood and the open eyes of Wilson Franks. He spoke to himself: "This is a shit job."

Powers and Johnson arrived, and it was difficult to see a close associate who was a good cop die so violently. Bud knelt down next to Franks, being careful not to step in the blood. He put his hand on the officer's head as he bowed his head and prayed. Paul looked at Bud and gave him a few seconds. Bud spoke to Franks when he picked up his head: "I'm sorry, Officer Wilson Franks. We will find whoever did this to you. Thank you for being such a good man, a good cop, and a good friend." He took his hand and he closed the eyes of Officer Franks forever. Powers sent O'Malley to question the occupants of the building, while he tried to control his emotions as leader of the squad.

"Bud," Powers said, "get the digital film from the elevator."

Without saying a word Bud was making a call to find the tenant manager to locate the film. Powers barked to one of the officers to find out from Priority 1 where the hell Detective Wyatt was, as the young officer started running.

"Bud," Paul looked at him. "The video."

Bud looked at his partner and said, "I'm not leaving him till they take him. He should not be alone." He looked at Franks then turned back to his partner. "A good man, and yet he dies in an elevator. For what? For bullshit."

Paul knew that as crazy and off-the-wall as Bud could be, his heart was worth all the gold in Fort Knox. He waited another thirty minutes until the medical team arrived and went to apartment 4D to speak to the manager of the building. The manager was concerned and cooperative as he brought Bud to the control room to play back footage. Bud watched as Franks entered the elevator and was caught completely off guard as the intruder ran in, put the knife into his throat while putting his arm out to keep the doors from shutting behind him.

"You never had a chance, friend," he said to himself as he watched the footage over and over again. While the killer had the same hat and mask on, it had to be a different person. The body motion and body type were different, yet it was the same mask. Bud looked at it five or six times, then had the manager stop the footage to look at the hand and watch of the killer. It was silver, about an inch wide and an inch and a half in length. It was a rectangular watch that had Roman numerals instead of numbers. The detective made notes as he continued to watch the footage again.

He said aloud, "You're not going to get away with this."

Paul Powers was on his way to notify Franks's ex-wife and sixteen-year-old son in St. James when he got a text from Bud that he had reviewed the footage and they needed to meet as soon as possible. Paul replied he would be back at the precinct within the hour and that he would have to be prepared for a press conference. Bud called him when he received that text.

"Paul, if we have no answers, we can't expose the bounty list. It would endanger too many people."

"Bud," Paul replied, "we have lost cops, with two more in the hospital. Whether we have a press conference or not, the bounties are on, and don't forget you are the top dog in this."

"I don't care about me, Paul," Bud answered. "I care about the others. And what about the girls?"

"Bud," Paul said, "do you think there is any way possible that Rachelle could be mixed up in this?" There was dead silence on the other end, so Paul decided to speak again. "Someone sent me a voice message of Rachelle speaking to someone that they needed to take care of me because she couldn't. I'm sick over this."

"Listen to me," Bud replied. "You and I are going to the mall to straighten this shit out. By the time you are finished in St. James, the girls will be on their way to the mall. Hold off on the press conference."

"See you there," Paul answered. "By the way, Wyatt never met O'Brien to go to Milford to take a look at Tangretti's residence. Check his house before going to the mall." Bud got off the phone and drove to Detective Wyatt's house. The door of the house was open as Bud pulled out his 9mm Glock. He identified himself as he walked around for ten minutes with no sign of disruption or Wyatt. He called it in to Gina to document it as he headed over to the mall.

O'Connor was outside with a few of the other inmates, but he was playing one-on-one basketball with Reynolds when he was told he had a visitor. When he walked in with Correctional Officer Louis Roberts, he had a smirk on his face when he saw ADA Ashley sitting there.

"How's it going, former Agent O'Connor?"

"Fuck you," the inmate replied.

"People continue to die, now another cop, because of the bounties. Where are Branca, Tangretti, and Simpson?" While it was a question, the tone of his voice did not ask it like it was a question.

"I don't know anything," he replied.

"That's right," Ashley replied. "You don't know anything." O'Connor sat there silently with the remark as Ashley spoke again.

"Your friend, Wiley or Wakefern or whatever the hell you call him, he tried to kill me last night for the bounty money. Now he's dead."

O'Connor laughed. "No way you killed him."

"Well," Ashley said, "you're right about that. You see, my friend behind the mirror shot him dead, and I think he enjoyed it." O'Connor looked up as the mirror window lit up and the figure of Detective Lieutenant Cronin was staring at him. O'Connor started to shake as he kept repeating to himself, "No, no, no, no!" as he backed up toward the wall. He went into the corner as he shook more, saying, "No! No! Impossible! No!"

The mirror window went dark as O'Connor, still shaking, spoke again. "See! See! It was a ghost!" He started to fall and curl in the corner as the door to the interrogation room was kicked in, which startled the guard as well.

"I'm sorry," Cronin replied in a sarcastic voice. "I forgot to knock." He turned around to look at Correctional Officer Roberts.

"You have been a very naughty boy; we will speak to you later," he said, as two other guards grabbed Roberts. ADA Ashley had received the reports he asked for, and the common denominator of Linda Tangretti was solved. They went to high school together, and while it was thin in a court of law, they felt comfortable he was the source of communication between O'Connor and the rest of Simpson and Branca's team.

Cronin turned around and looked at O'Connor sitting in the corner in shock. The detective walked up to the former FBI agent and leaned over to be closer to his face.

"Now you are going to tell me where Simpson and the rest of the gang are, or I am going to haunt you in this place forever."

Paul Powers gave the news to the next of kin and gave them information on what to do and whom to contact. He was trying to hold it together for the sake of himself and the rest of the Priority 1 Task Force team. While on his way to the mall, Bud gave him a call to inform him that Wyatt was missing and the girls were on their way to the mall.

"OK," Paul replied. "See you there at the entrance next to Macy's. Give O'Malley the update on Wyatt. Have Gina get a location on his vehicle. I need to straighten this out with Rachelle before the chief and the press take hold of what is going on." He was at the Suffolk County Mall in Lake Grove within fifteen minutes, and Bud was waiting for him. He sent Lynagh and Healey a text asking for their location, and they answered the Red Robin restaurant. Powers and Johnson met up with Lynagh and Healey at the restaurant to speak with them briefly before heading in to greet the girls.

Rachelle looked up and met Paul with her usual beautiful smile as he leaned over to kiss her as well as Deborah. He sat down with a nervous grin on his face and spoke. "Rachelle, I need to speak with you about something."

"OK," she answered. "What a surprise to see you." She continued to smile.

Paul looked at Deborah and said, "Bud is outside. May I have a few moments with Rachelle?"

Deborah looked at Rachelle and replied,

"Sure." She got up and met Bud outside the restaurant as Lynagh and Healey were two stores down keeping an eye on the surroundings.

"Hi there," Bud said as he poked her in the arm.

"You're a funny guy, Bud Johnson," she answered.

Bud looked over at Lynagh and Healey and could tell they

were upset over the death of a fellow officer. He looked back at Deborah. "That's what they tell me, sweet Deborah. Let's take a walk. Did you know Rhode Island is the smallest state with the longest official name?"

"What?" Deborah replied, looking at him.

"That's right," he answered. "The formal name for Rhode Island is the State of Rhode Island and Providence Plantations."

Deborah shook her head. "Where do you find all this stuff, Detective Johnson?"

"I don't know, Ms. Lance. I just like to see your reaction."

"You're a funny guy, Bud Johnson," she answered.

"That's what you've been telling me," the detective answered.

Paul started to speak when his smartphone buzzed and he saw it was Ashley, so he picked it up.

"I've got the info you wanted," he said.

"Give it to me," Paul answered. "Thanks." He hung up and called O'Malley, directing him to find the location of Caulfield and to get back to him. He looked at Rachelle, and he could see she was getting restless. He looked at her for a few more seconds and spoke. "Do you love me?"

Rachelle grabbed his hands with a puzzled look on her face. "What's wrong, Paul. Why are you asking me such a silly question?"

He pulled out a mini-cassette recorder and pushed the button to play Rachelle's voice: "It's time you take care of Paul, because I'm not sure if I can. Please call me." Rachelle pulled her hands away from Paul with a startled look on her face.

"You are bugging me? You are recording me?"

"No," Paul said. "Someone called my apartment and left it on my machine."

Rachelle got up quickly to leave. "I don't care what they did. What do you think this is about?" She hit him on his shoulder and tried to storm out of the restaurant, but Paul grabbed her arm.

"Rachelle," he said, "you know what we are going through here. Don't hold it against me because I need to know what is going on."

She tried to walk away, but he continued to hold on to her arm. Rachelle looked at him with silence as he could read her eyes to let go of his grip on her. The detective let go of his grip as Rachelle stared at him with a mix of sadness and anger on her face before she spoke.

"Paul, not everything is about police work. We do have a personal life; at least I would like to think so. I can't get into this right now, but your tone and approach make me feel like you don't trust me." Paul started to speak, but Rachelle interrupted him, "It's OK, we will talk later." She kissed his cheek as she left. The detective was feeling conflicted and was worried he was once again letting his emotions get the best of him.

Rachelle entered the mall and spoke. "Come on, let's go." Her voice was erratic and she had tears in her eyes, so Deborah did not resist leaving with her. She turned her head to Bud with a *sorry* expression on her face as they walked to the bench in front of Forever 21. Rachelle sat down, covered her face with her hand, and started crying. Deborah held on to her as Bud went into the restaurant to find Paul. He sat down across the booth from him before saying a word. Paul played the tape for him.

Bud stared at him before finally speaking.

"Unless you think she is involved in this, you've got bigger problems to worry about. Paul, you are a good cop. Trust your instinct, trust her, she loves you." They got up to leave as Bud spoke again. "It will be OK."

They went out to the mall and headed for the door to exit. Paul turned around and saw Rachelle staring at him, her face flushed with red and covered in tears. He looked at Deborah and she had that protective, angry look on her face toward Paul and Bud.

"Well," Bud said, "I guess I'm in trouble as well. Normally, I think I would be hungry, but losing Franks made me lose my appetite." The detectives went outside to their vehicles and waited for O'Malley and Caulfield to show up.

When they did, Paul looked at Detective Caulfield and asked, "Do you know why we can't find Detective Wyatt?"

The detective didn't have time to answer, for Paul Powers was in interrogation overdrive. He asked,

"What were those numbers you called when you were notified Jake Wiley was dead? Why haven't you visited Detective Chapman and Baker in the hospital, other than when you were assigned?"

O'Malley took out a bag of pumpkin seeds as Powers kept asking questions. "Most important, why did your fingerprints show up at Linda Tangretti's apartment that is paid for by the City nightclub?"

Before Paul could ask the next question, Bud took out his Glock and held his weapon by his leg, saying, "I knew you were a dipshit."

Caulfield remained calm and said he could explain.

"No, you can't," Powers answered back. "The video of Franks getting killed was helpful. Hold out your arm."

Caulfield resisted as Powers spoke again.

"OK, Bud, shoot him."

"Wait!" Caulfield yelled. He held out his right arm and dropped it.

"Your left arm, hold it out," Powers answered.

Caulfield held out his left arm and Powers reached over to pull his sleeve back and put it in Bud's face. Bud could see the watch that the camera caught as the killer held the elevator doors open.

"You fuck," Bud said. "You killed a fellow police officer for bounty money?" He raised his gun to Caulfield, and Paul shoved

Caulfield toward O'Malley, who now was reaching to get his gun. Bud was staring down Caulfield, for it was all he could do to keep from shooting him.

Paul's phone rang, which he would normally ignore, but it was his father so he answered with a curt "Not a good time, Dad. Let me call you back."

"Listen to me!" his father yelled. "Don't you dare hang up!" It was the first time in years that Paul heard his father yell at him, so he hesitated.

"I'm not going to let you throw away your relationship with this girl because you have insecurity problems." Paul looked over at O'Malley and Bud and raised up his finger requesting a minute.

"Sure," Bud said. "I'm in the middle of an arrest for murder."

"OK," Anthony Powers answered. "Before you age another minute or before you do something you regret. The message that you heard from Rachelle, about taking care of you, well it was left for me. She has been frightened about you and what is going on. Whoever played the tape to your machine is setting you up to do what you did. Now fix it!" With that he heard a click.

He looked at Bud and O'Malley and said, "I've got to go back into the mall and resolve something. O'Malley, come with me. I think it is better to keep you away from a former partner. Bud, stay with him until the officers get here and take his cell phone."

Bud had Caulfield lean up against the car before Powers and O'Malley left and handcuffed his hands behind his back as Paul and the elder detective went inside the mall. Paul felt sick about what had happened with Rachelle, but it seemed like every time something happened that had any relation to the Face of Fear investigation there were doubts raised. He sent Lynagh a text as to their location as they entered the mall. Both the girls had just taken a turn to the hallway to go the mall bathrooms. Lynagh and Healey waited in the mall areas for Powers as they saw Deborah and Rachelle walk toward the restrooms.

The walkway leading to the restrooms was separated by two-foot columns extending from the wall, each separated every six feet leading to the men's room and ladies' room.

As Rachelle and Deborah turned right behind the column, they were startled by a man with long hair and a beard. "Hello, Debbie, or should I say Deborah now?" Rachelle grabbed Deborah to try and pull her away, but Robert Simpson spoke again. "No problem, Deborah. I'll be right here waiting for you." Simpson looked at Rachelle. "You were a part of ruining my life by going along with Cronin's game. I should shoot you where you stand, but I think I'd rather hug you and kiss you, then leave a note to my Debbie."

Rachelle squinted her eyes and looked at Robert Simpson. "You have gone mad; you are really crazy."

"Robert," Deborah interrupted, "you killed those girls and cops to get back at all of us because of our breakup?" He took out his gun as people started running from the hallway. Lynagh pulled out his Glock and pointed it toward the column, which was protecting Simpson.

Robert raised his voice. "Come any closer, Officer Lynagh, and your friend Healey will be blown away. I have people in the mall ready to fire upon him and innocent bystanders as well."

Lynagh grabbed his phone and sent Paul Powers a text about what Simpson had just said. Paul had just reached Healey when he got the text.

He looked at O'Malley. "Get mall management and security to empty the mall now," he said as calmly as possible. "Try not to cause a panic, but get this mall emptied out now. We have a threat of bystanders and cops being shot."

O'Malley took off as Paul called Bud, who was in the car waiting for uniforms to take Caulfield in.

"Bud, get in here right away. We have a life-threatening situation in the mall with bystanders, but . . ." he hesitated.

"But what?" Bud asked.

"It's Deborah and Rachelle. Simpson has them."

Bud clicked the call. "Leaving you, shithead," he said to Caulfield. "Are you going to attempt to escape if I leave you handcuffed in the car?"

"You never know. After all, I am a cop," Caulfield said sarcastically.

"You're right," Bud said, "you never know, so I guess I have to shoot you." He pulled out his gun as Caulfield started to protest, but it was too late. Bud shot him in his kneecap as he left the car. You could hear Caulfield screaming bloody murder within thirty yards of the vehicle.

"You fuck! You shot me in the fucking knee. I'm going to kill you!" He couldn't even hold his leg due to the handcuffs. Bud entered the mall and started running toward the area designated by Powers.

Robert Simpson stood calmly behind the column as he continued to speak to Rachelle and Deborah.

"When you're fucking Detective Johnson, do you listen to any music, Debbie? Or do you just talk to him? Are you in the dark, or do you do it with the lights on?"

"Stop!" Deborah yelled as Lynagh moved a couple steps closer as he looked back at Paul.

Simpson looked over at Rachelle and said, "You can leave; I want to talk with her alone."

Rachelle held on to Deborah as she said, "I'm not leaving her alone with you."

Simpson was impressed with her bravery.

"Suit yourself," he replied. Rachelle looked back at Paul, who was eyeing her as he crept forward about ten yards behind Lynagh. She had a look on her face that she might be looking at Paul for the last time. She looked at him as he gave her the circular motion with a closed fist on his chest. It was the American Sign

Language for "I'm sorry."

Rachelle smiled as she looked back at Simpson and spoke. "I never wanted to hurt you. I was asked to set up that lunch with you to throw off everyone. I only did it to prove Paul was not a killer. I didn't have the affair with Patty Saunders. You did."

Simpson raised his gun at Rachelle, which could be seen from where both Lynagh and Powers were standing.

During this time Healey was scouting who else could have guns on them as Bud arrived at the scene and spoke.

"Go around the back of one of the stores. These malls have back hallways, and I'm sure there is one leading near the restrooms."

As Healey left, Bud could see people were anxious to leave the mall as officers and security were pushing harder to get everyone out.

Robert Simpson looked at Deborah Lance with his gun pointed at Rachelle. "Is he as good as me in bed?"

"You're sick," Deborah answered. "Give us a chance to get you help."

"There is no help for me now," he answered. "Tell me now if he is better than me or I do your friend here, now."

"Robert Simpson," Paul Powers yelled. "This is Detective Sergeant Paul Powers. Let the women go, and you and I can discuss this and why all this happened."

"You know what happened," Simpson yelled back.

"I don't know the whole story," Powers yelled back. "Let's talk about it while the women come over to Officer Lynagh."

"There is a gun aimed at Lynagh's head," Simpson replied. "If he gets any closer to me, he will be shot by one of my friends."

"OK," Powers replied as he looked at Lynagh to stop where he was. He was now about eight yards away from Simpson, but the column extending from the wall was still protecting him.

Lynagh's neck was already feeling the pain from turning his head back and forth from the mall to the column.

"Tell me the story, Robert," Powers answered. "Tell me why it has come to killing innocent women and our cops. Tell me how you got Detective Caulfield on your side." Paul wanted to use as much time as possible, hoping for a chance or opportunity for either him or Lynagh to take him out.

O'Malley was scouting the mall with management looking for any signs of a shooter or shooters in place. He had pulled his weapon out fifteen minutes ago and was no longer taking any chances. It also helped people adjust their attitude in leaving the mall a little quicker.

"Have the stores shut down and turn their lights off." He was hoping if someone was hiding in them they would be forced to expose themselves. He had to get forceful with some people who really didn't seem to care about what was going on and still wanted to shop. He walked up to two young girls staring at a dress in a window and in no uncertain terms spoke bluntly: "You two, get your petite little asses out of here. Don't you see what's going on here?" It was all they needed to start moving quickly as they eyed the gun in his hand.

Outside, Caulfield was still writhing in pain as he kept kicking the side of the car window with his good leg. Suddenly there was a shot and the door opened. The Ghost Face mask looked in as Caulfield tried to back away as best he could. Caulfield kept pushing toward the back of the car, but it was useless. He screamed for mercy as he even tried to bang his head against the window to find a way out. His only weapon was his one good leg to try and fend off the masked intruder. His screams got louder as his leg violently tried to fight off whoever was wearing the Ghost Face mask. The intruder stabbed Caulfield in the side as he continued to struggle to get away. Ghost Face managed to get into the backseat and told Caulfield to look. The mask came off as he was told why this was happening. He was stabbed one final time before he was gone. The masked killer opened a bag and threw a Ghost Face mask with blood splatter on the dead body of former detective Peter Caulfield. The killer knew by leaving the mask worn as a calling card it would show DNA. Instead, the masked killer took off the mask, put it in a bag, and disappeared into the night and left a mask never worn in the car.

Healey ran around the back of the Passion for Fashion store into the back hallway as Joseph Talison, an employee of Branca at the club, fired, catching Healey in the leg.

"Damn it," he yelled to himself. Another shot was fired, which just missed Healey's ear. He rolled to a clothing rack and turned it over to try and cover himself as he returned fire. The shots were heard by Powers and Johnson as well as Lynagh and O'Malley ten stores down.

"OK," O'Malley barked, "if you don't have a gun get out of the mall now." He fired a couple shots into the ceiling of the mall to have people start running from inside. Someone actually asked O'Malley why he shot the ceiling, and he answered, "It means 'Get the fuck out,' dumbass!" The crowd was now running as the shots rang out. He started to think how Powers and Johnson had rubbed off on him.

Powers yelled at Simpson as he looked at Rachelle and Deborah still standing. "Listen to me, Robert, shots are being fired. What is that about?"

Simpson shook his head. "I told you I have people here ready to kill and collect bounty money." Powers looked at Lynagh, who had taken another step closer. More shots were heard from the hallway. They knew Healey was in a gun battle as O'Malley reached Powers with three uniformed officers. He directed them to get to the hallway where Healey was sent. He turned his attention back to Simpson as he took another couple steps closer with Bud next to him.

"Tell me the story, Robert. Why kill Kate Summers?"

Simpson lowered his gun from his arm, getting tired as he began to talk.

"I worked for William Lance for over fifteen years. I fell in love with his daughter. We had a life. A good life. But when Deborah was kidnapped, your boss, Cronin, blamed me for Patty kidnapping Deborah. He forced me against my will to play a fucking game to solve his case. I lost my job. I lost my Debbie. As for Summers, you have no proof it was me."

The sound of Simpson saying "my Debbie" made her cringe, and he noticed it. Yet he continued talking.

"So what happens? Bud Johnson threatens me to leave forever, and what happens? He takes over where I left off. So I want to know right now who is better at fucking," he said as he pointed the gun at Deborah. "Rachelle can leave if she wants. I want Debbie and me to leave this world together." He repeated the words he wrote on the bodies of the dead girls. "If I can't have her, no one will."

"OK," Paul said. "Rachelle, start walking here." He had a chance to get her out of the way and save her life, and then he would work on saving Deborah.

"I'm not leaving Deborah," Rachelle answered. She held on to her friends arm as she looked back at Paul.

"Rachelle," Paul replied, "don't do this. Please come over here."

She looked at Paul and gave him the American Sign Language symbol with her hand for "I love you." It was the two middle fingers bent down with the thumb opened out with the index finger and pinky finger straight up as she spoke again, shaking her head. "I'm not leaving Deborah." It was in a tone of voice that indicated she knew she might not make it out of this one.

Lynagh looked back at Paul as he was getting restless as more shots were fired from the back hallway. O'Malley and the three uniformed officers had reached Healey, who had tied his leg up with a couple of shirts he pulled from the clothing rack. O'Malley quickly sent Powers a text that Healey was injured as he kept turning his head looking for a possible ambush in the corridor.

"Give it up," O'Malley yelled, "there are five of us. We are coming to you, and you won't get out of this alive if you don't drop your weapon now."

"Be my guest," the reply came. "You're worth $50,000, and Healey is worth $100,000."

"You got Healey," O'Malley answered as he motioned for Healey to stay quiet. "I'm coming in. It will either be me or you, but there are cops everywhere all over this mall. You will not get out of here alive even if you get me."

"I'm willing to take the chance," Talison replied as he fired another shot.

O'Malley kneeled down to Healey and whispered, "Don't say anything or fire a shot. Let him think you're dead in case there is someone else here listening. If someone comes up from behind us, then fire." Healey nodded his head as O'Malley and the officer crept forward. It was apparent that Talison was guarding the back entrance to the hallway near the restrooms while Simpson was there.

Lynagh took another step as a shot was fired at his head.

"I told you," Simpson spoke, "if you got any closer you would be shot. You are worth $100,000, so you most likely won't leave here alive anyway."

"OK," Paul said as he motioned for Lynagh to come back. "He's leaving, he's backing off." Lynagh took three steps back as more shots rang out as he barely took cover behind one of the columns.

"Robert," Powers said, "how did you know about the women being here at the mall?"

Robert Simpson laughed as he looked at the two women holding on to each other.

"I had the Lance mansion bugged in the foyer and living room. I heard everything these two had been talking about, including your sweet Rachelle calling your daddy that she was worried about you. I even heard my Debbie screwing that Sean Martin when your Detective Johnson got tired of her." Deborah covered her face as Rachelle held her arm tighter.

"Robert," Paul replied, "tell me how we all get out of this alive."

"We are not," Simpson answered. "Debbie will leave this earth with me. I only took the bounties off them because Cronin is dead. But I want Deborah with me for forever and eternity."

"And Wyatt?" Paul asked "Where is he?"

"He has passed on, Detective," Simpson replied. "It seems Linda Tangretti accidently shot him when he located her from a tip from Caulfield." He laughed as he spoke again. "Yes, he's been quite a help to me. It's amazing what money can do."

"Yes," Paul answered. "You embezzled millions of dollars from William Lance during your employment. That's how you are paying for all of this, right?"

"So what?" Simpson answered. Lynagh caught a glimpse of store lights going out and a figure running and he decided to make a move toward the mall. He began to sprint toward the open mall area as Simpson laughed. "Go get him, Lynagh, save yourself. Oh, where was I? The money was for me and Debbie. No one else. Her father didn't miss it."

Deborah was now crying as Paul spoke again.

"You love her, Robert. You know you're not going to shoot her. Let them go. We can make a trade, me for them."

Lynagh sprinted toward the figure he had seen, but somehow he disappeared again. There were at least twenty-five uniformed police officers now spread out through the mall, but all were told to stay away from the walkway leading to the restrooms. Still he could not see where the shooter was. Bud called Lynagh to check on Healey and O'Malley as the officer ran to the back hallway where the shots were originally fired.

Ashley picked up the call from the precinct as to what was happening at the mall as Cronin was driving. "Tell them to have four or five ambulances with a medical team standing by," Cronin said. "We have to get where we are going. Besides they can't know I'm alive just yet."

Ashley relayed the message as he hung up and looked at Cronin, saying, "You're a dangerous man, Detective Lieutenant Cronin."

Simpson barked back at Paul, "There can be no trade. I will take Debbie with me to another life. Somewhere where no one will ever have her again."

He raised his arm as Bud spoke.

"Then you will never have the satisfaction of seeing me dead, you sick motherfucker."

Paul put his arm on Bud, but his partner looked at him and said, "It's me and only me that will give us a chance to save the girls. He got Cronin and he put the big prize on me. Our only chance to take him out is for him to try and finish me. He's right. Cronin and I went out of our way to use him as a pawn in the Face of Fear case."

Bud started to walk toward Simpson, when Paul grabbed his arm again. Bud looked at him and said, "It's OK, partner. I've done a lot of praying." With that he started walking slowly toward Simpson and the girls. "I have no gun, my hands are up. I'm coming to see you, you ugly son of a bitch."

Simpson was clearly getting agitated as Bud continued to walk toward them.

Bud continued, "I love Deborah, and the big difference between me and you is that I also respect her. I am willing to sacrifice myself for her. That's how much I love her."

As Bud continued to speak, Paul called Lynagh who was now in the back hallway.

"Get to the sniper and get through the backdoor! If you don't make it we could lose Bud." Lynagh saw Healey leaning against the wall with his gun out and yelled to him.

Healey acknowledged and told him O'Malley was down the hallway to eliminate Talison.

"Anyone else here?" Lynagh asked.

"Haven't seen anyone," Healey relayed.

He tried to get up, but Lynagh held him down, saying, "Make sure no one else comes in behind us. Cops or crooks, we don't want an accidental shooting." Healey nodded as Lynagh moved further down the hallway in search of O'Malley and the other uniformed officers. He was slowed by the cartons, both full and empty, as well as the clothing on the racks. *So much for keeping fire escapes clear*, he thought.

"Really," Simpson replied to Bud, "you will give your life for Debbie?"

"I will, but can you keep a promise not to hurt her if I do, or are you a lying fish that's just jealous I have been with her."

"A lying what?" Simpson asked.

"Oh," Bud replied. "I meant a lying fuck."

Simpson was puzzled by the exchange.

"Jesus," Paul said to himself as he moved closer as Bud spoke. A uniformed sergeant walked up to Paul asking if there was anything more they could do. Paul told him quickly to be sure the mall was secure and to keep the uniformed officers present and visible to discourage snipers.

"Tell O'Brien to search for the sniper from one of the stores through the back hallways."

Lynagh was moving further down the hall between garment racks and boxes when he spotted a figure taking aim at O'Malley and the three officers. He raised his gun, took aim, and lost sight of the figure again. In another few seconds he saw him move closer to get a better shot, and Lynagh kneeled and fired two shots, injuring the man. It was the bartender from the City nightclub. O'Malley turned around and fired back as Lynagh started yelling. Talison fired from the other side, hitting one of the uniformed officers in the arm.

"Listen!" O'Malley yelled. "You won't leave here alive! Is it worth it? You won't get any bounty money anyway. Don't get in this any deeper than you already are. Cops have been killed. Your only chance of leaving here alive is me."

He looked back at one of the young uniformed officers who looked like a baby to him. "Get out of here before you bleed to death, and take that asshole over there with you," he said, pointing at the injured suspect. The officer started to resist until O'Malley spoke again. "It's OK; I have enough backup here," he said as he pointed to Officer Lynagh about twenty yards away. The young officer started heading the other way as O'Malley turned his attention back to Talison. "You're running out of time, and most likely bullets. No one else needs to die."

To his surprise Talison answered,

"All I wanted was to have a job in the nightclub business. Work nights, sleep late. Enjoy life, and then this guy enters our lives and offers us a chance to never have to worry about the bills again. I never thought so many people would be killed. Just the cops with the bounty on them. They convinced me you guys had to die. I just wanted to know what it was like to not have to worry about opening up a bill at the end of the month."

Lynagh had reached O'Malley while Talison kept talking and spoke. "He needs to surrender now or I'm going in. There will be a bloodbath in about two minutes in the hallway, and I need to get through that door."

O'Malley nodded and yelled to Talison, "We are out of time. We need to get through the door or both of us will be coming to you. You will not make it out of here alive."

A few seconds went by, and finally a rifle was laid on the floor as Lynagh ran up and pulled Talison away from the door leading to the mall hallway. O'Malley grabbed the rifle and Talison as Lynagh opened the door and saw Simpson standing behind the column as Rachelle was holding Deborah as they stood only a couple feet from him. He could see Bud walking up toward them as Paul was creeping closer and closer.

Lynagh raised his Glock and looked for a way to shoot, but the girls were too close. "Shit," he said aloud to himself. "Move a little, Rachelle."

Simpson was anxious to see Bud face-to-face. He let the detective come all the way up to them as Deborah grabbed him. "Oh, how sweet," Simpson said. "Why don't you tell the girls how many times you had Lynagh pick me up and bring me to the precinct during her kidnapping? Tell her how Cronin threatened me; tell her how you slapped my face, telling me never to come back. Tell her how you told me that you would fuck me up forever if I ever contacted her. You made me feel like a complete asshole. All because of killings I had nothing to do with. Tell her!"

Paul moved closer as Simpson was focused on Bud as another shot rang out. Paul grimaced as he focused on what was going on. Lynagh was turning his head sideways trying to get a clear shot. He was still speaking to himself for Rachelle to move.

Bud turned his head to Deborah and winked, saying, "It's true, he is a complete asshole."

Simpson was getting enraged that once again Bud was not serious with him. Yet Detective Bud Johnson was doing just that. He knew if he could distract Simpson even for a couple seconds someone might be able to take him out.

Bud looked at Rachelle. "Rachelle, go ahead, leave; he only wants me and Deborah, right?"

"No," Simpson answered. "I think I like this little group. We can all go to heaven together."

Bud pushed Deborah away from him, hoping to distract Simpson even more for someone to get a clear shot. "You're going to hell, you sick son of a bitch, and Deborah is too nice to tell you but I will tell you. I am better than you in bed. You needed the music to get it up and all I needed was Deborah. As for Kate Summers you forgot to take the strands of your hair from her hand when she was fighting for her life, you dumb shit. Your DNA is all over her death."

Simpson had enough. He leaned forward and started firing as Paul rushed in. Simpson fired three shots all at Bud as the detective went down. Lynagh fired, as did Paul, who unloaded his Glock at Simpson, hitting him in the head twice and the neck. Lynagh struck him dead center in the chest as blood splattered onto Deborah and Rachelle during the exchange. The sniper Simpson hired was none other than Ken Anker, who was behind a table of clothes in the Uptown Girl clothing store. He had Paul in his sights to finish him, but Officer O'Brien pulled the rifle upward as the shot went off and then struck him in the head with his firearm, knocking him out. O'Brien spoke in a whisper. "I should have blown your head off so you could go to hell."

Paul bent down to Bud and pulled his shirt open to find his vest, but he was unconscious. He checked his pulse and could not feel his heartbeat.

"Defibrillator!" Paul screamed. One of the officers in the hallway pulled one off the wall and rushed over as Paul attempted to use it on Bud.

Deborah was screaming as a crying Rachelle was trying to pull her away from Bud. Deborah was uncontrollable, and in the way, so Lynagh finally grabbed her and picked her up to get her away as they continued to work on Bud. Rachelle was on her hands and knees and her hair was covering half her face looking at Paul as he kept working on Bud.

As Lynagh carried a screaming Deborah Lance over his shoulder toward the exit he yelled for the medical personnel that they needed to get to the hallway. The medics arrived and they pushed Paul away to work on Bud. The two EMS men quickly used the paddles to defibrillate Bud to break the rhythm of his heart. Finally, on the third try his heart was beating normally. Paul fell to the side with tears in his eyes as he looked at Rachelle still on all fours. He was exhausted as he stared into the blood on the face of his lover as she kept turning her head from Bud to him. Finally she fell on her back near Paul as he held her. He held on to her as her cries echoed through the hallway. His heart ached like he never felt before.

O'Malley walked Talison out to the mall parking lot to hand him over to uniformed cops who were anxious to get their hands on someone who was involved in the Music Club Murders as well as responsible for killing cops. O'Malley took his cuffs off Talison and began to walk back into the mall when a single shot rang out and struck Talison in the head. O'Malley ducked down behind a car as he worked his way back to where Talison was shot. O'Malley reached the vehicle and saw blood coming from Talison's head. "Who fired the shot?" he yelled. The uniformed sergeant came up to O'Malley and told him it was no cop, that it was a sniper shot, and one hell of a shot at that.

O'Malley yelled, "We need to find out where it came from. I've got to get back into the mall!"

Lynagh finally put Deborah down outside the back of an ambulance. "Listen to me," he spoke firmly. "You've got to get yourself together. Bud is going to need you. You're going to the hospital, and you will be there for him, but you have to calm yourself down." Deborah was still crying, but she was attempting to compose herself. Lynagh spoke again. "One of the officers is going to take you to Stony Brook Hospital. You are going to clean yourself up and be there for him. OK?"

She was still shaking and nodded her head and spoke. "Is he dead?" she asked as more tears came out.

"Listen!" He grabbed her arms. "He had a vest on, but they were close range. There is always a chance with a vest, but he doesn't have any possibility without you there supporting him. He is not dead. Listen to me," he repeated himself. "You need to hold it together." He loosened his grip on her.

"OK," she said. He motioned for the medics to take her. The driver got out and asked if there were any more injured before taking her to the hospital.

Lynagh turned around and yelled, "There are another ten fucking ambulances here. Get her there and have her looked at before I shoot you myself!"

The driver got back in the car and took off. Inside the ambulance, Deborah realized she no longer had her phone and asked the medic to borrow his. She dialed the number and said, "I need you, Dad." She told him what happened between her cries, and he said he was on his way.

She pushed the buttons on the phone again as the voice on the other end picked up.

"Hi," Deborah said, "you made me promise to call you if anything happened to Bud. Well, something did. He saved my life by sacrificing himself for me. I'm so scared I'm going to lose him."

She began to cry again as the voice on the other end said,

"I will see you soon, and remember what I said almost two years ago. God works in mysterious ways." The call ended.

As Deborah sat in the back of the ambulance, she never felt so alone. Deborah remembered the night Lindsey told her about God working in mysterious ways and mentioned it to Bud the night she gave him the CD after the Face of Fear investigation.

The medics got a steady heartbeat from Bud as they feverishly worked on him by putting an endotracheal tube, or ET as doctors referred to it, in him to pump air into his lungs. One of them came over to Rachelle and examined her as she lay on the floor of the mall. Paul sat up to look at her as she just stared at him without saying a word. A third medic attempted to look at Paul, but he pushed him off, telling him to help with Bud. Paul lay back down on the floor, unable to get up.

The medic yelled back, "He's got enough help. Stay still, you've been shot."

Rachelle turned her head to Paul as he looked at her through his glassy eyes.

"No," she said as she touched his face. "No, not now," she said again as she cried. Paul's eyes stayed on Rachelle as he drifted off and lost consciousness. Paul had been shot by two of the sniper's bullets in the mall. One hit him in the back, which the vest saved him from serious injury. The second one hit him just above the waist on the left side, just missing the vest. He kept control in the mall by trying to deal with the pain. He needed to know Rachelle was going to be all right. The medics got Bud and Paul on stretchers as Lynagh was back in the mall to see what else was happening. Rachelle was alongside Paul's stretcher as they loaded him into the back of the ambulance. She took Paul's smartphone from his pocket and called his father. Lynagh met up with O'Malley and informed him he was now the ranking officer for Priority 1.

O'Malley looked at him and said, "Maybe they should call it Priority 2 since you and I are the only ones left that can do anything. Let's get back to Caulfield."

When they reached the vehicle they saw Caulfield cut up and butchered. Lynagh spotted the mask and picked it up.

"What is this about?" O'Malley asked.

Lynagh looked around the parking lot as he spoke. "We have a vigilante killer again, and unless Madison Robinson is Houdini, it's not her."

"Come on," O'Malley said. "Let's make sure the mall is clear and you can fill me in on the blanks before we go to the hospital."

When they got back to the mall, O'Brien was still in the Uptown Girl store with an unconscious Ken Anker. O'Malley ordered the medics to take him out through an exit other than where the vigilante shots had been fired.

As they loaded him up in the ambulance, Lynagh grabbed one of the drivers and spoke, "Make sure he is not on the same floor as our fellow cops."

"Sir," the driver said, "I have nothing to do with where he is put."

Lynagh repeated himself with a much stronger tone.

"Make sure, he is on a different floor."

The driver put two and two together as he shook his head and got behind the wheel as O'Brien jumped in the back.

Uniformed Officer Sergeant Church and his officers continued to search the parking lot and the small amount of cars that were still there. It was another ten minutes before they found a Ghost Face mask on the ground. The Sergeant called O'Malley who informed Lynagh.

"Looks like you were right. The spot where it looks like the shot that may have been fired from left another mask as a calling card. That's one hell of a shot."

Lynagh shook his head in agreement as they walked the mall. O'Malley called over three uniformed officers and told them the mall was to be sealed off until further notice. He then notified the Fourth Precinct commander to get three detectives to the mall to investigate any possible information and evidence, including video in what O'Malley feared would be nationwide news. Both Lynagh and O'Malley waited another 35 minutes till detectives arrived as well as the crime unit to search for evidence that would help in the investigation. It was another thirty minutes of filling the detectives in before they could get to the hospital. They reached Stony Brook Hospital which now had Officers Chapman, Healey, Detective Ellyn Baker, as well as Powers and Johnson. O'Malley got into the elevator with Lynagh as he spoke.

"The place is just filling up with cops." They reached the eighteenth floor where they were met by other uniformed officers that asked for ID. They no longer cared that Lynagh had a uniform on or that O'Malley was a thirty year veteran of the force. They were told that Paul was in surgery and it was determined that he was hit in the Iliac Pelvic bone which stopped the bullet. He was bleeding in the pelvic cavity but the doctors felt he would be stabilized in a short time. Although he was in excellent physical condition, Paul would not be walking for at least two to four weeks. Bud had slipped into a coma while Healey was satisfactory after the bullet was extracted from his leg. O'Malley and Lynagh went to Bud's room as doctors would not allow anyone else in the room. There were two uniformed officers by the door on the orders of the DA's office. Deborah was in the hallway being consoled by her father, and Lynagh could hear her telling him what happened in the mall.

"We need to get home, honey," he said.

She stood up, telling him she couldn't leave Bud or Rachelle while Paul was in surgery.

"OK, OK, honey, we will stay," her father relented.

Michael Corbin and Billy McAdams were in the club waiting for Linda Tangretti to tell them what was next. It appeared that Billy the bartender had been promoted a couple times since Detective Ellyn Baker had been beaten up. Tangretti had gotten a call from Caulfield before he was killed that it was OK to take the rest of the cash and that no one would be at the club for the next twenty-four hours. He also told her about the mall and that Franks, Lynagh, Healy, Powers, and Johnson were most likely dead, as well as Simpson. Linda got to the club at 9:45 pm and went to Brian Branca's office. She entered his bathroom, flushed the toilet, and held the knob down for ten seconds until the wall, where the sink and washbasin were, opened up. It was a hallway. She walked down the stairs that led her to another room, which opened up to an 1,800-square-foot hideaway apartment. Linda went to the bar and poured herself a drink and sat across from Michael Corbin and Billy the Bartender, as she called him.

"They're all dead except for Detective O'Malley and Officer Lynagh. We should take the money and leave. Patty has been avenged and Simpson got what he wanted."

Corbin leaned over toward Linda and stopped her from taking a sip of her drink.

"If Simpson is dead, how do we get the money?"

Linda put her glass down and spoke. "The only way this would happen is if Simpson put the money in an account controlled by a bank trustee. Once their deaths are announced in *Newsday* the money is transferred to the individual accounts." Linda held on to her drink then threw it in Corbin's face. "Don't ever stop me from taking a sip of my drink again."

Corbin moved back on the sofa without wiping his face and looked over at Billy. He spoke again to Linda. "As of now, you claim there are only two left. How do you know for sure? Did you see the bodies?"

Linda was getting upset with Corbin as she replied, "Look, you small, little dickhead. Cops are out of the way and you seem to forget we lost a few of our own along the way. Those left in the hospital won't make it out with our contact from within."

"Who is our contact from within?" Billy asked.

"Let's just say," Linda added, "he has a badge."

Corbin stood up. "If it's one of the two cops left uninjured then it might look a little obvious, don't you think?"

"You don't need to know who it is right now," Linda replied. "You just tell Branca when it is over, I want half of everything from this building."

Corbin was surprised by her remark. "You know that since Sysco ratted us all out that Branca will never see a dime from the club or this building."

"You're right," Linda answered. "He's a smart man; that's why this building and club are in his sister-in-law's name. She's never even been to this club, living in South Carolina and all."

Corbin shook his head as he stood up again. "Who is telling you all this? Who is your source?"

"Like I said," Linda answered, "he is a smart guy, but I'm smarter." She looked at Billy. "Any questions?"

"No," the bartender replied. "Except, where is Caulfield? Is he your source?"

"No," Linda replied, "he was an asset, but he is either dead or long gone. I have not heard from him since we hooked up."

"Hooked up?" Corbin said.

"Yes," Linda answered, "screwed, fucked, had sex."

"Oh, nice of you to mix business with pleasure," he replied.

"Any more questions?" Linda asked.

"Just one," a voice from the backdoor said as Cronin stepped forward with his Glock out, pointed at Linda. "Who is the source with the badge that is helping you on this?" Linda held it together and did not have a surprised look on her face while Corbin and Billy moved to the end of the sofa.

"You," Linda answered, "just don't want to die, do you?"

"Sorry to spoil things for you," Cronin answered.

"How did you find us?" Corbin asked.

"I have my own sources," Cronin answered. "It's called technology. I really haven't been a fan, but it's growing on me. There's a cop called Lynagh who placed hidden cameras in here when you guys almost killed Baker." He held his Glock by his side and looked at Linda. "Who is the source?" It was no longer a question, even though he phrased it like one.

"He is right behind you," Linda answered, "and he will shoot you in the back of the head if you don't drop your weapon now."

"I'm already dead, remember?" Cronin replied. He moved his gun to Linda's head. "I will kill you unless whoever is behind me is an incredible shot." Cronin's mind was racing as he started to visualize what cops were left who had been taken in by all this. The door shut and footsteps could be heard going up the stairs.

"Seems like your man had second thoughts," Cronin said to Linda Tangretti. The detective was so focused on her that Billy tried to go for his gun but Cronin shoved Linda to the sofa and fired a shot, which hit him in the leg. He moved his gun back toward Linda's ear as he looked at Corbin. "Have enough people died or been injured for you?" He continued to speak. "Because if not, I can oblige and shoot you as well."

Corbin put his hands up. "No, there has been enough killing." Cronin turned his attention back to Linda. "Your cousin started this shit by kidnapping her best friend eighteen months ago, but you couldn't let it go. Justice was served with Madison Robinson serving the next five to seven years in prison. So don't tell me you wanted revenge. You, like your cousin, wanted the money. Simpson wanted vengeance against me and the others. Not you; it's the money you had to have, and only Simpson could give it to you. Now," he said as he touched her head with his gun, "who is the source giving you all this information and giving orders?"

Linda looked at Cronin and spoke. "I was supposed to meet him here tonight for the first time. Simpson and Branca were the only ones that met him and know who he is. Like you, he wants everyone to think he has nothing to do with this case."

Cronin's expression on his face changed with those words. He had Linda sit on the couch as he took out his phone and called Gina. She picked up the phone and knew who it was.

"Yes, sir."

"Gina, where are Lynagh and O'Malley?"

"Both at Stony Brook Hospital waiting for Paul to get out of surgery," she replied.

"Have Lynagh get over to the nightclub here, and give him my new number so he can reach me."

"Sir?" Gina said.

"It's OK," Cronin said. "He's one of us; I trust him. Have

three officers each stay with Rachelle Robinson and Deborah Lance at the hospital. No one gets in or out of the eighteenth floor without my approval. Get Officer Wright over to the Wilkerson house immediately. Whoever the source is knows I'm alive, and I want to be sure the bounties are not reinstated. Simpson is dead, but I don't want to take any chances."

"Right away, sir," Gina answered as she hung up.

Both ADA Ashley and Cronin decided it was best to tell Gina that he was still alive after a couple days. She was so distraught that work was not getting done, and no support for Paul was making his job difficult. Cronin knew he would be questioned and second-guessed again, but he knew the only way to save the three girls was to be "killed." It also allowed him to roam freely while the case was being handled by Paul and Bud. Now all that was on his mind was who the source was. The leak, or the one responsible for this madness. Cronin had thought Ashley or O'Malley was possible, but it was Linda's words that struck a chord with him: "Like you, he wants everyone to think he has nothing to do with this case."

Lawrence Stone kept saying to himself over and over, "Cronin is alive, Cronin is alive," as he ran up the stairs and opened the wall to Brian Branca's bathroom. He ran like a deer through his office, ran through the main dance hallway leading up to the main room of the club, reached the door, and turned a fast right toward his car, and as he put his hand on his door he was grabbed from behind and thrown to the ground.

"What's your hurry?" the masked figure asked.

Stone got up and tried to run, but the Ghost Face killer caught him again and threw him to the ground. "What's the hurry?"

Stone was already half in shock between Cronin being alive and now this. "I need to get out of here!" Stone yelled.

The man who was the DJ at Skyline, known as Ace of Clubs was now too frightened to calm down.

"One last time," the masked figure said, "what are you

running from?"

"He's alive," Stone said. "Cronin is alive; I have to get to my people."

The Ghost Face hesitated and looked over to the club, then back at Stone. "You're not telling anyone, sorry." The figure took out a gun and hit him over the head with it. He was unconscious as Ghost Face put him in the car and locked the doors and took the keys with him. He ran off, taking off the mask and the black top. The mystery person walked three blocks to a vehicle, handed cash over to a woman, and drove off. Minutes later, a teenage boy was spotted with friends, and the mysterious person called him to come over. He walked up to the vehicle and he was offered five $20 bills to speak in a recorder, disguising his voice. He was handed the note to read into the recorder.

He began to speak.

"ADA Ashley, you can pick up Lawrence Stone in his vehicle in the parking lot. It's a piss-yellow Kia. I suggest you get to him within the hour; he knows your secret about Cronin and was ready to contact his boss. He is only alive because I have no proof he is responsible for the bounties." The boy disguised his voice like a high-pitched Minnie Mouse. He was handed the money for his time and voice. The caller then dialed ADA Ashley's number, which went to voice mail. The button on the recorder was pushed as the message played. When it was over the disposable phone was smashed and thrown in a dumpster near a deli.

It was a matter of minutes before ADA Ashley picked up his voice message, and he immediately called Cronin's temporary cell phone.

"Yes," Cronin spoke as he picked up the call.

"You may have a perp in the parking lot inside a yellow Kia. He is unconscious according to the voice mail I received. Be careful."

"I can't leave until Lynagh gets here," Cronin answered. "I figure another twenty minutes."

Ashley spoke quickly. "Let me get there with an officer. You stay there. We can't risk letting out you are alive just yet."

ADA John Ashley got to the little Kia with two uniformed officers who answered the call. He stood by his car as the officers, with their guns drawn, approached the car. They saw Lawrence Stone unconscious with his legs on the seat and the torso of his body down toward the floor of the car. They inspected the rest of the car top and bottom to be sure there was not a bomb attached to the vehicle. When they were satisfied, they opened the door to verify that Stone was still alive. He was out cold as the officers laid him out on the ground and checked the rest of the inside of the car. Lying on the front seat of the car was the now-famous calling card: the Ghost Face mask with the blood splatter on it. The officer picked it up to show Ashley, who was about twenty yards away. The ADA called Cronin in the club to tell him. Cronin was always good at puzzles, but even he was having a difficult time understanding the reason for the symbolic gesture. As the officer walked over to Ashley, a gunshot rang out. Cronin heard it over the phone and started yelling,

"John! What's happening?"

"We are under gunfire, and behind vehicles for cover."

"I'm on my way," Cronin yelled. He hung up and ran to Corbin and the injured Billy to handcuff them together, then looked at them. "If you are gone when I get back I will make sure you won't get out of this alive." He looked over at Linda. "You, I don't trust at all, so you are coming with me." He grabbed her as she struggled to get away. "Don't make me shoot you," Cronin said as he practically dragged her through the mystery stairwell, then through the bathroom and through Branca's office and the hallway. Linda fell, and Cronin got restless and dragged her by her collar to keep moving. Linda started screaming as her clothes moved up on her and the floor was giving her body burns. Cronin wouldn't stop as he could now hear more shots being fired. He had to make a choice to save Ashley and take a chance to let Linda get away or take the chance that Lynagh was close enough to hear the shots and get to the ADA while he held on to Linda. He dragged her another five feet and decided he couldn't take a chance on losing another life. He grabbed Linda, picked her up, and threw her against the wall, where she fell onto a sofa and then to the floor. The detective lieutenant ran to the car where Ashley was with no gun and started firing back.

"Talk to me, Officers!" he yelled. "Is everyone OK?"

The other officer behind the yellow Kia acknowledged they were OK but Lawrence Stone had been hit. Another shot was fired as Cronin looked at Ashley sitting against the car. Then shots were fired at the car as the officers sat still waiting for backup. The windows of the car shattered as the shots continued.

"It's not fun having a $75,000 bounty on you, is it?"

"Hey," Ashley said, trying to make the best of it, "don't short-change me, I'm worth $100,000." Cronin smiled as he reloaded his weapon.

"You're starting to sound like Bud."

Ashley's face turned serious. "He might not make it, Kevin. He took three dead center. His heart stopped from the impact. There is only so much a vest can do."

Cronin stared at Ashley as he finished reloading.

"If anyone can make it through something like that, it's him." As another shot hit the car Lynagh drove up and got behind his car, ready to fire. It was apparent the sniper no longer wanted to be part of the scenario, and the firing of rounds stopped. Cronin yelled to Lynagh to come with him as two other Suffolk Police cars pulled into the lot. Cronin was waiting for Lynagh to say something about the fake death, but he said nothing as they entered the club to find Linda gone.

Cronin shook his head as he spoke. "Ten minutes and she is gone. I thought she was in too bad of shape to get away."

Cronin and Lynagh went back downstairs through the mystery stairwell to find Corbin alongside the bartender. "Billy's leg wound is mine. Get Corbin down to the precinct and this asshole to the hospital."

Cronin's cell buzzed, and it was Ashley telling him Stone was dead. The sniper apparently only wanted to kill Stone.

"Damn," Cronin added as he hung up. "We need to go back to Sysco. There is more to this than getting rid of us for revenge."

He looked at Lynagh. "Call O'Malley and tell him to meet you at Priority 1 with Ashley. I want him to know I'm alive for the first time in person. Make sure security is in place at the hospital and on the girls. Including the Wilkerson girl. Tell Wright not to leave the scene or the girl without my authorization. Once it gets out I'm alive there may be a bounty placed on them, but I have a feeling now that Simpson is dead that won't be the case. The bounties may have been a diversion from the 'boss.'" Lynagh called in the directives from Cronin. He then looked at him with the expression on his face that he deserved an explanation.

Cronin read his mind and said, "In due time, Officer, in due time. Call Detective Stedman from K-9. Tell him we need the dogs to do a run-through of the entire premises."

Lynagh made the call, and as soon as the other uniformed officers arrived they left to meet O'Malley back at the precinct. When he walked into the precinct the eyes and actions stopped. It reminded Cronin of the old commercial when John Hancock speaks . . . everyone listens. There was such an uncomfortable feeling that Cronin could not wait to get to the Priority 1 Task Force area. When he walked through the first area of desks, he stopped and looked at the name plaques of Chapman, Dugan, Franks, Wyatt, Caulfield, Baker, Lynagh, Powers, and Johnson. He looked over at Gina, who smiled when she saw him but held herself back from giving him a hug.

"Hi, Gina," Cronin said. "Please get Caulfield's desk checked out, top to bottom, and then get it out of here. I don't want it here with the others."

"Yes, sir," she answered. The smile returned to her face as she walked away. She felt like there was a warm security blanket being put on her. She was impressed with the way Paul Powers handled the investigation, but after ten years of working with Detective Lieutenant Cronin, she knew this was going to be over very soon. One way or the other. Lynagh walked into the conference room to find O'Malley and Ashley waiting for him. He sat down as O'Malley looked at the officer.

"Do you want to tell me what this is about?"

"Sir," Lynagh spoke. "Quite frankly I don't even know how to explain it. You will know in a couple minutes, though, and I can't wait to hear it myself."

O'Malley looked at Ashley, who was checking his watch. Cronin walked in as O'Malley dropped his jaw and stood up.

"Please sit down," Cronin spoke.

O'Malley ignored the request as he answered, "What the fuck is going on here?"

"Sit down," Cronin said. This time it was not a request. O'Malley sat down with an angry look on his face as he waited for the detective lieutenant to speak. Cronin informed Lynagh and O'Malley of the undercover reporter that had been in the same section as O'Connor for the past fifteen months. How he befriended the former FBI killer, gained his trust, and had been able to transfer information. Ashley interrupted Cronin to lend support that the move did save lives. An example was that the bounties of Rachelle, Deborah, and Lindsey Wilkerson were all canceled upon his death.

"Why?" O'Malley shot back.

"This is about revenge on us," Lynagh replied.

"No," O'Malley answered. "Why would they give a shit about the bounties on the girls just because Cronin is dead?"

"Because," Cronin said as he looked at Ashley, "Robert Simpson claimed Bud and I ruined his life by forcing him to play a part in a game of cat and mouse."

"And?" O'Malley asked. "Did you?"

"Yes," Cronin said. "I needed him to confuse the killers and play a part in a game to draw the others out."

"So," O'Malley answered, "you risked more lives by making him a participant during the so-called famous Face of Fear investigation."

Ashley spoke up again. "I was with him, Detective. It would have never closed if we didn't play it out. Besides, Cronin didn't orchestrate Simpson fucking around on Deborah Lance or embezzling millions of dollars from William Lance."

"OK," O'Malley answered. "What about now? I suppose you didn't think this asshole would come back and put money on Priority 1's heads. You saved the girls lives, but what about the task force? Shit." He took out a bag of pumpkin seeds and started to pop them in his mouth before he spoke again. "What now? I hate to second-guess at this point, but there is only me and Lynagh left, so I'm not so sure what was gained other than the girls being saved."

Cronin was silent for a few seconds and then spoke. "First of all, no matter what you think, saving the girls is our number one concern. It will be our top concern until the ramifications of the Face of Fear case are finally over. As for the Priority 1 Task Force being down to the three of us, I didn't count on one of the cops being involved and a cop killer. I don't understand how he fooled you."

"What!" O'Malley replied. "Wait, are you accusing me of something?" He stood up as Lynagh pulled his Glock and pointed it at O'Malley. The elder detective stared at Cronin, Ashley, and the officer who now had O'Malley in his sights.

"Just what in the living hell is going on here, gentlemen?" O'Malley said.

Cronin stood up and spoke while ADA Ashley continued to sit. "You see, Detective O'Malley, you have a case from the City nightclub and the Pajama Club. Young girls getting their necks broken. They have notes put on them from Simpson, who happens to get turned on by music he loves to have sex to. Bounties are put on our heads, and for good measure your detective Hansen gets blown to pieces. My car is set to explode, two cops from the East End get arrested, and now Wyatt is missing. I don't understand why everyone on your team except for you is missing, dead, or responsible for some of the killings."

O'Malley stood there as Lynagh continued to hold his position. Cronin continued.

"This brings me to Caulfield. He worked for you for over five years. You had no idea he would go rogue?" Cronin walked over to O'Malley and spoke again. "Convince me you are not part of the killings. Convince me you want this resolved as much as we do." O'Malley looked over at Lynagh still holding his 9mm on him as Ashley stared at him in silence.

He turned his head back to Cronin and spoke. "You son of a bitch. We have one of my detectives who gave his life, with another one missing, plus two of your officers dead while other detectives are fighting for their lives, and you have a gun on me because I happen to be here with no injuries? I was told to give this case to Priority 1. Why? Because no matter what you want to call it, someone thought you treated them unfairly. Yes, Caulfield was dirty and a killer. Someone got to him. Who? I'm not sure yet, but I will say I'm not a fan of what is going on here. You are going to have to do better than this to rattle me. I've been a cop for thirty years and a detective for twenty years. You need my help to close it out unless you think you and Lynagh can do it by yourselves."

At that moment the intercom buzzed in, and it was Gina's voice.

"Sir?"

"Yes, Gina?" Cronin bellowed.

"I'm sorry," she replied, "but I thought you should know Detective Wyatt has been found. He's badly injured but alive. They have taken him to the trauma center."

"Goddamn it!" O'Malley yelled as he sat down and covered his face with his hands. Cronin looked over at Lynagh and nodded as Lynagh holstered his weapon. Cronin sat down next to O'Malley.

"Are you going to help us or are you going to retire?" O'Malley removed his hands from his face, and a line of a tear was across his face.

"You want to close the case, let's close it, but first I want to know who all the players were in the Face of Fear case."

Cronin nodded his head and looked at Officer Lynagh, saying, "Get down to the club; I want you there when the K-9 gets there. Report back as soon as you can."

Cronin looked back at O'Malley and spoke. "OK, you'll see the reports, but do me a favor. Next time you guys want to get tough in a garage with these thugs, don't leave your pumpkin seed shells behind."

O'Malley shook his head, knowing he had made a mistake. His thoughts were consumed by calling himself an idiot for leaving a clue to his presence.

Officer Janet Gates was sitting near the door about thirty feet from Madison when she got a call from Officer John Bay. "Janet," he said, "there has been a shooting at the Suffolk County Mall. Officers and detectives are down, including Madison's friends Powers and Johnson. Her sister was there; they saved her life."

Janet looked down the hall as her fingers started to tremble with nervousness. Bay gave her the details of who was shot and in the hospital.

"I have to tell her," Gates answered.

"Is she still having nightmares, Janet?"

"Yes. She is seeing a therapist, and it seems to be helping a bit, but she's not back to normal."

"Let's face it," he answered, "she will never be normal again."

"OK, thanks," she replied, as she pushed the *end* button. As she walked down the hall to speak to Madison, she got a text from John Bay that read, *Don't say anything to Madison, her attorney Al Simmons is on the way to speak to her. You hung up on me before I could finish.*

By the time she finished reading the text she was already standing in front of the jail cell with Madison reading a book that Rachelle had given to her. She put the book down and smiled at Janet until she read the details of her face.

"What is it, Janet?" She stood up with worry. "Is my sister all right?"

"Madison," the officer spoke, "I was asked not to tell you until your attorney got here."

"Please!" Madison yelled. "Please!"

"Your sister was at the mall with Deborah and they were threatened by Robert Simpson and others when Detective Powers and Johnson shot and killed him and others."

"Then why the look on your face. I thought something life-threatening happened to her."

Gates looked at Madison as she touched her hand on the bars. "Officer Healey was injured. Powers was shot in the lower back above the waist. It missed his vest. Johnson was shot three times in the chest. The vest helped, but the impact stopped his heart. He's in a coma. They're not sure if he's going to make it."

Madison reached for Officer Gates through the bars and said, "You have to let me make a phone call. Please?"

Officer Gates nodded. "I know, give me your sister's number."

Rachelle picked up on the third ring, and Madison could tell her sister had been shedding tears.

"Where are you right now?" Madison asked.

"Maddie," Rachelle said, "I'm here at Stony Brook Hospital. I have failed." The call ended with Madison yelling Rachelle's name over and over.

Lynagh got to the club and called Cronin to tell him the dogs were just arriving. He met the K-9 handlers and let three dogs run through the club. He slowly walked around the deserted club as he waited to see if the dogs would find anything. Currently the Suffolk K-9 unit had German shepherds, Belgian Malinois, and Labrador retrievers. It was only twenty minutes before the dogs arrived for their search of the club. Currently there were about twenty-two K-9 dogs, mostly German shepherds because of their "born to protect" attitude and extreme loyalty to their owners and handlers.

As the K-9 dogs continued to run through the building, Detective Lieutenant Cronin was finishing up with the players involved in the case that had gone national eighteen months prior.

The Music Club Murders were now in the local papers, but they did not have the exposure of the first case, with exceptions of the major city papers. Cronin believed that omitting the link to the Face of Fear investigation and Ghost Face calling card was a part of it, and he wanted to keep it that way. Now that it would be known he was alive, he expected escalation in everything involved, including the media.

"Sounds like you guys had fun," O'Malley said as he popped a few pumpkin seeds into his mouth. The experienced detective took extensive notes of all the people involved during Cronin's review of the case. O'Malley asked for Powers and Johnson's reports on the case to further review Cronin's statement. He even asked for the articles that Rachelle wrote, including her tweets during the course of the case. Detective Cronin had Gina give the detective everything he requested.

"I'm going to the hospital, then over to the club to meet with Lynagh," Cronin said. "You study the reports with your fresh set of eyes, and let's meet in the morning."

O'Malley nodded, as his head was buried in papers.

When Cronin and Ashley got into the hallway the ADA spoke.

"I'm guessing you don't think he is involved since you are telling him everything, including showing the reports."

"No," Cronin replied. "If he was involved he would not have asked for everything and been sitting there for almost two hours listening to the prior case. His file is perfect, and work ethic from his personnel files and case reports are outstanding."

"When did you get to those?" Ashley asked.

"It's amazing the amount of time you have when you are dead," Cronin replied as they walked to his office.

"Good point," the ADA answered.

Gina walked in with a smile, and Ashley could tell she wanted some private time with her boss that she had not seen for over a week.

"I'm going to question Sysco in the morning; let me know if you want to be there," Ashley said.

"Will do," Cronin said. "I'm going to the hospital."

"OK," Ashley replied, "give them my best. I will check in on them in the morning. You can count on the chief and commissioner to get in touch with you also, now that you have come out."

Cronin looked up at Ashley. "Was that a joke coming from you?"

"I thought it sounded humorous," the ADA remarked as he waved good night.

Cronin looked at Gina. "We can talk, but make sure there is an officer near Ashley until this is over. Check on Officer Wright at the Wilkerson house. The girl will need an escort as well if she leaves the house. If Wright needs relief, get her one. Check on O'Brien and Myers."

"They are on different shifts, sir," she answered.

"Not anymore," he replied. "They're on my shift now; get them up and over there."

"Yes, sir," Gina said as she turned around and smiled. She thought, *He is back.*

October 10

William Lance arrived at Stony Brook Hospital at 9:00 am. He took the elevator to the eighteenth floor and walked to Room 233. Bud Johnson was connected to an IV with standard saline solution, a feeding tube through his nose to his stomach, and a Foley catheter to monitor his urine output.

Lance's daughter Deborah was sitting in a chair near his bed with her head leaning against the wall. He stroked her hair as she raised her hand to take his.

"I can't lose him, Dad."

He tightened the squeeze on her hand and replied,

"I know, honey. He is strong." He kissed the top of her head and told her he was going to try and find out more information.

Deborah's father went to the nurses' station and asked to speak to the doctor. He was told it would be at least thirty minutes, so he walked to Room 242 to visit Paul Powers's room. He found the detective resting comfortably while Rachelle was sitting in a chair next to his bed holding his hand.

"How is he, Rachelle?"

She turned her head and smiled when she saw Deborah's father. "He is going to be fine," she answered. "He was lucky. The bullet went straight through without hitting any organs. It was probably the reason he was able to hold on until it was over. He was shot but wouldn't go down."

William Lance put his hand on her shoulder. "It's amazing what people do for someone they love." She looked up at him and smiled, her expression saying *Thank you*. Lance spoke again. "Have you been home yet?"

Rachelle shook her head. "No, I'm waiting for his father to get here. Then I will freshen up a bit before coming back. He should be here within the hour. He flew up from Florida early this morning. He couldn't get a flight last night."

Rachelle spoke again. "Would you mind staying with him for a few minutes while I see Deborah and Bud?"

"No worries," he answered. "Go ahead."

Rachelle looked at Paul sleeping, leaned over, and kissed the side of his face. She didn't stand up right away. She stayed leaning over him and put her hand on the side of his face for a few seconds before leaving the room. It took her four minutes to reach the intensive care unit, where she found Deborah asleep near Bud's bed. Rachelle stroked her hair as she opened her eyes to see her best friend. She grabbed her hand and held it tightly before she spoke.

"Am I going to lose him?" Deborah asked.

Before Rachelle could answer her, a voice from the door spoke.

"No, Deborah, you are not going to lose him." Both Rachelle and Deborah looked over to see Lindsey Wilkerson. She was now a beautiful fourteen-year-old girl who had grown three inches in the past year. Deborah wanted to rush and grab the girl, who had been a major part of the Face of Fear investigation but decided to speak instead.

"How do you know, Lindsey?"

The young girl walked over to Deborah and Rachelle and replied, "My prayers are usually answered, and I will be here until they are."

She smiled as she fell into a three-way hug with them. "Thank you for calling me, Deborah." Both the women squeezed the teenager tighter as Deborah looked out the window and saw Officer Wright and Lindsey's mother, Sharyn Wilkerson, with her hand on the glass as if to show support.

Deborah silently mouthed the words "Thank you" to her as Sharyn nodded. The mother of Lindsey Wilkerson kept her daughter out of the spotlight and felt strongly she needed to have a normal life. Part of having a normal life was requesting that Bud Johnson and Justin Healey respect her wishes to let Lindsey grow up before reentering her life. Yet when Healey was shot in the leg, and now with Bud at death's door, there was no stopping Lindsey from coming to the hospital. Somehow, the mother was coming to grips that Lindsey was not going to have a normal life. As a mom, she was frightened for her child, but she knew somehow Lindsey would eventually be with whom she was hugging in the hospital room.

The young girl broke away from Deborah and Rachelle, walked over to Bud, put her hand on his arm, and began to pray.

"Dear Lord, I pray for our loved one Bud Johnson, to watch over him, to protect him, and to heal him. We understand that life in the physical world is not forever, but I ask you Dear Father to keep him with Deborah, Rachelle, and me. I promise to watch over him in this world while he is here. I promise to continue to live and to make you proud while I am here. Please keep this man in our world to allow me to help him and have him protect me as well. I have always kept my promises to you, and now I need to remind you of a promise from you, Dear Father, God I thank you, it is written in Jeremiah 29:11. 'For I know the plans I have for you, they are plans for good and not for disaster, to give you a future and a hope.' I ask you, Dear Lord, to give me the promise to save Bud Johnson and allow him to fulfill his destiny. Only you and I know what that is, and I ask this in Jesus's name. Amen."

Lindsey looked at Bud unconscious in the bed and touched his hand as she looked over at Deborah and Rachelle, who were in silence as they watched Lindsey pray over him.

She walked over to the door and looked back at them.

"Stay with him, Deborah. He will return to us. I have information from the highest authority." She winked at them as she began to leave to visit Officer Healey.

"Lindsey," Deborah spoke, "why did Bud say those things to Robert? It was almost as if he wanted to get shot."

The fourteen-year-old who was already strikingly beautiful replied, "'Greater love has no man than this that a man lay down his life for his friends.'" Deborah recognized it was from John 15:13. Lindsey walked out of the room as she glanced back at Bud with a smile before visiting Officer Justin Healey.

Lindsey Wilkerson walked to the elevator with Officer Carol Wright and her mother as she passed the rooms filled with traumatic injuries. She grabbed her mother's hand as she could see doctors standing over a young boy, with his mother by his side. As she got closer to the elevator there was another room where she saw a man sitting in a chair. As his head touched the metal railing of his wife's bed, Sharyn Wilkerson looked at her daughter, who had a trail of tears on her face.

"Mom," the teenager said, "I wish I could help them all, but I can't."

"Yes, you can," her mother replied. "You keep them in your thoughts and in your prayers."

"That's easy, Mom, and yet so difficult," Lindsey replied.

Sharyn knew it was true. Lindsey's photographic memory would never let her forget what she saw at the hospital.

As soon as Lindsey walked in, Justin Healey lit up like a Christmas tree. The young girl went to his bedside and gave the man who was her protector during the Face of Fear a long hug before speaking.

"You got yourself shot again, Officer Healey."

He nodded with a smile. "Only in the back of the leg this time. It's so great to see you. Let me look at you."

Lindsey stood up by the side of his bed as the officer looked at her. She was now 5'5" with dirty blond hair. Her face was starting to look like a young woman's instead of a young girl's. She was slim and carried a pocketbook over her shoulder and an iPhone in her hand. A typical teenager who happened to remember everything she experienced and saw.

"So," Healey said, "what were you doing four days ago at 4:00 pm."

Lindsey laughed it off and just said,

"Boring."

The officer could see that as Lindsey was getting older, she was modest about her special gifts. It was only eighteen months before that she had fun showing them off. Now the maturity in her was bittersweet to him.

Lindsey interrupted his thoughts as she spoke.

"Thank you for continuing to protect me. I know you and the others have been close to the house. I feel like there is so much I know, hear, see, and remember, but my Mom won't let me read the papers or have certain apps on my phone."

Justin Healey grabbed her hand. "You never have to thank me, Lindsey. We are doing our jobs. We just want to be sure you are

OK until we believe it is finally over."

Lindsey put her head on his chest and the officer could see by Sharyn Wilkerson's eyes that she wanted to speak to him in private. He pushed the nurse's button, and it took another five minutes before someone came to his room. When Nurse Lorin came, the officer asked her to escort Lindsey to visit Chapman, Baker, and Powers so he could speak with Lindsey's mom.

"OK," Lindsey replied, "but make sure I'm far enough away so I don't hear you talking about me."

"Ahh," Healey replied with a laugh. "Some of the old Lindsey is still there." One of her gifts was her hearing. While she did not have perfect pitch hearing, her hearing skill only complimented her eidetic memory.

Justin Healey could see by Sharyn Wilkerson's face that while she was concerned, she was not happy.

"I don't know whether to say thank you for staying away from Lindsey the past year or be angry with you for getting yourself shot with Bud," she said. The officer had a puzzled look on his face as Lindsey's mother sat down in the chair next to his bed and spoke again. "There was no stopping her once she found out Bud was critically injured and you were shot." She looked away, then back at the officer, who was waiting for her to continue. "Is she in danger? Be honest with me."

"Sharyn," the injured officer replied, "her life will never be normal. I believe her gifts were given to her for a purpose. When I first met the little twelve-year-old girl I knew her life was going to change lives." He hesitated as he spoke again. "When the Music Club Murders started and we found the connection to Face of Fear, we had been watching the house, and someone has never not been far behind when you took her out. There was a bounty on her, but it was canceled after Cronin was killed. There has never been any evidence or indication that she has been in any danger since this case began. Our details watching her have simply been a precaution."

Sharyn was silent as she looked at the officer. He was getting frustrated with her silence, so he spoke again. "We have stayed out of her life, Sharyn, as you requested. We get it. Bud and I, we love her, but we understand. We will honor your wishes."

Sharyn looked away toward the door and back at the officer. "She's getting older and she's getting stronger. She loves both of you as well, and I know it's just a matter of time before she insists to be in your lives. Please, as she gets older, try to respect my feelings as much as possible. I don't want to lose my only child."

"I understand," he answered.

"You understand what?" Lindsey said from the door. Sharyn looked at her watch and realized twenty minutes had gone by quickly.

Healey looked over at her.

"I was telling your mom how I understand how much you mean to her." He looked over at Nurse Lorin to thank her for escorting Lindsey to the rooms.

"No need to thank me," the nurse replied. "I just love hearing someone recite the entire Declaration of Independence to me. All I said was all men are created equal and women disagree, and she corrects me and tells me the whole thing." She put up her hands with a half smile as everyone laughed.

Healey looked at the teenager and thought, *It is good to see Lindsey again.*

"Tell me about your school," Healey said.

"Well," Lindsey answered, "I graduated high school this year and I'm in my first semester of college."

Not bad for a fourteen-year-old girl, Healey thought. "And?" he said. "Are you still going to be a judge?"

"Yes," she replied. "I have to finish school and get my master's by the time I'm twenty-one. I want to be a detective while I work on my law degree. I want to practice law and then become a judge by the time I'm thirty-five. This will give me time to help people as a policewoman and a lawyer." Healey looked over at Sharyn, who had the look of concern on her face again.

"You know, Lindsey," Healey said, "there are many ways to help people."

"Yes," she said, "there are, but it is my destiny. The lord has told me"

Healey decided it was time to change the subject. "How is Monte doing?" Monte was the King Charles Cavalier owned by Lindsey, and the father of Rachelle's dogs.

"He is doing great," Lindsey said with a smile. "I taught him to read this past year."

Healey looked over at Sharyn before looking back at Lindsey. "Excuse me?"

The teenager started laughing as she spoke. "You're so silly. Dogs can't be taught to read."

The officer let out a sigh of relief because he would put nothing past Lindsey Wilkerson. He asked,

"How is Bud doing?"

The smile left Lindsey's face as she said, "He will be fine. He is in my prayers. He will be OK."

"Yes," Healey answered, "he will." He could see how traumatic Bud's injury was to her, and he decided it was time for a nap.

"He will be OK, Lindsey, especially with him in your thoughts. I'm getting sleepy."

"OK," Sharyn Wilkerson replied. "We have to go anyway. I'm sure we will be seeing you again soon."

Officer Healey thanked her as she left the room to give Lindsey some private time with the man who had saved her eighteen months earlier. Lindsey walked over to him and put her hand on the side of his head. She closed her eyes and he watched her lips move ever so slightly. *She is praying for me,* he thought. After about thirty seconds she opened her eyes and he spoke.

"It will be OK, Lindsey. I know it will."

She looked at him, smiled, and replied, "I trust you." She kissed the top of his forehead and left.

He was emotional as he watched her disappear into the hallway. He remembered the last time she said "I trust you," when one of O'Connor's men had a gun at her head in her bedroom. He saved her then, but hearing her say it again put pressure on him like he had never felt before. *You are something special, Lindsey Wilkerson,* he thought.

Deborah walked over to Bud as she stroked his hair.

"I better get back to Paul," Rachelle said. She kissed Deborah good-bye and touched Bud's hand as she returned to her room to find Correctional Officer Janet Gates waiting for her.

Janet Gates stood up and told her they needed to go somewhere and speak privately. Rachelle looked at William Lance and he gave her the OK sign that he would continue to stay with Paul until his father arrived. She looked at her iPhone and noticed a text saying Anthony Powers would be arriving within thirty minutes.

Rachelle and Janet went down to the cafeteria and got a cup of coffee and found an open table after searching for a few minutes. Janet took a sip of coffee and began to speak.

"I don't know why I'm getting involved, but I am. You told your sister last night that you failed when it came to Paul. Then you hung up. She needs to know what you meant."

Rachelle seemed confused but answered Janet.

"I have known Paul for a few years now, and it was always a flirtation relationship up until eighteen months ago. I fell in love with him, and everything was wonderful except for a few rough patches here and there. Then all this. I thought it was all over and we could move on, talk about marriage, kids, have a couple of dogs . . . oh damn, the dogs, I have to let them out."

"Wait," Janet replied. "I will take care of the dogs for you when I leave here. Just, please go on."

Rachelle pulled out an extra key to the house and gave it to Janet as she started to speak again. "My life the past two years has been consumed by Paul when I'm not working at Z Pita, or writing or visiting Madison. Even when I'm there, I know he lives above the restaurant. Someone sent Paul a tape of me leaving a message to his father telling him he needed to take care of Paul because it seemed like I couldn't do it. Well, it made Paul suspicious of me, and I can't tell you how much it hurt. I know he's a cop, but I need him to separate our personal and private lives. He apologized, but it did make me realize that maybe I have failed in my personal relationship with him."

Janet Gates let out a long sigh of relief, which prompted Rachelle to ask her what it was about.

"Rachelle, your own sister thought you did something crazy like being involved in trying to kill Paul when you said, quote, 'I have failed.' How can you hold something against Paul or think you have failed because of a message sent to him? Do you hold it against your sister that she sent me here?"

"No," Rachelle answered.

"OK," Janet replied, "then stop these insecure feelings about Paul."

"I guess," Rachelle answered, "I am insecure when it comes to him. I love him with all my heart, but our life hasn't exactly been normal and I can't remember the last time he did anything romantic unless I initiated it."

"Don't you think you are being a little selfish? Is this about you or the two of you?"

Rachelle shook her head. "I understand what you are saying. I guess I really need to think about all this when Paul is out of the hospital. The important thing is he needs me while he is here."

"No," Janet said, "he needs you, period."

Rachelle smiled and got a text that Anthony Powers had arrived in the room.

"Go," Janet said. "Just give me directions to your house so I can take care of your dogs."

"Thank you," Rachelle answered. "I live at the top of Prospect Street in the village of Port Jefferson," she said as she wrote directions down. "The dogs' names are Wes and Craven, and Wes will be happy to see you while Craven will be suspicious for a while."

"Wait," Janet said. "You named your dogs Wes and Craven?"

"Yes," Rachelle said with a laugh.

Janet shook her head. "And you want to have a normal life? Girl, you are in a dream world." And she laughed.

Rachelle got off the elevator and greeted Anthony Powers with a long hug when she got to the room. He wanted to know the whole story about what happened at the mall.

Detective Lieutenant Cronin was going over the photos and the report that Lynagh had given him. It still wasn't making much sense to him. He called Gina and asked her if Paul had kept a folder of notes for himself as the case progressed. She brought him a folder that was about a half inch thick with handwritten notes from Paul. His notes were detailed, and he had lines that connected from the Face of Fear investigation to the Music Club Murders. The lines showed names that were connected to both. He even wrote notes on the lines from one case to the other, with explanations as to the reason they were connected.

Cronin was fascinated with the details that Paul wrote. He studied the names one by one. Rachelle had a line from Face of Fear to Music Club Murders with the explanation, *Friend of Deborah, Paul Powers's lover, would not leave Deborah's side, writer of cryptic messages on Twitter.* Bud Johnson—*Lead investigator, antagonized Simpson, shot Kyle Winters and Jason "Jack" O'Connor at the Lance mansion.*

Cronin continued to read., Jason "Jack" O'Connor—*AKA the Voice, FBI agent, masterminded to have the Winters brothers eliminated, gain control of ransom, now in Bedford Hills Prison.* Detective Lieutenant

Cronin—*Game changer, manipulator, dangerous, controversial, great detective.*

He continued to read the rest of the names from his notes, which included Lindsey, Sherry Walker, Deborah Lance, Justin Healey, and George Lynagh. Paul Powers had to have spent hours writing in such detail on the connection of everyone between the two cases. Even ADA John Ashley and attorney Al Simmons were on the list. Anthony Powers, Deborah Lance, William Lance all had spots on his chart with lines showing the connections. Linda Tangretti showed—*Fun mom on twitter, Patty's cousin, from Face of Fear to killer and leader in Music Club Murders.*

Cronin's eye went to Robert Simpson's name: *From lover of Deborah Lance, employee of William Lance, affair with Patty Saunders, responsible for killings of Officer Dugan, Kate Summers, Michelle Cartwright, and Alicia Hudson, and embezzled money to pay for the bounties of Priority 1 Task Force.* Cronin shook his head with great pride at the work Powers had done.

"Gina," he called out, "why did you have this file?"

"He wanted me to type it up for him," she answered. He looked back on Powers's chart and saw a name on the Face of Fear chart that showed an arrow to the Music Club Murders with a question mark and the words *insurance fraud.* Cronin's eyes became intense as he kept reading the name with the question mark and the line that was unfinished leading to the Music Club Murders. He sent a text to ADA Ashley asking the whereabouts of the person named and what he was doing now and where he lived.

"Where's Lynagh?" he asked Gina.

"Home resting," she answered.

"Give him another two hours, then tell him to get here within the hour." He waited at his desk, expecting ADA Ashley to call him, and he wasn't disappointed.

Only ten minutes had gone by when the ADA gave him a call. "Detective Cronin, are you sure you want to do this?"

"John," the detective answered, "he needs to be paid an informal visit. We still have Tangretti and Branca out there somewhere. We can't do anything with the fat man because he is in custody; my team is down to O'Malley and Lynagh. Powers was on to something here. We have to see it through. Can you get the information for me?"

"Yes," Ashley replied. "Give me two hours, pain in the ass." Cronin smiled as he pushed the *end* button. Gina walked back in to inform Cronin that Paul's father was on the line to speak to him and the detective lieutenant told her to put him through. His conversation with Anthony Powers was brief, however when he finished his call, he asked Gina to come back in. "Gina, get my source over at Verizon communications on the line for me as quickly as possible"

Rachelle had her head down on Paul's bed when he put his hand on her head and moved his fingers through her hair. He looked at his father and said, "I'm OK, Dad. It was close, but I'm fine. It's Bud I'm worried about."

Anthony Powers looked at Rachelle with her eyes closed. "What about her?" He pointed at her. "Is she going to be all right? She has been through a lot with you, Son. Is this what you want for her?"

"What are you saying, Dad?" Paul asked.

"You know exactly what I am saying," the elder Powers said.

"I love her, Dad. She is everything to me."

"Yet," his father replied, "you become suspicious over a message she leaves for me."

"Dad," Paul said.

But he was interrupted by his father, who said, "I think you better take a long, hard look at what you two have been through the past two years. I think it's time you decide what you really want out of life. There is more I need to say to you, but I don't want to disrespect Rachelle by speaking while her head is on your bed. I'm going to check in on Bud."

Paul shook his head. "Thanks for cheering me up, Dad."

"Any time, Son," his father replied. "I love you, Son, and I'm glad you're all right," he said as he exited.

As Anthony Powers walked toward Bud Johnson's room he wasn't sure if he should be upset with himself for giving tough love to his son after being shot, or be upset that he was so concerned about Rachelle. He wanted her for his son, yet he grew to love her and was concerned about her if she chose a life with him. He shook his head, trying to clear his thoughts as he entered Bud Johnson's room.

The two hours went by fast, and Gina called Lynagh to inform him he had an hour to get to the precinct. Cronin had gone over all of Paul Powers's charts and notes and was tapping his fingers waiting for ADA John Ashley to call him back. It was another ten minutes before Gina walked in with an email sent to her with all the information that Cronin had asked for. Everyone had learned a long time ago not to send Cronin emails. Even in 2015 he hated using the computer. Only if he absolutely had to would he type a note, but he was usually a few steps behind when it came to technology. As Gina walked out, the detective lieutenant placed the information flat on his desk, side by side with Powers's charts. His fingers touched each set of papers as his eyes went back and forth from Ashley's note to the lined chart from the thoughts of Detective Powers. As he looked, the call from his source at Verizon returned Gina's call.

Detective O'Malley drove to St. James, and once he got to Cherry Street took a right on Maplewood. He drove to the blue-and-white house and parked in front of it. There he sat with his pumpkin seeds and watched for about an hour.

Officer Lynagh made it to the precinct and Cronin told him he would fill him in on the way to St. James. Detective O'Malley, who had been watching, decided it was time to approach the blue-and-white house. He left his vehicle, walked up to the door, and before he knocked, he sent Gina a text where he was. As he pushed the doorbell Gina contacted Detective Cronin, informing him of O'Malley's text.

"Damn it!" he yelled. "Step on it! No siren, just lights!" he yelled. Cronin answered back on the radio, "If you don't hear from me in twenty minutes, send backup automatically." Lynagh weaved in and out of traffic and stuck his arm out a few times warning other drivers to let him get through.

O'Malley was standing on the step when the door opened. Standing there was FBI Agent Robert Sherman. He was O'Connor's partner during Deborah Lance's kidnapping. The detective flashed his badge and asked the FBI agent if he could come in. Agent Sherman waved his hand with a smile as O'Malley walked into the foyer of the house.

"What can I do for you, Detective?"

O'Malley took out his bag of pumpkin seeds and led himself to the living room, which annoyed Sherman.

"Have you seen your ex-partner lately?" O'Malley asked.

Sherman was even more annoyed. "Why would I see him? He was responsible for lives being lost, including cops'. That's long behind me."

O'Malley continued to look around and placed his pumpkin seed bag down to pick up some photos from the mantel over the fireplace. "I read through the files of the last case. There seems to be a connection to everyone from the Face of fear case to the case we are working on, except for you."

"Detective," the Agent replied, "I've moved on. I was promoted after the case just like Cronin and his team, God rest his soul." O'Malley was amused by Sherman's comment about Cronin being dead.

"I guess you haven't got the memo yet," O'Malley replied. He had always wanted to use that line ever since he saw the movie *The Dark Knight*, and now he was thrilled he was able to.

"Excuse me?" Sherman asked. In the next room there were two men listening with guns drawn, waiting for the signal from Sherman to remove O'Malley's body once he was killed.

"Oh, nothing," O'Malley answered with a smile. "I just wanted to come by and meet you since your name kept coming up in the files from Face of Fear. If you can think of anything, please call me. I appreciate your time." The detective's experience felt a bad energy coming from Sherman and wanted to be lighthearted to get out of there alive. The two men hid before O'Malley came to the foyer. One was in the bathroom and one up the stairs.

When O'Malley reached his car he started to drive down the block, but when he got five houses down he turned his vehicle around and parked on the opposite side of the street just to see if anything happened in the next five minutes. He picked up his radio for Cronin, but he saw the detective lieutenant and Lynagh get out of their vehicle in the same exact spot where he had just left.

"What in the living hell?" O'Malley said to himself out loud. He watched as Cronin moved to the front door and Lynagh went behind the house. O'Malley was confused, but he wanted to stick around and see how this played out.

Cronin knocked on the door as Sherman's men went back to the bathroom and upstairs. "Look," Sherman said as he opened the door, "there is nothing else . . ." He could not finish his sentence when he saw it was Detective Lieutenant Cronin. His jaw dropped as he stared at him.

"What's wrong?" Cronin said. "You look like you've just seen a ghost."

Sherman continued to be startled as Cronin spoke again. "Thank you for inviting me in," he said as he stepped through the door.

Sherman shut the door and looked at him.

"It's been all over the papers that you are dead. What type of game are you playing now?"

"Why?" Cronin asked as he stepped down into the living room. He scanned the room to give Lynagh time to enter from the back. He saw O'Malley's bag of pumpkin seeds on the mantel and started wondering if he was even alive. Had O'Malley not called in his location, he would have suspected him of being involved with Sherman.

"Everything in life is a game. Most just don't want to admit it," Cronin said.

Sherman walked into the living room and sat down in his lounge chair.

"Please sit," the agent said.

"No thanks," Cronin replied.

"What can I do for you?" Sherman asked.

Dave, a bouncer from the City nightclub pulled out his weapon and added a silencer to it. He left the bathroom and approached the end of the wall to prepare to shoot Detective Lieutenant Cronin. He was within five feet when he felt the barrel of Lynagh's 9mm in the back of his neck. He froze as he heard Lynagh's whisper: "Give me a reason, any reason, and I will shoot your Adam's apple across the room."

Dave Lander didn't move, including holding on to his gun.

"Now," Lynagh said, "we are going to listen and see what Agent Sherman here has to say about what the hell is going on." He grabbed the silencer away from him.

Cronin walked over to Sherman before speaking. "What have you been doing with yourself since you lost your partner to jail?"

"I was promoted to another division," the agent replied.

"Doing what?" Cronin asked. The tone of his voice did not make it sound like a question.

"White Collar Division," Sherman answered.

Cronin nodded his head as he replied, "So you're dealing with a lot of insurance fraud."

"What's up, Detective Cronin?" Sherman asked with an annoyed tone.

"Well," Cronin replied as he walked over to the fireplace to look at the photos on the mantel.

"Do you like pumpkin seeds?"

Sherman shook his head as he opened the drawer of his end table and pulled out a bag of sunflower seeds. "No," he answered as he held up the bag.

Cronin picked up the bag of pumpkin seeds and held it up to the Agent.

"Somebody does."

"Your cop, O'Malley, was just here asking questions about Face of Fear," he replied.

"I wonder why," Cronin said.

"Why don't you ask him?" the agent replied. "Listen, I know how you operate, Detective. I don't have time for games. Just tell me what you want to know."

"You're right, by the way, I just love that word games," Cronin answered, "but then again, if you knew how I operated then you would have known I played dead when you had Caulfield attach a bomb to my car. You would have also figured out I wasn't dead. The thing is this, as much as you wanted the insurance money from the closing of the nightclub, you couldn't control Simpson. He was so bent on revenge toward me he became the loose cannon in all of this. You have Jake Wiley aka Jerry Wakefern kill a good cop; you bribe Caulfield over to the dark side with money and the Tangretti girl too. You didn't count on him getting sliced up in the back of a car. Tell me, how did you manage to keep O'Connor quiet through all this? The guard Roberts, maybe?"

"Are you finished?" Sherman replied. "I have no idea what you are talking about."

"Let me be clear," Cronin spoke quickly. "I received a phone call from Detective Power's father who played me a message that Rachelle Robinson left for him. Somehow, that message ended up on Powers voice mail machine, So, what do I do? I call my sources at Verizon to see how that could possibly happen without a court order or subpoena. Gee, I thought, someone other than me, thinks they are better at playing games, and you know how that pisses me off. I got a hold of my people over there, and low and behold you have your own sources and relationships over there in this grey world of law we live in. You made a mistake Agent Sherman. And, that's not all. You work for the White Collar Division, yes. Yet it's your group working on the insurance investigations of the three clubs. You manage to save two of them, but it is the Decades nightclub that would be collecting millions from the loss of business. The K-9s found the area where money was hidden behind a wall in Branca's office. You guys were in such a hurry you left some bills behind and did a lousy job putting the wall back together. I'm mad at myself that even though I was able to end Face of Fear, I still made mistakes. One, I didn't pursue Linda Tangretti more, and two, when I realized O'Connor found out about the letter written by Phil Smith, it had to have come from you even though you denied it at the mansion that night. I gave you the benefit of the doubt, but I told you in the hospital when Deborah Lance was brought in to keep it to yourself. You didn't, you told O'Connor, he opened his mouth, and yet he took the fall even while you were calling the shots. I made a mistake, and you took advantage of it by wanting even more instead of just going away. Did I miss anything other than the $5 million life insurance policy you took out on yourself two years ago?"

The detective lieutenant looked down on the floor and was wondering where he could buy some time for backup to arrive. "I bet when you were a kid they called you Bobby."

"So what?" the agent replied.

"Well," Cronin replied, "Bobby Sherman was a teen idol. 'Easy Come, Easy Go.' You must have been teased a bit."

Sherman wasn't amused as he stared down the detective, who spoke again.

"You let Simpson think he was running the show, just like you did with O'Connor with Face of Fear, and all you did was use them to get what you wanted."

"Look in the mirror!" Sherman yelled. "Look in the fucking mirror! I am no different than you!"

David Biggs was at the top of the stairway with Lynagh in his sights. The back of his head would be gone in 5 . . . 4 . . . 3. As his finger touched the trigger to squeeze, he heard movement on the carpet as he slanted his head enough to see out of the corner of his eye. The figure wearing dark clothes and the blood-splattered Ghost Face mask ran toward him as he let out a yelp. The knife went through his chest as he tried to grab the mask. There was no resistance, but Biggs fell to the floor. The masked killer picked up his rifle and dropped it down the stairs and ran back toward the back bedroom window.

The noise startled Lynagh, as Lander made an attempt to wrestle the gun away. Cronin started to go to the foyer as Sherman pulled out his gun.

"The only place you're going is hell. The old saying of when you need things done right you have to do it yourself rings true."

"You think you're going to get away with killing me?" Cronin asked. He looked at his watch. "In five minutes there will be backup here." The stare-down continued as Lynagh and Lander wrestled for the gun.

"You don't have five minutes," Sherman said. A shot rang out as Sherman fell over. Cronin looked over to see Detective O'Malley run to the other side of the wall opening and kick Lander in the head, allowing Lynagh to regain control of his weapon.

Cronin walked over to Sherman's lifeless body, kneeled down, and spoke.

"For the time being, at least I can look in the mirror, and like I said, easy come, easy go." O'Malley came back to the living room as they heard police cars outside.

"Why did you come back?" Cronin asked.

O'Malley let out a sigh of relief before he answered.

"Lucky for you, I forgot my pumpkin seeds," he smiled as Cronin nodded a thank-you. Cronin stood up as O'Malley spoke again. "I could have been with him and Caulfield. You took a chance."

"I know," Cronin answered. "It was a risk I was going to take. Besides now think of all the notoriety you are going to have. Plus I had informed Ashley to have you shot if I didn't come out alive." He smiled at O'Malley to let him know he was kidding, but O'Malley wasn't sure.

"What do you mean about notoriety?" O'Malley asked.

Cronin checked on Lynagh in the foyer before turning to O'Malley and saying, "The first time you shoot someone with your gun in your long career, you save the life of Detective Lieutenant Cronin. Now that's something you will be remembered for." He winked at Lynagh.

"Just great," O'Malley answered. "I won't get much sleep thinking about that. I'm wondering if I did the world a favor." He walked out as other officers walked in.

"Boss," Lynagh said, "how did you know O'Malley wouldn't be here with a gun on your head? Besides a rifle was dropped from upstairs." They handed off Lander to one of the officers as they walked up the stairs with guns drawn to find Dave Biggs with his eyes wide open and a knife wound in his chest. Four feet down the hall on the floor was the Ghost Face mask with blood splatter on it.

"Have the crime unit check for DNA, but most likely it's just never been worn."

Cronin looked at Lynagh. "As for O'Malley, he has been on the force for thirty years. He never fired his weapon. He wasn't about to start by being on the wrong side of the law." Lynagh nodded as they went down the stairs and drove off to the precinct, where ADA Ashley was waiting for them.

"Is he in custody?" Ashley asked.

"Yes," Cronin replied. "The devil has him."

The ADA shook his head.

"You killed him?"

"Not me," Cronin replied. "O'Malley did it."

"What the hell happened?" Ashley yelled.

"Well, I guess he decided my life was more important than Special Agent Sherman's."

"What about Tangretti and Branca?" he replied.

Cronin looked over at Lynagh before answering. "They are long gone. This woman Linda Tangretti, she used all these men to get what she wanted, the money and, I have a feeling, Branca. She worked with Sherman through her ties with Simpson, her cousin Patty Saunders, may the devil rest her soul, and the correctional officer Roberts at the prison. She was underestimated from the start."

Ashley sat down in Kevin's chair and spoke. "Now you're talking about Face of Fear."

"Yes," Lynagh answered. "She was Fun Mom on the twitter accounts from that case. We looked at her only as the cousin of Patty Saunders. Nothing more."

"Now," Cronin said, "it's all about insurance fraud. Sherman cut a deal to get money from the club closing, but the surprise was getting himself killed off to get life insurance paid out to his wife and to disappear together. The club was hiding cash thanks to some good accounts but must have found out collecting on the business loss would have been a paper trail nightmare."

"Branca and Sherman used Simpson's revenge as a distraction from the real goal. Simpson utilized their contacts and put bounties out on Priority 1, knowing that the women getting killed in the club would 'hide' the insurance fraud. They might have gotten away with it if it hadn't been for Powers's notes and charts. It was a well-thought-out plan. Get rid of me and most associated with Face of Fear. Use the revenge motive; use Simpson's money he embezzled from William Lance. What gave them away was the attorney, Edward Larson, when he verified the coverage of the BI clause from the insurance company."

"BI?" Ashley asked.

"Business Interruption clause. He checked six months ago and confirmed how it would work, what triggered it, and how they would be paid. When they found out murder was not a qualifier for the payout the way they wanted it, they took a different route. Powers checked it, but somehow it was discreetly hidden. He did an incredible job of investigating in the case."

Ashley looked back at Cronin. "But it's not over?"

"No, not yet," Cronin replied with a tone of annoyance. "We still have to find Branca and Tangretti."

Ashley looked back at Officer Lynagh. "Would you excuse us, please?" The officer looked over at Cronin and left as soon as the detective lieutenant made a motion with his eyes signifying it was OK to leave. The door shut behind him as Ashley spoke.

"You're right about this with Branca and Tangretti, but there's one thing. Who killed Phil Smith in the barn that night eighteen months ago? I ask because I don't believe it's over till all loose ends are taken care of. Now I'm going to ask you, because I know how you were desperate last time and a few things backfired. So did you kill Phil Smith that night?" Ashley stood up to hear Cronin's answer. "And where is the missing money?"

Cronin hesitated, which made Ashley uncomfortable.

"Kevin, I'm waiting for an answer," he pushed.

"No," the detective lieutenant replied. "If it was me, I would have only needed one shot, and it wouldn't have been in the throat." He opened the door and walked out of the Priority 1 area with Lynagh behind him. ADA Ashley stood behind Cronin's desk, not sure whether to feel relieved that Cronin told him he wasn't involved in the shooting or upset with himself that he asked him the direct question he had thought about over the past year and a half. His cell phone rang and he saw it was DA Steinberg.

"Shit," he said out loud. He was sure it was about the death of FBI Agent Sherman. He sat back down as he picked up the call and wrote on a big piece of paper for Gina to see through the glass, *Where did they go?* She wrote back in bigger letters, *The hospital.* He nodded as he began to speak to his boss.

9:00 PM

It was getting unusually late for Madison to get a visit from her attorney, Al Simmons, but Correction Officer Steven Jacobs brought her down to the attorney-client room anyway. It was one of those rare times when Janet Gates and John Bay were not on shift. When she walked into the room she greeted Simmons with a hug as always. Even in a jail outfit Madison was as sexy as could be, and thanks to Paul, she had the reputation of having legs equal to Kimberly Guilfoyle of Fox News's *The Five*. As she sat down, Officer Jacobs informed them that Officer Gates would come back for her in forty minutes because there would be a shift change.

Al Simmons reviewed everything that was going on in the hospital and the case. Cronin had Gina send him an email for him to find out if there was anything he needed to know. Madison thought about telling Simmons about having Gates make a couple calls and going to the hospital to speak with Rachelle, but Simmons was shaking his head sideways as if he was hoping she would not. She thought about the exact words he asked her because she did not want to lie to him. His question was, "Is there anything I need to know about this?" She decided that there wasn't anything he needed to know as of now, so she simply said no. Simmons started nodding his head up and down as if to say he agreed with her answer.

"Has the doctor helped with your nightmares?" the attorney asked.

"A little," she replied. "He told me it will take a while, but I'm not going anywhere." She had a smile on her face, which Simmons was happy to see when she cracked the joke.

"Are they the same?" he asked. "The nightmares?"

"Pretty much," she answered. "The Ghost Face mask finds me in different locations, stabs me, then pulls off the mask, and it's me. It's frightening." Her attorney put his hand on hers.

"Someone is killing with the mask, but this time they're leaving it behind as a calling card. You wouldn't know anything about that, would you?"

Madison looked at Simmons. "I'm in here. I can't get out. It's not me."

"OK," he said, "we can talk again later in the week." He was concerned she did not answer the question directly. Their conversation turned to the condition of Powers and Johnson at Stony Brook. It was felt that Powers would be up and around within twelve days, while everyone had Bud in their thoughts. The forty minutes was stretched to forty-five by the time Janet Gates opened the door to lead Madison back to her cell. Madison hugged Simmons good-bye and then Janet led Madison back to her private cell. When Madison got back in her cell she asked Janet to talk to her inside her area, out of view of the camera. The correction officer knew what it was about, so she complied. Janet Gates sat down so Madison would sit. With Gates height at 5'4" Madison towered over her when they were standing.

"How did it go with my sister?" she asked Janet.

"She's OK, Madison. She is emotionally stressed out over her worries about you, Paul, and Bud, and I get the feeling there is insecurity setting in over the relationship."

Madison seemed puzzled as Janet continued. "The shooting at the mall was traumatizing for her, yet she is the one trying to be a source of support for everyone. I'm concerned about her. Don't forget she will be missing work for a few days, if not more."

Madison Robinson stared at Janet Gates as the officer continued to explain to her about Rachelle. They talked for over an hour about everyone. In between even a few jokes were cracked, and Madison thought Janet had the most attractive laugh. The smile on her face disappeared as she looked at Janet totally differently, as their eyes focused on each other.

The correctional officer knew she was getting in over her head emotionally with Madison but couldn't help herself.

"I better get back to my post," Janet said.

She got up to leave and didn't see the disappointment on Madison's face.

When she got back to her desk, she covered her face with her hands and spoke to herself. "Oh my God, what am I doing?" Her breathing got heavier as she spoke to herself again. "Get control." She knew she had already crossed the line in her job with Madison, but she felt an overwhelming urge to help her even if she wasn't sure why.

Detective Lieutenant Cronin knew once he set foot in the hospital he would officially be alive. Rumors of his sighting were already taking effect. Suspicions rose even more once the escorts were assigned to Rachelle, Deborah, and Lindsey Wilkerson.

As Cronin and Lynagh stepped off the elevator on the eighteenth floor, heads started to turn. Police officers were not even sure how to react. It was so awkward that Cronin actually thought it was amusing. He went to Bud's room and saw Deborah Lance curled up on the chair trying to get some shut-eye. The officer standing guard at his room didn't know how to acknowledge the detective lieutenant so he decided not to say anything. Cronin stood outside the window looking at Bud Johnson lying with all the tubes inserted in his body. Deborah opened her eyes and glanced up to see the man she thought was dead. She tried to fix her hair but gave up since she figured she didn't have any makeup on anyway. She didn't bother to put on her shoes and came out into the hallway with bare feet. Cronin looked over at Lynagh and nodded toward the officer at the door.

Lynagh put his hand on Officer Phelan's arm. "Let's go get a cup of coffee." Deborah was already standing there with her arms folded, waiting for an explanation of why he was standing there alive. Cronin turned his head to look at Bud lying there, and then turned back toward Deborah, who was still waiting for him to speak.

"You must be confused by this, but you will understand soon enough." He looked back at Bud and added the word "unfortunately" to the end of his sentence.

"There was a bounty on you, Rachelle, and the Wilkerson girl. It was set up by Robert Simpson to get revenge on me for what happened during the Face of Fear investigation. Once I was pronounced dead there was no need for Simpson to spend the extra money. He wanted you for himself or he would have taken care of you. FBI Agent Sherman allowed him to do it as a distraction and an alibi for an insurance scam he had going on."

Deborah did not say a word, but he could see the anger in her eyes as he spoke again. "The only way to resolve this was to have the freedom to go where I needed to go and keep you safe while they thought I was dead."

Deborah just nodded her head as she backed away from him to go back in the room. Her face had disgust all over it as Cronin spoke before she entered the room.

"Nothing to say?"

Deborah stopped and turned back toward Cronin with her arms still folded and finally spoke. "What about Bud? He thought he lost you. Did he know about this? I know the answer. It's no. Why do I know? Because I know this man, his heart, he would give up his life to bring your killers to justice. His whole way of thinking and his actions are based on his heart, whether it's right or wrong. He should have known."

She started to walk away again as Cronin spoke.

"You will understand why he didn't know. The last case,

both Powers and Johnson were so conflicted over you and Rachelle, I had to take the lead. This case is a direct link, and I was not going to have the conflict again. This case will be closed soon, and as for Bud it may have been me on his mind, but it's you that controls his heart. We have him on tape at the club telling Branca to put all the bounties on him to be the target. He wanted all of us safe, but it's you that dictates his heart."

She looked back at Bud and wiped the tears from her face as Cronin spoke again.

"Now I need you to continue to support him emotionally and make him stronger so we don't lose him."

She nodded as she went back to the room. She turned around and saw that Officer Phelan and Lynagh came back to Cronin. They spoke for a few seconds as she saw the detective pointing at Phelan before walking away with Lynagh. Her thoughts were simply, *You're a mysterious man, Kevin Cronin.* She turned around and looked at Bud and bent over to kiss his forehead.

Paul Powers was talking to the doctor when Detective Cronin walked into his room. Rachelle was standing on the other side of the bed and grabbed ahold of Paul as soon as she saw it was either Detective Cronin or his ghost. Paul was dumbfounded as it became awkward with the doctor standing by the bedside.

"Well," Doctor Ng spoke, "I will be back in a couple hours to discuss your rehabilitation when you are out of here. I'll be sending you to St. James Medical Center. I know the director there very well. You're in great shape, but you should have therapy and limited walking for at least another two weeks."

Doctor Ng was an Asian American doctor from Hong Kong who studied at Stony Brook and ended up being one of the doctors on staff. He left the room as Lynagh poked his head in to acknowledge Paul. The injured detective nodded to him with a half smile before turning his attention to Detective Lieutenant Cronin. His boss gave him the same details he gave to Deborah, except he added one more thing.

"Paul, the work you did on this case as lead is outstanding. I'm beyond proud of you. Especially the work with the charts between the two cases."

Powers looked at Rachelle as he tightened his grasp on her before he spoke.

"There was no other way, I suppose, but I don't agree keeping it away from Bud and myself. Ashley knew and yet we didn't."

Cronin respected Paul's feelings but he was clear in his reply.

"I needed the freedom to roam as I saw fit. It was approved by the DA's office and the commissioner. As for you and Bud, you didn't need this on your plate. I didn't want what I was doing interfering with your decisions. With me dead and the bounty off the girls, it served a couple of purposes. With a dirty cop in the squad it could have been much worse." He looked at Rachelle and he could see the anger in her eyes. "I'm a real hit with the ladies today."

Paul looked at Rachelle and she could tell he wanted a few minutes alone with Cronin. She got up without saying a word to Cronin and joined Lynagh in the hallway.

"Good thing," Paul said, "you missed Lindsey. She would have had a few things to say as well." Cronin ignored the comment and spoke to Paul in detail about his chart. He told him about Sherman and the insurance premiums fraud and how it was all set up with the murders allowing Simpson his revenge on Priority 1 and giving Sherman the distraction he needed.

Paul nodded as he spoke.

"Am I still the lead on this case?"

"Yes," Cronin replied. "It was your charts that made the connection to Sherman. It is likely that Tangretti and Branca are out of the state. I put holds on their passports, so unless they paid big bucks, they're in the country somewhere. There is one more thing. Someone is still killing with the Ghost Face mask, and we know it's not Madison Robinson. They are using a gun as well as a knife and have no problem leaving the mask as a calling card."

There was no reaction from Paul, which bothered Cronin as he spoke again.

"Make no mistake, if it's someone from my team, I will take them down."

Paul answered with a firm voice. "I don't know who it is, but aren't you the kettle calling the pot black? There are rules for all of us except for you."

Cronin started to walk away but turned back.

"You may not like my style, Paul, and I know it seems I'm on the edge, but make no mistake, the law will be followed. You are the lead, but right now I'm more concerned about Bud. With Branca and Tangretti gone with the money, it will be an FBI case. Besides, we put an agent behind bars, and now with O'Malley killing the other, we are not exactly on everyone's favorite hits list. Hurry up and get out of here. My old cell number is back on."

He got to the door when Paul called to him,

"Boss." Cronin turned around as Paul said, "I may regret saying this, but I'm glad you're back."

Cronin nodded as he entered the hallway where Rachelle and Lynagh were talking. Rachelle walked back into Paul's room, again without saying anything to Cronin.

"You're a popular guy," Lynagh said with a smile. It quickly disappeared as the detective lieutenant stared at him.

"Sorry, Boss," Lynagh said as they walked to the elevator.

"Just bring me to Wyatt and Baker's rooms, please." Cronin said.

They drove back to the precinct as Cronin rearranged some of the things that Paul had done while he was "dead." He asked Gina to give him a list of all the officers borrowed from the

Fourth Precinct that were now escorting Deborah Lance, Rachelle Robinson, Lindsey Wilkerson, Chapman, Healey, Baker, and now Powers and Johnson.

He shook his head at all the injuries and touched the names of those who were killed. The three girls as well as Dugan, Franks, Hansen, and that bastard Caulfield. He went over the Face of Fear case in his mind a few times and was starting to second-guess his actions with Simpson, which many believe resulted in the ramifications of the Music Club Murders. A voice interrupted his thoughts.

It was ADA Ashley. "Don't second-guess yourself, because if you have doubts you will not be good for anyone."

The detective lieutenant looked up at his old friend Ashley.

"John, we have to make sure Branca and Tangretti are caught."

"And," Ashley replied, "the same goes for whoever shot Phil Smith that night."

Cronin nodded his head. "That too." Ashley started to leave when Cronin spoke again. "You are never going to let me live that down are you?"

Ashley slapped the side of the doorway as he continued to walk.

"Don't make a promise that you can't keep. Have a nice evening."

Cronin went back to the chart from Paul's folder and called Gina into his office. He wrote a name on a piece of paper.

"Give me every flight he has been on between July 1 and July 9 of 2013." She looked at the name, nodded, and went back to her desk.

Cronin walked over to Gina's desk and looked like he was staring at the air behind Gina. She glanced up at him and finally turned around to see what he was looking at. When she turned around he was now tapping the tip of her desk, still staring into space. She had known him long enough to let him be and continue to entertain his thoughts until he was ready to speak. It was another ten seconds when he did begin to talk. He looked at Gina and said, "Have the tech man, Tillman, gather all the video in the surrounding blocks of the City nightclub when Stone was shot and Linda Tangretti got away. I want a six-block radius of the club fifteen minutes before, during, and after the shooting. Everything we got. I also want him to check all social media of the names I will give to you, Facebook, Twitter, Instagram, all that shit, within the same time frame. If he needs help, fine, let's pull strings to get him the help."

He started to walk away when Gina asked him if he was sure if that's all he wanted.

"No," he answered, "I'm not, but I will get back to you."

Gina smiled as she picked up the phone.

October 10

Janet Gates relieved John Bay and tried to stay at her location, but she couldn't. Her conflicted feeling on what she doing for Madison kept her from sleeping. She waited another five minutes and walked down to the cell and tried to keep a straight face when she saw Madison, but when she smiled at her, the correctional officer couldn't help but smile as well. In a trembling and unsteady voice, Janet began to speak, "Listen, I . . ."

Madison interrupted her before she could finish.

"It's OK, Janet, I understand you have a job that you can't lose. I don't know what is happening, but I want you to know I genuinely care about you. I'm sorry."

The correctional officer nodded her head slightly as she spoke.

"I'm not sure if I'm sorry, and that is what scares me."

She smiled as she walked back to her desk. Madison stood there not sure of what she just heard, but she too had a smile on her face as she prepared to get ready to turn in. The next day she would see the doctor again about her nightmares that were now only once a week instead of every other night. She looked forward to exercising again as well. Her thoughts turned to Janet as she put the blanket over her. She would never forget how kind she was to her during this time of having nightmares and risking her job for her. Madison was honest. It ached her when she told the petite guard that she really cared about her. She also knew that she did not want Janet to lose her job. Two things would happen. She would lose her job, and Madison would lose having her around almost every night.

316 | R.J. Torbert

She drifted off to sleep peacefully as Janet watched her from the monitor screen at her desk. It was a camera that did not record film but allowed the officers to be sure everything was going OK. The entire cell was on camera except for the small space where Madison would shower, use the toilet, and the back wall where Janet would sit with Madison. She kept shaking her head with her thoughts running wild. *You are a kind person, Madison. I can't believe you could really kill all those people.* She shook her head again, hoping to get her thoughts under control.

Ken Anker, Kevin Sysco, and a new inmate that had just arrived at the precinct on a unrelated charge by the name of Rob McDonagh were all in the three holding cells at Priority 1. Normally Sysco would have been moved by now, but he never asked for an attorney, and Branca never sent a new one in. Cronin decided to keep him in the holding area in case he was needed. The big man never complained as long as they were feeding him. The three of them never spoke to each other in the holding cells until now.

Ken Anker broke the silence and spoke through the bars. "Whoever is shitting their pants, please stop."

"Sorry," Sysco replied. "It must be the food they serve here."

Rob finally chimed in, "Man, you need to see a fucking doctor, seriously, you have issues."

"Sorry," Sysco said again. "I can't help it."

"Not normal, guy," Anker said. "Passing gas is one thing, but it literally smells like you dropped a load. Just go on a fast."

Officer Walsh, who was standing at the end of the hallway, came over to speak to the three jailed men. "What's all the fuss about, boys?"

Anker spoke first. "Tell monkey scratch ass over there to stop the shitting. I can't breathe."

Walsh looked at Sysco. "He's got a point. Get it under control, or I'll have you hosed down." Walsh walked back to his post, where he was met by a young African American officer.

"What's up?"

"Nothing," Walsh answered. "Tell the cook we need to serve Sysco bread and water for a while. Either that or we will have to drop a fumigation bomb in here."

Five Days Later
October 15

Paul was getting ready to be released from the hospital with his father by his side. Healey and Chapman were released the day before, and Baker was set to be released in a couple days. He asked to sit with Bud before leaving the hospital. The staff put him in a wheelchair and rolled him to his partner's room. He was still in a coma, and still Deborah Lance was in the chair near his bed reading the book *Intelligence for Your Life*. She got up and hugged Paul and pushed him closer to Bud Johnson's bedside. He touched his hand and looked up at Deborah. "Thank you for being here for him."

She smiled at Paul and replied, "It's where I need to be."

"Have you seen Lindsey?" he asked.

"She's been here every night, Paul. She sits with him for an hour every night and prays over him." Paul was touched by the information.

"That's really nice. I guess her parents are not thrilled, but it's really nice." She looked up at Anthony Powers and grabbed his hand to say hello.

"I thought Rachelle was coming to be with you when you got out?" she said.

Paul looked over at Bud then back at Deborah.

"She has missed so much work. I told her to go to Z Pita so Joey Z could catch a break."

"Oh, OK," Deborah said in an awkward tone. Paul let go of Bud's hand and asked his father to push his chair instead of the nurse.

"Thank you again, Deborah," he said. "You are very special to him."

She smiled at him, but she sensed something was wrong.

"What's happening, Paul?" she asked as she followed him to the hallway.

"All this," he said as he pointed to himself. "All this killing and they get away. No one knows where they are, and for what? Revenge? Insurance money? What kind of world are we living in? Is it worth it?"

He started to push away again as his father stayed silent as Deborah spoke again.

"What about Bud? I love him, but it's you he needs right now. What about Rachelle? I love her as well, but it's you she needs. As for me, I love you too, and I need you to not give up, because if you do, it will affect all of us." Paul sat frozen for a few seconds as his father turned his head from his son to Deborah.

She continued to speak. "I don't know why, but we are in this together. We haven't given up on you. Please don't give up on us." She turned around and returned to Bud's side. There continued to be silence as Paul and his father went to sign papers for his release.

EIGHT DAYS LATER
OCTOBER 23

It was now October 23 in Key West, Florida, which has average temperatures between seventy-eight and eighty-six degrees during the month of October. It was relaxing and the perfect place for Linda Tangretti and Michael Branca to hide out in plain sight. The little home in which they were staying in the winter was a rental they paid cash for under the names of Betty and Joseph Thomas. She cut her hair short and dyed it black while Branca shed ten pounds, grew his hair longer, and wore glasses when he was out in public. They had escaped from Long Island ten days earlier and their lives had been a nonstop party of sex, alcohol, and leisure ever since they hit the Keys.

The first week was filled with nervous laughter that they got away with everything. From the beginning they were barely together yet planned it out so carefully that it worked. They had sex over twenty times the first week and were already down to four times a week by the beginning of their second week. The money that was hidden in the walls of the club from Simpson bounties, and what money they had from Simpson's bounties gave them over $3.5 million in cash that they could live comfortably on without having to show IDs the rest of their lives if they didn't get crazy.

The two of them were getting comfortable in their surroundings, and while it was fun and exciting the first couple weeks, Linda was getting bored. Branca knew it was time for something different, so he surprised her with a weekend trip to the Royal Coconut Palace Hotel and Spa. It was the newest hotel in the Keys and it had a main building with about twenty-five separate detached bungalows near the water. He couldn't wait to spice up their sex life on the beach. In addition he never forgot what she told him about her ultimate fantasy, which was to have sex with someone dressed up in a Halloween costume. He made the reservation for the weekend of October 31 to November 2. He was proud of himself as he entered their small little home on Peacock Circle.

Paul Powers was back at his apartment and was able to convince his father to return to Florida a few days before. He was still in pain from the shot he took to his pelvic bone, but he was getting restless for the job. He would be returning to the precinct on desk duty along with Ellyn Baker, who was now back at work on desk duty as well as Officer Healey. Chapman would be home for another week before returning.

Paul walked up the hill to Prospect Street, knocked on the door, and walked in to be greeted by Wes while Craven lay by Rachelle's feet. He walked over, gave her a kiss, and sat down. Rachelle was prepared for what was going to happen next but still wasn't sure if it would become a reality. Paul was different since the shooting at the mall and she wasn't sure why, but she had been thinking how ironic it had been that it was Deborah and Bud who grew apart before the shooting, and now after the shooting it was Paul who was withdrawing.

"Rachelle," he said, "I think it's best if we have space for a bit."

"You mean," Rachelle shot back, "you're tired of having sex with me. Is that what you mean?" She was sarcastic in her tone because her heart was aching. She had realized Paul was becoming distant with her, but it was difficult to actually let go. Instead she fought back by being defensive.

Paul was startled by her comeback but replied, "I can't live with myself anymore knowing I put you in danger just by being a part of my life. Any time someone wants to get to me all they have to do is use you."

"Oh," Rachelle said, "that explains it. Now I understand. Just how selfish are you? I have been through hell and back with you because you mean the world to me. It's my choice how to live my life and who I'm with." She shook her head and held back the tears. "But you are right. The last thing I want to do is be with someone who doesn't want me."

"I want you to live," Paul answered. "I can't deal with the chance that something may happen to you."

Rachelle continued to shake her head as she spoke. "So the old cliché: it's not you it's me."

Paul pet Wes before speaking again. "I'm going to take time off. I'm not sure about my life anymore. I just want to make sure Bud is OK before I leave. I'm not sure what I will be doing or where I will go, but I need to do this." He got up and went over to kiss her before he left, but she moved her head. He hesitated for a moment before turning away and leaving the house. Rachelle burst out with a loud cry as she covered her face. Her dogs knew something was wrong as they stood up trying to get her attention. It was over an hour before she could even get herself up. She was so worn out by all the crying that she fell on her bed and cried herself to sleep.

Deborah was reading her book when Bud opened his eyes and touched her hand. She dropped her book and touched his face as the heart monitor indicated to the nurses' station that there was a change. Nurse Lorin came in and notified the doctor on staff to get to his room.

"Welcome back to the world, Bud Johnson," Nurse Lorin said. "Is there anything I can get for you?"

Bud tried to speak but seemed groggy and unable to finish his sentences. One of his sentences involved the words *gummy bears*, which brought a smile to Deborah's face. Nurse Lorin looked over at Deborah and told her not to worry, that it was common for patients to appear "out of it" when waking from a coma. Just as Nurse Lorin turned her head back to Bud, he attempted to pull his tubes out, but she prevented him. Deborah stood up as she began to get nervous.

"Listen, Bud," Nurse Lorin spoke. "You are OK. You are in Stony Brook Hospital. You are going to be OK, but you need to leave your tubes in. Do you understand?"

Bud nodded his head as the nurse continued to speak with him while Deborah held his hand. Bud looked over at Deborah, who was standing beside the nurse. He grabbed her hand as tears rolled down her cheeks.

"Don't cry," he said. "I'm . . ." he stopped and struggled to finish with the word "here."

She smiled as she replied, "Yes, you are." She sent Rachelle, Paul, and her father a text that Bud had awakened.

Bud looked around, still seeming out of it, but managed to take sixty seconds to ask how long he had been there.

"It's been almost two weeks," Nurse Lorin said. "You had periods of wakefulness and you opened your eyes at times, but you never fully woke up till now." Doctor Ng came into the room and asked for privacy for a few minutes with Bud. As they went into the hallway Deborah questioned Nurse Lorin about Bud's periods of wakefulness.

"I didn't know that," she said. "No one told me."

"It's quite common," Nurse Lorin replied. "Except . . ."

"Except what?" Deborah asked.

"It was unusual that it happened the same time every night the past ten days. From 6:00 to 8:00 usually."

"Are you sure?" Deborah asked.

"Honey, when it comes to my patients, I'm sure of everything." Nurse Lorin had been a nurse for twenty-six years. An attractive woman who was very strong-willed when it came to looking after her patients. Blond, single, and always wondering why there were so few "hot" male patients over the years.

Deborah looked back at Bud trying to talk to the doctor,

but her thoughts were of Lindsey Wilkerson. It was 7:00 to 8:00 at night when the young girl would visit Bud and pray over him. She covered her mouth and kept thinking to herself, *Lindsey, Lindsey, sweet Lindsey. Who are you, my dear sweet child?*

It was another hour when William Lance came to the room for a visit. Detectives Baker and O'Malley stopped by as well as Officer Lynagh. Doctor Ng finally put a limit on the visitors and asked Deborah to limit his visitors to only one person after 6:00 pm for the next couple days. She wrote on the pad for Nurse Lorin the one person would be Lindsey Wilkerson.

"Excuse me for asking," the nurse said to Deborah. "I can't help but ask since Bud Johnson has had so many visitors and friends. I noticed no blood relatives have been by. Does he not have family?"

Deborah hesitated for a moment and spoke. "He lost his mother a few years ago and his father before that from his abuse of alcohol. His older brother and he had a falling out and don't keep in touch."

The nurse reached out her hand to Deborah. "So you are his family."

The woman who you could tell shed many tears over the previous two weeks smiled with nervousness at Nurse Lorin and said, "Yes, I am his family as well as his friend. His blood family doesn't know what they are missing from this kind and gentle soul."

Doctor Ng came out to the hallway and told Deborah if things went well, Bud would be out of the hospital within the following seven to nine days. He began to walk away as he stopped and called to Nurse Lorin, "Oh, and see if we can get some gummy bears, the . . ."

He was interrupted by the nurse, "I know, I know the Haribo kind. He is a gummy bear himself." She walked down the hall waving her arms.

Deborah laughed as she went back to the room. She stared at Bud as he spoke slowly. "I guess you missed me." Bud drifted off to sleep.

Three Hours Later

Bud spoke again as Deborah grabbed his hand. "I thought I lost you."

Still struggling with his speech, he spoke. "Never," he said. "Unless I don't get any damn gummy bears." She laughed again as she put his hand to her face. "Wait," Bud said. "If I've been here for two weeks, what happened with my move? What happened to my homes to leave and close on?"

Deborah sat down next to him. "Don't worry," she replied. "You are moved out of one and now a resident of the Henry Hallock house on South Street."

"But how?" he asked. "The money? The closing?"

Deborah smiled as she answered, "I took care of everything. The transactions were done through my accounts, but since you were not there I worked it out with the Marchese family for you to rent the house for a year. To show faith I gave them six months' rent in advance. They were very understanding, and when and if you are ready to buy, they will discuss it with you. Everything is in your name. You can pay me back when you are out of here." Bud looked at her in amazement over her trust in him.

"What about my things?" Those four words took him almost a minute to say, but Deborah was patient.

"My dad hired movers to take care of everything," she said, "including what needed to be cleaned, Mr. Johnson. You are such a man," she said with a smile. Her expression changed and she got serious. "But a sweet, wonderful man. Listen," she said, "you're only allowed one visitor after 6:00 pm the next few days, and I hope you don't mind but I gave them a name I think will make you happy."

"It's not you?" he asked.

"No," she answered. "You have me all day," she said with a laugh.

"OK," he said, "it's Paul."

"No," she answered. "I think you will be happy and surprised. Just be patient."

Bud was a little confused but he decided to wait it out. Deborah said good night to him with a kiss on the lips. "Welcome back." He looked at her and thanked her.

Deborah got in the car and drove to Rachelle's house on Prospect Street. She opened the door and found Rachelle not showered, her hair a mess, and her face red from crying most of the day. She held Rachelle and just kept saying, "Get it out of your system, I'm here for you."

It was another thirty minutes before Deborah let go of her, saying, "Come on, you are going in the shower." Deborah helped her undress and stayed by her as she showered to wash all her emotions away. Deborah even helped dry her off, combed her hair, and made her put on her Benjamin Franklin lounge pants and a T-shirt and then brought her to the kitchen to make her a cup of tea. They sat for the next couple hours as Rachelle vented about what happened to her relationship with Paul. The shower, tea, and Deborah were just what Rachelle needed to feel a little better. Deborah listened as Rachelle told her why Paul wanted to split.

Deborah touched her wrist and spoke. "Do you love him, Rachelle, or are you in love with him?"

Rachelle looked at her. "Both," she said, "but I know it's over. He can be so loving, so thoughtful, yet when I saw him shooting Robert in the mall over and over again, I was so frightened by what I saw in his eyes."

Deborah touched Rachelle's chin to get her eyes focused back to her. "I had a conversation with Bud a few months ago and he told me there was no one more loyal than Paul. He said that

Paul told him the most important people in his life were his father; you, Rachelle; Bud; and I don't know why, but me. So you need to consider that three of the four people he cared about most were in danger of being lost to him. Give him his time, Rachelle. I have a feeling."

Rachelle smiled at Deborah.

"You are good for the soul, Deborah Lance." She smiled gratefully as she continued to drink her tea.

It was now after 7:00 pm and Bud was texting with Paul when Lindsey walked in. Bud almost dropped his phone but couldn't help but smile at the girl he thought he would never see again. She walked over to him, bent over, and hugged him and wouldn't let go.

"I'm so happy to see you, Lindsey. I would ask you how you have been but you would tell me everything that has happened in the past year and a half."

She laughed and spoke. "No, I don't really do that anymore, but it was fun with you." The detective was referring to Lindsey's desire to torture Bud as a twelve-year-old with her photographic memory and gifted hearing.

"How is school?" he asked.

"Good, thanks. I'm in college now and will graduate when I'm seventeen."

Bud nodded but was not surprised. "And then what?" he asked.

"Well," she answered, "let's just say you will be seeing a lot of me."

"Umm," Bud answered. Lindsey interrupted him and changed the subject.

They spoke about the past eighteen months and what she had done. He knew he would get caught up with her life because she remembered every single detail of her life. He used to joke with her about her memory and she would challenge him constantly.

She went from being annoying to someone he cared about very deeply. It was now close to 8:00 pm when Sharyn Wilkerson came into the room to bring Lindsey home. Bud acknowledged her with a thank-you for bringing Lindsey to see him.

"You're welcome," she answered, "but it was difficult to keep her away."

Lindsey hugged him good-bye and she got to the door, when Bud spoke again.

"Will I see you again, Lindsey?"

The young girl smiled. "Oh, yes, it is your destiny, Bud Johnson."

Bud looked at her with his head cocked. "Are you messing with me again, girl?"

Lindsey's smiled disappeared as she answered, "You are a good cop, a good man, a good friend, and a good partner. You will know your destiny, Bud Johnson, as you continue to get closer to God." She kissed her hand and blew hard to push it to him as she walked out the door.

He looked at the empty space in the doorway for at least a minute before he turned his head and noticed Deborah had left her Bible and her book *Intelligence for Your Life*. He picked up the John Tesh book and spoke to the Bible, "One step at a time," and began to read. He was reading for over an hour when Detective Cronin walked in with O'Malley and Lynagh. Bud put the book down, thinking, *So much for the one-visitor rule.*

"I was wondering when you would be here. Deborah and Paul told me over the phone today you were alive."

Cronin looked at Lynagh and O'Malley to give him privacy for a few minutes. He sat down in the chair and Bud listened while Cronin reviewed the case and why he disappeared by death during the investigation. He explained that Branca and Tangretti got away with the cash and Paul would be taking a couple weeks off for vacation and most likely an additional three weeks' leave of absence. As Bud was listening he began to text Rachelle, Deborah, and Paul. He wanted to see them in the morning. They were talking for over an hour when the nurse on duty told Cronin he had to leave or Nurse Lorin would skin her alive in the morning. Before he left he told Bud that Priority 1 would be working on other cases, including the undercover at the correctional facility.

"This is not like you, Boss," Bud said. "Loose ends, and we move on."

The detective lieutenant stood up to leave and spoke. "There won't be any loose ends, Bud. Get some rest. I'll see you in a couple of days."

Bud nodded as O'Malley and Lynagh said quick hellos and good-byes before the nurse pushed them out.

OCTOBER 26

Paul arrived at Stony Brook Hospital to see Bud at 9:45 am. Bud waited patiently for his partner to bring up that he was leaving for a few weeks, but Paul never did. After about ten minutes of small talk Bud started the conversation.

"Cronin tells me you're taking time off."

"Yes, I need to get away."

"When were you going to tell me?"

"I was waiting to be sure you were OK and out of the hospital."

"What about Rachelle, how does she feel about it?"

"Bud, I've told Rachelle that we needed time and space from each other for a number of reasons."

"Oh, I see, the girl risks her life to be with you, and you tell her good-bye."

"It will never be good-bye with her, but I need to clear my head and I need her to be safe."

"Sounds like bullshit to me."

"I didn't come here to have you upset while you are in the hospital. You asked me to come."

"Paul, you are one good cop, but you don't know a good thing when you have it."

"I almost said the same thing to you a couple of months ago."

"OK," Bud replied, nodding his head, "you made your point, but you've almost lost her a few times in the past couple of years."

"Because of me. Bud, my life is dangerous to her. If she was lost I would blame myself forever."

"So," Bud answered, "when it comes to Rachelle, you're a coward, is that what you are saying?"

Paul looked away, then back at this partner and best friend. "I guess I am."

"Paul," Bud replied, "if you need to go and get yourself together, then do it. But do me a favor. If you guys go your separate ways, then let it be. Don't keep anyone hanging. Let her move on with her life and really give her space."

Paul nodded as they spoke police business and Cronin's latest maneuver on the case. It was another thirty minutes before Deborah came in, and while she gave Paul a kiss he could tell she was upset with him. He knew there was no doubt she had spoken to Rachelle. Paul gave Bud a handshake and a hug before leaving, allowing Deborah and him to talk about what was happening with their best friends. Deborah stayed with him for the day, and at 2:30 pm Rachelle walked in with a short haircut and a different look with her makeup.

Deborah gave her a puzzled look and Rachelle simply said, "A new start, a new look."

Bud was afraid to comment other than to say, "You look beautiful no matter what you do." She stayed for an hour until Bud was prepared for therapy and left with a smile and a hug.

As Bud left the room with Nurse Lorin, he looked back at Deborah and said, "You better keep a close eye on Rachelle, before she cuts off other things."

Deborah just shook her head at him.

"You're still a clown, Bud Johnson."

"See how I get when I don't have my gummy bears."

She laughed as Nurse Lorin was yelling,

"Gummy bears my ass; let's get to work! Don't talk to me about gummy bears unless they are sitting at the bottom of a vodka martini."

Deborah was shaking her head with a smile as she looked

back at all the cards that were sent to Bud the past few weeks he was in the hospital. She sat down on his bed and started picking them up one at a time, reading them. They were from Paul and Rachelle together and then cards from each of them separately. There were cards from the precinct, the mayor of Port Jefferson Village, the Brookhaven town supervisor, Joey Z, and the Wilkerson Family. More cards from people throughout the community and the general public. Some were stacked laying flat. She noticed two cards on the other side of the bed that were separated from the rest. One of them was a card she had written to Bud. She read it again to herself.

Dear Bud,

When I think about our lives the past two years, I want you to know that you give purpose to me. A sense of security that only my father has been able to give to me. You "touch" me and have "touched" me. I will be forever grateful that God brought you into my life. With much love, Deborah.

She put the card down and picked up the other card that was standing next to her card. It read,

Dear Detective Bud Johnson,

You asked me when I was twelve years old what I thought about faith. I told you that faith gives you the strength to do more than you originally intended to do. It is also written that faith is being sure of what we hope for and certain of what we do not see (Hebrews 11:1). I have faith, Bud, that you will fulfill your destiny. You are in my prayers every night. With much love, Lindsey.

Deborah smiled as she placed the card down on the bedside table. She picked up her iPhone and called her father while she waited for Bud to return from his therapy.

Correctional Officer John Bay brought Madison down to the visitor center not knowing for sure who was waiting for her. Madison didn't recognize Rachelle at first with her short haircut and different-color lipstick, but she knew something was not right. She reached her hand over the top divider as always, so they could hold hands.

"What's wrong?" she asked Rachelle.

"We are no longer together," she answered.

"What happened?" Madison asked.

Rachelle hesitated for a few seconds before giving Madison eye contact and speaking. "I'm not sure, really. I'm not sure at all. He claims my life will always be in danger if we are together, but I think it's an excuse to move on." Madison let her speak until there was silence.

"I don't believe that, Rachelle. There is more to this than you being another notch on his bedpost." Rachelle didn't answer her sister, so Madison spoke again. "Do you love him, Rachelle? Enough to spend forever with him?"

"I thought we would always be together, Maddie, but I guess . . ." Rachelle struggled to get the rest of the words out, "I was wrong."

"Is that why the change in your hair and makeup?" Madison asked.

Rachelle laughed. "Well, I needed to feel good about myself."

Rachelle stayed another forty minutes as she brought Madison up to date on Bud, Deborah, and the ever-mysterious Detective Cronin. Rachelle said her good-bye and drove to Z Pita restaurant for her shift for the evening, where Joey Z informed her that Paul had given him a month's rent in advance but that he would not be staying upstairs until further notice. Rachelle nodded, as Joey Z told her someone would have to check on the apartment every other day to be sure everything was OK. Again she nodded as she walked to the front. She did not want Joey Z to see the tears filling up in her eyes.

She went out to the sidewalk on Main Street, where she covered her mouth to keep the sounds of her crying to a minimum. Joey Z saw her through the window and almost went out to console her. He decided to let her have her privacy. She returned inside the restaurant within ten minutes, and because of the professional she was, no one could tell how much she was hurting inside.

HALLOWEEN
OCTOBER 31

Brian Branca and Linda Tangretti were getting ready for their weekend getaway at the Royal Coconut Palace Hotel and Spa for Halloween. It was perfect for them. While there were *wanted* notifications by the FBI and Suffolk County Police, the Halloween getaway was the perfect way for them to get out and have a disguise for a fun weekend. The hideaway bungalow was a two-bedroom mini-house surrounded by trees and bushes with about twenty yards between the other bungalows. The costume party would start at 5:00 pm by the pool, with a buffet of lobster, fresh fish, shrimp, clams, and different prepared dishes of chicken and steak. After, they would board the dinner cruise ship, the *Atlantic Princess*, where 140 passengers would party into the night, enjoying wine, beer, champagne, music, dancing, and a light buffet of fish and salads until 1:00 am. The cruise ship would sail the Atlantic Ocean for the night before returning the following evening. The thought of sharing all this with complete strangers who didn't know their identity was exciting to both Linda and Brian.

They checked in at 4:00 pm and found their little bungalow within ten minutes. They unpacked their costumes and took a shower together. Linda was so excited and turned on about the weekend she enjoyed getting Brian aroused with the water coming down on them. She had never had sex in a shower before, and she made sure today she would take advantage of the opportunity. It was awkward and not like what she had seen in the movies, so it was only a few minutes when they moved to the floor of the bedroom and had rough sex with their soaking-wet bodies. Linda spoke to Brian as she encouraged him to be rough with her. He was so turned on, it was over within five minutes.

Linda noticed how hard he was breathing from it and told him to please not have a heart attack until at least they had a chance to enjoy the weekend. He laughed as he kissed the side of her face. It was another five minutes before they got up off the floor to dry themselves. Linda jumped in the shower again to have another cleansing as Brian put on his Zorro costume. He loved the black outfit and the small mask. He even shaved cleanly to look more like the character. He had a fake sword with the authentic costume. Linda did not want to wear a mask on her face, so she became a police officer with all the accessories—the fake gun, mace, nightstick, and sunglasses.

Once she was dressed, Brian grabbed her and spoke. "You know I've always had a fantasy about women police officers."

She kissed him and told him she would "arrest" him later. They could not believe the world they entered when they arrived at the outdoor buffet between the two pools. The costumes ranged from Hercules, Tarzan, the Blues Brothers, and Zombies of all kinds to humorous costumes such as bananas and a couple peanut butter and jelly sandwiches to Cinderella and the sexiest costumes Brian had ever seen. He laughed at the Lucy and Popeye costumes, and he loved the thought of not knowing who anybody was. The chance that he could be standing next to a celebrity or a cop gave him an adrenaline rush. He was amused by his own thoughts and wondered if the other guests entertained the same feelings. *If they only knew they were partying with a wanted killer.* He laughed out loud as Linda poked him with a look on her face that was saying, *What the hell are you thinking?*

The advantage for the people dressed up like Hercules and Tarzan and some of the sexy outfits was that they could jump in the pool if they wanted to; however, it did not bother Linda and Brian. This was the first real time in many weeks where they were mingling and talking with other guests.

Linda was eyeing a male cop who looked like a Chippendale

dancer in disguise until his partner dressed up in a sexy firefighter costume pulled on his badge. The food was the best Linda had since they left Long Island. The hour of 7:00 pm came fast, when the host, dressed as a naval commander, ordered everyone to start boarding the *Atlantic Princess*. Only toiletries and a small bag were allowed for the cruise. You would either keep your costume on or you would have nothing on for the cruise. As they boarded the ship there were mannequins dressed in some of the most famous costumes of all time. On each side of the black carpet there were Power Rangers, Ninja Turtles, Michael Myers, Star Wars characters, Jason, Batman, and Spiderman, and as they got to the end of the walk entrance there was Ghost Face. Branca gave the mannequin the middle finger as Linda laughed.

They entered a huge ballroom with more food on the side tables, in addition to couches and high tables to mingle and talk. There was a DJ waiting for them as he started playing music to get everyone in the Halloween mood for the evening. Linda shook her head over how much detail was given for the party. It wasn't five minutes before she dragged Brian to the dance floor. She was feeling so comfortable that she took off her hat and sunglasses and let her hair down as she moved to the club music. The lights flickering with the sound of music and champagne brought her to a level of escapism she hadn't anticipated. For the first time in years she didn't have a care in the world. The main floor was filled with so many different characters, from Marilyn Monroe to the Great Gatsby to vampires and politicians. It was a room filled with familiar faces.

As Linda moved closer to Brian Branca and put her hand on his groin, she spoke in his ear.

"Tell me, Zorro, is that your sword or are you happy to see me?"

He laughed as he brought her closer to him. "Let me show you." Two hours had already passed as the big boat was now over three miles out to sea. He started walking toward their room holding her hand as they left the dance floor. They walked through the black carpet of Halloween legends and Branca did not forget to give the Ghost Face mannequin the middle finger again, but this time he did it with both hands as he said, "Here's twice as much for you." He was so amused he almost knocked the glass of champagne out of Linda's hand.

They walked up the spiral staircase to the second level and turned right into the hallway that led to the suites with balconies looking over the beautiful Atlantic Ocean. They opened the door to the room that had a king-size bed surrounded by plush carpet that looked like a painting on the floor. A bar fully stocked, a mirror on the ceiling, a long sofa on the side of the room with a glass entrance leading to a 15'x10' balcony that made them feel like they could touch the ocean.

They fell on the bed as Branca started to unbutton Linda's police shirt. She took his mask off his face and told him she would be back in a few minutes. Linda got up and went into the bathroom. She fell in love right away. It had a hot tub, a shower, two sinks, and a marble tile floor with a hand-painted picture of the ocean. She felt like she was standing on the ocean. The wall had a flat-screen TV so you could enjoy shows while relaxing in the hot tub. She was thinking how she could stay in there for hours.

Brian Branca lay on his back as he looked at the moon through the sliding doors to the balcony. He got up off the bed, opened the sliding door, and walked over to the bar and dropped his cape in anticipation of fulfilling his fantasy of being with a female cop. He poured himself a glass of champagne and walked out to the balcony to take in the view of the moon and the ocean. They were now out about three miles from Key West as Brian held out his glass to the moon.

"A toast to all of you assholes. Who's the king of the world now?" He loved the sound of the water brushing up against the side of the boat. The swishing sound was so relaxing in a calm ocean.

He closed his eyes as he heard a noise behind him. Thinking it was Linda he turned around and smiled, but it was a figure dressed in dark clothes. The mysterious figure came up on him so fast he barely got a glimpse. It was enough to know it was Ghost Face who came up on him, lifting him up so fast and with such precision that Branca was over the balcony and into the ocean within a couple seconds. The figure threw the mask from the moving ship as close as he could to Branca, and as it landed Branca swam toward it. He grabbed it, and just in time, the exterior lights of the vessel came on. The mask had the words *No Mercy* written on it in what looked like blood. Branca started screaming for his life as he suddenly realized the boat was not stopping. It was only now that he asked for God to enter his life. He started to make up words to pray for forgiveness, but there was no hope. Within four minutes the vessel was out of sight and within the shark-infested waters off Florida it was only another ten minutes before Brian Branca experienced a slow, merciless death.

Linda was oblivious to what happened for she took a full twenty minutes before coming out completely naked except for the badge on a chain around her neck. "You're under arrest, you bad boy." She looked around the room and saw the sliding door open to the balcony. "Come back in, and I'll show you what it's like to be the most wanted."

She walked over to the bed and noticed there were photographs spread out on top. Her facial expression changed as she got closer and picked up one of them. It was a photo of Officer Franks. She dropped it and looked at the others as her breathing became heavier and her heart started beating faster. Photos of Detective Hansen, Officer Dugan, Chapman, Baker, and Wyatt bloodied with their injuries. She shuffled through the photos as she looked around to see if anybody was in the room.

"Brian!" She started yelling his name over and over as she

saw the photos of the three young women that were killed in the nightclubs. She started ripping up the photos as she yelled for Brian again. There was a frightening silence in the room that was too much for Linda. She put on her uniform pants and was in such a hurry she didn't even bother to button the shirt when she put it on. She ran down the hallway almost bumping into a couple dressed as Mickey and Minnie Mouse. She walked quickly down the spiral staircase to go back to the large room where the party was. She was hoping that Brian had played a silly joke on her and she would apologize for taking so long in the bathroom.

As she went toward the room and past the Halloween legends on the black carpet she stopped when she got to the mannequin that had the Ghost Face mask on it. Staring at her was a male mannequin. The mask had been taken off. Linda started screaming as she ran into the party. She was grabbing both men and women to help her. Most of the party attendees were aware of what was going on, but they were trying to avoid her. Finally one man dressed in a captain's uniform was able to grab hold of her and he finally convinced her he was part of the ship's crew.

"Help me!" she said. "Someone is trying to kill me, please help me!"

"Hold on," the captain said, "how do you know this?"

Linda dragged him to the hall of mannequins outside the party and showed him the male head. "He's missing the white mask! The Ghost Face mask."

The man looked at her like she was crazy but still tried to calm her down. "Ma'am, we have a doctor on board, let me take you to him."

"Oh, fuck you!" she screamed as she ran down the opposite hallway.

There was a door half open so she entered. In the room it was a young couple making out on the sofa in full costume of Robin Hood and Maid Marian. Before Robin could say anything Linda left the room not sure of what she was going to do.

She started to walk slowly toward the center of the ship when the famous white mask appeared all the way at the other end. Linda stopped in her tracks as she began to cry. "Stop, please stop!" The masked figure started walking slowly toward her as she backed up, taking a few small steps before turning around and running to the hallway exit and up the emergency stairs. She didn't even notice the three guys dressed as the three Stooges in full character.

"Hey, Moe, it's a sexy cop."

"Never mind." Curly received a slap.

Even Larry had a comment.

"That's what I call a wardrobe malfunction."

Linda ran up two flights of stairs and asked a sexy zombie if she knew where the purser's office was. The pretty zombie pointed to the third level as Linda ran to the center of the ship, where the spiral staircase was. She reached the third level within seconds in her bare feet and found the purser's office empty. She stood there not knowing what else to do, when an announcement came over the ship's speakers. It was in a whispered inflection but loud enough to be understood: "No Mercy."

She left the purser's office not knowing where to go or what to do, but her heart was pounding so hard she started looking for the doctor's office. Her thoughts ran wild as her hair was now soaking wet and she was shaking with fear. She crept slowly down the hallway and even jumped when a door opened. She decided she needed to get back to the party because it would be safer with the large crowd. Slowly, with her head turning constantly and her breathing getting harder, Linda made it back to the costume party. Her shirt was only closed at the bottom two buttons, so most noticed that depending on how she moved, her breasts were exposed, but she was sweating so hard with stress, physical activity, and emotion she didn't give it a second thought. Once inside the party she found the man dressed up as the captain again.

"I'm sorry," she said, "I need help to get off this ship."

He looked at her with a puzzled expression.

"We are over three and a half miles from shore and we are not scheduled to arrive back until tomorrow evening."

"I would do and pay anything to get off this ship," Linda said to him. "I'll even pay for a helicopter to come here and take me back. I have a family emergency."

The captain looked at her and said, "$3,000 for the helicopter expense and $10,000 for me."

Linda nodded her head. "Deal, just get me out of here."

"How do I know," the captain said, "that you won't screw me? You don't have the money on board. I need some collateral and the key to your room back at the hotel with the number."

Linda moved closer to him. "You can come with me to my room. I have cash there, and honey, if you get me out of here I will definitely screw you as well as . . ." She grabbed his crotch.

The man dressed as the captain nodded as Linda gave him her room key with the number. She had no choice if she wanted to get off the boat. "Let me make a phone call. I will tell them you have an emergency with immediate family and you will pay for the expense. Get your story together."

"How long?" Linda asked.

"It will take at least a couple of hours," the captain answered.

Linda was afraid to leave the party and realized something had happened to Brian. She was mingling throughout the crowd and party for twenty minutes when "Alone in the Dark" by Mystic Strangers came on. Her heart started beating faster. She tried to drown out the lyrics, but she couldn't. She pushed herself through the crowd to find the ladies' room.

"Move!" she kept saying. Finally, she found the ladies' room and went inside. She could still hear the song behind the door, but she couldn't hear the lyrics, which was good enough for her.

She went inside the stall, and before she could shut the door behind her a hand reached out, grabbed her hair, and in a second snapped her neck. Linda Tangretti died almost exactly the way Kate Summers and Alicia Hudson had died in the music clubs. Her death was a full circle of the deaths she was responsible for.

Linda's body was picked up and put in a wheelchair that had already been placed outside the door. The mysterious figure dressed in a mirror mask pushed the chair past the Halloween figures hallway. Still the Ghost Face mask was missing. The wheelchair was pushed to the elevator past the spiral staircase to the second level. Once the elevator opened, Linda's body in the wheelchair was pushed to her room. The chair was steered all the way to the balcony as her body was picked up and thrown over the side of the vessel. The killer went over to the bed and picked up all the torn apart photos that had been placed there for Linda. The mysterious figure touched each photo and said "For you" before tossing them over the side with the Ghost Face mask that was taken from the mannequin. The figure left the room and went back down to the party and disappeared into the crowd.

The helicopter arrived in two and half hours, and "Captain" Bob Langer could not locate Linda Tangretti. The expense was building as the helicopter was waiting. Finally he decided to get on the copter himself. It took twenty-five minutes to land about five miles from the hotel as Bob put the $3,000 on his credit card. He went straight to Linda's room and the key didn't work.

"Bitch!" he said out loud. She had given him the wrong room number just in case he betrayed her. Bob was relentless as he discreetly tried the door key to each of the bungalows. The more doors he tried, the more upset he was getting. All he kept thinking about was the $3,000 on his credit card. One hour later he was still checking the doors until finally it worked.

He entered the room and looked behind every nook and cranny until he looked under the bathroom sink. Inside a shoe box was a stack of $100 bills totaling $82,000.

Bob didn't want to waste time so he drove back to the helicopter pad and paid another $3,000 to be brought back to the ship plus the charge for the wait time for the helicopter. As he flew back, Langer was getting his thoughts together as what his alibi would be if Linda Tangretti ever came back for the money. He hadn't even thought about it till now. He was swearing at himself thinking about how many people knew and saw him take the helicopter back and forth. He was back on board by 1:00 am, which was only an absence of two and a half hours. He walked around the ship to try and find Linda but gave up after another hour. He reported to the real ship's captain that it was a false alarm, that the person needing medical attention was OK, and that the passenger did not leave the ship. It wasn't a lie, and Langer hoped there would be no more questions. All he cared about was that he felt like a different person with $82,000 in $100 bills in his possession. *It's true*, he thought, *it takes money to make money*, thinking about the $6,000 already spent.

NOVEMBER 1

S ince Linda and Brian paid in advance for the entire trip, no one thought twice about it when they did not check out. Left in their room was their only set of clothes they brought before changing their clothes. It was not that unusual for people to leave things in their rooms. Since everyone was in costume, no one missed them the next afternoon when the ship was returning to port. By this time, most everyone only had a portion of their costume on and was so hung-over or tired, no one cared about the way they looked. Only those concerned about their identities in front of strangers kept their costumes fully intact. The vessel hit port at 5:00 pm Sunday, and Bob Langer was in a good mood saying good-bye to the passengers hoping they had a good time.

It was a gorgeous day in Bermuda. Barbara just came out of the ocean, dried herself off, and laid in her lounge chair as she stared out into the beautiful blue ocean.

"Hello, Barbara," the man behind her spoke. She looked up to see a chiseled, good-looking man with dark sunglasses and a bathing suit.

"Yes?" she said. "Who are you?"

The man looked at the ocean, then took off his sunglasses as he spoke to her. "Barbara Sherman, wife of former FBI agent Robert Sherman. My name is Paul Powers, and you and I have much to talk about."

NOVEMBER 18

The Priority 1 Task Force was fully intact except for Bud, who was under strict orders to stay at home. Both Deborah and Rachelle took turns checking in on him over the past few weeks. Paul also kept in touch with him by phone on almost a daily basis and was returning to work the Monday after Thanksgiving. While Paul was away, he sent Rachelle a text once a week, but she never replied. She had accepted their life together was over and felt it made no sense to prolong the inevitable. It was difficult for her to check on Paul's apartment upstairs, and each time she did she would take some of her belongings out of the place until everything that was hers was eliminated. There were photos of her and Paul on the bureau and night table, but she did not touch them. Her friendship with Deborah grew closer as they both remained loyal to Bud in his time of need. She knew Deborah loved him, but she was worried she too would fall victim to a broken heart to a cop. She was there for her, and Deborah continued to visit the jail with Rachelle to visit Madison a few times a month.

Lindsey Wilkerson was insistent with her parents that she needed to be involved with Bud and Justin Healey. While she was only fourteen, her intellectual prowess made it much more difficult to hold her back from the lives of the two Suffolk County officers as well as Rachelle and Deborah. She would go over to his new home at 116 South Street and keep him company by playing games or getting into one of their famous debates that was amusing to everyone. The most recent had Rachelle and Deborah beside themselves. Bud was sucking on a couple gummy bears as Lindsey was explaining why she could not be hypnotized, which is common in people who are left-brain-dominant. Bud would argue with her that it made no difference but Lindsey was adamant.

"You will find, Detective Johnson," she said with a wink, "that most lawyers, mathematicians, judges, and lab scientists are left-brained people and that we are very logical people."

Bud shook his head. "And you read this where?"

"Never mind," Lindsey answered. She no longer liked to show she remembered exact times and dates, but she did enjoy her banter with Bud. "There are exceptions as in all things, but this is a fact."

"OK," Bud answered as he gave her a hug. "I believe you." He looked at Rachelle and Deborah and crossed his eyes as they both laughed.

Detective Lieutenant Cronin had just hung up the phone with ADA Ashley regarding the transfer of undercover reporter Gary Reynolds from Bedford Hills to go to the Riverhead facility with Detective Ellyn Baker. Both of them would be there for one month to get close with the inmates and find out what they could about the doctors giving out prescriptions for cash. They had worked it out that the transfer of Reynolds was now safe. Baker couldn't wait for the assignment and was chomping at the bit.

Detective William O'Malley accepted a temporary transfer to Priority 1 while Powers was on his leave of absence, but Cronin was going to try and pull strings to keep him with the task force until his retirement, which he insisted would happen within the year. Justin Healey was back at his role as George Lynagh's partner and occasionally would tease him about what he called "Lynagh's Luck." It seemed no matter what happened during the past few years, he came out unscathed. Officer Chapman was back on normal duty and was showing the ropes to Officers Dugan and Frank's replacements and what was expected of them at Priority 1.

Al Simmons, Madison's attorney, came by for a visit and told Cronin that the therapist was a big help for Madison and the nightmares were becoming much less. He also requested to see if Madison could have Rachelle spend Christmas Eve with her sister and a correctional officer.

Cronin looked up at Simmons and spoke.

"On the other side of the bars in her jail cell?"

"Yes," Simmons answered. "She was alone last Christmas, and I don't think spending a couple of hours with her only family should be an issue, do you?"

"Gina," Cronin said to the speaker, "please have ADA Ashley stop by in the morning."

"Yes, sir," she replied. Cronin looked back at Simmons and told him he would try and see what he could do through the proper authorities. The attorney nodded as he shook Cronin's hand and left the building. Cronin thought how lucky Madison was to have Simmons for an attorney. Then again, $300,000 missing from the briefcase that Phil Smith had from the night he was killed was a help. His thoughts stopped him from paperwork as he asked Gina to bring him the folder on what they had when Phil Smith was found dead in the barn eighteen months prior.

NOVEMBER 19

ADA Ashley was in Cronin's office at 9:00 am sharp.

"The request for Madison Robinson's visit on Christmas Eve will have to be reviewed by our office in conjunction with the commissioner at the jail. Regardless of what we or anyone else thinks, she is a criminal. We have to be careful."

"Yes," Cronin replied, "however, she was allowed to serve out her term there to be near her only family. So it's quite a contradiction if it's not allowed. I can just see the papers now: *Vigilante Killer Kept at Jail to Be Close to Family Is Denied Christmas Eve Visit.*" Ashley nodded with amusement at Cronin's sarcasm.

"We will do what we can to make it happen." He started to walk away but turned back. "Any news on the search for Brian Branca and Linda Tangretti?"

"No," Cronin replied. "I have a feeling they are long gone." He looked down at his papers as Ashley tried to get a read on his facial expression.

"Gone?" or "Long gone?" Ashley asked. Cronin looked up for a second as Ashley waited for an answer. He didn't give it to him. Instead he changed the subject.

"Powers is back Monday. I would like to keep O'Malley on our task force until he retires. He deserves to retire from Priority 1. It's only a year, and since he's been with us for three months already I don't think his precinct commander would mind breaking in some younger blood over there. His experience is an asset here."

Ashley nodded. "What about Powers?"

"What about him?" Cronin replied.

"He goes on leave of absence while Johnson is out on disability. Are you going to keep him in Priority 1?"

"There is not a team better when the two of them are together. Powers will get down to business Monday and Johnson will return January 3. In the meantime our team will hold things together. Bud not coming back till after the New Year is another reason we need to have O'Malley stay on."

Ashley looked at Cronin and waited for him to look at him. "Is Face of Fear going to be over and out before the end of the year?"

"I gave you a promise, didn't I?" Cronin replied.

"Yes, you did," Ashley said. "Have a nice Thanksgiving if I don't speak to you." Cronin nodded as he looked over the folder of papers related to the killing of Phil Smith during the Face of Fear Investigation.

Detective Sergeant Paul Powers returned to work Monday, and the six weeks he was absent only made the heart grow fonder from his coworkers. He was in better shape than when he left and his tan had heads turning from the female officers. He walked into Cronin's office and was there for twenty minutes.

Paul walked over to Cronin's desk and shook his hand.

"Nice to see you, sir."

His boss stood up and put his left hand on top of both their right hands.

"Please sit down," Cronin said. "Bring me up to date. How are you doing?"

"I'm feeling good and ready for things to get back to normal," Paul replied.

"Normal," Cronin said, "what an interesting word."

"It's pronounced *normal,* and it means not abnormal; regular or natural, but I think that's a good thing."

Cronin shook his head.

"Yes, whoever thought that *good* meant *normal*?"

"I'm ready for things to be the way they were," Paul replied.

Cronin nodded again.

"So you are ready to put everything in the past and look toward the future."

Paul looked at him with a bland stare. "The past is the past. That part of my life is over. I just want to move on."

"Do you want to tell me what you have been doing for the past seven weeks?" Cronin asked.

"Well, as you know, two weeks of it was locating Barbara Sherman."

"And?" Cronin asked.

"She knew he had a policy and their marriage was over. She thought once he was pronounced dead and he got his money they would split it and go their separate ways. She had no part in any of it. Let's just say she fell into a pile of shit luck by ending up with everything from the policy. Why did you have me track her down?"

"I wanted to be sure," Cronin said, "that she was just lucky and not an accomplice in all of it." He leaned back in his chair and looked at Powers before speaking again. "Your charts and the Sherman connection, how did you find out?"

"The night in the garage," Paul answered, "with Branca. He told me there was a connection. It's amazing what people remember when they think you will kill them. I whispered in his ear to be sure no one would hear me and he told me there was a connection. I just needed to put some evidence together. Following the letter of the law can be difficult at times." He looked at Cronin as if to give him a message.

"Yes," the detective lieutenant answered. "It can be difficult."

Paul asked, "Did we ever find out who killed Lawrence Stone in the parking lot?"

"No," Cronin answered, "not yet."

Cronin leaned forward and decided to try and change the

subject. "Tell me how you are feeling."

"It would take too long, but I can tell you the rest and relaxation did me good," Paul answered. He spoke again. "I visited friends, my father, worked out, and even traveled a bit."

"You know," Cronin replied, "we never found Linda Tangretti and Brian Branca. The FBI thinks they have either smuggled themselves out of the country or they are just that good at disappearing inside the country." He looked at his detective sitting across from him. "Do you have any thoughts on what happened?"

Paul answered immediately. "I don't know, but if you want me involved in looking for them, I will be happy to help the FBI."

"No, it's OK," Cronin replied. "I think it would be a waste of taxpayers' money." He turned around and pulled a file open and began to speak again. "Our notes from Face of Fear showed that Linda Tangretti's handle at the time on Twitter was Fun Mom. So I went to Connecticut, and lo and behold, she had a nine-year-old son staying with his grandmother who had a number that the kid could reach his mother at. The phone would ring and ring, only going to voice mail. So we traced the location of the calls and it showed the person using the cell was in Florida. The FBI took the info and covered the state and found video of some guy by the name of Bob Langer using a key to try and get into bungalows in Key West on Halloween. He was brought in for questioning and he told some story of a woman he met on a cruise ship party who disappeared."

"Why did he go back to her room with her key if she disappeared?" Paul asked.

"I wondered that also," Cronin replied. "He told us she begged him to help get her off the ship that someone was trying to kill her."

Paul shrugged his shoulders. "Did he identify her as Linda, and where is Branca?"

"I think," Cronin answered slowly, "that either Langer

is a good liar, which we can't charge him for with no bodies, or whoever did kill them is pretty damn lucky with Langer getting himself involved. If any bodies were to be found, he most likely would be on trial for murder since there are records of him taking helicopter rides from the ship to her hotel and back. Either way I don't think we will be hearing from them again. I'm sure the money was involved. The love of money is surely the root of all evil"

Paul nodded. "1 Timothy 6:10" Cronin looked surprised that Paul quoted the bible as his detective spoke again. "Bud, he taught me that. What would you like me to get started on?"

"Get your things together, get settled, go home, and make sure your personal life is squared away. We have Detective Baker and an undercover person going in to the Riverhead facility in a couple of days. Also get things back in motion with your partner. He will be back in about five weeks. Your work on the Music Club Murders brought Sherman and his crew down. Good work, Detective."

Paul went to the door, turned around, and spoke.

"You did the right thing by faking your death. You saved the girls' lives. Thank you, but . . ." His hesitation caught Cronin's attention as Paul continued to speak. "Bud, I can't stop thinking about what he did. He took three bullets to the chest and was ready to sacrifice everything for us. Although you saved lives, we would have probably lost them anyway if he hadn't done what he did. I can't get my head around it."

Cronin leaned back in his chair and was silent for a few seconds.

"Is that why you're letting your personal life go to hell?"

Paul was taken aback by the comment. He did not want to get into a confrontation with Cronin within the first few minutes of his return, but he couldn't help himself.

"Why don't you say what you really mean?"

"You know exactly what I mean," the detective lieutenant

replied firmly. "Your personal life, you may think it's none of my business, but it is because as good a detective as you are, there is difficulty in having the separation between the two."

"She is in danger as long as she is with me," Paul answered.

"Yes," Cronin replied, knowing he meant Rachelle Robinson. "She is, but you should give her more credit. She is a smart woman who agreed to my plan with Face of Fear. She put her life on the line to prove to me you were not some nut running around with a mask killing the bad guys. Instead, it was her sister, and what does this woman do? She sticks by you. Knowing what the consequences could be. Whether you like it or not this girl is inside your head. Do what you think is best, but I have to tell you, being great at your job means jack shit if you don't have someone to share your life with. You may think you're saving her life, but from where I'm sitting you may need her to save your life. As for Bud," Cronin continued, "Dr. Ng at the hospital has advised us that it's going to take time for his brain to fully recover from the trauma and the time it was lacking oxygen. Most who had that experience would go out on disability, but if I were a betting man, Bud will be back."

Cronin's words felt to Paul like someone just hit him in the chest. He looked at his boss with silence and nodded as he tapped the side of the door molding before leaving. There was no use to continue to look at him. No one ever won a stare-down with Kevin Cronin. *Except maybe his wife,* Paul thought. He managed to smile, reflecting on that thought as he walked to his desk.

Everyone in the office gave him his space for a few minutes until Ellyn Baker walked over and welcomed him with a big hug, bare feet and all. She was followed by the others who were in the precinct, including Gina, who didn't realize how much she missed him until he walked through the door. Officer Carol Wright came over and introduced herself as a new assignee. Paul couldn't help but notice she had black sneakers on while Baker refused to wear any shoes at all. How ironic it was that the high heels of her shoes may have saved her life that night at the club with Sysco. Ellyn Baker couldn't help but notice how muscular he had gotten in his arms, and she tried not to stare long enough for Paul or anyone else to notice. He looked over at the desk with pumpkin seed bags and smiled that O'Malley was still with the task force.

The detective sorted through his desk and stopped long enough to look at the framed photos sitting left to right across the top. Two of the photos were of him and Rachelle. One of them was of Rachelle, Bud, Deborah, and himself wearing Santa hats from the previous Christmas. One was of his dad and mom, and the last one was of Rachelle with the dogs. He reached to put them away but stopped as he thought to himself he needed more time before he could put them in a drawer.

Lynagh and Healey came into the precinct and hugged Paul at his desk. They exchanged comments about how each of them looked, and Paul got everyone laughing when he told Healey he was impressed he had not been shot in the past six weeks. He looked at Bud's desk and examined the photos on his desk. Deborah, Lindsey, one of himself with Bud, his parents. He had two greeting cards from Deborah with notes to him. Paul knew that Bud even kept a drawer of notes and cards in his desk. The other drawer was full of various sunglasses. He would tire easily of the same style, buy a new pair, and then forget to wear them. He was a tough cop, but he was turning out to be the most sensitive man Paul ever knew.

He looked over the folders of cases that the team had worked on the past two months until 3:00 pm and said good night to drive over to see Bud in his new home, the Henry Hallock house on South Street. When Bud opened the door his face lit up and he hugged Paul until his partner begged him to let go. He showed Paul around the house, starting with the basement.

"Jesus," Paul said, "it looks like nothing has been touched for fifty years."

Bud shook his head. "Aw, come on, maybe only forty-five years. The street is terrific; all the people are really nice. I have a great neighbor across the street. Louise loves to cook for everyone, her fish fries are the best!"

Bud continued, "I swear, the place is not haunted. I like to call it 'occupied,' and if it wasn't for the fact they were friendly ghosts, I would have moved already. And are you ready for this? The owners of the house own Marchese Motors on Route 112. I get free oil changes as long as I'm a tenant."

Paul was laughing and was starting to feel good again seeing Bud returning to being "Bud" again. Even his love of eating was returning. By the time Bud and Paul were upstairs in his bedroom he almost had convinced him there was a ghost in the house. There was an awkward silence for a moment as the two detectives, who had been through more together than any partnership on Long Island as cops, looked at each other.

"Why?" Paul asked. "Why did you bait Simpson for him to shoot you?"

Bud looked at him and then smiled.

"I was sure he was going to kill Deborah and try for Rachelle if he wasn't taken down. When you love someone, Paul, you forget about yourself and think about them."

There was a noise at the front door and Paul could hear Deborah and Rachelle's voices as they walked in.

Paul looked at Bud.

"You didn't tell me you were expecting company."

"What a great detective you are," Bud answered as he walked down the stairs.

Paul followed him and watched Bud kiss Deborah and Rachelle. He walked over, but the dogs rushed to Paul and were jumping on him. Even Craven, who was normally less anxious to say hello, was happy to see him. Rachelle forced a smile but could not help that her heart was beating fast. She thought she was over

Paul, but looking at him playing with Wes and Craven she felt heartache, nervousness, and suddenly missed him. She couldn't help but notice what good shape he was still in. She attempted to talk to Bud, but Paul walked over and gave Deborah a hug and a kiss and then reached over and did the same to Rachelle, who found herself putting her arm over his back. She was mad at herself for doing it, but it was an uncontrolled response.

"You look good," Paul said. "I like your hair this way."

"Thank you," Rachelle answered.

The dogs were still trying to get Paul's attention, and he was doing his best to give it to them. Deborah looked at Bud with an evil eye, trying to tell him through her facial expression that she hoped he had not set up this particularly awkward meeting. He shook his head at her as he tried to grab some gummy bears and she hit his hand hard to be sure he only took a few.

The meeting was so uncomfortable for everyone that Deborah told Bud they were going shopping and they were leaving the dogs with him for a couple hours.

"It was wonderful to see you, Paul," Rachelle said. He moved in to kiss her good-bye and she adjusted her head so he could kiss her on the cheek when he hugged her. He hugged Deborah, but he could sense she was still a little upset with him.

They left the house as Paul turned around and looked at Bud, who threw his arms up in the air when he spoke.

"You came over unannounced after being away for six weeks. This is going to happen often, being you are my best friend and partner, so we all have to deal with it."

Paul nodded as Bud looked at the dish that held the gummy bear packets. It was empty. Deborah had taken the packets so he wouldn't have too many while she was gone.

"I know they were not supposed to go shopping, Bud. You can call them in a few minutes and tell them I'm gone."

"No," Bud answered. "Just like you have to deal with this,

we too have to deal with it as well. It's been a couple months, and when she is dating someone new, then we all have to adjust."

"Wait," Paul answered, "is she already dating?"

Bud looked at his partner with a surprised look.

"Paul, you haven't seen her in a couple of months and you sent her a few texts while you were gone. I would say that qualifies her to be dating someone."

"You didn't answer my question," Paul replied.

Bud hesitated for a few seconds before replying.

"Not yet, but Deborah wants her to move on, and she has been trying to set her up with one of the teachers at the school."

"Oh," Paul replied. "I see. OK, I will see you later. I need to get with Joey Z and get settled back in the apartment."

Bud grabbed his arm as he reached the door. Paul looked at him as Bud spoke. "I suppose one day we are going to talk about what you have been up to the past couple of months."

"Yes," Paul replied. "We will." He gave Bud a hug and walked down the stairs as he looked at his partner behind the screen door.

"When did the doctor say you can do one of your famous dances for us?"

Bud laughed as he told him, "Not till I'm ready to go back on duty."

"OK," Paul said. He looked at Bud for a few more seconds before speaking. "Thanks, Bud, for being my partner."

"You're welcome," Bud replied. "You are one lucky son of a bitch."

Paul nodded as he turned to start the walk down the hill to East Main Street toward Z Pita.

DECEMBER 17
FOUR WEEKS LATER

Joey Z's restaurant was decked out for the Christmas season. The red-and-green tinsel with the floating snowman and Santa from the ceiling put the casual restaurant in the spirit of Christmas. Detective Sergeant Paul Powers and his Priority 1 Task Force had solved a cold case from three years prior that was a kidnapping that resulted in a murder. Detective O'Malley had proven to be an asset to the team, and Paul had agreed with Cronin that he should remain on the task force once Bud returned to duty. The task force had brought closure to a family, and it was very rewarding to them. Detective Ellyn Baker had now been in the Riverhead facility for almost three weeks and she was relaying important information to Lynagh and Healey, who were now working as correctional officers in the jail. Powers figured he would pull them all out within the week and decide the next course of action. Even Detective Lieutenant Cronin was back to his administrative ways. Paul had accepted that as long as things were moving along normally, Cronin would stay out of most of the decisions he made.

Officer Chapman was working with O'Malley on a recent cold case that was solved. Cronin threw a folder of another cold case in front of O'Malley from 1974. Kathleen Kolodziej from Ronkonkoma, NY, who was brutally murdered by multiple stab wounds in Upstate New York. The billboard showing the picture of the seventeen-year-old college student is still up on Route 7 West on Interstate 88 off of exit 22 in Richmondville, NY. "You will be working with the FBI on this," Cronin said. "Her uncle is still alive on Long Island, and it would be nice if we can close the books on it." Cronin continued as O'Malley went through the folder, "Crime

Stoppers has a reward of $2,500 for anyone that leads to a conviction or closure on the case."

Chapman, a man of few words spoke up. "It will take more than that for someone to speak up."

O'Malley nodded. "yes, someone with a conscience. Well, we will see about that. Let's get to work."

It was now 5:00 pm and Rachelle had come in early to cover for Joey Z, who had to leave early. She was always in the holiday spirit and she was not going to change. She had received a text a couple times from Paul to talk since they had seen each other at Bud's house, but Rachelle was strong. She politely answered that she needed more time to be "friends" with him. She noticed she could handle her life better when she was not around him during this transition of their lives. She had on her Santa hat that lit up, which the regulars always got a kick out of. She greeted Joey Z as he said good-bye, and he told her Paul was at his usual table for an early dinner.

"It's OK," Rachelle said as she grabbed Joey Z's arm, "it's OK." Joey left through the back kitchen as Rachelle walked to the front, then around to the other side, and saw Paul sitting with a very attractive woman who appeared to be about ten to twelve years older than him. Her heart sank as she went back to the front desk, but she quickly got angry and couldn't hold it in any longer.

She walked up to the table as Paul looked up at her with a smile, but it quickly disappeared as Rachelle spoke in a high-pitched voice for most to hear.

"It's one thing to move on for whatever reason you want to give. But to disrespect me by coming into my restaurant with a date while I'm here!"

Paul tried to stop her, but he had no chance as Rachelle continued to speak. "Thanks for showing me the kind of man you are. No romance unless it is about sex!" Paul stood up, trying to get her to calm down, but it was apparent the other customers were enjoying the show as Rachelle continued. "Be careful," she said as she looked at the woman. "He will get tired of you in a year and then you will see him bring in another girl, God knows what her age will be." The patrons were smiling and laughing at Rachelle's show, and Paul was mortified.

"Rachelle!" he said.

"Don't you 'Rachelle' me," she answered. "I'm not through talking yet."

As she was beginning to start again, she saw Anthony Powers come out of the men's room, which was about six feet in back of the table, separated by a half wall to allow the walkway to the bathroom. The elder Powers walked up to Rachelle as she was silent and gave her a hug.

"It's so nice to see you, Rachelle. I would like to introduce you to my fiancée, Susan."

Rachelle was clearly embarrassed as Paul moved his lips to try and keep from speaking.

Rachelle looked over at Susan and said, "I'm so sorry for the misunderstanding, Susan, but as you will soon find out there can be communication issues."

Susan nodded and put out her hand.

"Nice to meet you, and please call me Sue."

Rachelle smiled and hugged Anthony Powers again, saying, "I'm sorry." She walked away without saying anything to Paul.

"Well," Paul said, "nothing like first impressions. I think I need a drink."

"Son," his father said, "I think you need more than that."

There was a young boy who could be heard two tables away saying, "Just when it was getting good!"

"Shhh," his mother said.

Rachelle was now on the other side of the restaurant and was shaking her head. She felt like such a fool that she did not go to the other side to check on the patrons until Paul, his father, and Susan left. Joey Z would have had a stroke if he had known about the episode. Deborah had invited Rachelle to spend the week before Christmas with her and her father in Belle Terre with the dogs because she did not want her best friend to wake up alone during the holidays. It was at this minute that Rachelle decided to take her up on it. She sent her a text that she would be over later that evening and would be staying until the 26th.

Even though the Pink Mansion was only five minutes away from Rachelle's house on Prospect Street, it was a world apart, and Rachelle needed the hideaway. She got to the house at 10:00 pm and Deborah was waiting for her with blankets and hot chocolate to watch TV by the fireplace.

"I can't watch TV tonight," Rachelle said as she began to tell Deborah what happened in the restaurant.

Deborah tried to keep from laughing as Rachelle explained to her what transpired in the restaurant. "Listen," Deborah said. "You'll feel better after watching your favorite, Suze Orman."

"No," Rachelle said "I just want to go to bed."

Deborah grabbed her shoulders. "Rachelle, you are going to watch Suze Orman with me."

Rachelle was startled by her insistence. "OK, gee whiz, OK." They snuggled under the blankets as Deborah's father, William Lance, kissed them good night. Rachelle wasn't sure about Deborah's insistence on watching the show because it appeared they were having conversation through most of the show. Finally, Deborah said, "Shhh, this is my favorite part." She made the television louder.

Suze Orman began to speak. "Tonight I'm going to end my show differently. I've been asked to do this before, but I had refused until I got this particular note. I made a phone call to the person who seemed to have connections to get this in my hands and to verify the information."

Orman continued, "Dear Rachelle. . ."

Deborah looked at her friend as she sat up when she heard her name being spoken by Suze Orman.

"There are so many things I need to say to you, yet for reasons I understand, you have been hesitant. My life has been filled with so much good and so much bad that all I could think about was how I would feel if this happened or that happened. My judgment about you or us did not have clarity because of my lack of confidence in you believing in me. My insecurities have made my personal life something that means nothing if you are not part of it. I miss you, and everything you are, whether funny or sad, angry or happy. You told me once, quote, 'I believe in you.' You believed in me more than anyone, and yet I believe I let you down."

Rachelle had tears in her eyes as Deborah held her hand while Suze Orman continued to read.

"I let you down because I was so busy worrying about how I would be if something happened to you that I was willing to experience the journey without you. There would be no journey worth it if it was not shared with you. Therefore, Rachelle Robinson, I am asking you to share the journey with me, to believe in me again, and to marry me and be my wife and be the mother of my children. I promise to give you everything I have to show you how much you mean to me. I promise to be there and always be by your side when you need me. I promise to be a better man. I promise to make you believe in me again. Love Always, Paul."

Suze Orman put the letter down, looked at the camera, and spoke. "If that isn't romantic, I don't know what is." Then she signed off with her famous sign-off, "People first, money second, things third."

Rachelle put her hands in front of her face and cried as Deborah held her.

"Why are you crying?" Deborah asked as she held her tightly.

Rachelle looked at her as she spoke. "I made an ass of myself at Z Pita tonight. He must have made this arrangement a week ago."

"It was three weeks ago," Deborah said. "You wouldn't let him speak to you, so he went this route. Thank God my father has connections."

Rachelle put her head on Deborah's shoulder as tears flowed from her as well. She ran her fingers through her hair and kissed the top of her head. She let a minute of silence go by before she spoke to Rachelle. "Well? What are you going to say?"

There was silence as Deborah leaned her head forward. Rachelle was sleeping. It was the first time since the breakup that she has seen Rachelle fall asleep so fast. She sent Bud a text asking him if he had seen the show, to which he replied *Yes*.

He also sent a text to Paul that read, *I'm proud of you, Detective Powers*. His message was answered, *Thanks, Detective Johnson. Sleep tight with the ghosts tonight*. Bud smiled as he put the phone down and said to himself, "The ghost can kiss my ass tonight; it's a great night."

DECEMBER 18

It was 8:00 pm the next night when Paul got out of his vehicle and started to go up the stairs to his apartment. He reached the fourth step when the door behind him was opened by someone who had a key. He turned around and it was Rachelle. She shut the door and leaned against it with her arms folded. Paul stood on the fourth step, not sure what to do or say, but the silence was getting awkward.

Finally Rachelle spoke. "Thank you for the romantic proposal." The detective was a little taken aback by her words but let her continue. "I need to know where you were these past six weeks and what you were doing."

Paul started walking down toward the bottom of the stairs as he replied, "I was sent on a confidential assignment to track down Barbara Sherman. Then I took time to spend with my father and his fiancée in Florida." He let out a half smile as he tried to continue, "You know the woman you confronted in the . . ."

Rachelle held out her hand and interrupted him, "Yes, I know who she is." She turned her head, looking for more to say, and finally said, "Did you get done with what you had to?"

"Yes," he answered.

"Did you hurt anyone?"

"I'm a cop, Rachelle."

"Did you abuse your authority?"

"What's this about, Rachelle?"

"I want to know for sure what kind of man you are."

"I will do anything to protect what I love."

"That was my sister as well; she is in jail. Am I going to lose you also because you would do anything?"

"No," he replied. "No," he repeated to himself.

"Did you sleep with anyone during the past six weeks?"

He moved closer to her as he replied with a half smile, "Rachelle, I . . ."

She interrupted him again, "What are you smiling about? I need to know if you would ever betray me. Did you sleep with anyone while you were away from me?" She continued to stare at him, looking for his answer.

He slowly shook his head side to side as he tried to touch her, but she moved her arms to avoid contact.

"I would never betray you, Rachelle," he answered.

She had learned from a detective, so she pushed further. "So the answer is 'No'?"

"No," he replied. "I didn't sleep with anyone."

Rachelle was satisfied but not yet ready to forgive. She smiled and spoke. "I will see you soon."

She opened the door and shut it behind her as Paul stood there and realized she never accepted his proposal. The dampness in the back of his head was starting again, which was a sign he needed to get upstairs and calm himself down. He didn't understand what had just happened, but he was depressed she didn't fall into his arms. The past two years had made Rachelle a stronger woman. She was, after all, the centerpiece of the Face of Fear. From the original notes of, *who do you love?* It was about her, Madison's actions, his indecisiveness, and the repercussions of her writings to draw out the kidnappers, to the attempts on her life. He sat down on the bed and recalled the night both he and Bud arrested Madison and took her to the precinct. When they got there, he asked Bud for a couple minutes alone with her. The conversation was imprinted in his mind forever.

"Why, Madison?" as he stared at her crying in the backseat of the car.

"Why?" he asked.

She answered, "You tell me, Paul," through her cries. "Who do you love?" It was obvious the answer to the question was Rachelle. Everything she had done was out of love for her sister, and he was doing the same for the woman he loved. It seemed to always come back to Rachelle. He wanted to call her back and go downstairs, but he decided to take a shower instead.

Things were suddenly becoming very clear as to what was truly important. It was another forty minutes when Paul walked down the back stairs, cut through the alley to Main Street in the village, and took a walk in the cool, brisk air. Paul passed Starbucks on the corner of Main and Arden and continued past the Gap, Pindar Wine, and Kimi Japanese restaurant. He stopped at Tommy's Place, which had been Timothy's Bar and Grill during the Face of Fear Investigation. He started walking again past Vincenzo's Pizza and came to the famous corner where people still look at the ladder going up to the roof of what was now called the Frigate. Even the Ocean City Café was now called the Steam Room.

Life goes on, he thought as he turned right on East Broadway. He looked at the cars coming off the ferry and was happy to see K-9 dogs waiting to check cars before boarding to go back to Connecticut. He walked to the dock at Danfords and remembered how much he enjoyed holding Rachelle's hand as they looked at the names of the boats in the marina. It was always his most favorite thing to do when it came to walking the marina dock at Danfords. *Reel Therapy*, *Luna Sea*, and *Irish Wake* were his favorites in tonight's walk, but the one that made him laugh was *Broke but Afloat*.

He left the dock to cross the street to the Fifth Season restaurant parking lot and went by the back of what once was Best Bargain Bookstore to Trader Cove's parking lot to get back to his apartment. The one constant that did not change in this beautiful village was the parking space problem. No one seemed to know what the answer was, but it was a detriment when Paul wanted to have dinner with friends who needed a vehicle. The walk was just what he needed to clear his head.

DECEMBER 23

It had been almost a week since Paul spoke to Rachelle in the stairway, and he had not heard from her. He was confused that she did not accept or decline his proposal. He drove out to the Riverhead Correctional Facility, where Lynagh, Healey, and Baker were undercover to get a final report before pulling them off the assignment. He and ADA Ashley met with them in a secure room for an hour.

Baker handed over fourteen names of doctors who were given to her as accepting cash for samples of oxycodone and Vicodin or prescriptions for them. There was more. Gary Reynolds was given the name of a prominent male doctor from the Hamptons. Reynolds was given the name by over half a dozen inmates. ADA Ashley looked the list up and down as Paul asked many questions of Ellyn Baker and Gary Reynolds. By the time they were finished Paul looked at ADA Ashley and suggested it might not be a bad idea to have more undercover reporters and/or cops serve time in jails. Ashley didn't reply, but he nodded in agreement that it may need to be looked at seriously. Not only did he have fifteen names of doctors breaking the law, there was a problem with young girls aged sixteen to seventeen who were in the same cells as adult women. The overcrowding had become such an issue that Ellyn Baker was almost in tears recanting stories of possible abuse to these young girls who were afraid to talk.

"Why did they talk to you?" Ashley asked.

"They didn't have to," Baker replied. "Remember I've been here for the past three weeks. We are not helping anyone by crowding minors in a large cellblock with women of all ages.

Yes, some women are protective, but many in here are too strong physically to fight. If this is the case in jail, what the hell is going on in the prisons?"

Powers looked over at Ashley. "We should have a meeting with DA Steinberg and Cronin. I agree with Ellyn, we need to do more than investigate these doctors." He looked over at Lynagh and Healey, who had been standing by the door dressed in their correctional officer uniforms.

"Anything to add to this?" They both nodded as Lynagh spoke. "The staff here has been very helpful, and no problems."

Powers nodded and looked back at Ashley. "What would you like to do?"

Ashley responded quickly, "We will try and get a warrant for the records of the prescriptions based on this undercover assignment. If we get it, I'll send auditors in and have them crawl up their asses with their own stethoscope. Prescriptions, samples coming in and out, plus we will match up the names and see how many inmates we have in here that received prescriptions from the names of doctors we have on the list. We will go from there."

Powers nodded and looked back at Reynolds and Baker. "Gary, I want to thank you for not only being here for the past three weeks but for the past fourteen months at Bedford Hills. It was a crucial part of saving lives." He looked at Baker and smiled. "Take Christmas Eve and Christmas off, both of you are leaving today. Thanks very much." He touched Ellyn's hands and she felt a rush go through her. *Stop*, she kept thinking, *stop, and get control of yourself.*

Paul looked over at Lynagh and Healey. "This is your last day here as well. Finish out the day and be ready to accompany Ashley to some of our favorite doctors on the 26th." They both nodded as Powers and Ashley left the room and asked to take a tour of the women's cellblock section. They walked through and saw what Detective Baker had informed them of. There were at least half a dozen girls under the age of eighteen in the same cellblock. One of them looked even younger, but Ashley was assured she was sixteen but just looked younger.

Powers shook his head.

"I thought the reason Yaphank jail was built was to stop this shit."

"Yes," Ashley said, "it was the reason, but apparently it's not the answer."

"Well," Paul replied, "we better find it fast."

Ashley and Paul went their separate ways as the detective sergeant drove home alone. He suddenly found himself getting depressed. He was alone, he missed Rachelle, and he missed the dogs. Most of all he was depressed he did not get a reply from his proposal. In some ways he could not blame her, but he thought he would have heard from her even if it was a no. His thoughts were interrupted with a phone call from Bud, who invited him to have dinner with him at the restaurant. "8:00 pm, OK?" Bud asked.

"Great," Paul answered, "I need to vent anyway."

Bud laughed, "That's what a partner does. No problem."

He met Bud, who was waiting for him on the front side of the restaurant where the TVs are on the wall. Usually, Paul would be at table three, but there was a couple already there. Paul looked around and was hoping Rachelle would be there, but she was not. Bud sat across from Paul and had him laughing within minutes. Paul could hardly keep down his food when Bud told him the jail in Yaphank had to clear out a section because Kevin Sysco had a serious intestinal problem and the attorneys and public defender were able to convince the judge it was inhumane and cruel punishment to have the other inmates around him. Paul was laughing so hard he thought he was going to pass out.

"I love you, man," he said as he looked at Bud. His partner nodded and looked at his watch and nodded for Joey Z to make the Fox News channel a little louder.

While the restaurant was quiet, Bud wanted Paul to see the Hannity program. Tonight it was Monica Crowley, Paul's favorite, subbing for Sean Hannity.

"Tonight," Monica Crowley said, "I'm honored to do something very, very different. This is for you, Paul Powers." The detective looked up startled at Monica Crowley saying his name on television.

"People have found so many ways to propose, but I'm here to say to you that I am honored to accept your proposal on behalf of Rachelle Robinson for marriage. In her words:

'Dear Paul,

I accept your proposal and your promise. I too promise to always love you, be there for you, but most of all to always believe in you. I accept whatever life brings as long as you keep your promise. With much love, Rachelle.'"

Monica Crowley folded up the paper, looked at the screen, and said, "I don't know how to follow that up, but we'll be right back." Her trademark smile faded out as Bud grabbed his partner's hand while Joey Z stood about five feet back with a huge smile on his face.

"I need to see her," Paul said.

Bud smiled. "She's upstairs waiting for you, my partner."

Paul tapped Bud's hand and ran out the backdoor, which Joey Z normally didn't like, but he made an exception this time.

Bud looked at Joey Z and said, "Well, I guess the Budster did it again." He looked around at the dirty dishes and spoke again. "I guess I'm stuck with the check." Joey Z laughed as he handed Bud the tab for the meal. "One thing about you, Joey Z," Bud said, "you never forget the check."

Joey Z always had a comeback. "Yes, my friend, but I don't have your life. I'm just a sixty-two year-old man trying to make a living." He walked away with a smile and spoke again. "Hey, Brett! Don't charge Bud for the Pita bread." Bud just shook his head as he laughed.

Y ou couldn't have asked for a better Christmas Eve. It was lightly snowing and about twenty-nine degrees. Deborah had asked Bud to spend Christmas Eve with her and her dad as well as close friends of theirs that had made a tradition of going over to the mansion. Bud was uncomfortable intruding on their tradition and instead he asked her to come over later and stay the night with him. While she was now twenty-eight and wanted to be with him, she was struggling with telling her father she would be with Bud for the night, especially on Christmas Eve.

She picked up Rachelle on Prospect Street to drive over to the jail to visit Madison for a couple hours. Rachelle was herself again. She jumped in the car and hugged Deborah and enjoyed giving her details of their first night together in months. Deborah was almost jealous listening to her talk about it. They got to the jail about 1:40 pm, and Madison was brought in to a special room to meet her sister Rachelle and Deborah. Correctional Officer Janet Gates was in the room as an escort during the meeting. Madison was informed that her attorney, Al Simmons, would also be stopping by.

They were in the room only twenty minutes when Paul walked in as a surprise, and it was the first time in over sixteen months that Paul had hugged Madison without a sheet of glass between them. He kissed Rachelle, who didn't want to let go of him, but he finally explained what he was doing there.

"Maddie, I wanted to let you be the first to see this." He took a little box out of his pocket, opened it up, showed it to Rachelle, and said, "Thank you for accepting my proposal. I hope you like this." It was a two carat marquis diamond with two round half carats on the side. Rachelle knew they were engaged, but seeing the ring and Paul putting it on her finger still made her misty-eyed. Madison looked at her sister and how happy she was, and she too became emotional. She looked up at Janet Gates, who was smiling at Madison.

2:00 PM

Detective Cronin drove up to the house and parked in the driveway and sat behind the wheel of his car for a few minutes and wondered if he should turn around and drive away. It was a fleeting thought, for he got out of the car and walked to the door. He rang the doorbell and walked into the foyer and was led to an office where there was a shadow of a figure sitting in the dark in the corner.

"It's over," Cronin said. "It's over; you need to turn yourself in."

"What took you so long?" the figure from the shadow said.

"I needed the evidence to back me up," the detective lieutenant replied. "Quite frankly, whoever killed Phil Smith in the barn that night was not a major concern for me. He was a no-good murdering piece of shit. I didn't even care that people thought it may have been me. But you slipped up by not telling me you came back the night before instead of the following night. The money, the payoff, the high level of technology on the briefcase all had me thinking. Then the shots that were fired, one missed, then one in the throat. A cop wouldn't have missed on the first shot, and speaking of the shot, the ballistics on the bullet showed the gun was owned by Steven Anderson from the paper Rachelle worked at, and I'm sure if we look hard enough we would find it somewhere in the house unless you destroyed it. I have the flight information and I checked; the only place that sold that kind of briefcase was your chain of stores before you sold it. You should have left another for Simmons. The cash was yours, so it's not illegal for him to keep it. The briefcase was too expensive for me or anyone else to have.

I know it wasn't me who shot him, and only you had the means and money to do this. The money that went missing really was not missing. Anyone else but you would have made a fuss about where all the ransom money went to. Well, there was no fuss because you got your money back after you shot Smith. However, it was your love for your daughter that fired the bullet. Love, something so great can create hate toward others. I checked the technology used on the briefcase. It's the same as what's used on the mansion here. Everything has a signature."

"What do you want me to do?" the shadow spoke.

"I want you to enjoy Christmas Eve tonight, Christmas Day tomorrow, and then I want you to turn yourself in before New Year's."

"Don't you understand?" the man said as he came out of the shadows. "I would do anything to protect my daughter. Any father would."

Cronin looked at William Lance. "Yes, I know, which is why I'm letting you turn yourself in. You can afford the best attorney, you were under extreme pressure. Public sympathy will be on your side. More important, there were only two people in the barn. One of them is no longer around. If you say you reacted out of self-defense it will be difficult for a jury to convict you."

"You think so?" Lance said.

"Yes," Cronin replied. "A jury is made up of people like yourself. There is only one version of the story, and that's yours. Get your attorney and turn yourself in. I'm sure he will want you to testify before the grand jury."

"That's it?" Lance said. "You are going to leave and not take me in?"

Cronin took a step closer. "As I said, I won't take you in if I don't think you would do harm to yourself or others. William, your daughter needs you; she has been through a lot the past couple of years. Don't just think of yourself. Think about her."

William Lance nodded as he spoke. "I'll turn myself in on the 27th. I will need the 26th to talk to Deborah."

"OK," Cronin said, "bring the gun with you when you do. Put it in a box and make sure there are no bullets in it." He hesitated before speaking again. "Don't disappear, William. I will find you if need be, so think about Deborah. With a good lawyer, you won't do much time, if any."

The two men stared at each other for another thirty seconds before Cronin said, "Merry Christmas."

He nodded and turned around as William Lance said, "Thank you."

Cronin got in his car and called ADA Ashley, who picked up on the second ring. He barely said hello when Cronin spoke. "I kept my promise. Merry Christmas, you son of a bitch."

Ashley looked at the phone when he heard the click. He shook his head and thought to himself, *Same to you, mystery man, same to you.* He smiled as he rejoined his parents at the dinner table filled with his thought, *I'm sorry, Kevin Cronin, for giving you those promissory notes, but it was time, my friend.*

4:00 PM

Jason "Jack" O'Connor was in the TV room when the guard yelled, "O'Connor, you have a Christmas gift in your cell!" The former FBI agent smiled as the guard escorted him back to his enclosed room with the small window. He walked in and always had a sarcastic smile on his face because he had won the right not to have the victims' families on his walls as Paul Powers had threatened numerous times. The photos were put up numerous times, but lawyers had gotten them removed each time.

On his bed was a shoebox-sized package wrapped in Christmas paper. He sat down on his bed and unwrapped the paper, opened the box, and found more tissue paper. He moved the tissue paper slowly to discover it was the white Ghost Face mask with the words in blood red, *No Mercy*. He jumped up from his bed and threw the mask against the door and started screaming.

"Get this out of here! Do you hear me? Get this out of here!" He started kicking the door. "Open up! Open up!" He picked up the mask and started throwing it against the wall. "Get this fucking thing out of here! Do you hear me!"

In fact the whole cellblock could hear him, but the burly guard smiled as he walked down the hallway listening to O'Connor's screams.

5:10 PM

Sherry Walker loved to walk along Cedar Beach in Mount Sinai. This snowy day was no exception. She had enjoyed her time off away from the task force. The officer who saved Rachelle Robinson's life and took a knife to her abdomen eighteen months prior was now concentrating on starting a new life. She walked out to the end of the pier, took out her disposable phone, and pushed the buttons. The call was picked up as Sherry said, "It's over, time to move on."

"OK," the caller said. "Any last messages for her?"

"Yes," Sherry said, "tell her . . ." she hesitated for a moment trying to think of the appropriate words. "Tell her, her nightmares should end." The call ended as she threw the phone in the water.

As she started walking toward the beach with the snowflakes coming down, a figure started walking toward her. She stopped to see the figure of a man approach closer to her. He stopped about ten feet from her and spoke.

"Hell of a day for walking on a pier in Mount Sinai."

"I guess so," Sherry answered.

"This is over, right? No more calls, no more killings. Many lives have been lost for the sake of revenge."

Sherry nodded as she replied, "You're a smart man. No matter what side of the law you are on, revenge has no mercy." Both of them stood still and did not move as Sherry spoke again.

"Why did you kill Lawrence Stone in the parking lot? I left him alive for the cops to pick up."

"I was asked to help clean up the dirt surrounding this case. I did it for Madison. It's the same reason I got rid of Tangretti and

Branca in the Keys. Madison has her revenge. and so do you"

Sherry nodded. "I guess we all got our revenge. How did you find them?"

"Oh," the man answered, "like you, it's amazing the connections I have in my job. You found Caulfield at the mall, saved Lynagh at Sherman's house, and took good care of business at the garage, so we make a good team." He laughed. "And you," he continued, "are right, there is no mercy when it comes to retribution. They were shown none, and I did as you asked with the calling card. It had *No mercy* on it." He took another breath as the conversation continued. "Why the use of the mask, Sherry? This could have been done without leaving calling cards that could gain national attention."

She put her hands in her pocket to warm them up as she replied, "I wanted to be sure both sides of the law knew there was a connection to the Face of Fear investigation. I knew it would raise the stakes and keep Tangretti, Branca, and that asshole O'Connor a little more stressed. I'm sure O'Connor is enjoying his Christmas present right now."

The man smiled as she continued, "His men tried to take my life and took the lives of people I cared about. I knew Powers and Johnson couldn't go outside the law. I wasn't going to see them go down without my help."

The man nodded before speaking again and moved a step closer. "Now for the big question. You know Cronin; he won't stop. The case may be over, but the killings of Caulfield and Talison in the mall parking lot and that other asshole Stone won't just go away by themselves. Cronin, as well as Powers and Johnson, know about the mask, and it wasn't cops who killed them. The bodies of Tangretti and Branca have been eaten by sharks, so that's not a problem."

Sherry smiled as she spoke. "Did you notice there has been nothing in the media about Ghost Face being involved in this case?

I have a feeling it's going to stay that way, and as long as this is over, I don't think Cronin will be spending tax dollars on a calling card left at the scene. Call it woman's intuition."

"Well," the man said, "I guess we are done here. You and I will never meet again."

"I hope not," Sherry answered. "It would not be wise. It's time to concentrate on a life."

"So," the man answered as he waved, "Merry Christmas."

"Same to you," Sherry answered.

The man turned around and started walking away to where she could barely see him when he turned around and gave Sherry one last nod before turning back toward his vehicle. *You're lucky I'm married, you delicious-looking man*, she said in her thoughts.

As his car pulled away, John Bay made a phone call. "It's over," he said, "Merry Christmas."

"Thank you," came the reply, and there was a click. Al Simmons put the phone down and went over to pour himself a drink. He raised his glass in the air and said, "Here's to you, Madison."

6:00 PM

Bud was walking up Main Street holding hands with Deborah as the light snow continued to fall. She thought he looked so adorable in his knit hat. "I'm sorry," she said. "I will come back later and see you. I want to spend Christmas Eve with you, but my Dad, it's uncomfortable."

"No worries," Bud said, "as long as you have dinner with Rachelle, Paul, and I for Christmas. It's fine, Deborah. Really, it's OK."

"Thank you for understanding," she answered. He kissed her on the lips and told her he would see her later. She started to get in her car as she watched Bud walk up Main Street. She looked at him as he kneeled down to a man who was sitting down on the park bench between Elements retail store and the Salsa Salsa Eatery. She waited in front of Spy Coast Bar as she saw him continue to talk to the man, who had his arms folded across his body to keep warm. She moved away from her car and took a few extra steps to get a closer look at what was going on. Bud put his hands on the man, then took off his snow hat and put it on his head. He then took off his gloves and put them on the man's hands. Deborah took out her phone and pushed the buttons to make a call.

"Dad," she said, "I hope you're not upset with me, but I really need to be with Bud tonight. I love him and don't want him to be alone. Will you be OK with your friends?"

"I'll be fine, sweetheart. Merry Christmas, my love," her father replied.

"Thanks, Dad. I love you."

"Deborah," her dad replied, "I want you to know how proud I am of you, and I know your mom would be proud as well."

It was rare for her father to bring up her mom, she thought, as he continued to speak.

"Your mom knew that the name Deborah came from a woman who was a prophetess of the god of the Israelites and was the only female judge mentioned in the Bible." Deborah tried to push the phone closer to her ear as her father continued to speak. "She was a strong person, a warrior and 'The Song of Deborah' is considered the earliest sample of Hebrew poetry from the twelfth century."

Deborah looked back at Bud walking up Main Street as she replied, "Dad, is everything OK?"

William Lance let out a small laugh to reassure his daughter before he spoke again. "I'm fine, honey. I just wanted you to know that your mom demanded you were named Deborah because the only female judge from the Bible was a strong, independent woman, and I think your mother would be so proud of you. Life gets in the way, and now I think it is appropriate that you know."

"Dad," Deborah replied, trying to keep her emotions in check. "I love you, and thank you for telling me. I'll see you tomorrow." She kissed the phone and pushed the *end* button. William Lance wiped the tear from his eye as he walked past the giant Christmas tree to his office.

Deborah walked as fast as she could in the snow as she yelled for Bud to wait up for her. He turned around and had a look of concern on his face when she walked up to him and gave him a hug.

"What's wrong?" he asked.

"Nothing," she answered, "everything is right. I'm staying with you tonight," and she kissed him.

He looked at her. "You are my Christmas present?"

She smiled and answered, "Your Christmas past, present, and future, Bud. You have always been there for me since the day I met you." He kissed her again as they started walking toward South Street to the Henry Hallock house.

Bud turned his head as he put his arm around Deborah and saw Lindsey across the street looking at them with a warm smile on her face. She looked so beautiful under the streetlight that shined brightly on her. He nodded to her as he kissed Deborah, looked back again at the young girl, and noticed that there was no streetlight at all yet there was light on Lindsey. Bud felt a warmth throughout his body as he turned his attention back to Deborah. The beautifully decorated village normally played Christmas music from the Pie restaurant, but now at this moment it played a Christian song titled "Me, Without You," by Toby Mac.

Lindsey took her phone out of her pocketbook and sent Bud a text, *Merry Christmas Bud. May God bless you.* She was still looking at them through the falling snow as her phone made the sound when she received a text.

"Lindsey! What are you doing? Let's go home," Sharyn Wilkerson said.

"Yes, Mother," Lindsey answered. As they got in the car she looked at her text message. The young girl let out a long sigh, closed her eyes, looked up in the sky, and said, "He knows, Dear Lord." She smiled as she looked at the text again. It said, *Merry Christmas to you as well, my sweet guardian angel.*

Epilogue

THREE WEEKS LATER
JANUARY 18

As Kevin Cronin sat in the Mount Sinai diner waiting to meet a potential witness, his thoughts drifted to what occurred during the past few weeks and where everyone was. William Lance, as promised, turned himself in with his high-powered attorney claiming self-defense. Based on the nature of the crime he was released on bail after surrendering his passport. William Lance had gone before a grand jury satisfying them on his justification of the use of force. Deborah Lance took a leave of absence from the school and stayed by her father's side each time he appeared with his attorney. Her initial reaction was shock when he spoke to her, but after a long cry and hug she became strong with the help of Rachelle and Bud.

Bud still had not returned to the task force but he informed Powers that his doctor at the rehabilitation center gave a date of March 1 for his return. He was never hurting for company, so he was never lonely. Even when he was alone at the Henry Hallock house he would hear voices downstairs, so he would just say, "Please, Grandma, let me sleep."

Cronin smiled as he continued down the list in his thoughts. Justin Healey would meet up with Bud and became a fan of the Pie and its owner, Kristen Pace. As Bud predicted, the young officer developed a crush on her. While she was older than him, you would never know it from the way she kept herself in shape. They became a couple and Cronin noticed the maturity in him since dating her. Bud would sometimes tease her and bring in a microphone to read the news like she was on Fox News. She always took it in stride, and Justin loved the way she laughed. Even the staff created a hot and spicy pizza called the Foxy Pie.

Rachelle continued her studies at Empire State College and knew there was a book in her future as well as a life with Paul Powers. Cronin's smile disappeared as his thoughts turned to Officers Blair and Lawrence from East Hampton. Lawrence's involvement with Branca and in the attempted murder of police officers landed him in the Nassau County Correctional Facility with no bail. It was ADA John Ashley who made arrangements for Lawrence to be placed there instead of the Suffolk County Correctional Center. The ADA felt strongly that Lawrence would not survive being in a facility run by the Suffolk Sheriff Department after shooting at Suffolk cops. The move most likely saved his life. Regardless, he was placed on suicide watch and was in Enforcement Protective Custody at the jail. Officer Blair was arraigned at his beside in the hospital and had bail posted. Still, Ashley had a police escort at the hospital to be sure he wasn't eliminated. Cronin's relationship with Ashley continued to be of utmost respect for each other, yet when there were disagreements there was no backing off from each other. Cronin knew they complemented each other more than ever. If actual details of what went down and the protocol utilized to solve the case went public, it would most likely be career ending for both of them. The Detective Lieutenant knew in his heart he did the right thing regardless of the outcome and it was important to him that good won over evil.

His thoughts were interrupted when the teenage boy came into the Mount Sinai diner with his mother and saw the man raise his arm. Tanya Fillmore and her son Jeremy walked to the booth as Kevin Cronin asked them to sit down.

"Thanks for coming," he said.

"We didn't have much choice from the way you made it sound," Tanya responded.

Cronin tightened his lips to her remark as he looked at the boy. "You are a tough young man to find."

Jeremy looked at his mom and did not speak.

"On October 9 of last year you are on video taking money from someone in a car and speaking into a phone. Please tell me what that was about," Cronin said.

The mother spoke with her hand out to be sure Jeremy was quiet until it was OK with her. Her voice had a sound that appeared to be regretful that she came.

"Mr. Cronin, you told us . . ." she could not finish the sentence, for the man interrupted her.

"It's Detective," he said with a smile. "Detective Lieutenant, actually."

Tanya stared at him in almost disbelief as she started again.

"Detective Lieutenant," she said and hesitated for him to acknowledge it. "You told me if Jeremy came here and tried to help you that you would leave him completely out of it. No matter what the fallout. I have your word on this?"

The detective tilted his head and looked out the window at the cars driving by on Nesconset Highway. He looked back at Tanya Fillmore and spoke.

"Ma'am, I always keep my promises. Just know that."

The mother looked at her son and nodded that it was OK to speak.

Jeremy said, "The car drove up and she called me over and offered me $100 to make a call for her disguising my voice."

"Do you still have the money?" Cronin asked.

His mother laughed. "You would have been too late if you asked the next day, Detective. You don't have teenagers, do you?"

Cronin ignored her comment as the boy told him the money was spent within a couple days.

"I'm going to show you photographs. I want you to point to the photo if any of them are the person that gave you the money." He laid out six photos on the table as Jeremy looked over at the photos for what appeared to be a long time. Cronin almost expected the boy to point to Sherry Walker's photo, but he did not.

"It's none of these photos," he said.

Cronin pushed the photos closer to the boy as he touched Sherry Walker's photo.

"No," the boy said. "The woman who gave me the money was white."

There were few times when the detective was surprised, and this was one of them.

"Anything else?" Tanya Fillmore asked.

"No, no thank you for your time," he answered with a tone of disappointment. The mother and her son left the booth without saying good-bye as Cronin sipped his coffee with his mind filled with thoughts.

He shook his head as he continued to think about the car and who was behind the mystery killings. He looked at his phone, picked it up, and sent a text to ADA John Ashley. *Let's get a list of everyone who has visited Madison Robinson from October until now.* He grabbed the photos to put them back in his briefcase and looked at Sherry Walker's photo. He was nodding at her image and almost grinned when he closed the case on the photographs.

JANUARY 19

Madison was surprised to see Sherry Walker visiting her at the facility.

"I didn't think you would ever come."

"Well," Sherry said, "I think enough time has passed."

"Is it completely over?" Madison asked.

"There's no evidence, no link unless John loses it."

"He won't," Madison replied. "What about you?"

Sherry was quick to answer, "Those people were the fallout from the Face of Fear. They took my ability to ever have a child when I was stabbed. I have no regrets."

Sherry smiled. "Cronin questioned a boy that was given the money to call Ashley. Thank God I paid another $300 to a stranger to take the vehicle and do the transaction for me."

"What about video where you paid the stranger and how did you know where to be? The club garage, the Sherman house?" Madison asked.

"Not every building and street has video cameras, Madison. As for the other places, I still have friends."

"I don't want to know who your other friends are, do I?" Madison asked.

"No," Sherry answered. "There was someone who knew where everyone was, including videos from the buildings, but I will tell you this . . ." Madison smiled as Sherry said, "Payback is a bitch."

TO MY FATHER HENRY

You came into my life at age 12 and gave me all the milestones every child growing up into a adult should have. And you gave my Mother the best years of her life. You gave my bride to me at my wedding and you lit up the world with those blue eyes and your sense of humor. You are loved and will be missed.

About the Author

R. J. Torbert continues his work at Fun World, which includes protecting the trademark and copyrights of Ghost Face. R. J. has entered his twentieth year at Fun World, creating and developing over one thousand items sold around the world. He is currently working on his third novel, R. J. holds a Bachelor's degree in English and Creative Writing.